SEDUCED BY THE DARKNESS

With unfathomable speed he pulled her away from the desk, twirled her around and maneuvered behind her. He massaged her shoulders and kissed her neck. The edge of his teeth grazed her flesh, and a shiver arced through her.

"I've thought about bringing you across," he said.

She opened her eyes. Why couldn't she speak? Across what?

"Into my world," he responded, as if she'd spoken aloud. "A life of darkness, but a life of eternity. We'd belong to each other." His voice remained a whisper. He massaged her arms, his hands tracing a line to her fingertips, then back across her palms and pausing on her wrists. He increased pressure there, on her veins, as if he could feel the blood pulsing through her.

His breath tickled her ear. "The temptation to take you is overwhelming."

Sensations flooded her mind. Waves of pleasure rolled over Lara, pleading for the destruction of a barrier he'd not yet penetrated.

Take me.

LOVE WITHOUT BLOOD

RAZ STEEL

LOVE SPELL NEW YORK CITY

To my father, Irving, who passed away unexpectedly
and was never able to share my dream to be a writer.

LOVE SPELL®

January 2009

Published by

Dorchester Publishing Co., Inc.
200 Madison Avenue
New York, NY 10016

ISBN 10: 0-505-52800-2
ISBN 13: 978-0-505-52800-1

Printed in the United States of America.

10 9 8 7 6 5 4 3 2 1

Visit us on the web at www.dorchesterpub.com.

ACKNOWLEDGMENTS

The list of people to thank is brief but important. It begins with a mentor, Laura Szabo-Cohen who put my writing on track; my critique partner, Cindy Cox, who kept my writing on track and assured me nothing I said would provoke the undead to seek retribution; Bucks County Romance Writers, a group of talented, supportive writers who have encouraged me at every turning point; my editor, Chris Keeslar, who has offered excellent advice; my agent, Kelly Mortimer, who has offered my editor plenty of advice; Shannon Aviles and her wonderful team at More Than Publicity; Douglas Michael, MD., for his medical advice, (not all of which I heeded—part of my personality); Jenn Urban, RN., for technical advice about St. Mary's, (also not all of which I heeded. I've always wanted to claim "Literary license," so I will.) and Mimi Michael for last minute research.

Finally, what acknowledgment would be complete without thanking Mom? She prefers I call her Charlotte. From my heart, thank you, Charlotte.

All of the characters and events in this book are fictitious. Any resemblance to actual persons, living or dead, is purely coincidental, except for Theresa; I really did have a crush on her in eighth grade.

Raz Steel

One

Dr. Lara West's brain replayed the day's events in the ER, searching for a loophole, a mistake, some way she might've saved the child's life. There was none. She remembered trying to help the parents accept their loss. How could they? Her stomach twisted into knots as she pulled on a nightshirt, crawled into bed and cried.

She didn't remember the moment sleep overtook her, but when her cell phone rang at 4:00 A.M., it sounded like a fire bell. Her mind jumped into crystal-clear focus. The hospital used her pager; the service used her house phone. That didn't leave many options for people calling the cell. She didn't have any real friends. She didn't have time for them.

Her stomach still hurt from her earlier turmoil. Was this unrelenting pressure a constant companion for any head of ER? Should she withdraw from competition? No. Resolve washed over her. No way would she give up her dream to be chief of emergency medicine at Jefferson Memorial Hospital.

The continued ringing of the phone snapped her back. Propped on one elbow, Lara grabbed the cell and flipped it open. Its blue light shimmered in the dark bedroom. Only one bar appeared at the bottom of the screen. Damn. The cell beeped: low battery.

"West," she answered.

"I need a doctor."

She spoke fast, before her phone died. "Sir, if you're ill, go to the nearest emergency room."

"I can't. I need *you*, Dr. West."

She'd been around pain long enough to recognize it in the caller's voice. He forced his words out, his breathing uneven. An unexpected chill snaked across Lara's shoulders, and she shivered inside her summer nightshirt. "I don't make house calls."

"I can't stop the bleeding."

"Sir, if you're bleeding, hang up and dial 911. You need immediate attention."

"I know. Come downstairs."

Adrenaline shot through Lara's system. "What?"

"Dr. West, come downstairs. I don't have much time." Agony edged the words.

Lara's eyes widened. Air poured into her lungs, and she held it. Her mind flipped into overdrive. She'd locked the front door when she came home. No windows were open. Had she checked the back sliders? If the call was coming from downstairs, the caller had forced his way in.

She glanced at the second-floor window, too high to climb out. Pins and needles ravaged one foot. Her sun tattoo burned on the small of her back.

Call 911, you dummy.

Panic rose in her throat and Lara shuddered. *What if this man dies in my house?* As a second-year med student, she'd witnessed a car accident, and fear of the unknown had prevented her from responding. That victim had died at the scene. She'd sworn she would never let it happen again.

As if he read her thoughts, the intruder said, "Would it help if I were already dead?"

"If you want my help, go outside and wait for me."

"I can't move."

His presence belied that. The man was trying to lure her. He'd violated her home. No way would she respond.

"Come downstairs." The words floated around her, weaving a delicate pattern in the air, searching for sympathy. "I'm in pain."

Lara jumped, seized by compulsion. If this man was bleeding, possibly dying, did it matter that he'd broken into her house? She was a physician first, a victim second. Wasn't that the Hippocratic oath? Hadn't she sworn that upon graduation from Johns Hopkins?

She snatched the robe draped over the foot of her bed and fastened it somewhere between her belly and hips, a line less distinguishable in recent years. Darkness layered her bedroom; shadows swept in from the hall. Weight of the unknown pressed on her shoulders. She wanted to cry, but her eyes were dry. She had to go out there. Must she also help those who broke into her home?

Reason won. She ended the call with the intruder, then dialed 911 and pushed send. The cell beeped. Dead battery.

Undeterred, she seized the house phone from her nightstand, still intending to call the police. Breathing rasped on the line, then a voice, *his* voice, weaker, naked. "I won't survive without help."

The words preyed on Lara's emotions. How could this intruder know what she felt?

I can't go out there.

He'd used her house phone to call her cell. Her dead cell. Wait! She kept a spare battery and charger in her medical bag . . . downstairs on the kitchen counter.

"Shit."

A new thought came to her. She could save herself, and not at the expense of this man's life. She'd go downstairs, grab her bag, slip in the new battery and dial 911. The police would arrive before she finished examining him.

The intruder coughed, struggling for breath. "I hear you moving around, Doctor. Please, are you coming?"

She had no time to reconsider.

Lara dropped the house phone on the bed. Her feet dragged across the carpet as if they had a will of their own, fighting her all the way down the hall. Below, a splash of lamplight shone in the living room. She hadn't left one on.

She squeezed her cell phone, staring downward. Perspiration sliced past her ribs, and she fought to unclench her teeth. But fascination warred with fear. Lara's bare feet continued to move toward the steps.

She spied the intruder slumped in an easy chair, his back to her. Because he sat in the shadows, she couldn't distinguish his age. From behind, she could tell his left hand pressed against his right shoulder. She had to reach her medical bag.

She gripped her cell phone tighter and stared down the steps. Goose bumps traced across her flesh despite the lack of air conditioning. *I am not going downstairs.* True to her thoughts, Lara didn't move.

"I don't know if I can hold on." The man spoke to her, but no longer over the phone. His words were hypnotic, drifting up from where he sat, tearing at her, compelling her to actions she didn't want to perform. "I need your help."

Lara surrendered. The carpet burned cold into the soles of her feet like an icy pond. Each tentative step tightened the embrace of duty—she navigated the stairs as if she approached an uncontained virus, but his words and need compelled her.

His arm and hand rested on the arm of the chair, his palm open. She recognized the house-phone extension. But how the hell had he gotten her cell number? With no time to wonder now, doctor mode kicked in. A dark stain spread across his shirt and seeped between the fingers of his hand. She had two goals: save the man, save herself.

Her hair spilled across her shoulders as Lara leaned closer and made a quick assessment. The intruder pushed out a shallow breath, his lips deathly pale and pressed together, his eyes dark but alert. His open hand trembled. Lara switched on the reading lamp next to the chair, and light glistened off her polished nails. The intruder twisted his head away. Jaw set hard, he refused to admit how much pain he felt.

An animal scent wafted from his clothing, and Lara's nose twitched. "A patient break-in is a new experience for me." Her voice steadied. She bent over and lifted the man's blood-soaked fingers away from his shoulder, careful not to get gore on herself. "How'd you find me? No, never mind. What happened?"

His last finger finally conceded, came away from his wound, and Lara peered through the hole in his shirt before he could respond. "You've been shot!"

"A new experience for *me*." The man's voice slithered around Lara's spine, winding itself into her soul.

Why did I come downstairs? What am I doing?

As blood gushed from the intruder's wound, necessity forced all other thoughts into a tiny recess of Lara's mind. She glanced around the room, still organized and neat. She stored towels, sheets, everything sanitary upstairs. But she couldn't leave him. She turned away, unfastened her robe and shoved it off her shoulders.

"Doctor, some other time." The intruder coughed. "I'm not up for that."

I'm saving his life and he's joking.

"Shut up," she said. She pulled her nightshirt up and off, then replaced the robe. She turned around, then pressed the nightshirt against his wound and brought his hand back into place. His cold skin seared her flesh. Tension tightened the muscles in his arm.

She hadn't fastened her robe securely, and it flopped open. She flushed as spring air danced across her bare breast. "Keep pressure on it," she directed as she retied her sash. No time for ridiculous thoughts. She had to call the police, report a shooting. Blood had already soaked through the nightshirt.

Lara didn't remember flipping her cell phone shut or slipping it into her robe pocket, but she felt it kick against her thigh. She grabbed for the house phone. "We need an ambulance."

A hand grabbed her wrist and twisted it behind her back so fast she screamed. She screamed a second time when she realized the wounded man had one hand pressed against his shoulder and the other resting on the arm of the chair. Someone *else* was in her house.

"No ambulance." A gravelly voice spoke from behind. "Do your doctoring crap here. *Capisce?*"

"Let her go, Tony," the wounded man commanded. Tony obeyed.

Lara rubbed the red marks on her wrist and glanced over her shoulder into the shadows. A massive guardian of indeterminate age, Tony glared at her. Did she imagine that repugnant odor?

The wounded man's voice drew her attention back

to him. "Dr. West." He struggled to speak. "I came to your house because I can't go to a hospital. Do what you can for me." His steely expression contradicted his defenseless words.

Lara's wrist throbbed. She replaced the house phone on the arm of the chair and tightened the sash of her robe. "I need my medical bag." She fired a defiant glance at Tony, implying she didn't need permission. Tony followed her, his footfalls faint for a man his size.

The bag sat on the kitchen counter where she had deposited it earlier. Her colleagues laughed that she still carried one, but to Lara the black bag proved a portable emergency kit. They'd stop laughing when administration named her the youngest-ever chief of emergency medicine at Jefferson Memorial. Doctoring in a gangbanger neighborhood didn't need to be male dominated or heartless.

The lemon scent of dishwashing liquid filtered upward as she scrubbed her hands in the sink, but that motion was more important to clear her thoughts than to kill germs. She grabbed a glass of orange juice along with her bag and hurried back to the living room. Tony melted against the wall, deep in the shadows.

Lara's patient closed his eyes.

"Hey. Stay awake," she ordered. She set her bag on the floor and the juice on the end table.

The intruder opened his eyes and stared into hers. Lara tingled. The intruder spoke without words. She squeezed her thighs together. A quivering assaulted her, and she blinked to break the spell.

The man wore a fathomless expression, and his pupils and irises blurred together. *Not possible. Must be the light.* Lara pulled latex gloves from her bag, stretched them over her slender fingers and applied pressure to his shoulder.

She handed him the juice. "Drink this."

"I'd rather not."

"Drink it. If you're going to break into my home and demand that I doctor you, you're going to damn well do what I say. Drink it."

He held the glass to his lips.

"Every drop."

His eyes flashed. He drank as if the liquid burned his throat.

Lara rummaged through her bag. "Who are you?" She straightened, stethoscope around her neck, the device she used to peer into patients' eyes in hand. She'd been a physician for ten years and suddenly couldn't remember the name of the damn gadget.

"What's your name?" Had she asked the man or the instrument?

The intruder hesitated, perhaps unsure how to answer, or if he should.

"Robert."

Lara flipped on the nameless gadget and shone the light into Robert's eyes. He winced and twisted away.

"The bullet is in my shoulder."

"Would you rather do this yourself?"

"My eyes are sensitive to light."

She cupped his chin, turned his head back toward the reading lamp and peered into his eyes. Pupils and irises remained blurred. He had no pulse.

"What kind of meds are you taking?" she asked.

"None."

This makes no sense. This man is alive, not dead. . . . Isn't he? "We have to get your shirt off, but I don't want you to move."

She unbuttoned his collar and couldn't help but notice hard muscles sweeping across his chest. She pulled the shirttail out of his pants. Blood trailed over a washboard stomach. She helped him lean forward. Pain slashed across his face, and she eased him back again into the chair. "Never mind. We'll cut it off." She extracted scissors from her bag.

Robert managed to frown. "It's six-hundred-count Egyptian cotton."

"What do you care? It's bloodstained."

"I don't mind that."

Her lip curled as fabric gave way beneath her tool. She handed Robert the carved piece, slid the remainder from his other arm and dropped that in his lap too. "Don't worry," she said. "It's still Egyptian cotton."

She probed the edges of the hole, then inspected his back. "There's no exit wound."

"You have to remove the bullet."

"No." The wound seemed almost superficial, yet she'd been unable to stanch the bleeding. The bullet must've nicked a vein. If he refused to go to a hospital, how could she save his life?

"Remove the bullet," he repeated. The words wrapped around her like a shroud around a corpse. What choice did she have? The man had lost a lot of blood.

Lara needed a moment to gather her thoughts. She cleaned the area around the wound and talked as she did. "I don't have a sign out front or an office in my home. How'd you find me?"

"GPS. OnStar. We made two rights, then a left on Pennsylvania Avenue just past the Washington Monument." Robert coughed. When Lara applied extra pressure to his shoulder, he jumped. "That hurt. What are you, a doctor or a quack?"

"I'm a doctor who wants a straight answer. What're you doing here? How'd you know I'm a surgeon?"

"WebMD."

She pinched his shoulder.

"Ouch!"

"I can remove that bullet with a scalpel or a spoon."

"I made a few phone calls. You're the top surgeon in a city ER that sees a lot of gunshot wounds."

"Should I ask how this happened?"

His eyes told her not to ask. The bleeding slowed and she irrigated the wound. She tore off her gloves, then pulled on fresh ones. Next, she unrolled a cloth bundle on the floor. An assortment of surgical instruments glistened in the light. Wait—when had she made the decision to operate? ER pressure paled by comparison.

The man observed with cold precision.

Odd, he should be losing alertness. "Normally I wouldn't do this with the patient awake," she admitted.

"We have no choice. Don't worry, I'm not squeamish about blood."

"How're you with pain? You think it hurts now? Wait till I start digging."

"Do what you have to, Doctor. I'm familiar with medical procedures. I've worked in a hospital."

Tony glided out of the shadows, one finger in the air. Robert rolled his eyes. "Yes, Tony, you can go pee."

"Thanks, Boss."

Tony moved another half step. Lara glanced over her shoulder. The goon was staring at her back. A hospital security badge dangled from his belt. His stomach bulge prevented her from reading the hospital name. "You don't need *my* permission, Tony," she sneered.

"Where do I go? I need directions."

"Try the GPS."

Tony fidgeted for a moment, shifting weight from one leg to the other. Lara continued to arrange instruments. The goon's focus returned to Robert.

"Try one of the doors down the hallway." The wounded man flicked his chin, and Tony hurried away.

"That wasn't nice," Robert said to Lara. "He has bladder issues."

"Hey, you two broke into my house, and my wrist still hurts where he grabbed me."

"More harm may still come your way."

The veiled threat spiked a chill down Lara's spine. Her feet itched. With Tony out of the room, she could run. . . .

The image of the car-crash victim unfolded in her mind. That man had died. Lara swallowed hard.

The flow of blood increased again, and her patient looked pallid. She had to act. Her hand trembled. Eyes closed, she inhaled deeply. Her pulse skidded back to normal. She opened her eyes and refocused on the job.

This patient's life rested in her hands. In the ER, with X-rays and a staff to assist, the angle of extraction would be obvious, complications dealt with. Not here. Complications now might mean disaster. She didn't want to do this. She wanted these men out of her home.

Would she get her promotion if this man died of a nonmortal wound while in her care? Would the board of governors pick some administrative clone for the post? Would the hospital remain a model for Tinman, heartless doctoring?

Yet, what about her own well-being after his surgery? Liar and criminal, Robert threatened her safety. Her duty as a physician might come first, but that didn't preclude saving herself afterward or maintaining her front-runner status for Dr. Byra's job. Surinder Byra may've been the first female chief of emergency medicine at Jefferson, but she was still callous.

Lara winced. The grandfather clock ticked. It was like exploding shrapnel in her brain.

She glanced at Robert, his eyes shut against the pain. Tony hadn't returned, and she hadn't heard the toilet flush.

Maybe he locked himself in the coat closet?

Her cell phone pressed against her leg deep in her robe pocket. *Flip up the cell, slip in a new battery, dial 911,* she told herself.

"I don't think so, Doctor." Robert's eyes flashed open.

"What?"

"Don't call the police."

Did he read minds, too? "Neat trick."

"I'll take the phone."

When had she put her hand in her robe pocket?

Her fingers tightened around the tiny device, her only safety line. Personal desire warred with what Robert wanted. His thoughts wriggled inside her head, her hand guided by his desire, his will.

She resisted. The urge grew stronger. Robert wanted that phone.

Call the police. She gripped her cell tighter, but her fingers refused to obey. It didn't matter anyway. Her breath trapped in her throat, speech was out of the question.

Robert's eyes locked onto hers, pupils and irises impossibly blended. Unnatural feelings wove a subtle pattern of tingles across Lara's skin, forbidding her to look away, insisting she remove the cell phone and hand it to him. Her eyes remained locked with Robert's, but her hand stayed true to her will, buried in her pocket.

Two

Robert Eyre slept in a converted church set far back from the road. Robert's agent had purchased the abandoned building, removed all religious artifacts and arranged for renovations. He found the circumstances amusing.

"You know, Boss—in case you need to confess your sins," the agent had said.

Robert had hissed in pretend anger.

He spent days asleep in the church loft, buried in six-hundred-count Egyptian-cotton sheets. A window in his sleeping cell overlooked a farmer's field that stretched across to a hospital. The St. Mary's Medical Center in Langhorne, Pennsylvania, where he worked.

He woke with a start. The sun hunkered down below the horizon and bathed the hospital in an eerie glow. The full moon rose bloodred, a harbinger of Robert's surrender to his beast. Full moons meant nothing specific to vampires, but like Pavlov's dog conditioned to the ring of a bell, Robert had tied his rhythms to moon cycles. Full moons meant time to feed. He'd been feeding this way for centuries.

Moonlight reflected in his eyes. *Feed now.* He made ready and hurried toward the hospital. Time for his shift.

Day nurses teased him as they went off duty. "Hi,

Bob-by." They exaggerated his name as he sashayed by. Heads shook, and eyes gave his toned frame an up-and-down. "Such a waste." Robert smiled and shrugged at the innuendoes. It was easier to pretend being Bobby and gay. Especially after the suicide of his lover, Marilyn. He was doomed to a lifetime of solitude, but such was the curse of his nature.

His body required fresh blood to survive, and the beast within him—Roberre, he had christened it—preferred females. Roberre cared nothing about human life. Decades ago, Bobby realized he owed society a debt for the crimes of his beast. Nursing paid that debt. He also found blood and women more accessible when he worked in a hospital. No more killing.

Day-shift nurses giggled. Bobby ignored them. Coworkers didn't appeal. He'd encountered hundreds of nurses during his career. He thought about nurses but fed from psych patients. He could stop thinking about nurses, including Meridian Jones, anytime. Couldn't he?

Yes. Simple. He'd evade Nurse Jones.

Once a day, when they changed shifts, her gaze probed him. Green, sparkling with laughter and a hint of inner self, those eyes were everywhere. Nurse Jones saw more than he wished to reveal.

Bobby tried to push Meridian from his thoughts. He needed to feed tonight. Marty Connor in Human Resources and Admissions had inadvertently informed him of a new psych patient, Kelly DiRico. He'd pay Ms. DiRico a visit after rounds.

An unshaded window left him awash in moonlight, and he growled. He rounded a corner and stopped short. Too late. His hands balled into fists. Meridian Jones paused on the edge of his personal space. Her scent preceded her, intoxicating and alluring. He didn't want confrontation, so he forced his hands to relax. A trace of anger and frustration flashed across her expression.

She studied his face. "You're avoiding me." Her words floated past, cast a spell over him. Her voice massaged his passion with an urgency few females had ever provoked. He invoked Shakespeare.

When she's angry she is keen and shrewd.

Their eyes locked.

"Why?" she asked.

He hadn't expected to be challenged by this woman. Not directly. "Why don't you act like the other nurses?" he replied.

"What do you mean?"

"They take me as I am." He struggled to keep his fangs from erupting—sexual attraction increased his hunger. Her eyes enticed him to continue. "Why are you searching for something else?"

"Because I'm not really a nurse," Meridian said.

Bobby frowned. Lavender tickled his nose. He detected Nurse Jones's increased respiration, her dilated pupils, and imagined the sweet taste of the blood that pulsed through her veins. Hunger gnawed. His awareness heightened.

Her shift was over; she'd probably had a late meeting. He could escort her to her car. Under shroud of darkness, he'd control her mind with whispered words. He'd kiss her lips, caress her cheek and let his hand slip across her breast as he lowered her to the ground. He'd push back the hem of her dress, his head would slide between her legs and his teeth would sink into the soft flesh of her inner thigh. He'd take enough blood to quench desire, then wipe her memory.

His tongue raked across his pulsing fangs, drawing blood. He swallowed, and the wounds healed.

"I've never been the person people expect," Meridian continued.

Bobby's lust cooled. Her cryptic nature didn't appeal. Feeding from coworkers presented risks, even with a memory wipe. He swallowed again and kept his lips pressed together, then stepped around Meridian and headed away.

She spoke to his back. "Why are you angry?"

Bobby spoke over his shoulder without turning, his voice low and guttural. "I'm not a nurse, either."

Obscurity turned him off. Meridian would no longer haunt his thoughts. What did she mean, she wasn't the person people expected?

Hunger forced him to refocus. Rounds before feeding. He turned a corner and encountered a workman on a ladder installing a camera in a stairwell.

"What's that for?" Bobby asked.

"Don't know, Doc. Got the work order from Security. Putting up three dozen of these all over the place."

Doc. A woman in scrubs was taken for a nurse, a man in scrubs for a doctor. How amusing. Cameras, however, were a problem. *All over the place* probably included nurses' stations. Bobby's image wouldn't register. How could he explain that?

Nervousness chased Bobby through his rounds. As Meridian claimed about herself, he wasn't the nurse people expected. Blood hunger dwelt in his soul. Security cameras increased his risk. The obvious solution was to move to a hospital in a smaller town with less security. Damn it, he enjoyed living here. The refurbished church provided a secure sleeping fortress and easy access to the hospital.

An agent could investigate a job in another hospital, he supposed, but renovating new living quarters might take months. Hiding until he found a new position meant drinking animal blood. He grimaced. Animal blood caused unnerving nightmares.

No, he didn't want to move. He would just have to elude the security cameras.

Before he met Sigmund Freud and developed Vampirical Harmony, he'd lived for decades with tortured dreams. Freud had delved into his unconscious mind and helped him find a different path. No torment. Bobby didn't want to go back to animal blood.

Philippe D'Paltrow sashayed past, interrupting Bobby's reverie. Thin, shorter than average, with a touch of eyeliner and lip gloss, the man had a sexuality that preceded him—and that, unlike Bobby's, wasn't pretend. He looked thirtyish, younger than Bobby. Transferred to the night shift two months before, Philippe had made friends with his fellow nurses—at least the women.

A second pass within five minutes identified Bobby as Philippe's next targeted friend.

Bobby's fangs erupted, and he spoke in a low voice to Philippe's back. Hypnotic words. "Stay away."

Despite this—Bobby hadn't met many people able to resist his suggestions—Philippe returned in a few minutes and stopped at the nurses' station where Bobby worked. He leaned over the counter with an engaging smile. His soft voice accompanied a wave of his hand. "I'm not going to beat around the bush." His index finger flipped back and forth between them. "We're ostracized by almost everyone. I'd like the opportunity to get to know you better."

The plea of someone leading a lonely existence. Bobby might empathize, but vampires don't make friends.

Bobby maintained his gay front. "I don't want a date."

Philippe arched an eyebrow and tilted his head. "Someone to talk to, man-to-man or girl-to-girl, would be nice. I can chat with the other nurses about shoes and what color blouses bring out their eyes, but I can't talk to them about what's *in here*." He touched his breast. "They don't understand. They're not like us."

Bobby concentrated on withdrawing his fangs. "No, they're not like us."

"Maybe we can meet during break? I notice you're still using the men's locker room. Why don't you join the girls? They really are friendlier toward gay men. I'll ask. I'm sure it'll be okay."

"I have to finish my rounds." Bobby picked up a stack of charts and headed down the corridor. Ahead, Meridian ducked down a side hall. Had she been watching them?

Philippe's words trailed after him. "Some emotions are difficult to express. Trust me. You'll feel better when you know someone won't judge you. I'll be in the locker room for my break."

Bobby rounded the corner without answering. What could he say? Should he get friendly with this man who wanted to share gay experiences, then confess, "I'm not gay; I'm a vampire"? Philippe resisted Bobby's suggestions. There'd be no memory wipe.

Above the usual hospital sounds, a familiar voice reached Bobby's ears and wrapped itself around his spine. Damn! He sidestepped into an alcove. Why was *she* still here during the night shift? Meridian Jones angled toward the second floor nurses' station.

She'd lost a few pounds since coming to St. Mary's, but she still had a curvy waist and hips that narrowed into delectable thighs. Bobby licked his lips. Her voice, her eyes, the soft curve of her ass aroused him, but Nurse Jones defied all he understood of human behavior, and that niggled. She'd stop her rounds and offer encouraging words to patients. He'd discovered her one night reading to a comatose Jane Doe. The book was embedded in Bobby's mind: *Faking It*, by Jennifer Crusie. That described Bobby's existence.

So what? It didn't matter now. He refused to think about Meridian Jones.

He pretended to tie his shoelace and watched her walk away from the nurses' station. Her hips swayed, enticed him. He liked to drink from a woman's inner thigh. Lazy vampires attacked necks. Drink and fly—a younger generation. Imagination took rein. What if Meridian followed him home one morning to his solace, high in the church loft? He'd caress her skin, stroke her ego and delve into her mind. Then he'd drink her blood.

Bobby blinked. What was he doing? There was no time to fantasize. The new security cameras presented issues.

Meridian stopped to talk with Head Nurse Cron. Her weight shifted, and the voluptuous line of her body struck a seductive chord. An involuntary surge of blood made Bobby flinch.

The doors behind him popped open, banging into the backs of his legs and forcing him into the hall. He spun around as two young nurses emerged. "Didn't see you, Bobby. Sorry," the taller one said.

Bobby's fangs hadn't retracted. He couldn't open his mouth to speak with these nurses in his face, nor could he hide the bulge in his pants. He forced a tight-lipped smile and noticed the nurses' eyes drift lower.

"Ohhh, Bobby," the shorter one said, "what're *you* daydreaming about?" Giggling, the pair headed down the corridor, but the disturbance drew the attention of Nurse Cron. Meridian glanced over her shoulder, too.

Bobby fought the temptation to invade Meridian's thoughts. He couldn't risk involvement, and he couldn't expose Roberre. The women whose thoughts Roberre assaulted had died. Bobby would expose no one to that again.

A new thought surfaced. He had to escape before Nurse Cron asked about patients and forced an encounter with Meridian. He didn't want to breathe in the familiar scent of lavender that perfumed the air every time she drew near. Though the blood of involvement was like nectar, he forbade himself caressing this woman's soul. Drinking a liter of blood from a sleeping female psych patient would have to suffice. At least the psych patient would stay alive.

Nurse Cron signaled. Bobby pretended not to notice. He'd be forced to talk with Meridian, tempted. Worse, Roberre might make contact.

Bobby headed for the roof, a refuge at night. The darkness wrapped around his skin, and the evening breeze carried sounds and smells that flooded his mind with humanity. Doctors used this roof as a smoking lounge, but a creature of the night could elude these occasional intruders.

He pushed open the emergency exit door and found himself face-to-face with a security guard. Hands up, palms out, the man offered professional assurance.

"Sorry, Doc, access is forbidden."

"You're new?" Bobby asked.

"The hospital added six of us to the force until the situation gets sorted out."

"Cameras and more guards. There's a security issue on the roof?"

"Access throughout the hospital is restricted."

"I won't be able to go wherever I want?"

"You won't be able to go anyplace not directly related to your job. Visitors will be limited, and sensitive areas will be under surveillance twenty-four-seven."

"Someone walking off with bedpans?"

"Blood," the guard said.

"Excuse me?"

"When a hospital loses blood, that's not an everyday occurrence. People get scared. A scared community is bad for business."

"Blood is being taken from patients?"

"You mean, like a vampire?" The guard laughed. "Nothing that far-fetched. We assume packets are being switched and stolen from the blood bank. Can't tell for sure."

"Why deny roof access?"

"The thief comes and goes. Administration doesn't expect us to catch him, but they want him stopped. They figure he might be using the roof."

The moon shone above the guard's shoulder. Shadows danced across the rooftop. A dog howled. Bobby's stomach grumbled. His skin itched everywhere, but with no good place to scratch. His fangs throbbed, and every sense registered heightened awareness.

He needed to feed. Now.

Three

Lara didn't hear Tony return. She screamed when a giant paw grabbed her already sore wrist, yanked it above her head and pried the phone from her fingers. He released her and tossed the phone behind Robert's chair.

"I have one question, Boss."

"What's that, Tony?"

"Why would she use a spoon?"

Robert's eyes narrowed. He licked his lips once, then glanced at the chiming grandfather clock. "Would you mind finishing up, Dr. West? It'll be sunrise soon."

"And what, you'll turn into a pumpkin?"

"Tony turns into a pumpkin. I turn into something else. The bullet, please. I want it after it's removed."

Night was fading, and Lara sensed the urgency in his words. She trembled and fought back the fear rising in her throat. A single mantra kept her focused: *I'm a physician first.*

She edged alongside her patient, scalpel in one hand, a bottle in the other. She'd decided to skip the Novocaine. Robert could deal with the discomfort. Lavishing antiseptic on the wound, she watched as the surface bubbled and Robert clenched his teeth—a victory without celebration.

How far would she go to save herself? She thought about poking around the wound longer than necessary, allowing Robert to grow weak, eventually to pass out. She'd still have Tony to deal with, and he'd proven agile and observant. Since she hadn't been allowed to call 911, was this her only option?

Robert spoke again as if he understood. "I'm familiar with hospital procedures, Doctor. Don't try anything stupid." His eyes flashed. "Get on with it."

How could he know her thoughts?

Maybe rendering Robert unconscious wasn't the answer. Certainly it wasn't ethical. *Doctor, do no harm.* Escape meant eluding both men and harming neither.

She gritted her teeth. Her eyes squinted. No plan leaped to mind, and she refocused on saving her patient.

Fear wouldn't steady her hand, so she latched onto the only other available emotion—anger. Her face burned and her jaw ached with tension.

The extraction proved the toughest she'd encountered. The slug had seared its way into Robert's flesh and fused to everything it touched. Lara tugged, but it refused to let go. Every time the bullet shifted, Robert winced. Finally Lara cut the flesh surrounding the wound and yanked the bullet free before it reattached.

Staring at the slug, she felt a sudden urge to keep it, examine it. Cutting-edge technology? She'd never seen anything like this. Probably no other physician had, either. There might be a monograph in it.

Robert exhaled through his mouth. His eyes closed for a long moment. He breathed in, and his lungs expanded—he was clearly relishing the air. His skin lost its grayish hue, and his face became animated and darker in color.

Lara exhaled, too. Her latex gloves were stained red and she felt perspiration slide down her ribs. She'd forgotten her predicament and that she hadn't yet finished the operation. The internal lacerations required stitching. She needed to close the wound to avoid additional blood-vessel damage. The patient needed hospitalization.

She gripped the compressed bullet with forceps, examined it in the light, then glanced at Robert. With the loss of so much blood, his pressure should have dropped and his respiration should have been up. Instead, he spoke with clarity and surprising alertness.

"I'll take that." As if he'd thought better of the idea, Robert retracted his hand. "Give the bullet to Tony." The large man glided forward from the shadows.

Lara twisted and relaxed tension on the forceps. The bullet dropped into her medical bag. "Oops."

Robert cocked his head. His face darkened and his eyes narrowed. "Clumsy of you. The bullet. *Now.*"

Lara jumped, let out a yelp, and her bloody hand dove into her bag. After a moment she recovered and displayed the bullet, also covered in blood, and faced Robert, not Tony. "I don't think I want you to have this." She clamped her hand shut.

"Don't test my patience, Doctor. You'll find I have none."

Lara jerked her hand with the bullet back toward her stomach and covered it with the other.

"You're playing a dangerous game," Robert warned.

"I like to play," she retorted.

Before Lara could react, Tony yanked her hand over her head, pried open her fingers and confiscated the bullet. He released her unceremoniously. She lost her balance and fell to the floor.

She rubbed her bruised wrist. "I swear, Tony, if you touch me again, I'll take that scalpel, cut off both your hands and shove them someplace none too pleasant."

The goon chuckled and glanced at his boss. A silent command passed between them, and Tony held a different finger in the air, this one aimed in Lara's direction. He swaggered, paused near the hall, peered in the direction of the bathroom but went the other way through the swinging door.

"Don't you pee in my kitchen!" she called out.

"I don't think that's what he meant when he held up the finger this time," Robert said.

"Thanks for that insight."

A grim look replaced Robert's smile. His eyes reflected decision. "I'm sorry we're intruding in your life, Dr. West."

Cabinet doors rattled in the kitchen.

"What's he doing in there?"

"It doesn't matter."

"It matters to me. My roommate will be mad in the morning if there's a mess."

"You live alone."

"I like to dream."

"I'll give you something pleasant to dream about."

A carnal image swept through Lara's thoughts. She shook her head, trying to eradicate it. The vision clung, tingles winding their way across her shoulders and tripping down her spine.

Criminals didn't appeal, so what induced this feeling, the stirrings in her breasts and between her legs? She'd denied them since she'd first heard Robert's voice, but they were there. Unwanted, but there.

The command in his tone, the handsome lines of his chin . . . Hadn't she caressed that chin when she turned his head? The chiseled muscles of his bare arms, the cavernous depths of his eyes, the air of mystery—everything about this man left her languishing in a sea of je ne sais quoi.

It had been a long time since she'd felt anything like this—she hadn't even dated since med school. She'd refused all overtures to love. Fellow students, then colleagues, cast her as an outsider. Hell, that was a natural role. She had her work now, no time for relationships or friends. And no need. She even refused when her surgical team invited her to join them for lunch. Lara liked her solitary life. She maintained her *essence*, what made her Lara West, and shared it with no one.

"Doctor."

Lara blinked. A sensual reflection of Robert tangled with her soul. Her stomach cramped, and a dull throb beat around her eye sockets. She had to do something to free herself from the unwanted image of them making love.

Stay focused on medical issues.

"I have to stitch that wound."

"Tape a bandage over it," he replied.

"If you move, it will bleed again."

"I'd rather not have stitches. I have something else in mind."

"I hate to ask."

A moment passed. "You have beautiful eyes," Robert said.

Whether Lara's eyes were beautiful or not, red flags danced in front of them.

I have wide hips, too, but you didn't mention that.

Suspicion made her feet itch. Why did a man tell a woman she had beautiful eyes? Two reasons—either he was in love with her or he wanted something. Love? She'd never experienced it. It would play no role in her life. She was happy alone. Love didn't enter this equation, and Lara had removed the bullet. What did that leave?

Lara sat where Tony had dumped her. Robert glided out of the chair and onto the floor nearby. Muscles rippled across his bare chest. His wound looked smaller. Nothing oozed.

"A bandage, if you don't mind," he said.

Kneeling up, Lara pulled a large patch bandage and a roll of tape from her bag. She made quick work of tearing the tape, stretching it long enough so that it covered as much hair on Robert's chest as possible. At least when he pulled it off, it would hurt.

As she pasted the last piece into place, his hand danced through the air, and his fingers caressed her cheek. His nails glistened. She hadn't noticed that before.

What happened to the blood that had stained his hand? Not a trace remained.

"You shouldn't be moving around."

"Your skin is soft."

"You'll bleed again."

He leaned closer. She felt his breath on her neck. "I can hear your heartbeat."

"You should be resting."

"Then I wouldn't be able to do this." His lips brushed across the skin just below her ear. "Or this." His tongue traced a half circle behind her lobe.

"Your blood pressure is liable to drop."

His mouth curved down her neck to her shoulder. Lara was unable to control the small moan escaping her lips. She blinked. The idea of sex with this handsome stranger elicited excitement, despite the circumstances. Though the notion remained ridiculous, she could not prevent the urge washing over her or the warmth spreading between her thighs. Robert wanted something. Was it simply her?

She'd never wanted a significant other, never needed that intimacy. Her *essence* was sacred, not to be shared with friend or foe. Maybe that made her different than most people, but she rejoiced in her difference. What was happening to her now?

Lara's heart beat faster. Veins throbbed in her neck. Her robe gaped open, and Robert's eyes focused there. His gaze strayed across her skin, stripping her of dignity and any vestige of hope.

When their eyes locked, a shudder traced its way down the back of her skull. Another person's feelings wheedled their way into her mind: memories of living in dark, desperate loneliness, the scent of blood, hunger for something such as Lara had never felt before, then the overpowering urge to sleep.

She fought the urge. She didn't realize she was holding her breath.

Robert's nostrils flared. "I can smell it."

"Smell what?"

"Fear." He bared his teeth.

Fangs appeared. Lara's eyes widened and her jaw dropped. Her heart thudded against her chest. Robert growled. His face contorted. He leaned forward as if to attack.

Lara's consciousness slipped away, but . . .

No. She couldn't sleep.

Why not? There must be some reason.

Try to focus. Where am I? Not the hospital—wrong sounds, wrong smells. Home?

Yes. I'm home. Safe.

Sleep, intoned a voice, not in her ears but deep in her mind. *Sleep.*

Giving in would be easy. She just had to concede consciousness to the voice.

No!

Footsteps and more voices. These voices rang in her ears.

"You're hungry. Why not take her?"

She knew that voice. Who was it?

"No trail."

She knew the second voice, too. It matched the voice in her head.

"Why not wipe her memory?" the first voice asked.

"Memory could resurface. You have the bullet?"

"This bullet almost killed you."

"I'm already dead. The bullet could've destroyed me. Allowing myself to be shot was a risk worth taking. We wouldn't get a bullet to examine any other way. Ready?"

"Yeah."

"Start the fire."

The words didn't make sense. Lara wanted to scream, but she wasn't really awake, and the sound evaporated in her throat.

Four

Anticipation fed hunger. Bobby melted into the bowels of the hospital. He now shared consciousness with his alter ego, Roberre.

Roberre the hunter. Roberre the seducer.

Roberre the beast.

Bobby worked on the second floor and preferred to feed on the fourth. Until they finished construction of the psych ward, the hospital used any available space for such patients. With security already in place, unused maternity rooms were currently being utilized. Late at night around the full moon, Bobby always found a female psych patient alone in one of these rooms. Familiarity with hospital procedures facilitated his exploitation of this; it was easy to avoid other nurses making rounds, and security guards didn't question the presence of any hospital employees—until now.

Bobby and Roberre used the stairs to move between floors rather than elevators. The stairways were vacant, but for junkies and occasional lovers seeking seclusion for an illicit tryst. Both proved avoidable. As Bobby climbed to the fourth floor, his urge to feed expanded. His tongue traced his fangs and a low growl escaped his throat. Roberre desired taking Meridian instead of a faceless woman in the dark.

"No," Bobby asserted. He wouldn't risk emotional involvement with anyone.

Dim lights stretched along the empty fourth-floor corridor. Screams erupted from one of the birthing rooms, and a smile twisted Bobby's lips. The renewal of life ensured an endless blood supply. He hadn't asked for this existence, but he had a right to maintain it.

Not at the expense of human life.

For a long time, it had seemed he had no choice. When his fangs erupted and the beast overtook him, bloodlust—the need to survive—overpowered every other emotion. Roberre had taken many lives. But Bobby controlled the beast now and worked in hospitals to repay his debt to humanity.

Still, Roberre wanted more than just blood.

Bobby stiffened. He embraced his immortality, but he hated the beast.

Immortality? Vampires are dead.

Animal blood nourished his body but tortured the last dregs of his human soul. Nightmares, terrifying images of suffering women and pain inflicted by a monster always followed when he drank animal blood. He'd awake sweating, breath jagged, fangs aching. . . . No, it was human blood or nothing. He could keep himself from being a murderer.

Roberre the hunter glided down the corridor unnoticed. He slipped into an alcove across from room 431.

In the next room, the floor nurse woke a new mother for her midnight feeding. Bobby had timed his arrival with practiced expertise. Soon, the nurse trundled the newborn to the nursery. Room lights were doused, the door closed and the new mom slept. She wouldn't hear anything coming from room 431.

Bobby refocused. He sensed the psych patient, Kelly DiRico, drugged for sleep, drifting in a dreamworld.

Roberre's senses carried him beyond the smell of hospital antiseptic. He smelled X-ray film and wrapped bandages. He tilted his head back and inhaled the scent of baby. Something compelling laced the musk of a newborn. The aroma swirled in the corridor, and Roberre inhaled more deeply the collage of odors and sounds.

Fresh blood had burst fragrant in the birthing room down the hall, but now the woman's screams had abated, and a baby's first cry filled the air. Roberre paused. The hard drive whirled at the unoccupied nurses' station, the second hand ticked around a clock mounted on the wall, the electrostatic charge crinkled the air around the exit sign at the end of the corridor. This was the catalog of sensations in a heightened awareness.

A pinprick of empathy welled in Bobby for Ms. DiRico. He quashed it. Hunger filled his every pore, drove every muscle, surrounded every aspect of his being and ignited a relentless desire. The beast took rein.

Roberre glided across the corridor and caressed the door of 431. He sensed his prey behind it: female, vulnerable, asleep. Blood gurgled in her veins. Perspiration, faint and sweet, tainted her skin. Roberre emitted a low hiss.

Bobby imagined the lavender scent that wafted from Meridian. Would the blood of involvement taste sweeter? Why was he denying himself, again?

Hunger redirected his focus to the present, and he twisted the doorknob. Someone should've locked it to keep him out. Someone should've sprinkled the door with holy water, strung garlic across the frame. Someone should never have left this psych patient alone.

No one anticipated a vampire in the maternity ward. The door wasn't anointed with holy water or lined with garlic. The knob offered no resistance, and Roberre the seducer slipped into the darkness with Ms. DiRico.

Her breathing slowed, the soft, steady exchange of someone in deep sleep. Her neck veins bulged as blood surged toward her heart. Bobby drifted to her bedside. The angelic face didn't deter his desire. Plump breasts filled the hospital gown. A nurse had strapped the patient's wrists to the bedrails.

Bobby pinched the sheet and tugged, teasing himself, as more and more of his victim lay exposed. His mind touched hers and the two blended, and he used her thoughts to keep her asleep. For the moment.

Arteries throbbed in the soles of her feet, and Roberre massaged them with both hands. A sigh escaped Kelly's lips as Roberre caressed her flesh, encouraging the blood that would soon be his.

Gruesome thoughts swept Roberre, but Bobby imposed his will. He withdrew his hands. Roberre needed to feed, and he wanted to make love sheathed in violence. Bobby needed female blood, and he wanted his prey to live. His goal remained clear—keep Roberre in check while maintaining his own existence.

In the dark shroud of the maternity ward, Bobby twisted his hands in the air, examining them with Roberre's heightened senses. Their slenderness belied the beast's strength.

How could violence appeal to anyone? He'd experienced viciousness with Genghis Khan, discussed tragedy with Will Shakespeare, but it wasn't until he'd explored the dichotomy of his personalities with Freud that a glimmer of reprieve from Roberre's brutality took shape. The great psychiatrist had suggested Bobby make a trade with the beast. Bobby needed human blood to calm his soul but couldn't abide taking a life. The beast drank his prey to death.

Couldn't he take blood without killing? Yes. One obsession existed more powerful than the beast's bloodlust, one way to rein in the bloodsucking monster. Sex. Freud helped Bobby concoct a mutually satisfying experience involving both sex and feeding—Vampirical Harmony.

Bobby stiffened as Roberre massaged Kelly's feet again. "I want to take her now." His voice emerged deeper than Bobby's, more guttural.

The dangerous moment expanded. If unleashed, Roberre the beast would physically tear into his prey and satisfy both his sexual lust and need to feed. Bobby would be sated by female blood, but his victim's life would be ended. Killing, even to maintain his life, was unacceptable.

Bobby allowed Roberre to caress her calves, to touch Kelly DiRico's tender skin and simultaneously entwine his thoughts with her dreams. In her mind, Roberre the seducer could take his victim wherever he wanted her to go. In her dreams, he would take Kelly on a journey culminating in multiple orgasms, all of which would be real. During the five stages of Vampirical Harmony, she would experience sensations, the intensity of which would rock her soul.

Roberre relished the entire experience. The power to fulfill a woman fed his ego. Her climax fed his id. Part of Vampirical Harmony depended on recognizing a woman's fantasies and re-creating them, so Roberre had a unique advantage. He read a woman's thoughts. He understood what pleased her.

In Kelly's dream, Roberre lashed her to the bed.

Her first dreamworld climax arrived quickly, and the woman's body arched up, her face and neck flushed, her breathing ragged. Roberre's feelings mirrored hers, and this amplified the expanding intensity of her contractions. He sensed the tension in her calves. The exquisite interaction was enough, and his victim exploded in the first stage of Vampirical Harmony.

"She's mine," Roberre said. All the while, he shared her ecstasy.

By the time they'd reached the fifth stage an hour later, Kelly's body was drenched in sweat, the sheet beneath her soaked. Time for Bobby to reassert control.

"No," Roberre said. "I'm not through yet." He grabbed the young woman's ankles and forced her real-world legs apart.

The room smelled of sex. Bobby's tongue traced across his fangs. The jagged edge ripped his flesh, and he tasted tart blood before the wound healed itself. Bobby stood on the precipice of his own climax, on the edge of losing control to the beast. Roberre verged on domination. Bobby had to act now.

His hands slid up Kelly's legs and his tongue trailed along the flesh from ankle to knee. Bobby imagined Meridian in Kelly's place. Excitement surged. His tongue circled higher, searching for Neverland. In her dreamworld, Kelly was reaching the threshold of a final climax, her back arched, and her hips thrust forward.

"Time to wake up," Bobby whispered.

"No!" Roberre said.

Kelly's eyes sprang open as Bobby sank his fangs into the soft flesh of her inner thigh. Blood gushed into his throat, the nectar of death. He imagined the taste of Meridian. His victim's orgasm coincided with his and Roberre's, and Bobby stifled all of their screams—three parts ecstasy, one part fear.

He withdrew his fangs before Kelly passed out. He hovered above her, eyes locked to hers, holding her immobile in action and thought. "You will not remember. . . ."

The memory wipe always followed the final stage of Vampirical Harmony. Kelly would waken in the morning with an incredible afterglow most likely explained by drug-induced sleep. She might wonder why sleep made her breasts ache and her toes curl. The two welt marks on her inner thigh would itch like crazy for a day or two before they dissolved. No other trace would remain of her experience.

Bobby drifted out of room 431. "Someone should've locked this door," he said.

"Let's find out if Meridian's door is locked," Roberre suggested.

"No."

"I'll treat her to Vampirical Harmony and she can keep the memory."

A tempting female voice interrupted, wound around Bobby's passion. "What are *you* doing up here?"

Meridian. What's she doing here in the middle of the night? Careless of me to be seen like this.

He needed an answer. A believable answer. They stood in front of the glass-walled nursery.

"Babies," he said.

"Excuse me?"

"I like to watch babies. Theirs is the blood of innocence."

She tilted her head. "That's a peculiar way to talk about a baby. Babies *are* born innocent, though. Society corrupts them all."

He looked at her. "You mean there's no hope for any of us?"

"To remain innocent? Our culture won't allow it," Meridian said.

"A depressing thought."

"Not really. We may not remain physically pure, but we can choose to remain innocent in our hearts, to treat people with care and respect."

"Not many people choose that path," he finished.

She glanced over his shoulder. "Whom were you talking to a moment ago?"

"You ask a lot of questions. I thought you worked days."

"Double shift tonight. I didn't see anyone else. Whom did you say you were talking to?"

"Why do you always stare at me?"

"Why do you always answer a question with a question?" A sly smile creased her lips.

"Easier to avoid giving answers. Something my mama taught me." He refused to allow his smile to engage. "And . . . I talk to myself. Oh, I am fortune's fool. Why do I think you're going to be trouble?"

His tongue glided across his fangs. The beast lurked, waiting for Bobby to make a mistake. He had to escape before that happened, before Roberre captivated Meridian.

As he angled toward the emergency stairs, he could sense Meridian's smile. "You keep walking away." She raised her voice. "And trouble is my middle name. Something *my* mama taught *me*."

"I'll teach you something your mama didn't," Roberre remarked, his voice too low for the words to be discernible.

"Excuse me?" Meridian said.

Roberre laughed. "I just need an hour of your time."

Bobby blinked and ground his heel into the floor. He needed to control his alter ego. He knew he could submerge that part of his consciousness—though suddenly, he wondered if Roberre sometimes did the same to him. Was he ever entirely submerged? What if Roberre led a clandestine life, controlled his body and did whatever he wanted? Would Bobby even know? What would Roberre be doing?

He dragged his mind back to the present, and something about Nurse Meridian Jones tugged at the slim thread of humanity left to him. She was a mystery, and to humans, a mysterious woman always appealed. She was irresistible.

And dangerous.

He shook his head and pushed open the stairway door. The latch clicked shut as the door closed behind him. He hopped over the railing and glided down into darkness.

Five

Lara needed to escape.

Wait. They think I'm unconscious. When they leave I can call the police and walk out.

"Start the fire."

What fire?

Sleep, the inner voice said.

Lara snuggled inside of herself, her mind folded over, then folded again, and darkness enveloped her thoughts. An image of trees bending in the wind blended with a star-filled sky and the sound of a gurgling stream. Wind and water called to her, as did the heavens, and Lara sank deeper into oblivion.

Sleep, the voice repeated.

Where am I?

She imagined fingers caressing the nape of her neck, warm breath, a tongue tickling her flesh. The pattern of her thoughts didn't match anything familiar, and the engulfing sensations filled her with tranquility. Had a voice said something about harmony?

Sleep, the voice said.

Oh, yeah. I'm home, safe.

Her nostrils captured a faint woodsy odor before her ears recognized the crackling of drywall. Real voices and footsteps faded.

Wake up.

Sleep, the voice cajoled. *Sleep.*

Her feet itched, shoulders ached, eyes shut tighter. She inhaled, and her lungs filled with smoke. A coughing fit racked her body.

Wake up! Lara's eyes popped open.

She remembered sinking to the floor, the reading lamp splashing its feeble light around her. Her cheek was now pressed tight against the carpet. Dense smoke obliterated the ceiling. She couldn't stop coughing as foul air forced its way down her throat.

Get out of the house.

She realized then that her arms were stretched behind her back. She tried to bring them to her side and push up. They didn't budge. She was hog-tied. She wrenched her neck and smoke burned her eyes.

Robert intended to kill her!

She clenched her jaw and gnashed her teeth.

That son of a bitch. He has no right—

There was no point in complaining. She tugged, but her arms refused to budge. How had he tied her? Not with rope. She twisted her neck and peered at the bonds.

Newspaper, rolled tight on a diagonal. Her father used to roll newspaper like that and tie it in a knot for fire kindling. Lara's ankles were crossed and bound, and her wrists were bound to her ankles.

He'll never get away with this. It's newspaper.

Very strong newspaper.

Her gaze darted around for a sharp object: scissors, broken glass. Nothing helpful appeared. She tried to roll onto her side, because she had no other ideas, and rolling always worked when people were tied up in the movies.

Hell! The first way she rolled hurt her shoulder more, so she rolled back onto her stomach. What movies had she watched, anyway?

She needed to clear her head, breathe deep and slow. That brought more smoke into her lungs. How long before the fire reached this room?

Emergencies cropped up every day in the lives of trained professionals. No panic. Dr. Lara West knew what she wanted and how to get it. Right now she wanted to escape from a burning house. All she needed in order to do that was—

Lara screamed as panic shoved its way into her life. She kicked; paper bit her flesh. She wiggled her arms; carpet burned her cheek.

Helplessness cast its shroud as more coughing racked her. If she didn't get out of the house, she'd die of smoke inhalation. Her mind raced, and it was then she realized how Robert would get away with it. She'd be discovered overcome by smoke, restraints burned away in the fire, charred flesh hiding the marks. She'd examined enough fire victims. Most *had* died from smoke inhalation, and the bodies had burned afterward.

The official report? Fire started on the stove when the victim walked into the living room. Accidental death. There'd be no suggestion of murder.

What could she do?

Get out of the house.

She rolled to the right and rolled to the left. She brought her feet closer to her shoulders and her hands closer to her knees. Both hurt, and neither helped. She rocked, slithered, wiggled, squirmed. She struggled against the newspaper and lost again.

Fire erupted around her. Flames had escaped from the kitchen and now licked the living-room ceiling. There was no way to reach a phone, and she was too far from neighbors to wake them by screaming. She couldn't die like this.

Mom. Dad. Help me.

Tears flowed across her cheek. With a huge sob and uncontrollable shaking, Lara collapsed inside herself, surrendering to circumstance. She squeezed her eyes tight and conjured an image of her parents, long since dead.

An odd thing happened: her father spoke. *Honey, there are two times when you're excused for peeing your pants—when you laugh too hard, and when you're scared out of your gourd.*

Lara wasn't laughing, but she felt a trickle of urine escape.

"I *have* to pee."

Her eyes burned. Tears streamed across her cheek.

"I'm a surgeon. I save people's lives. I can save my own."

Another drop of urine warmed her inner thigh. Embarrassment warred with disgust.

Hold it in. Roll over.

She rocked and rolled between coughing fits. On the fourth attempt she found herself nearly faceup, bonds beneath her, the strain on her arms and legs unimaginably worse.

Go ahead and pee.

Nothing came out.

Come on, damn it.

Fire leaped across the living room, the walls now engulfed in flames. Heat seared her exposed flesh. Lara's medical bag rested on the edge of the dining room table, out of reach.

Concentrate. Pee.

She didn't have to go anymore. "Eughh, I can't do this."

Lara failed again when she tried to scream. No sirens interrupted the early morning quiet. Her neighbors were busybodies, except when she needed them to pay attention.

Someone sound an alarm! No paperboy, no garbagemen, no dog walkers, no joggers—what's wrong with this neighborhood?

Mrs. Polansky across the street knew the time and date of every delivery to Lara's house.

"Wake up, Mrs. Polansky. Look out your window now!"

Mrs. Crider next door knew the number of tulips blooming in Lara's garden and spotted dandelions within minutes of eruption.

"What's up, Mrs. Crider? Doesn't a *house fire* play havoc with aesthetics on our block?"

The clock chimed 5:00 A.M. and all's well—if you like charred neighbor. That made Lara laugh. Laugh, cough, laugh . . . and pee.

A stream of hot urine poured out of her, brushed her inner thigh, and tumbled through space, splashing on her hands and feet. "Eughh." She grimaced in disgust.

However, it was what she needed. Lara grunted and tugged and groaned and tugged harder. She rolled onto her side and struggled with her urine-soaked bonds. She jerked her arms and wrenched her legs, her face contorted with effort. One of the papers finally shredded, and she had some wiggle room. She twisted and pulled and another paper shredded. One hand whipped free. She clawed at the remaining paper.

Fire raged all around her. Part of the ceiling crashed onto the dining-room table and knocked her medical bag to the floor. Lara tried to jump up, but her legs buckled.

She crawled toward the table, grabbed her medical bag by its brass handles and burned her hand. "Shit!" She needed that bag. She doubled over the bottom edge of her robe like a pot holder and, with her other hand, gingerly reached for the handles again. They were hot but bearable.

Another huge chunk of ceiling crashed down. She'd never get out crawling, so she forced her legs beneath her and pushed hard to stand up. Dense smoke burned her eyes. She covered her nose and mouth, her throat already blistered. Dodging burning furniture and a collapsing ceiling, she escaped out into the night.

Hog-tied with newspaper and left to be burned alive by a man whose life she'd saved—that's what Lara reported to the police. Maybe. She didn't remember. Time stretched out and rushed forward. Had she mentioned two men, or just Robert? The next few hours blurred with sirens and flashing lights, a blanket tossed over her shoulders, convulsive coughing, oxygen mask, a ride in an ambulance.

She argued with paramedics. "I need my medical bag."

"We'll take care of that later. Let's just get you to the hospital."

"I'm a physician. I need my medical bag with me."

The paramedics finally relented after a harangue convinced them she wouldn't calm down without it. They refused however to take her to Jefferson, where she worked. Policy demanded they deliver her to the closest hospital.

Lara knew St. Bonaventure's Medical Center, though she'd only visited there once. She was now rushed through the ER and admitted for observation. Her coughing hadn't stopped. Pain overwhelmed her consciousness before the drugs took hold. She'd been burned a few places, including on her hand.

She stretched out on a gurney, aware of being wheeled onto an elevator, medical bag pressed against her hip. Finally sleep overcame her. Sleep without voices.

Six

Meridian wasn't just working double shifts. She wandered into view far too often for coincidence. She'd been stalking him for two weeks since their encounter at the nursery. Her pursuit added difficulty to feeding, but it also added a spice of mystery. A woman tracking him? It lured his mind out of decades of complacency. The more he risked, the greater the craving to risk more. Bobby hadn't played such a game in over a century. He was enticed enough to weave his rounds in and out of her sight.

Of course, eager as he was to engage a mind that challenged his, he held on to one specific tenet: he would not get involved. He would maintain emotional distance. This game could be a fun pastime, an extraction of flirtation and whimsy from what was once his human soul, but that was it. His humanity simply surfaced so that he might glimpse the sunlight, soon to fade into darkness for eternity.

Before he rounded the next corner, tingling overcame

his body. His palms itched with no good place to scratch. His eyes widened, throat constricted, fangs erupted. Head tilted back, he encountered a scent. Meridian.

She stood near the nurses' station at the far end of the hall, talking with Marty Connor. Bobby sidestepped into an alcove and sniffed again. Lavender. He slipped one doorway closer. Her back faced him, and she didn't know he approached. Marty didn't notice, either—his eyes were old and weak. Bobby wanted to hear their conversation. He continued his dance down the hall.

Meridian wore a tight uniform, and when she shifted her hips, she oozed seduction. She ran her fingers through the back of her short hair, an innocent yet sensual gesture. Bobby imagined her hands entwined in his hair, her nails digging into his scalp. The image made his fangs ache.

A sense of familiarity washed over him. How could that be?

Unlike most of their coworkers, Meridian kept her mind narrow in focus. She masked her thoughts as if concealing a great mystery. She stalked *him,* so he'd unearth that secret. He had time and proximity. Her guard would slip, and he'd slide inside her thoughts. She'd be unmasked eventually.

Someone tapped his shoulder. Bobby jumped. Weren't there rules about sneaking up on vampires?

Philippe grinned. "Didn't mean to startle you."

Something protected Philippe from mind control. Did it also stop Bobby from sensing his presence? This wasn't his typical human experience.

"I was wondering if you'd have a few minutes later to talk?" Philippe said. "I'm having issues with Nurse Cron and could use advice from someone who's known her longer."

Philippe's genuine nature appealed to Bobby. He hadn't made friends in decades. He nodded. "I'll find you after I finish my rounds." *And after I feed.*

"Great!" Philippe hurried away.

Bobby refocused on Meridian. She still chatted with Marty. Bobby maneuvered down the hall.

Meridian turned just as he got within earshot. Bobby sensed Nurse Cron suddenly exit a room behind him. Trapped!

Meridian smiled as if she'd heard his approach. She pivoted back to Marty, who said good-bye and left without even noticing. With Nurse Cron behind him, Bobby could only proceed.

His stomach knotted. Had Meridian truly sensed his presence? She held his gaze, her eyes a blur. Bobby could get lost in those eyes.

Her devilish smile said she understood his predicament. He didn't want her to understand, but he couldn't stop himself from wanting her. Desire snaked down his throat, through his stomach and beyond.

What hope did he have to win the upcoming skirmish without controlling his passion? He clenched his teeth and forced his fangs to recede. Stepping forward, he paused in her personal space, making clear that the next words were for her ears alone. " 'As if increase of appetite had grown by what it fed on: and yet, within a month—let me not think on't— Frailty, thy name is woman!' "

Meridian blinked once. "*Hamlet?* Have you no words of your own, sir?"

"Actions speak louder."

Meridian cupped her ear. "I'm sorry, what did you say?"

Bobby frowned. " 'Raindrops on a rainy day and a contentious woman are alike.' "

"Proverbs now? And rain? Haven't you seen the night? The moon is nearly full, the sky is cloudless . . . and I almost never argue." She stepped close, and Bobby flinched, surprised to find her unmoved by his assault. Or at least undeterred.

Her lips pursed. "Touch me. What're you afraid of? I don't bite."

Bobby bit back a smile as a memory flooded his mind. He'd attended the execution of Mary, Queen of Scots. Someone—was it the Master of Gray?—had uttered, *"Mortua non mordet."* Being dead, she will bite no more.

He settled for a less amusing response, himself. "This is neither the time nor the place for touching."

"Not the right time? Not the right place? We're in a hospital." She glanced at the wall clock behind the nurses' station. "It's ten minutes before twelve. Would ten minutes after be more suitable? Perhaps in the X-ray room? With a candlestick?"

Bobby stared at her, trying to fathom her depths. He almost began, "A friend of mine . . ." but caught himself and instead said, "Freud once wrote, 'The great question that has never been answered . . . is "What does a woman want?" ' "

Meridian gave a small smile. "To know what a woman wants, you need to understand the woman."

"You suggest the impossible!"

The woman cocked her head and dropped her voice to a whisper. "So that's it. You're afraid to try."

"I'm afraid of nothing," he growled.

Meridian smiled. "The X-ray room it is, then—in twenty minutes."

Bobby fought his desire. After a moment he won. "When you get what you want, it won't be planned and you won't have advance warning."

The woman simply stared into his eyes. "Then I

have a surprise to look forward to—and the thrill of spontaneity."

Did she mock him? Those voluptuous, moist lips curled. Her eyes danced with laughter, yet she sounded serious. He had issued a threat, thrown down a gauntlet. She had picked it up as one might pluck a flower from a garden. Challenge accepted. This woman was strong. She begged for Vampirical Harmony. She deserved such exquisite pleasure, and deserved to remember it. No memory wipe.

Guilt stabbed at the fleck of humanity still lodged in his consciousness. He'd been responsible for Marilyn's death, the same as if he'd snapped her neck. He couldn't leave another woman so vulnerable. Meridian would enjoy the encounter, but he would have to wipe her memory.

Roberre snorted. "Don't worry, I'll handle it for you."

Bobby drew a deep breath. "No!"

"Excuse me?" Meridian asked.

Bobby escaped just before Nurse Cron reached them.

Seven

Lara registered myriad aches and pains, from the enlarging twinge behind her eyes, to the foul taste in her mouth, to the stiffness in her knees. The bandage wrapped around her burned hand throbbed. Whatever she'd been given for pain had worn off.

One eye creaked open. A man stood at the foot of her bed reading a chart. A physician? No way. Nor the police—they'd come and gone, their report filed. Reporters weren't allowed in private rooms. Who did that leave?

A crew cut, a chiseled face, close-set eyes, pointy teeth—all suggested a wolf in government man's clothing. But what did the Feds want with her? This particular Fed wasn't tall by any standard. His suit hung from his frame as it would from a hanger. He reminded her of the assistant administrator at Jefferson who wouldn't take no for an answer. *Just want to be friends,* was his line. *Want to go out?* Lara's head hurt.

Questions didn't fit her mood. She needed answers. The clock indicated she'd slept almost twelve hours.

Like that of a startled wolf, the Fed's head twisted around. "I see you're awake."

"Who're you?" Her voice rasped.

He ignored her question and refocused on her chart. "West, Lara. Accomplished surgeon." He cocked his head, his words accusatory. "You helped a wounded man last night."

"A man bleeding to death."

"Not likely."

"How would you know? You weren't there, and you're not a physician." She couldn't believe she was defending the man who broke into her house, threatened her life, delivered to her a slice of heaven—what else could one call that incredible feeling?—and then burned her house down with her still inside.

"What makes you think I'm not a physician?"

"What makes you think I'll answer your questions?"

He flashed a badge. WPAVU.

Lara raised her eyebrows and shrugged, tired of manipulation. "That means something?"

"Witness Protection Agency."

"And the *VU*?"

"Special branch. Doesn't matter. I need you to describe the man you helped last night."

"Is he a criminal?"

Lara wasn't sure why she asked. She already knew the answer. She hated Robert for violating her life. He'd threatened her. But . . . he'd also touched her in the most intimate way. He hadn't forced himself on her. What she'd felt had transcended sexuality. He'd understood her thoughts. How could that be? Hadn't she allowed his touch? Hadn't she encouraged him? Her body language, the uncontrollable moaning?

Lara's face contorted with the memory. That man had *tried to kill her.*

The government man raised an eyebrow.

Lara closed her eyes. "Go away, please. Don't you have a mug shot? I'll pick him out of a photo gallery."

"Not possible."

Her eyes popped open. "Why not?"

"I need a description, Lara."

"Dr. West."

"Don't play games."

"I like to play." Uh-oh. This conversation sounded familiar.

The man lifted the bottom edge of her bedsheet and peered at the soles of her feet. "Come on, Lara, a little cooperation."

Lara curled her legs in. A movie scene flashed in her mind of a character who'd lost her shoes. *That's all that's left, just the ruby slippers.* What role did Lara play?

"Get out of my room," she growled.

"Testy, are we?"

The man sauntered to the window, brushed aside the curtain and stared at the fading sun. "I have all the time in the world, *Dr. West.* But you may not."

"What's that supposed to mean?"

"I'm here to interview you."

She'd saved a man's life, the man had tried to kill

her, and now a witness protection agent was conducting an interview? Lara blinked.

"You think I'm in danger?"

"Personally, no, but I have orders. It's my job to certify that you don't need our program."

"Witness protection?"

"The man you treated last night. A description, if you please. Height?"

"Don't know."

"You're being contrary."

"No, I really don't know. He sat the whole time."

"Best guess, then."

"Best guess? Six feet."

"Age?"

"Couldn't tell. Might've been forty or a hundred and forty."

The agent squinted and lowered his chin. "You're more perceptive than I gave you credit for. Did your patient have a name?"

"Robert."

"Robert Helstrom. Aka Robert Burns, aka Bobby Kennedy—there may be more. Our file goes back a long way. Last night you helped him escape."

"I most certainly did not! I helped him to stay alive."

The agent mocked her tone. "You most certainly did not." He edged around her bed. "Look, lady, you may think it's all a joke or a misunderstanding, but this is serious. Once Robert Helstrom sinks his fangs into you, he doesn't let go." He laughed, as though he'd made a joke. Lara had the distinct impression the agent was talking around whatever he really wanted to know.

Her eyes glazed over. Events were moving too fast. How had she gone from overworked surgeon performing an operation to an out-of-shape woman seduced by a criminal and made a hog-tied barbecue? Her thighs tingled and her nipples hardened with the more powerful memory. She didn't have the energy for this government agent who wanted to play twenty questions.

Or was it that Lara didn't want justice, but a repeat performance of the sexual fantasy?

The agent turned away and spoke over his shoulder. "I guess we're finished here."

She didn't respond.

The agent walked to the door, then turned. "Police report said you removed a bullet from his"—he flipped through a notepad—"right shoulder. You gave him the bullet, he tried to kill you, end of story." He flipped the notepad shut, slipped it into his pocket and put his hand on the doorknob. "Have a nice life, Dr. West."

She smirked at his waving hand, recognizing it as an empty gesture. "I gave him *a* bullet." Dropping it in her bag first had been no accident. She had a bullet collection from the ER. Robert had gotten one of those.

The agent's chiseled face turned back as he froze in the doorway. "What's that supposed to mean?"

Lara had finally realized the point of the interview. Cutting-edge technology or whatever. "I didn't give him *the* bullet."

"He'll have figured that out by now." The government man rubbed his chin and paced. "Smart girl. Dangerous, but smart. Lost in the fire?" He didn't wait for an answer. "Robert will be back tonight looking for it in the ashes. Without knowing it, Doctor, you've baited the perfect trap."

"Why will he wait until tonight?"

The agent chuckled, yanked a cell phone off his belt and searched his contact list. Lara eased back into her pillow and stared at the ceiling. She didn't understand what about the bullet he was so fixated on, but she knew she'd saved something important.

"He probably won't come himself," she offered. "He didn't want to touch the bullet. He'll send Tony."

The agent hesitated midcall. "Who's Tony?"

"The man with Robert last night."

"The police report didn't mention another man."

"I didn't mention the other man to them."

The agent frowned. "Hold on," he said into his cell phone. "This Tony. He's . . . a regular guy?"

"Except for a weak bladder and surprising quickness."

The agent latched onto that, his focus intensified. "What do you mean, 'surprising quickness'?"

"He was unexpectedly fast for such a fat man."

The agent nodded. "No . . . inhuman movements?"

"Inhuman? Only when he grabbed my wrists." She glanced at the flesh there, noticing the dark bruises for the first time.

"You're right. Tony would've been there and gone. Too bad. We really didn't want Robert Helstrom to have access to that technology." As an afterthought he added, "I'll send a team to check through the rubble, just in case."

He made a half arc around the bed and peered past the curtains again. The sun had fallen onto the horizon, a fiery orange ball. He continued his phone conversation as if Lara weren't in the room. "It'll take him months to synthesize an antidote. With her help, we may still have time to find him."

When he flipped the cell phone shut and his eyes narrowed, Lara's foot tingled. The agent turned partway toward her, and the dying sunlight cast a shadow across half his face. "Experience has taught us that Robert doesn't leave loose ends. Funeral arrangements will fool your colleagues, but they won't fool Robert. He'll come looking for you soon enough."

"What funeral arrangements?"

"There's a reason why Robert tried to kill you."

"To avoid my fee?"

"You can identify him."

"As what? You already know he's Robert."

"Identify him as the man from whom you extracted that bullet. It means that if we're forced to capture him we can take judicial action. Our case would be stronger if we had the bullet. You're a doctor, you examined him, you can prove he is who we say he is."

"Robert?"

"We have to get you out of here right away."

"I seem to be missing something."

The agent waved a dismissive hand. "Something he said or something he did will lead us to him. We can figure it out later." He flipped open his cell phone again and barked, "This is Special Agent Jake Plummer. Get me a secure line, then put me through to Dog."

Lara fought annoyance. "Listen, Special Agent Jake Plummer of the WPAVU, whoever you are, what are you talking about and who the hell is Dog?"

"Agency head honcho. Omnipotent."

"You call him Dog?"

"I'm dyslexic." He paced, and peeked down the hall in both directions. "I need a better description of Tony, besides 'fat.' "

"Dark eyes, receding hairline, over six feet tall, somewhere between thirty and forty, perspires a lot. Check bathrooms."

His cell beeped, and Special Agent Plummer refocused as he answered. "I need an extraction. Now. St. Bonaventure's Medical Center, fifth floor. Code yellow." He pushed the curtains aside as the last crease of sun disappeared below the horizon. "I know, I can see it. Don't worry, she'll be in my care. By the way, she'll be perfect."

He flipped his cell shut, reattached it to his belt and pushed the emergency button to summon a nurse.

"What are you doing?" Lara's eyes leapfrogged from the window to the hall to Special Agent Plummer. "We're not on the fifth floor."

"How do you know? You weren't awake when they brought you up here."

She pointed to the embossed door as a nurse scampered in. "Room number seven twenty-two. We're on the seventh floor."

"Not for long," Agent Plummer said.

Lara peered up from her wheelchair at her escort as they left her room. Dizziness kept her seated. Her knees ached and her eyes burned. Agent Plummer was insisting she change rooms for safety, but she wasn't changing lives. No way. She liked her life and she wasn't going into any witness protection program.

She snapped orders at the nurse. "I need my medical bag."

"No, she doesn't," Agent Plummer said.

"I *need* my bag," Lara commanded. That bullet was the one thing she had that gave her any control. Pain seared behind her bandaged hand. "I want a painkiller too. Demerol, fifty milligrams."

The nurse glanced at Agent Plummer, who nodded. The woman disappeared and reappeared a moment later, deposited Lara's black medical bag in her lap and a pill in her hand, and escorted both Lara and the Fed as far as the seventh-floor elevator bank.

Lara clutched the bag and popped the pill, dry.

Inside the elevator, Agent Plummer pushed the button for the ninth floor. He glanced down at Lara, his face screwed tight. "How can you swallow a pill without water?"

Lara didn't answer. The elevator rose before she spoke again. "Perfect for what?"

Plummer considered her. "The VU part."

"What's that? You said it didn't matter."

"That was then."

The elevator dinged, and Special Agent Plummer whisked Lara past a giant nine painted on the wall. They hurried down the first hall they came to.

"This isn't the fifth floor, either," Lara grumbled.

"Nothing escapes you. That's what makes you perfect."

Lara squeezed the hand brakes. Her wheelchair screeched. The Fed banged his knee and cursed.

"Don't you know how to use a wheelchair? What are you, a doctor or a quack?"

"A woman who wants to know what's going on."

"Did you think the Witness Protection Agency runs a free program? Hardly. Not in the VU." Agent Plummer's shoulders hunched. "You have to pay for it somehow—service." He slapped her hand away from the brake, rubbed his knee and started moving again.

"I don't want to be in the Witness Protection Program. You're talking about giving up my family, my career, my friends."

"You don't have family."

"I like to dream."

"We'll give you something to dream about."

"A new identity? For what? To protect me from a man whose life I saved? I'm not going to do it." She clutched her black bag. Robert wanted it.

Agent Plummer spoke fast. "The government needs you. There's no choice. You're in. Dr. Lara West is dead. The funeral will be day after tomorrow. Too bad you can't attend."

"Can't attend my own funeral?"

"You'll be busy."

"Busy being dead?"

"Busy training."

"For what?"

"New job."

"Let me guess, in the VU?"

"Perfect."

"Are you learning impaired? No way. Not gonna do it," Lara growled. This man fantasized. No way would she enter the Witness Protection Program. She wasn't about to give up her life as a surgeon, let alone her dream to be chief of emergency medicine at Jefferson Memorial.

They'd stopped in front of the emergency staircase. Agent Plummer glanced around before he pushed open the door. He wheeled Lara through to the landing, spun her chair around, tilted it back and wheeled her down the steps backward. Each thunk jarred her skeleton and ignited a new headache.

Lara's head throbbed, and maybe that was what made her actually start considering. Dr. Byra, the outgoing chief of emergency medicine, had refused her request for a vacation. She'd refused Lara's appeal for a sabbatical. She'd ignored her demand for a leave of absence. Lara needed time away from ER pressure. She needed time to refuel, if she were to be awarded head of ER. What if she went along with Agent Plummer for two or three months? It would be her sabbatical. She could read journals, write a few articles, further her own career, all without job pressure. Agent Plummer could catch Robert Whoever-he-was, and then he could resurrect her. Dr. Lara West could return to Jefferson in time for Dr. Byra's retirement party and her own succession to the post.

"Where're we headed?" she asked.

"Haven't you been paying attention? Fifth floor."

The wheelchair thunked down another step. "I'm glad we didn't go to twelve first. Dare I ask why we went to nine if we want to be on five?"

"Misdirection. Consider this your first lesson. People on seven saw us leave. They think we went up."

"We did go up."

"No one on nine knows who you are, and no one saw you leave nine. Only the agency will know we're on five. Robert will track you, but don't worry. Your trail will end here, too." He watched her face carefully, and she had the sense he knew her thoughts.

Lara shrugged. "Why should I worry? Because some guy wants to kill me?" She stared at the government agent. "I had four years of college, four years of med school, three years of residency, and now that I'm four months from becoming chief of emergency medicine, you want me to chuck it all? You want me to give up my life, my friends, everything. All this, but 'Don't worry, Lara'?

"And don't tell me I don't have family. I've got a second cousin, Ed Farley. He's a detective. He'll find me if I disappear."

"Really? Where's Detective Ed now?"

Lara didn't know. She hadn't heard from him since her mother died ten years ago. "That's not the point."

"What is the point, Dr. West? You don't want to perform a service for your country? Didn't you take an oath to help your fellow man?"

"That's a medical oath."

"So, what—it doesn't count? You're in a high-pressure job. Wouldn't you like to escape the tension?"

Was he reading her mind? What if she slept for a week? No cell phone, no pager, no midnight emergencies. A tempting idea. Tension oozed from her at the very thought. The wheels clunked over two more steps and jarred her back to reality.

"This chair—new shocks, wider tires and it'll ride like a dream," she said sarcastically. "That's what I'm doing, right? Dreaming? I can't possibly be headed toward the fifth floor and the VU, whatever the hell that is, in the WPA, accompanied by Jake the Snake."

"You've got a wise mouth, lady. I'd dump you here, but I've got orders."

"I know. Orders from Dog." She shook her head. "I am not, under any circumstances, for any reason, going into the Witness Protection Program."

They reached the fifth floor. Agent Plummer donned a lab coat. He wheeled Lara past the nurses' station and grabbed a chart from the rack. The desk nurse didn't even look up. Jake angled them to the side, stopped and pretended to take a history.

"Clever disguise," Lara hissed. "I bet your mom wouldn't recognize you."

"Leave my mom out of this. She has enough trouble recognizing me as is. Don't worry. By the time we're done, nobody'll recognize you, either."

"I don't want to change identities," she repeated for the fiftieth time.

"You want to stay alive, don't you?"

Lara turned her head. She didn't know what to say. Robert had tried to kill her yesterday, but how could he really discover she'd survived? Why bother? She hadn't seen him commit a crime, though she knew he had done so. He just wanted the bullet. If she surrendered the bullet to the government, there'd be no reason for Robert to come after her.

Thoughts of a few days away from the ER seduced her. Her burned hand required time to heal before she could operate again. She could leave the hospital with dyslexic Jake the Snake and go see Dog. She wouldn't mention that she had the bullet, in case she needed a bargaining chip. Afterward, she'd go back to her life and deal with job tension. Somehow.

Her headache spread as she considered something else: to be a witness, you had to *see* something. "I'm not a witness," she grumbled.

Jake glanced at his watch. "When my people arrive, we'll get you out, but you'll have to listen to them and follow instructions."

"I always follow instructions," she replied.

"What is it that makes me doubt that?"

"I don't know." She tried to hide her disdain. "What's code yellow?"

Agent Plummer's eyes darted from Lara's chart to her face. "Doesn't matter."

"You mean, '*That was then*'?"

He shook his head. "You really don't think you're in danger, do you? You think this is a joke."

"I think there's no valid reason for giving up my life."

"That's what code yellow means. There *is* a valid reason, and if you don't see it, we'll convince you."

"I don't want to be convinced. This is my life. I like it."

Agent Plummer straightened up and scanned the hall. He touched the side of his head, and Lara noticed for the first time that, along with the lab coat, Jake had donned an earpiece. "Time to go," he said.

"What? What do you mean?"

"My people are in place."

"I don't see anyone. Where?"

"Trust me."

"Right. You're just going to wheel me out?"

"You're going to walk out."

"That won't be conspicuous or anything in this hospital gown?"

He pushed her away from the elevators and the nurses' station. Two orderlies mopped the floor in front of a storage room. Agent Plummer glanced over his shoulder, then spoke to them.

"Everything set?"

The taller orderly responded. "Katie's inside." He jerked his head toward the door. "The delay seemed necessary. Ralph has two suspects under surveillance near the main entrance. Suzanne followed two more inside, where they separated. She's with the one headed toward Administration." He touched his right ear, much the same way Jake had a moment before. "He's there."

"Not much time," Jake said. He tilted his head toward Lara. "We need to bring her into the program now."

Lara grabbed Jake's lab coat with her good hand. "Don't you understand English? I'm not going into witness protection. I'm not giving up my life!"

Jake pried open Lara's fingers. "Okay, Dr. West, I'm tired of arguing. You have a decision to make. We don't have much time. You give the word and we'll all walk away. You can face Robert's people on your own. You heard Owen's report. There are bad people downstairs, and it's only a matter of time before they finish searching the first floor. So, what's it going to be? You want us to get you out of the hospital safely, and you can decide later whether or not you're going to be in the program, or do you want us to leave you here?"

Lara couldn't swallow. She made life-and-death decisions for other people, not herself. What if Robert did want her dead? What if he'd sent Tony to get her? With one phone call, Special Agent Jake Plummer had mobilized a team of at least five agents.

Dizzy, sore, with a bad hand—why was she fighting

this? The prudent choice didn't seem hard to make. She just had to surrender control. Ha!

"Okay, take me out of here. But I'm not going into your program."

Agent Plummer glided into action. He held his hand up to his earpiece, listened again, then pointed to the two orderlies, who'd resumed mopping. He opened the storage room door and wheeled Lara inside. "We have to get you into a disguise before they track us to this floor."

"What disguise?"

"Don't worry. You'll be perfect. Katie's going to help you change."

A rugged woman in a nurse's uniform, old enough to be Lara's mother, grabbed the handles, spun her wheelchair around and backed Lara up to the far wall. Jake headed for the door.

"Where're you going?" Lara demanded.

"Worried about me? Ah, that's sweet. I'm going to wander around. The fourth guy nobody's watching fits Tony's description." He yanked the door open with one final comment. "Make her *believable*, Katie. And do a better job than last time. It's important that Dr. West survives."

Seven and One Half

The storage room door clicked shut behind Agent Jake Plummer and muffled the buzzing clippers inside.

"She didn't look scared," Owen, one of the fake orderlies, said.

"Good call with the code yellow," the other agent added.

Jake smirked. "Katie's got her now. Cutting a woman's hair off lowers her self-esteem and makes her more pliable. You guys do your jobs. She'll be scared by the time she's in Katie's van." He shoved his hands into his pockets. "Nice touch throwing in *surveillance*. Our people still haven't spotted anyone?"

"Not a soul," Owen said. "Robert won't dare come after her here. Too public. And it's not like someone Tony's size can hide from us. Believe me, she's not in danger in this hospital."

Jake nodded. "Get into position. Make it convincing."

"Don't worry, Boss. We'll make her a believer."

Eight

Hunger gnawed at Bobby, and he thought of Meridian.

What did the two have to do with each other? She invaded his thoughts. She haunted his dreams. Night after night, his rounds blurred. He hadn't considered intimacy with a woman for the last half century, and now it was all he could do.

He tilted his head back and sniffed. Her familiar scent chased him down hospital corridors. With increasing frequency, he wondered about her caress. Sweet blood? Would she sheath him in humanity? Would she accept his inhumanity?

Did it matter? These were mind games that diverted attention only in the moment. Greater amusement lay ahead. Another psych patient would occupy this room soon, and when she slept, Bobby would enter her dreams, make love with her in that ethereal world, then sink his fangs into the real flesh of her inner thigh. He would taste blood again before long.

He gathered the curtain sash and stared out the window of room 431. The moon, two days before full, bathed him in light. The urge to feed scratched his throat, and his tongue glided along his fangs. His hands balled into fists. Experience taught he could control this urge for two more nights. It was a constant struggle.

Bobby hurried from the room. His fangs withdrew, but he stiffened as he approached the emergency stairs. A worker labored by the door. A toolbox proclaimed the kneeling man a locksmith.

"That looks like a Carlsburg locking mechanism," Bobby remarked.

The locksmith glanced up and scratched his ear. "Not many folks familiar with lockin' technology. Anyone can open these doors from this side, but if the latch don't click shut in sixty seconds, an alarm'll sound. 'Course, once you're on the other side, ain't no openin' it. Have to call security, 'less there's a fire. Then these babies release automatic-like."

"Great," Bobby said. The locksmith missed the sarcasm. Bobby climbed the stairs.

"If you're plannin' on comin' back this way, I'll be finished in half an hour. After that, nobody'll be able to get through this door."

"Don't worry, I'll fly in through a window," Bobby said.

"Ha ha," the locksmith replied. "Very funny." He lowered his voice. "Every fuckin' doctor thinks he's a damn comedian."

The nights grew shorter with the onset of summer. The hospital installed closed-circuit cameras, added guards

and locked doors to beef up security. Unaccounted-for
drugs could be ignored by administration, but missing
blood alarmed everyone. The crime's ghoulish nature
put the hospital in an unwanted spotlight. Not surprisingly, officials clamped down. The extra security meant
feeding problems for Bobby.

He stopped in the corridor across from the blood
bank, annoyed. Few humans stole blood. Had another
vampire invaded his territory? What vampire in his
right mind would drink stale blood warmed in a
microwave? Bobby shook his head. The hospital kept a
record of every stored liter. How stupid could a vampire be?

"Want to take a break with me?" a nurse asked as
Bobby headed toward the second floor nurses' station.
Her smile was charming, and her coy glance made
clear her intentions.

Why flirt if they think I'm gay? Bobby winced, shook
his head and continued his rounds.

He considered his problems. Security was interfering with feeding, coworkers were interfering in his
personal life, and Nurse Cron was interfering with his
work. She no longer found typed reports acceptable,
and insisted he make verbal reports while she took
notes.

Bobby rounded a corner. Down the corridor, Nurse
Cron chased Meridian from a patient's room. Philippe
wheeled a crash cart from the same room, racing after
the preeminent cancer specialist, Dr. D'Lorien. Nurse
Cron's round face was beet red and accentuated by
short black hair. She wore one pair of glasses low on
her nose and a second pair on a chain around her
neck. Her voice carried over the usual hospital din.

"You're not authorized to perform that procedure!"
Meridian stopped. "The patient could've died by

the time a physician got there. His pressure plummeted. His heart stopped. The tube had to go back in." She didn't sound contrite, but matter-of-fact—the man's life needed saving, the duty fell to her.

Bobby chuckled. Such hubris would qualify as a mortal sin in the *Book of Nurse Cron*.

Meridian remained unfazed, and Bobby was struck by the fact that her actions paralleled his. She followed a code of behavior that she believed in, and neither hospital rules nor their enforcer would deter her from that path.

"You are *never* to overstep the boundaries of your position again," Nurse Cron was saying.

"As much as I like to cooperate, I can't promise that," Meridian said. She didn't wait to be dismissed, but acknowledged Nurse Cron with a tilt of her head and disappeared into the hospital hubbub.

The woman's passion for life pounded like the wild surf, drawing Bobby ever nearer. He clung to that fragment of humanity which demanded a connection, the fragment that knew that she was emotionally challenging.

Yes, the blood of involvement flowed in Meridian's veins, and Bobby yearned for satisfaction. Her blood *would* taste sweet.

The first night Meridian failed to be present when he arrived at work, Bobby could hardly focus. Her penetrating eyes and the alluring sway of her hips . . . he'd grown accustomed to seeing them, to anticipating his next glimpse. He imagined the soft skin of her inner thigh and felt his blood surge just to the left of his right pants pocket. It was disconcerting.

Desire for blood warred with desire for intimacy. He craved the caress that only souls in love could exchange.

He desired the understanding of a woman who stood on equal intellectual ground. Involvement heightened physical pleasure . . . but increased risk.

He stalked the hospital halls in a daydream, avoiding security. He wanted Meridian, but he needed to feed. In three days the moon would wane, and he'd have to control his desire for another month in order to keep suspicion minimal. His fangs ached. He itched everywhere, with no place to scratch. His last feeding had failed to satisfy hunger.

Meridian's image haunted him, chasing him along the hospital corridors. He ducked into an elevator, pressed *two* and closed his eyes. The mechanism engaged. At the last moment, a hand blocked the doors, which reversed and glided open. Footsteps padded to a stop. A trace of lavender floated on the air.

"No avoiding me now. I've been transferred to the night shift." The beautiful woman he'd been thinking of had appeared as if from a dream. She stared into his eyes and extended her hand. "I'm Meridian Jones. What's your *real* name, Bobby?"

He froze. Did she sense his dual personalities?

"Names mean nothing," he said, though he couldn't refuse her hand, the chance to touch her flesh. At the hospital, Bobby always kept his flesh warm and his pulse beating. Otherwise, someone might notice.

"They bring us closer. So says my intuition," she replied.

"Intuition? We're strangers, nothing more." She might even feel the spurious pulse through his palm. *And palm to palm is holy palmers' kiss.* What did Romeo reply? *Have not saints lips?* Or fangs?

"We're less strangers than you care to admit."

In the elevator her scent filled his nostrils and her sensuality excited every nerve. Bobby kept his lips pressed together as familiarity overwhelmed his senses. He withdrew his hand, certain that Meridian masked a secret identity, too, and that this created a bond between them. Was that what she meant?

Meridian stepped closer, invading his space. "You're not what you seem."

Excitement swelled. What exactly did she sense?

"I like my anonymity," he said.

"I'm not suggesting we do anything other than remain anonymous, but you give away some of your anonymity with every action."

"In what way?"

"In your words, your attitudes, in the emotions you try so hard to keep hidden." She touched his sleeve. "You quote Shakespeare and the Bible, you're the only man who talks with Philippe, and you look at me as if, I don't know, you're a starving man and I'm the last meal on Earth. So I'll repeat the question. *What's your real name, Bobby?*"

The beast surged forward, but Bobby couldn't allow Roberre to make contact. He exerted his influence, trying desperately to keep control. An answer flowed out, low and guttural.

"Some women call me Roberre."

The elevator door slid open on the second floor and Bobby escaped, dragging a laughing Roberre with him.

Nine

Muscles rippled in Agent Katie's arms and veins bulged in her neck. She either spent too much time working out or popped steroids. She waved buzzing barber's clippers in the air.

Lara twisted her head. "What's *that* for?"

"We're going to start with your hair."

"Shorten it?"

Katie half nodded, half shrugged. "In a manner of speaking."

"I don't want my hair cut." Lara knew she sounded like a petulant child.

"Sorry. Emergency call. No time to find a wig. They're looking for a thirty-something female patient with long hair. Disguise means changing your profile. Older with makeup . . . change your clothes, change your hair." She raised the clippers.

Lara snagged Katie's wrist. "I said I'm not getting a haircut."

Katie twisted out of her grasp. She dropped the tool in Lara's lap, spun the wheelchair around, grabbed the armrests and bent over, her beet-red face in Lara's. "Nobody asked you. Your government decided you're in danger. We're taking action. These are my orders. I'll strap you into this chair if necessary, so decide damn quick, lady, if you want to cooperate."

Lara wasn't used to taking orders. "You're scaring me."

"Do you have any idea who's after you? Of course not. Jake hasn't explained it." Katie straightened, drew her shoulders back, the lines in her face growing tight. "I work for the United States government Witness Protection Agency." She leaned closer, dipped to eye level, her voice soft. "Do what I say and we'll keep you alive."

Minutes later, Lara patted the top of her head. Nothing but the shortest bristles remained. "What did you do to my hair?"

Katie had already packed the clippers away. She handed Lara a fluffy, ecru linen garment. "Put it on."

Her eyes wide and her jaw hanging open, Lara brushed her hand across her scalp again, unwilling to come to terms with her new military haircut. Katie painted lines from the corners of Lara's eyes toward her ears, and more lines from her eyebrows across her forehead. Lara gasped when she caught her reflection in a storage container.

"Are we going trick-or-treating?"

Katie ignored her. "Ready to stand, ma'am?" She spoke with urgency.

"Ma'am? My name is Dr. Lara—"

"Not any more, ma'am." The woman yanked Lara out of the wheelchair.

"What're you doing?"

"Orders. Get dressed."

"I don't like being touched."

"What do you think is going to happen if they catch you in the hospital?"

Lara looked away and shook out the garment she'd been given. "This looks like a religious robe."

Katie pressed her palms together and bowed. "Hare Krishna."

"I need my medical bag." Lara took half a step toward the wall where her black bag had been deposited.

Katie's viselike grip fastened onto her arm again, immobilizing her. "Get dressed. You need to leave."

"My bag."

"I'll bring your bag."

Lara pulled the robe over her head.

As they left the fifth-floor storage room, Katie pressed pamphlets into Lara's hand, patted her back, and aimed her away from the elevators. The instructions seemed simple enough. "Take the stairs down to the third floor and switch stairwells there. Go down to the first floor, chant, pass out pamphlets. Jake will meet you in the lobby."

"Chant what?"

"Doesn't matter. No one'll listen to you."

"Why the third floor first? Why not go right to the first floor and outside?" Ventilated air whistled across Lara's bald scalp and entrenched her in her Hare Krishna role.

"There are suspects inside, and you're at the wrong end of the building. Most people would go to the closest elevators, then walk the first floor. They'll search for you on the first floor. Hospital records show you were on seven. When they don't find you on one, they'll go to seven. Walk the building on the third floor."

Lara's head throbbed.

Despite her misgivings, she breezed down the fifth-floor corridors with Katie at her back. The agents/orderlies had moved their work so that one mopped in front of the nurses' station and the other stood near the elevators. Escorted all the way, she knew nothing could go wrong here. Lara bowed to a couple of physicians, handed a pamphlet to a nurse and chanted. Katie followed her into the stairwell and peered over the fifth-floor railing until Lara swung open the door and disappeared on the third floor.

She held her breath as she passed Radiology. "What happened to simple?" she whispered.

Tony.

Tony loitered on the third floor getting a drink. What, were there no water fountains on the seventh floor in this hospital, or was this just bad luck?

Too late to back up, too late to duck into another room. Didn't Agent Jake know she needed help now? Lara kept up her act, hoping Tony didn't recognize her. She handed a pamphlet to an orderly. Tony turned and stared into her face.

He won't recognize me.

Lara's heart beat faster. She avoided eye contact and continued to chant. Tony spread his feet apart because his fat legs couldn't get any closer together. His mass blocked the hall and blotted out all light.

Gurney wheels clanked behind her. Doorbell chimes tinkled, like a department store's announcement for ladies' lingerie. The smell of antiseptic wafted through the air. Lara's nose wrinkled.

The hospital scents forced a memory rush. Tony had set the fire. It had been Robert's command, but Tony provided the match. Did he recognize her now? Imagining his gaze searing into her scalp, Lara tried to swallow a rising lump in her throat, knowing she had to maintain composure for another moment.

Tony's huge head turned as she offered a pamphlet to a patient parked in a wheelchair. "You," his gravelly voice exclaimed.

An incriminating tone, but Lara refused to acknowledge it. She continued down the hall, pace steady—unlike her heartbeat. She held her breath, hoping some other person might respond.

A second "You!" more damning than the first, echoed in the corridor and wrapped itself around her. Lara ran.

Tony ran faster. He lunged and almost snagged her robe with a giant paw. Lara sidestepped a nurse and a couple of doctors exiting an elevator.

"Security!" Tony called.

Would the guards really help him, or was Tony just proclaiming himself part of the hospital security force? Last night, before the fire, she'd seen a hospital identification badge dangling from his belt. Maybe he worked here.

"Out of the way!" Tony growled at passing hospital employees.

It was difficult to run in the damn robes, and Lara gasped for breath. Her knees ached. She needed to reach the lobby, and Fat Tony was gaining on her. She reminded herself that help waited downstairs.

She slid around a corner and banged her knee on a wheelchair parked next to a gurney. She spun the empty gurney into the hall just as Tony appeared. He crashed into it like a dead whale tossed onto a beach by a wave. Lara shoved the wheelchair against the gurney and thrust crutches into the spokes to lock it up. She slogged away as Tony wriggled backward to stand.

She couldn't keep running. Ragged breath burned her lungs. She had to hide.

Stay calm. Jake had said to use misdirection.

If she didn't reach the lobby, Agent Jake would search for her. Katie had told her to walk the third floor, so the third floor was where they'd look first, wasn't it? Lara sucked in air. Surgeons understood pressure.

She rounded another corner, hurried past a sitting area. Out of Tony's sight, she had ten seconds to hide. Pick a door, any door. X-RAY, MRI, EMPLOYEES ONLY, BLOOD BANK. In a hospital this size, X-ray and MRI were in use 24-7. *Employees Only* meant a lounge, so no hiding places. The choice proved obvious.

The blood bank door swung open. An island counter stared back, cluttered with microscopes, test tubes and flasks. A second door led to the refrigerated blood-storage area. More counters lined the walls, doors above and below, plenty of places to hide.

Lara opened closets and cabinets. Filled, filled, filled. Panic filtered into her thoughts. Her smoke-ravaged lungs burned.

Voices in the hall. She circled the island. All these hiding places and no place to hide! The inside door had a small glass window at eye level. A wooden wedge propped the door open so that the door touched the end of a counter, creating a dark, triangular cavity behind it.

Voices rang closer from the hall. "You!"

Lara knew that voice. It addressed a different *you* this time.

"Did you see a woman in a white robe?"

Lara wormed her way behind the door at the end of the counter and ducked, her back pressed to the wall. She held the edge with one hand while the other brushed the counter to replace the doorstop. She scraped her knuckles grabbing the doorstop and pulled it toward her, so the door was propped open as before, but with Lara ensconced behind it on her knees. She'd blocked herself in with no room to stand up without pushing the door closed.

Her heart thumped in her ears, and her breathing sounded like Darth Vader. Christ, Tony wouldn't have to see her to find her.

"Check for yourself. No one's in there," a second voice in the hall said.

She could sense Tony rumbling into the room, pausing to take in cabinets and closets before renewing his search. Doors opened, then slammed shut, as if proclaiming, *Not this one . . . try the next.*

"Did you find her?"

Someone else had entered the room, though Lara hadn't heard footsteps.

"Did you find her?" the newcomer repeated.

She recognized the voice of seduction, its subtle tones and false dreams. *Robert.* The throbbing intensified behind her eyes.

"Chased her into this hall," Tony said. "Then she disappeared."

"She's here," Robert replied.

Danger glided closer. Lara held her breath. Sweat made the cotton robe cling to her back.

Being stalked in a hospital seemed so unbelievable. What had happened to Agent Jake? Lara felt helpless, like she was falling in a nightmare. She squeezed her eyes shut, pinched the flesh on her arm, peeked at her surroundings. She was hunched in the small cavity behind a laboratory door and dressed in Hare Krishna robes.

Sorry, but you're not dreaming.

New footsteps tapped on the tile. Likely those of a lab tech. "Told you no one was here," one of the earlier voices said.

"The blood bank?" Robert's beguiling voice asked.

"Through that doorway," the tech said. "But you're not authorized to go in there."

The next few moments blurred for Lara. A voice spoke—to the tech or her? "You will not remember seeing me. Forget. . . . Forget. . . ."

One man's shadow crept beneath the door, yet two men entered the blood-storage room.

Forget. . . .

"Let's go," a seductive voice from inside the room commanded.

Lara jumped as if a compulsion had seized her. She kicked out the doorstop, grabbed its handle and slammed the door shut. A face vaulted to the window. Menacing eyes spoke to her heart. *Don't move!*

Lara backed away nonetheless. The tech stood to one side, silent, staring with an empty expression.

The door sprang open. A man dashed from the shadows so fast that his movements blurred. Tall, with a chiseled face. Irises and pupils blended together, age betrayed in those eyes. Tony stomped out after him.

Lara didn't have time to think. She extended a pamphlet. "Hari Krishna, brother—"

Tony grabbed her wrist, snarled and tossed the pamphlet on the floor.

Lara rubbed her sore arm. She glanced from one man to the other. Tony had tried to kill her. He'd set fire to her home. He'd tracked her to this hospital and trapped her in this room.

A voice spoke inside her head. *You will not remember seeing me.*

She stared at the man with strange eyes. Who was he?

It didn't matter. She had to escape from Tony.

"Help me," she pleaded with the tech.

He suddenly woke up, frowned and addressed Tony. "Is this the woman in white robes?" he asked.

Tony smiled. "Yeah."

"He's chasing me," Lara explained. "Call security. Please."

"He *is* security, lady. You'd better go with him," the tech said.

Insanity ran amok. Lara could run to the stairs and find Agent Jake on the first floor. In fact, that's what she was contemplating. But . . .

Don't move.

Lara blinked and twisted her head. A tall man, fortyish and with rippling muscles, blocked her escape. He looked familiar, those penetrating eyes with irises that blended into pupils. Was he Tony's man?

You will not remember seeing me. You will forget. . . .

Where had she seen him?

It didn't matter. She had to escape from Tony.

She lurched away, dodged down the length of the island, bumped into a stool and stumbled. Tony crept along the other side, mirroring her. Tony's henchman took a few steps and closed the distance, sealing her into a trap.

Lara panicked. She grabbed the nearest graspable object—a beaker filled with red liquid. Blood. She raised it, as if to throw it at the flunky.

For the first time, those dark terrifying eyes abandoned their focus on her and narrowed on the blood. Instead of backing up, the man continued to advance. Lara stood her ground. She cocked her arm. "Don't come any closer!"

From behind, Tony grabbed her wrist and twisted it high above her head. Lara grimaced as he disarmed her and slammed the flask onto the counter.

"Be careful with that," the tech said. "It's O negative." He frowned again and spoke to Tony. "Can you get her out of here? Is this guy with you, too? He doesn't look like security. Who is this?"

A look passed between Tony and the man with strange eyes, and then Lara blinked. The second man had been right in front of her, but now he hovered behind the tech, his mouth open and close to the tech's ear. He glanced at Lara and refocused.

Lara refocused too. The voice of command wove a delicate pattern in the air. *You will not remember seeing me. Forget. . . .*

Lara blinked.

The man disappeared.

Who had disappeared?

Lara's mind swirled. Tony wrenched her arm high behind her back and shoved her toward the door.

"I warned you about grabbing my wrists," she growled.

Tony chuckled. "I'll risk it, Dr. West. Seems I have a job to finish. I need that bullet. The real one, this time." He propelled her down the corridor.

"You're going to march me through the hospital as

your prisoner? You'll never get away with it." Two
nurses exited the employees-only door and headed toward them, the perfect opportunity to test her theory.

"Help! He's kidnapping me."

Tony shrugged and offered a wan smile. "Psych consult."

The nurses nodded and continued past as if this
were an everyday occurrence. Hell, in a city hospital,
this *was* an everyday occurrence. Maybe Tony would
get away with it.

He guided her past the nurses' station. Each time
Lara squirmed, his grip tightened. Frustration numbed
her mind. Tony's massive head leaned close to her ear.

"Where's the bullet?"

She remembered a bullet. Where'd it come from?
Not a gun. A surgical procedure. Not on Tony. Tony
had witnessed it, though. She remembered that, too,
but no other face came to mind. Why couldn't she remember?

The elevator chimed and the doors slid open. Two
men in lab coats, one with an unpronounceable name
monogrammed above his breast pocket, engaged in
conversation, waiting for the doors to close so they
could continue their journey. Stethoscopes looped
around their necks. Dr. Monogram had other instruments stuffed in his lab coat. The pockets substituted
for a black bag.

Tony directed Lara on board and stabbed *twelve*, the
control panel's top floor. As the elevator doors closed,
Lara interrupted the conversation.

"You have to help me. I'm a physician, and this man
is kidnapping me."

Tony flashed a hospital security badge and made a
grandiose gesture toward her robes. He nodded his
head and winked. "Psych consult."

Lara couldn't blame him—it had worked before. "I demand to speak with the chief surgeon. Dr. Grey, isn't it?"

Tony shoved her arm higher behind her back. "She's been making demands all day. I told you, Dr. Grey went to Seattle a year ago." He smirked at the other hospital personnel. "This afternoon she wanted to be a religious zealot, so she painted her face and put on a robe."

Lara caught her bizarre reflection in polished elevator chrome. Uh-oh.

"I *am* a physician." She pointed to a gadget in one of Dr. M's pockets. "What layman would know what that is?"

"Okay," Dr. Monogram said. "What is it?"

Tony squeezed tighter, and answered before she could. "I'm a layman, and I know what that is. It's the thing you use to look into people's eyes."

"Yes, but I know its technical name," Lara said.

Dr. M and his buddy looked at her with bored indifference. Dr. Buddy spoke. "Sure, lady, I don't think I've heard its technical name since med school."

Tony pushed her arm higher still. It was like being on excessive meds: brain-freeze struck. She frowned, glared, her forehead wrinkled, and no answer emerged from her lips.

Tony chuckled.

The elevator stopped at seven, the doors slid open and the two doctors stepped off. Lara felt her last chance slipping away. A surge of emotion welled up, and her throat constricted. The doors began to shut.

"Ophthalmoscope!"

Dr. Monogram spun around just in time to grab the doors and prevent them from closing. He glanced from Lara to Tony's massive face and back to Lara. "You've got our attention," he said.

"What floor is Psych on?" she asked.

"Five," Dr. Buddy answered.

Lara cocked her head. "We passed five." She stretched up on her tiptoes, leaned forward and winced. "Could you get him to let go of my arm? It hurts."

Dr. M refocused on Tony. "She's not going anywhere with us standing here. Why don't you release her arm and we can sort this out?"

Tony shook his head. "I don't think so."

Lara gained confidence. She fidgeted in place, her expression exhibiting more pain than she really felt. "Ouch!"

Dr. Buddy advanced into the elevator.

"Okay," Dr. M said. "That's enough." He tugged on Tony's arm. "Let her go."

Tony swatted him into the control panel. The elevator chimed. Dr. Buddy tried to stop Tony with no more success—except that to shove him, Tony had to release Lara. Off-balance, she fell forward and out between the closing doors. Tony wasn't fast enough to follow. The doors shut and the elevator rose.

Lara scrambled to her feet, alone in the seventh-floor corridor. She ran a few steps, then froze. What would Agent Jake do? *Take the stairs. Stay away from elevators. Walk the building on the third floor.*

The hell with Agent Jake and his cohorts.

Lara pushed the call button, hoping that one of the other two elevators would get there before Tony returned. She forced a smile at a passing doctor. No one manned the nurses' station. She pushed the call button again and stamped her foot.

At the far end of the hall, about thirty yards away, a lit sign proclaimed EXIT. The more time passed waiting for another elevator, the more the sign beckoned.

She could hear Agent Jake. *Don't wait. Run.*

She glanced down the empty corridor.

Not that way, Imaginary Jake said. *Find another way off the floor. Misdirection.*

She stabbed the uncooperative call button.

Not the elevators, Fake Jake reiterated. *Run.*

Lara peered down the cross-corridor, then back at the exit sign. The exit door popped open and Tony burst through.

Even from this distance, Lara could see his face redden. She punched the elevator button twice more. Her weight bounced foot to foot.

Run!

The elevator dinged. Tony gathered speed as he charged down the corridor.

Lara jammed her thumb against the call button and held it. "Come on, open!"

Tony loomed closer. The doors opened in slow motion. Lara scrambled into the empty elevator and stabbed at the controls. Her eyes darted back and forth between Tony and the panel. The doors started to slide shut. Lara held her breath.

Tony arrived a fraction too late. The doors closed on his furious face.

As the elevator descended, Lara kept one finger on the Door Close button and, with her other hand, flipped up the small red box that covered a toggle labeled EMERGENCY—EMPLOYEES ONLY. This was a speed-elevator switch that skipped other floor calls and took riders directly to the designated destination. She hit it, and like a plummeting rollercoaster, the elevator dropped, leaving her stomach, Tony and the seventh floor in the dust.

When the doors opened, Lara pushed all of the buttons, taking the elevator out of the running for Tony's chase. She angled across the first-floor lobby.

Agent Jake leaned against a pillar, ankles crossed. Visitors and hospital employees traversed the floor between them. Jake spied Lara, too.

Ready to run, Lara calmed her breathing. An air-conditioned breeze riffled her robe. Since Tony had seen her, why keep up the cover? Because Jake's people had said other men guarded the main entrance. They likely hadn't made her yet.

Lara tugged on her fingers. No more pamphlets. She pressed her palms together, bowed her head, and chanted. Katie was right, no one in his right mind would engage a robed, face-painted chanter.

A clear path opened to the exit. Jake allowed a smile to twist his lips. He cocked his head toward the doors.

A blurred movement drew Lara's attention. A tall man stood alone, his face set off by the strangest eyes. Those eyes focused on her.

Lara paused. The man glided toward her. Why did she wait? Agent Jake wanted her to get out now!

She took a few steps forward and hesitated again. A press of people obstructed her view. The stranger drew close. His eyes were dark, the pupils and irises blended together.

Oblivious of the other man's approach, Jake grabbed her elbow. "This way, ma'am." He aimed her toward the doors.

As she walked, a sudden chill creased the back of Lara's neck. A seductive voice echoed in her head.

You will not remember me. You will forget. . . . Forget.

Ten

The new locks made stairway travel as risky as the elevators. Bobby exited through the parking garage and onto the little-used driveway behind the hospital. He'd finished his rounds and the extra job assigned by Nurse Cron, which she hadn't expected him to finish before 3:00 A.M. He would've preferred at least an hour to accomplish his current task, but with increased security and Meridian stalking him, forty-five minutes would have to do.

He glanced at the stars. Moonlight reflected off the back windows of St. Mary's, and a light breeze tousled his hair. His palms itched with no place to scratch. His fangs had long since erupted, and the tightness in his pants conflicted with the pang in his stomach. A wisp of cloud danced across the sky, and when it dissipated, the half moon glared at him, daring him to take what he needed for existence but to leave his victim alive.

It was less than a month since he'd last fed, yet hunger gnawed at him, driving him with a relentless desire for blood—warm, human, female blood. And dreamworld sex while feeding satisfied a primal need better than feeding alone did. Decades had passed since he'd combined emotional intrigue with the process. Guilt had suppressed that need until now.

Meridian. She both stimulated desire and irked him. He'd met dozens of women—hundreds—and had suppressed the urge for passion. It had been easy with them. Not her. He couldn't think of that right now. He needed to feed. He needed Meridian out of the way.

He'd made it easy for her to keep him in sight tonight, hoping to lull her into a false sense of security. When she'd taken a bathroom break, he'd ducked out the back. He now imagined her conducting a room-by-room search of the second floor, and a smile creased his lips. Did she suspect him to be a nocturnal hunter, or was there something else? A desire beyond lust spread through him with reaching tentacles. Did the same yearning push Meridian to seek him?

Outside and staring up at the hospital, he counted seven windows from the left to find the fourth-floor entrance to his private Wonderland. Earlier tonight he had stopped in at the administration office. He'd told Marty Connor he wasn't feeling well and might need a quiet place to sleep for an hour, a vacant fourth-floor room. Marty had obliged with a room number. Darkness embraced him as he rose into the air. The window slid open and he floated into the unoccupied room.

Screams echoed from five nearby birthing rooms, and Bobby couldn't help but wonder if Bucks County obstetricians didn't believe in Demerol and epidurals. He tilted his head back. Blood scent laced the air. His fangs throbbed. He had to feed. Now.

The urge to feed two weeks before the full moon—it was overwhelming him for the first time in years. And his recent inability to get Meridian out of his mind . . . Were the two things connected? Was she at fault? The possibility of unrestrained involvement with Meridian engaged his mind and made his stomach ache.

He needed to focus. He heard the elevator gears

and the groaning cable, the footsteps of an orderly, the wheels of an empty gurney rattling down the hall. Maternity ward activity centered in the birthing rooms. Bobby headed for room 431.

His footsteps made no sound as he glided forward. He envisioned holding Meridian in his arms, he imagined caressing the soft flesh of her cheeks and licking the delicate milky white skin of her neck. He could feel her veins pulse and half taste the sweet blood coursing through her heart. If only he—

A doctor charged around the corner, headed for a birthing room, and Bobby ducked into a doorway. Careless! He scoffed at himself for being distracted. Desire for Meridian warred with his blood thirst. He didn't need Meridian. He did need blood.

The doctor vanished, and the now empty corridor presented no challenge. Bobby glided into the alcove across from room 431. His heightened senses indicated a new mother was one room over, dreaming.

He slipped across the hall and caressed the door. Beyond, St. Mary's newest psych patient's heart pulsed, and she breathed with the soft, steady exchange of someone in a deep sleep. He'd caught a glimpse of her being brought to this room before his shift. Young, pretty, exactly what he needed to quench his hunger. She would be as delicious as Kelly DiRico.

The image of Meridian again swept into his thoughts. The sway of her hips—it induced forgetfulness. The seductive allure of her voice touched the small piece of humanity he fought to maintain, but for good or ill? The wry twist of her lips combined with the understanding in her eyes dragged him into hot-blooded crisis. For her safety, he should move to another town. For the sake of her existence, he couldn't risk intimacy. He couldn't—

"The nursery is at the other end of the hall."

Bobby spun around.

Meridian! How long had she been standing there? How careless could he get? He struggled to keep Roberre submerged.

"I thought you were working downstairs tonight," he said.

Meridian shrugged. "I took a break to watch the babies. You know—the innocents. How about you?"

Bobby cleared his throat and aimed his thumb at the door behind him. "This patient . . . is a friend of mine."

"This is a psych room."

"My friend is a little daffy," he admitted.

"It's two thirty in the morning."

"I'm a little daffy."

Doubt etched Meridian's face. She raised her chin. "What's her name?"

Bobby thought back to the woman's chart. "Amy Pershing."

"High school sweetheart?"

Bobby's focus narrowed. His fangs wouldn't retract. Brutal hunger stabbed his consciousness. Satisfaction slept behind this door, and he had only thirty minutes before Nurse Cron missed him. Meridian's presence was a danger for them both.

He sniffed for Amy's scent. He'd had it a moment ago. Instead, his nostrils filled with the sweet scent of lavender. He turned and saw Meridian's pupils were dilated, and he sensed the uptick of her respiration. Desire wound fingers around his passion and squeezed, her pheromones tickling his senses.

He imagined the salty taste of her skin, the softness of her hair, the warmth of her breath. He could hear her tongue glide across her teeth and push against her lips just enough. . . . Enough for what? Enough for him to capture it if he kissed her? Enough for him to sense that her craving was as strong as his own?

What if he *did* kiss her now? What if their lips touched and fire arced through his body, curling his toes? What if his mouth were to slip across her cheek and his tongue to trace a line down her neck to her breasts and, while she panted and begged him to go on, what if his fangs were to sink into that rounded flesh? Blood would splash into his mouth and she would grip his shoulders with the passion of an unsatisfied lover, pleading for ascendancy. The blood of involvement would never taste sweeter. Meridian would be his. He could take her over and over again. If she were his, she could live in his house, sleep in his bed. Her blood and her soul would be his for eternity.

Roberre asserted his persona.

Take her.

You know where there's an unoccupied room.

Sweep the breath from her lungs. She'll melt into your embrace. Take her.

Now.

A low growl emerged from deep in Bobby's throat. Hunger, passion and lust pushed him to the edge. Roberre would not be submerged.

Attack her!

"She's not yours," Bobby said.

He strode past Meridian and around the corner. He could sense her following, but he'd ducked into a room and out of sight by the time she reached the corridor. He'd lost her, though he could hear her ragged breath and the exasperation in her whisper.

"If the two of us keep having these third-party conversations, I'm going to get jealous."

Eleven

"What took you so long?" Agent Jake said.

Lara opened her mouth, but he waved her off. "Never mind. No stories now. Tell me some other time. One block down." He pointed, "Turn right. There'll be a gray van parked on the street. Katie will be there."

"Where will you be?"

"Worried about me? That's sweet. I'll be following at a safe distance. Just in case."

"In case what?"

"In case someone attacks you."

"I've already been attacked."

"I know. That's why we're doing all this."

"I mean tonight, now, here in the hospital. Tony."

"Tony found you?" Jake's eyes widened.

Lara ran her hand through her buzzed hair. "Despite this clever disguise."

Jake peered into her eyes. "You okay?"

"Worried about me? That's sweet," she mimicked, and the sarcasm made him flinch. She bit her lower lip. "I've never been this scared in my life."

"Did you see Robert?"

"Who's Robert? One of your guys?"

He looked closer to see if she was serious. "Never

mind. Another story for later. Keep your chin up and keep chanting. You know where you're going?"

She nodded.

"Ready to be in my program yet?" he asked as she headed away.

Lara glanced back at him. "No. He wasn't trying to kill me. He just wanted the bullet. Give him the bullet or catch him or something and this nightmare will be over. I don't need to give up my life. I'm not frightened of Tony."

"You just told me you'd never been so scared in your life."

Lara shrugged, then she realized he was right. She didn't want to meet Tony again, exactly, but it was something else that had scared her. What was it?

"Second thoughts?" Jake asked. He tapped a button and spoke into his wristband. "We're on, boys and girls. Everybody stay alert. Tony *is* in the hospital. Code yellow is still operational."

Lara stared at him. " 'Code yellow' should convince me?"

Jake shook his head. "Why are you so stubborn? They turned your house into a barbecue. They tracked you to this hospital, chased you around it. What is it that you don't get? You're in danger. They want you dead. I want you alive."

Lara knew he was making sense, but there were things in her head that weren't adding up. "Who are 'they'? Tony—"

"Never mind." Jake gave her a gentle shove in the small of her back. "First right. Gray van. Don't talk to anyone."

"But—"

"Including me." He shooed her off and backed away.

Lara fell back into her role, but with less enthusiasm

than when she'd started across the fifth floor. She chanted and bowed and made it through the first-floor lobby to the world outside.

A warm breeze blew through the early-spring Washington, D.C. night. Stars twinkled beyond the city aura, and dogs howled at the full moon. Lara's respiration slowed. She could no longer feel her pulse pounding behind her ears. She tilted her head back and smelled garbage.

Tomorrow must be collection day in this part of the city.

She rounded the corner without incident, spied a van parked beyond an alley and sighed. In the dim light, she couldn't tell the color. With no other vans in sight, she headed for that one.

As she passed the alley, a movement in the shadows distracted her. Breath was trapped in her throat again. The passenger door of the van slid open.

"Duck!" Katie shouted.

A loud crack echoed behind her. Something whizzed by Lara's head and shattered the van's back window. Footsteps echoed off walls as someone disappeared into the darkness.

Tony? It had to be. He'd shot at her! Myriad emotions warred in Lara's mind.

"Tony," Katie announced, confirming Lara's thought. The woman glanced at the van's broken window, at Lara, at the alley. "Bastard," she muttered, and flashed a middle finger at the dark alley. She placed a guiding hand on Lara's shoulder. "Get into the van."

Lara scrambled into the vehicle without being asked again. She wanted to escape. She wanted to be safe. She didn't want to be chased. She didn't want to be burned alive. She didn't want to be shot.

She didn't want to give up her life, either. Would these things be mutually exclusive?

Katie climbed in behind her, slid the door shut and glanced again at the shattered back window. "Sit," she commanded, then scampered forward into the driver's seat, listened to her earpiece, started the van's engine and roared out of her parking space. The tires screech-ed, a horn blared, Katie cursed and Lara breathed again.

"Buckle your seat belt, and for God's sake, keep your head down," the government agent said over her shoulder.

Lara scrunched down and buckled. "Don't your ve-hicles have bulletproof glass?"

"That must be everybody else's vehicle." Katie re-peated her epithet: "Bastard."

"Where's Jake?"

"He's got our backs. He's going to meet us at the agency."

"I don't seem to have much choice here, do I?" Lara noted.

"Not if you want to live. You don't know what you're up against."

"Well, why don't you tell me?"

"Because that's Jake's job."

Lara grabbed Katie's headrest. "Woman to woman. You need to tell me, Katie."

"Tony attacked two doctors but slipped out of the hospital before our people could nab him. St. Bonaven-ture's confirmed he's worked there as security chief for almost three months."

Lara processed that. "Why does Tony want to kill me now?"

Katie glanced in the rearview mirror. "It's not Tony, it's Robert."

"Jake mentioned him, too. Robert. Who's Robert?"

"Uh-oh." Katie took a corner too fast. "Robert

must've reached you. No wonder you don't understand what's going on. He's wiped your memory. You're not going to be much help to Jake if you can't remember Robert . . . ."

"I remember the bullet."

"Bingo. You're still in play for both bastards."

Less than twenty minutes later, Lara glanced up and down the street. The Witness Protection Agency headquarters looked nothing like CIA or FBI offices. There was no impressive building like the Pentagon. No snappy address. No guards. No fanfare, no sign to designate their home turf. It looked like any other brownstone house in Washington, except it was gray and two stories taller than the buildings on either side.

Katie parked on the street and fed the meter. She snatched Lara's medical bag. The two women climbed a dozen steps to a portico.

Inside the foyer, eight narrower steps and a second door greeted them. The front door had opened with a key, but this door had no lock or handle. Katie stood on a pad in front of it, and a series of red lines crisscrossed her body much like a supermarket scanner. The lines slowly winked out and the door slid open.

"Finally, something to impress me," Lara said. "I thought the WPA was a second-rate agency or something."

"What do you mean?"

Lara glanced at her. "Look at the evidence. You people flub a simple evacuation assignment to get me out of the hospital safely. With five of you around, I'm attacked and no one's there to help. When I do finally escape—on my own—I'm nearly killed before you can tuck me into a car. You drive me to headquarters that looks like my Aunt Ruth's home, and—"

"You don't have an Aunt Ruth."

"How would you know that?"

"Everybody on the team did their homework before we arrived at the hospital, ma'am. The fact is, while you might've been scared, you've made it out of the hospital and to WPA offices without a scratch on you. We *didn't* flub our assignment.

"As far as our offices being impressive, I assure you that, on the walk from the front stoop to this foyer, you've been scanned, X-rayed and fluoroscoped. You passed through a metal detector and a bio detector, we've read your brainwaves, and we have a baseline on your respiration. You've climbed the steps of the eight mortal tests."

"You only mentioned seven."

"You're about to meet God."

The door beeped and slid open, and as they slipped through, Katie cocked her head, hand up, listening to an earpiece. She didn't speak, however. Crease lines furrowed her brow. After a moment she escorted Lara to God's fourth-floor office.

"Why do you call your boss God?" Lara asked as they walked.

"What else would you call someone with absolute power over life and death?"

Lara huffed and her palms itched. The sun tattoo burned in the small of her back. As they entered a corridor, Katie directed her to the second door on the right. Together they entered a huge room.

Books lined four of the chamber's five walls, and the ceiling loomed high. A spiral staircase led to a narrow upper-level walkway, giving reach to otherwise-inaccessible bookshelves. A wooden ladder on wheels seemed the only approach to others.

The door slid shut behind them. The absence of

windows created a sense of confinement. High-backed
chairs were placed at an angle near the fireplace. Despite a roaring fire, Lara shivered. At the room's center, a lone metallic chair snuggled into the dark
carpet. It seemed out of place with the surroundings.
Katie directed Lara to sit there.

The seat molded itself to her legs. Broad armrests
cradled her elbows and wrists. Hidden clamps jetted
out and fastened her to the chair.

"What the—?"

Katie spoke without stepping forward. "For God's
protection. You can imagine the unsavory characters
that march into our building."

"I'm not one of them," Lara said. "I demand to be
let go!"

Before Katie could respond, a stooped woman with
silver hair hobbled into the room. She carried a silver
tray with a porcelain teapot and a tea service for two.
Lara could smell freshly cut lemon wedges and something else that didn't match the smell of tea. Garlic.
Did the odor emanate from the tray or the old
woman?

The wrinkled face somehow matched the tea set. A
grandmotherly flower print housedress with a white
handkerchief tucked into the left sleeve somehow
screamed that this woman was in the maid service of
the Witness Protection Agency.

The old maid centered the tea tray on a desk corner.
She straightened the teapot and the saucers as if they'd
been disorganized during transport, rotated the lemon
dish a quarter turn, reangled the sugar bowl, and finally poured one cup of tea. She stood at attention, as
well as anyone of her age could stand at attention, as if
with anticipation of a grand entrance by God.

Lara tried to stand, but the metallic clamps of the

chair dug into her flesh. She could no longer distinguish if she huffed because of the climb or the circumstances. Her head spun. Panic accelerated. How dare the government strap her to a chair?

Katie remained silent and out of sight. No one spoke, and God failed to appear. Lara's stomach knotted, and she panted.

"I demand to speak to whoever is in charge. You can't hold me like this. I came to you for protection, not to be incarcerated. I demand—"

"Would you hold something for me, please?" the old maid asked.

Lara shook her head at the incongruity. Strapped to the chair, how could she hold anything? And where was God?

The old woman opened a desk drawer and removed a large wooden cross. She embraced the artifact, then hobbled to Lara's chair and placed the cross in Lara's lap. Her ancient eyes studied Lara's face. "If you'll just hold that for a few minutes."

Lara stared back, her eyes wide and her mouth dry. "Who're you? Where's Jake? Who's Robert?" Her foot twitched. Pins and needles ravaged the back of her head.

The old woman removed a vial from a pocket of her housedress, unplugged the top and sprinkled the contents in Lara's direction. Lara's eyes widened as drops splattered her face, buzzed hair, arms and Hare Krishna robe.

Lara struggled against her bindings. Desperation edged her voice. "Are you people crazy? What're you doing?"

The old woman responded as if annoyed. "Anointing you with holy water."

"Why don't you toss me in the Potomac, chair and

all? If I don't sink, you can burn me at the stake." Lara could hardly swallow. "You people are nuts. Where's Jake? When do I speak to your boss?"

The old woman hobbled back to the desk and, with shaky hands, picked up a teacup and sipped. When she put the cup down, it rattled in its saucer. She spoke to Katie. "Other than the clever wit, I see no evidence that she's been turned." The old woman eased herself into the desk chair. "Too many questions. Like Jake, Ms. Jones wants to know everything."

"Who's Ms. Jones?" Lara asked.

"You are," the old woman answered. She turned again toward Katie. "We've already made funeral arrangements." She took another sip, and the tone of her voice turned cold. "Waste her."

Lara's mouth dropped open as the old woman's words registered. What kind of loony bin had she been dragged into?

Perspiration beaded her forehead. She had to pee. Lara kept reminding herself the world made sense, but the dull throb behind her brow expanded. Fear beyond what she'd felt in the hospital raged through her mind. Why did she have a buzzed scalp, and why did she wear religious robes? For what possible reason would she be clamped to a chair in a room from a Sherlock Holmes mystery?

Her legs quivered. Moisture dripped from behind her knees and under her arms. Her sun tattoo shot off solar flares. Did her fear have more to do with an ancient housemaid ordering her death, or a paramilitary, steroid-pumped mother ready to obey?

"Waste her," the old woman repeated.

"I disagree," a voice of reason interjected.

Lara closed her eyes and held her breath. She hadn't realized Agent Jake had entered the room. He stopped alongside Lara's chair, but addressed the old woman. "I think she's perfect for our needs."

Lara forced the air from her lungs. "Perfect or not, I demand to be released. I'm done playing games." She twisted her head and glanced at Jake. "Where's your boss? Who's in charge here? Perfect for what?"

"Too many questions." The old woman made a slicing motion across her neck.

Jake chuckled. "We need another hunter. She's a doctor, and I submit that her personality is just what we need."

"Just what we need? Do you mean someone who wants to know everything, or just someone who's more obnoxious than you?"

"I'm not obnoxious," Lara growled.

Jake remained silent but adamant.

The old woman sank back into her chair, sighed and sipped tea. "She'll obey orders?"

"As well as any mule in the universe."

Lara glared at Jake.

"I'm joking," he whispered. He turned toward the old woman and cocked his head toward Lara. "She'll do whatever needs to be done."

"She'll be *your* responsibility."

Jake offered half a shrug. The old woman flicked a finger. Katie tapped a control panel, and Lara's arm restraints slipped away.

Lara stood and rubbed her already-sore wrists. "I came here under duress. I'll put myself in your protection for a couple of months until you catch Tony, but listen to me: I'm not giving up my life."

"Tony? Does she mean Robert?" the old lady asked.

Jake stepped forward. "Memory wipe."

"After your people secured the hospital?"

Jake shrugged again. "Robert. He slipped out of the

hospital before we could nab him. Tony eluded us, too."

The old woman twisted her chair 180 degrees and spoke to the wall. "We really don't need her then."

Katie whispered something to Jake, who approached the desk. "She has the bullet," he said. "Our scanner found it in her medical bag."

The old woman spun around. She pushed hard to get up out of her chair and shuffled forward. "You're suggesting we owe her something?"

"Don't we? Did you want Robert to have a bullet to study?"

The old woman hobbled away, but paused at the door and spoke over her shoulder. "Explain to her." The door slid open, and she disappeared.

"Someone want to tell me what's going on?" Lara accosted Jake. "Who *is* she?" She pointed at the closed door.

Jake arched an eyebrow and simply poured himself a cup of tea.

Lara pointed to the chair behind the desk. "What is this?"

Jake spun the seat around. "This, my dear, is the empty seat of God."

Katie rolled her eyes. "Excuse me if I don't stick around for the explanations. I've got a report to write." She waved to Lara and disappeared in the same direction the old woman had.

"Stick around for what? What is it you need to explain to me?"

"Your job."

"I'm a surgeon."

"You're still a doctor, but no one will know that. We'll give you something else to do. You can work in a hospital, but that'll be a cover for your new job."

"What job is that? I'm only going to be here until you catch Tony. Maybe a few weeks."

Jake sat in God's chair. "We'll discuss the time frame later. There are . . . undesirable elements in our society."

"Yes, I know. One of those elements is the reason I'm here." Lara gave an impatient sigh.

"Yes and no. You're not here because of Tony. You're here because of Robert."

"Who's Robert?"

"A vampire."

"Excuse me. I thought you said 'vampire,' and you weren't laughing."

"Someone has to protect our way of life."

"That's what you want me to do? Save the world from . . . vampires?"

"That's my job. Your job will be to find them."

"You're still not laughing."

"Owen, you jerk!" Katie punched the other agent's shoulder.

He spun around with a smirk. "Sorry about your window."

"Bastard. You know insurance won't pay for that. You could've aimed higher."

Twelve

Preshift meeting began at 9:50 P.M., and the almost-full moon tortured Bobby as he landed in the field behind the hospital and entered through the parking garage. Feeding only during the full moons had sated Bobby in the past. This month he'd tried to feed early. Meridian had interfered.

He emitted a low growl and joined the meeting, a minute in progress. Nurse Cron flashed a scowl— tardiness wouldn't go unpunished. At the back of the group, Bobby caught Meridian's lavender scent. If he'd been paying attention, he wouldn't have found himself behind her.

She shifted her weight hip to hip, the sway of her body as aphrodisiac as any drug. She turned and stared into his eyes. He refused to look away, and her eyes played with him, laughing, teasing, performing a seductive ballet.

"You're late," she whispered.

Bobby repressed a smile. He wanted to sweep her into his embrace. Not just a physical one, either. Loneliness gnawed at him.

"Nurse Cron will punish you," Meridian said.

Her eyes danced across his human soul. Bobby sensed their connection. It was strong—*so* strong. He could already read her mind, but he wanted more than that. He wanted to entwine Meridian's soul. He wanted Meridian to share her thoughts, her understanding, her essence of life.

"She'll boil you in oil," Meridian continued.

He could live vicariously through a woman's compassion, feeling those sensations, all those emotions that were no longer part of his own existence. He wanted that. He wanted Meridian to wrap herself around him, physically and psychically.

Meridian kept a straight face. "A good boiling may improve your disposition."

He would caress her skin, embrace her humanity, sink his fangs into the soft flesh of her thigh and drink the blood of true passion. But, no comfort level existed. Bobby required more than sex. Blood kept his ageless body functioning. Sex staved off his physical hunger.

Making love fed his burning spirit. Women excited him. He embraced a woman's mind first, then he caressed her soul. He held women sacred. Over decades, making love had evolved into art, and when Bobby's fangs erupted, he transformed into Roberre, artiste extraordinaire, a bloodsucking monster he could live with. He took all that he needed, except emotional closeness. The danger of involvement.

Involvement? Roberre could take Meridian without—

No!

"After you're boiled, she'll probably flay you and use your flesh to make a handbag."

What was she talking about?

Involvement meant exposure to his beast, and he was becoming involved. Bobby couldn't allow that. For Meridian's sake, he had to keep his distance.

He drew his features into a frown and angled himself in a negative posture. Disappointment flashed across Meridian's face. He knew she wouldn't understand, and he knew she felt the same connection to him that he felt to her. That connection remained forbidden.

Meridian turned to face Nurse Cron again. Bobby felt as though he'd been kicked in the stomach. His fangs erupted, and they ached with desire. He needed to feed—but it couldn't be on Meridian.

What if he drank from several psych patients tonight? Would that slake his thirst? He closed his eyes and imagined warm blood squirting into his mouth and swirling down his throat.

Roberre tried to assert himself. *It won't be enough, a sip that leaves each victim alive. Why not pick one succulent patient, sink your fangs in deeper and drink until she's drained? That'll satisfy our hunger and overwhelm these foolish human cravings.*

No. Bobby couldn't allow it. If he gave in to his beast, the monster would swallow him forever. The existence he knew would be ended.

Bobby's hands balled into fists. Hunger clawed every aspect of his being.

Nurse Cron droned on about the night's schedule. Bobby's tongue danced over his fangs, and the sharp points tore into his flesh. The tart taste of blood filled his mouth, and for a moment the urge to lash out at everyone nearby overwhelmed him. He fought for control.

Trying to feed before the full moon had been a mistake. He could wait two more days.

He had to.

Thirteen

"Why can't I leave this house?" Lara asked. It had been almost two months since Jake had saved her from God.

"Finish your makeover. We'll give you a new life in a new community," Jake said.

Lara had rested for a few days before Jake's people began prodding her with physical therapy. Between workouts, they kept her laughing with ridiculous books about vampires. "I'm not entering your program. I have rights. This is America."

"Glad you paid attention in geography class, but there're a few things you need to learn that aren't taught in school."

"I'll tell you one of the things I learned in school, and that's to be in the right place at the right time. In seven weeks, Dr. Byra, my boss, is going to retire, and

Jefferson Memorial won't hold her position open. I'm the heir apparent, and I intend to be there on coronation day."

Jake offered a sly smile but no words.

"Don't look at me like that. If you don't catch Tony in time, forty-seven days from now I'm walking out the front door. I'm keeping track. Don't think I'm not."

"It's Robert you have to worry about, not Tony. I'd hoped you would remember something about the night he burned your house down that would lead us to him." Jake waved his hand. "Doesn't matter. He'll turn up. In the meantime, you still have to report to the doctor. Second floor. All entrants in the Witness Protection Program are required to make a blood donation for the Red Cross."

Lara arched her back. "I am not making a blood donation. I'm a surgeon. I understand the importance of blood donations. I've devoted the last fourteen years of my life getting to this position and helping people, but I'm not donating blood. I never have, and I never will."

Jake rubbed his chin. "That's a strong statement. I must've touched a vein. It's not my idea, though. Dog requires a blood donation from everyone in the program."

"Well, you can tell Dog I'm sorry. I've agreed to go along with your program for a few weeks, that's it. As for my blood, it's not a religious thing and it's not a stubborn thing, it's personal. It's . . ."

"It's what?"

"It sounds funny."

"Hey, if you stop laughing when I talk about vampires, I promise not to laugh when you tell me about your blood."

Lara frowned. "My blood is serious. It's part of me, it's unique to me, it's as much my *essence* as my mind.

I'd never give away part of my mind, and I wouldn't give away any of my essence. My blood, as much as my mind, is what makes me *me*. Tell Dog this is where I draw the line. I am not under any circumstances giving away my blood."

"Right. I'll try explaining that to Dog." He laughed.

"You said you wouldn't laugh."

"I'm not laughing at you. Your blood is personal, it belongs to you—end of story, as far as I'm concerned. I'm laughing at what I'm sure will be Dog's reaction."

"I don't care about Dog's reaction. I'm not doing it."

"Good. Stand your ground. In the meantime, let me remind you, you'll have a new job."

Lara chuckled. "As a vampire hunter?"

"I thought you promised to stop laughing, too? Your cover will be as a nurse."

"My *cover*? Like I'm a secret agent." Jake had to be kidding. He'd been going on too much about the vampire stuff and Robert, a nonexistent felon he claimed she knew. Lara patted the top of her head, still unaccustomed to the feeling. Her hair had grown less than an inch. "I've lost twenty pounds. I'm hairless, nameless, and I almost don't recognize myself in the mirror. And I don't mind telling you I'm kind of scared. What if Tony is still looking for me?"

"Well, Tony is acting on orders, and you can bet his boss is still looking for you."

"That's comforting. Thanks."

"Vampires have excellent memories. They're ruthless and relentless. You know what Dog always says. 'The only good vampire is a dead vampire.'"

"Ha, ha. Aren't all vampires dead? Tony—"

"Tony is not a vampire. Robert is. I don't know how he got close enough to you in the hospital to wipe your memory."

Lara paused midexercise. Opposing mirrors enhanced several of the tiny gym's walls. Two other walls had doors—the one Lara used three times a day, and one that remained locked. (She knew. She'd tried it. Regularly.)

She now spent days with various trainers, and she couldn't recall ever feeling so healthy or strong—or so confined. A distinct line had reemerged between her waist and hips. That made her smile.

A different line, an indistinct line, blurred reality and fiction. Why couldn't Jake be serious about her imminent future? Vampire jokes grew stale with overuse. If Jake wanted her to be a nurse, she could be a nurse for a day . . . or a week. Maybe two. After that, she would be *Doctor* Lara West, chief of emergency medicine at Jefferson Memorial.

Though time had passed since Tony had attempted to murder her, nightmares haunted Lara and understanding evaded her. Every time she talked about Tony, Jake talked about Robert. It no longer sounded like a joke. Who the hell was Robert? Why didn't she know him?

Tony, she knew. Tony had left her to burn in the fire. He had chased her in the hospital and shot at her that night outside the hospital.

Jake talked her into a plan—albeit, a brief one. She tried to convince him to let her remain a physician in whatever was her temporary identity, but he said no. He insisted that would draw suspicion. It was dangerous enough that he was allowing her to stay in the medical profession, but he needed someone to work undercover in a hospital.

Of course, nursing jibed with Lara's goal to help people. Escaping the tension of a big-city ER had already relaxed her. Neither Jake, nor Katie, nor any of the personal trainers, nor even God, had objected to her reading medical journals. And there had been no repercussions about not donating blood. Perhaps they were simply relieved she'd stopped asking so many questions. Jake hadn't yet confided to which D.C.-area hospital she'd be assigned, but it was probably one of the quieter, suburban locales.

"I don't mind having a personal trainer six hours a day, but why am I spending so much time getting into shape?" she asked.

Jake didn't look up. "A healthy body reflects a healthy mind. In your new occupation, you'll discover that being in shape is an advantage you'll appreciate. The first day you got here, you huffed and puffed climbing three flights of stairs."

"I'm going to be a stair climber in my new job?"

"A nurse. Haven't you been paying attention?"

"I forgot. Memory wipe. A nurse hunting for vampires. Ahh . . ." Lara bent her arm in front of her face and hid behind her elbow. She employed her best Transylvanian accent. "Come closer. I *vant* to drink your blood." She pretended to attack Jake's neck.

He pushed her aside. "You've been watching too many movies. Most vampires don't drink from the neck."

"Oh, really, Mr. Expert? Where do they bite?"

"The wrist. The soles of the feet. Five years ago we had a report from Memphis, Tennessee, of one who was drinking from high on the inner thigh of women."

"Really?" Lara glanced sharply at Jake. "What happened to him?"

"Lost touch. Thought we were getting close, but he closed up shop and moved on. Probably he's established a new identity by now. Could be anywhere in the world—though rumor has it he's somewhere on the East Coast."

"Hm." Lara laughed. "Maybe that's whom I'll track down. I'll find a vampire who wants to drink blood from my inner thigh . . . and just as he's about to take a sip, you can drive a wooden stake through his heart. That way all three of us can have a good time."

She found the situation amusing but disconcerting. Jake continued to tease her with vampire nonsense, and she was no clearer on what he really expected her to do. It seemed all government agents were trained to avoid answering questions by making vampire jokes.

They sound serious, but I'm not that gullible. Vampires do not exist.

At least she could help people. She could employ her medical training and do it without ER tension.

Lara had a date she intended to keep, no matter how scared she was. Maybe it would be another month or two before they caught Tony, but she planned on being back to take Dr. Byra's position. There was no question. Jake had stopped arguing.

In the meantime, I can catch up on my journal reading, even though I haven't written anything yet. And . . . look at the shape I'm in! She flexed both arms and admired herself in the mirrors. A pipe and a can of spinach would complete the image.

Katie came in to take over the afternoon training. Again, Lara was struck that the woman had the look of an aging professional athlete.

"Is this the normal WPA fitness program?" she asked as she did her reps on the Universal machine.

"What do you mean?" Katie asked.

"Does everyone who enters the WPA go through this rigorous physical training?"

"Everyone in the VU," the agent replied.

Lara did five more reps. "You know . . . Jake mentioned something a long time ago. What's the *VU* stand for?"

Katie chuckled as if Lara had asked something silly.

Jake and the old woman watched through the one-way mirror as Lara and Katie worked out. He'd hoped his team would capture Robert, somehow coerce him to work for the WPA. He shook his head. Vampires treasured nothing. What would compel a vampire to cooperate? Besides, Dog had her dictum, and she was, after all . . . Dog! She'd never allow it.

Dog finally spoke. "She doesn't believe you."

"Neither did Katie at first. She turned out okay."

"Katie already was an agent."

"By the time Dr. West figures it out, she'll be an agent, too. We're going to deliver her to her new home tomorrow." Jake tapped the glass. "Are we really going to call her Ms. Jones?"

Fourteen

"Where are we?" Lara asked.

"Bucks County, Pennsylvania." Jake pointed to the black mailbox at the end of a short driveway. "Your new home, four-thirty-two Blackrow Court. By the way, your first shift is day after tomorrow. You're on from two to ten. St. Mary's Medical Center. You have until then to adjust and go shopping."

"A day and a half to adjust to a new life? No problem." Jake ignored the sarcasm.

"What am I shopping for?"

"You get to pick your own underwear. You'll find everything else you need already here." He handed her a couple of credit cards and a Pennsylvania driver's license. "You do know how to drive, right?"

Lara glared.

Jake held up his empty hand. "Just joking. I have a niece who lives in Newtown, a stone's throw from here. Terrible driver, but a good psychologist. Kerry Rand. Has some strange ideas, though. . . . Doesn't matter." He waved his hand again. "The hospital is a mile down that road on the left. If you were taller you could see it."

He handed her a large brown envelope. "House key, car key, and you'll find some other documents you'll need in there. Checkbook, name of a local dentist."

"I need a dentist for something?"

"You need a checkup every six months. A healthy body reflects—"

"A healthy mind. Yes, I know." She wouldn't need a dentist. She wasn't going to be here six months. Although, it had taken her long enough to get here. Lara stretched and felt the power of her newly trained muscles.

"You can continue your physical training in the hospital health club. I'll give you a few days to get acclimated to your new job. Then I'll detail your assignment."

"Won't the hospital administration do that?" Lara asked.

Jake offered a goofy grin. "If anyone asks about your past, you're not answering."

"How do I get away with that?"

Jake shrugged his shoulders. "Answer a question with a question. Now, one last thing." He handed her a cell phone. "The only number programmed is mine. Keep the phone with you. I'm on call twenty-four-seven. I don't need to remind you, under no circumstances are you to contact anyone from your former life."

"What if Tony finds me?"

"Not very likely. Not after that trip. As of this moment, only Dog and I know where you are, and I'm not talking."

"God has no faith in me, does she?"

"Doesn't matter. I have faith in you, and you believe in yourself. That's what's really important. Look at you." He stepped back with a gesture. "This is not the same woman I met lying in a hospital bed."

Lara twirled, arms spread in the warm summer evening. A thousand stars twinkled down from the heavens, and a thousand fireflies twinkled back at them.

Jake reached for the car door. "Don't worry. Remember, we shipped you here carefully. Not likely anyone else knows where you are."

True.

She'd worn a wig early that morning when they'd left, and her buzzed hair beneath had been dyed blonde. Katie had escorted her to the basement then through myriad tunnels. They'd emerged on a platform of the underground train not far from the Smithsonian. Lara had noted a sign on the door from which they'd emerged:

DANGER
HIGH VOLTAGE
EMPLOYEES ONLY

That door had locked behind them.

They boarded a train, rode to the zoo, where Katie had tucked her into the back of a van different than the one that had been shot at less than two months ago. The woman took a circuitous route to Dulles International Airport and deposited her at a US Airways flight gate to Atlanta just as the plane finished boarding. She handed Lara a tote bag saying, "A few personal things you might need. Take the wig off before landing. Jake will meet you at the other end. Good luck."

"But—"

An airline attendant interrupted: "Ma'am, they're closing the doors. If you want to board, you'll have to go now."

Katie smiled and dipped her head. "Keep your hair short."

When she deplaned in Atlanta, Jake was lounging at the gate. He escorted her toward car rentals, handing her a Virginia driver's license and a credit card to make the transaction. Lara scanned the documents.

"This is who I am now? Theresa Hull?"

"Give me a break. I had a crush on Theresa in eighth grade. I still hope she'll call someday."

"I'm your girlfriend?"

"Just until you get a car."

"What does that mean?"

She found out fifteen minutes later, bringing the paperwork back to Jake. He took it and handed it to a familiar-looking woman with nicely rounded hips, obviously in shape, who was the same height as Lara and who had a buzzed haircut.

"This is my vicarious Theresa. Follow her into the ladies' room and change clothes with her."

"Change clothes? Why?"

Jake handed Lara an airline ticket. "Hurry up. You have just enough time to make your flight."

"I just rented a car!"

"Theresa will take the car. You're going to Minneapolis."

"What's in Minneapolis?"

"You'll find out when you get there."

Lara followed Theresa into the ladies' room. Other women ignored them. They entered side-by-side stalls and passed clothes over the top. Lara emerged from the stall and glanced in the mirror. "I look a lot like you." She turned to face the girl. "You look a lot like me."

*Theresa never spoke, but she glanced at Lara's reflection
with a look that said it all.* Duh.

*Lara followed her out of the bathroom. Theresa's derriere
swayed with each step.*

"Is that what I look like from behind?" *Lara had asked her.
When Theresa didn't answer, she called to the departing
woman's back,* "No one's going to believe you're me. Your feet
are way too small."

*Theresa had already melted into the crowd, and Jake was
no longer in sight. The airline ticket flapping in Lara's hand
woke her up.*

Final boarding had been called on her next flight. She
didn't know what she'd do in Minneapolis, but she didn't
have to wait. When she arrived, as soon as she deplaned, a
woman barely five feet tall and about Lara's age approached.
The woman walked with a limp and spoke with a twinge of
a Spanish accent. "I'm Lisita. Jake told me to look after you
until your next flight." She directed Lara under a baggage
sign.

"I don't have a suitcase," Lara said. They'd already
stepped onto the moving walkway.

"What's your point?" Lisita asked.

Lara pointed to another baggage sign. "No need to go there?"

"Didn't Jake tell you? I'm contrary."

"Seems to be a recurring theme in WPA employees," Lara
mumbled.

The moving sidewalk dumped them off at the edge of a
huge concourse. They shuffled toward the same carousel as
the other passengers from her flight, but veered into a small
office nearby. A skinny Vietnamese man with a couple of gold
teeth smiled at them from behind the counter.

"Problem?" he asked.

Lisita answered, tilting her head toward Lara. "Can't
seem to find her luggage."

The man maintained his smile. "Try back there. Lost

suitcases are collected inside." He indicated a second door at the back of the office: BAGGAGE CLAIM—EMPLOYEES ONLY.

Lisita ushered Lara into a storage room loaded with suitcases of all shapes and colors and a musty smell, like the room wasn't used much. Behind them, the door shut and a lock clicked. The storage-room light was glaring, and airport sounds didn't penetrate.

They wove their way to the left wall, near the back corner. Lisita pushed a heavily laden cart to the side, revealing a trapdoor.

"You're joking," Lara had said.

Lisita glanced at her. "No. And don't worry. I have no sense of humor." She pulled open the door and let Lara climb down the stairs first. Lisita sealed the door over their heads, negotiated the steps and joined Lara in the maintenance tunnel.

"This must be the scenic tour. I'm getting weary of flying today anyhow," Lara cracked.

Lisita glanced at her watch. "You have time until your next flight."

"Where am I going now?"

"Right now you have an hour of information to absorb."

"About Minnesota?"

"Jake said you weren't up on your vampire lore."

"Ha ha. I thought you said you were humorless. Next time you talk with Jake you can tell him he's gotten all the mileage out of that joke that he's going to get. Really, where am I headed next?"

Lisita handed Lara a ticket and a sealed envelope. "Hard to say. Your flight stops in Chicago, Detroit, Cleveland, Philadelphia and D.C. The envelope is from Jake. He said not to open it until you board the plane, and to make sure I'm handing you a sealed envelope that hasn't been tampered with. Jake doesn't want me to know where you're going."

Lara had held the envelope up to a light. "Very mysterious."

"It's for your protection. Jake said he'll meet you." She hesitated and stared into Lara's eyes. "I wouldn't trust him if I were you."

"How long have you known him?"

"He recruited me into the WPA five years ago. Bastard."

"You've been safe the entire time?"

"As safe as you can be when you work for Jake. Safer than I imagine you're going to be."

"Why do you say that?"

"A feeling."

"Do you have these feelings often?"

"No."

Philadelphia *was what the note said. Nothing else. No greetings, no* Hope you're having a good time. *Just* Philadelphia.

Post flight, Jake met her at the gate, a procedure no longer permitted in that town. The flight had departed late, and Lara's stomach grumbled. Jake directed her through another door marked EMPLOYEES ONLY. *Tunnels, storage rooms— Lara no longer paid attention.*

They emerged outside near a baggage trolley, and Jake steered her into a black 4x4 parked on the tarmac. They found an exit ramp and scooted out of Philadelphia International onto I-95 North for forty minutes. There they got off at Exit 49, Newtown and Bucks County Community College. In five minutes, Route 332 brought them to Summit Square. Jake had turned left onto Summit Trace Road, drove past a shopping center, and wound his way back to Blackrow Court. Now here they were.

Lara hadn't spoken during the drive and wondered if Jake thought she'd slept. "Did I see a shoe store in that shopping center?" she asked.

"Not just any shoe store. That's probably the most famous shoe store on the East Coast. In-Step. A professional athlete

stumbled on the store a few years ago. The owner showed him how the shoes he'd been wearing didn't fit, put him in a new size, and he went on to have a career year. Attributed it to the change in shoe size. Told some of his friends. Now any athlete who's anyone goes there."

"I thought athletes get their shoes for free?"

"What good are free shoes in the wrong size?"

"You sound like a commercial."

"Owner's a friend of mine. Nice guy. Writes romantic fiction."

Lara got out of the car and breathed in Newtown night air. Or was it Langhorne? Neither the signs nor Jake had made it clear.

Lara watched Jake drive away. She held the screen door of her town house open with her hip as she inserted the front door key and stepped into her new life.

The dwelling smelled new. New paint, new carpet, new furniture. The foyer had a high ceiling and a skylight. An elongated kitchen with an off-white marble floor, granite counters and an island offered modern appeal. A large greenhouse window faced front. She could add plants to the shopping list.

The dining room and living room were combined. A two-story ceiling and a full-wall fireplace offset the narrow kitchen. Sliders led to a small back patio, fenced in. A hallway across from the dining room led to a laundry, bath and two bedrooms. It was more than enough space. Bureaus and closets lay empty in both bedrooms.

Lara scratched her head. "Jake said I had all the clothes I needed."

Hunger drove Lara back into the kitchen. Her mouth watered when she found food in the refrigerator. A sigh escaped her when she discovered a vase with a single daisy and a note attached: *Nice view from upstairs.*

She grabbed a handful of grapes and scanned her house. No staircase.

Two closed doors to the right of the entrance foyer looked like closets. She opened the first. A coat closet. The second door opened onto a carpeted stairway that climbed straight back. She tapped both wall switches, and soft light glowed above the railing.

A doorway at the top of the staircase slanted to the right, and she entered a bilevel bedroom with exposed beams and a back wall of glass. A four-poster king-size bed was centered under double skylights. A freestanding fireplace stood near the foot of the bed. Bookcases filled with romance novels lined side walls and extended partway into the room, and a little beyond that a step took her into a study with two blue glass desks and a PC in front of a wall of windows. Next to the bed, a small night table held a phone and a clock. A walk-in closet hid a long bureau and numerous shelves filled with clothes.

The bathroom was divided into two rooms. Clear glass walled off the shower, and a full moon smiled down at her through another skylight. Lara reflected its smile.

Hunger pangs filled her stomach, and drowsiness tugged at her brain. Sleep won.

The next day sped by, filled with eating, shopping and more eating. As the day exposed itself, anticipation gnawed Lara. She explored her new surroundings—including the shoe store—and satisfied her curiosity. She'd always found new situations exciting. Perhaps this explained her eventual acquiescence to Jake and the WPA. She'd eventually be back in Washington, but in the meantime she'd begin a temporary nursing career. Part of her found that thrilling.

Lara hiccuped. She did miss *something* about the ER. Was it the adrenaline rush that accompanied it? Possibly. Her nightmares of burning up in a fire had finally faded. She'd slipped into a tension-free zone after six weeks of workouts. Certainly no job Jake provided would offer stimulation, no matter how oddly she'd been sent here. Could it?

Thinking again about her real job as a surgeon, about the years of training it had taken her to get there, Lara chuckled. She'd return to the operating room soon enough. Meantime, she'd enjoy helping people without that ER tension or adrenaline. Tony— and Robert, ha ha—would be captured. Then she'd be out of here. Actually, in a few weeks she'd be out of here whether Jake approved or not.

On her drive around town, Lara stopped at the hospital to see what the other nurses were wearing. She didn't want to draw attention to herself on her first day.

Seemed like blue scrubs were the code.

Her first shift began at 2:00 P.M. on Thursday. She reported at 1:30. An assistant from human resources, Marty Connor, gave her the fifty-cent tour. Congenial, elderly and interesting to listen to, he wasn't what Lara had expected. She couldn't place his accent—perhaps from somewhere in New England?

Or the North Pole. His belly jiggled and his gait was wobbly. His pants were hiked up and attached with suspenders. Freckles dotted a receding hairline, and his mouth wore a constant smile. Lara smiled back.

At the end of the tour he introduced her to a head nurse, Samantha Esher. According to Mr. Connor, Sam rated as the second-meanest shift head in the hospital. Young, tall and pretty, she had a nasty, tobacco-chewing, son-of-a-bitch husband—which explained her orneriness at work. Mr. Connor made introductions and escaped before Sam could give him further instructions.

The head nurse maintained a tight smile. "This way, Ms. Jones. You'll start like everyone else, with scut work. I'll assign you a mentor later this afternoon. Doesn't matter if you're new to the hospital or new to our shift, everyone gets a mentor for a month to acquaint them with our procedures and the oddities of different departments and shifts."

Lara smiled. *Ms. Jones.* That would be the hardest thing to get used to.

She would manage, though. Lara was there to serve, to take care of patients' medical needs, and in some cases, their emotional needs. She'd learned long ago that good doctoring involves more than just taking care of the body. That principle seemed equally important to good nursing.

It didn't take her long to establish a routine to avoid her mentor, Nurse Lipetsky—at least during her off-duty time. She arrived at the hospital before 10:30 A.M., worked out in the health club for a couple of hours, showered, then went in search of someone to help until her shift began. Sometimes she stopped in occupied rooms to chat with patients, sometimes she read to them or straightened their pillows. She had a sense that maybe Nurse Lipetsky resented her attitude. Too bad. Lara ended her third day as a nurse with the same smile that ended the first two days. Nurse Lipetsky and Sam Esher aside, she could be happy here.

The night nurses gathered for their preshift meeting at 9:50 P.M., something none of the other shifts did. Each head nurse determined procedure. The night-shift meeting always ended just as Lara came off duty.

Though male nurses were no longer unusual for staff, Lara hadn't known any in D.C. St. Mary's night shift boasted one, and he was staring at her.

Lara didn't normally catch the eye of men. Of course, she didn't normally look like this. A bigger question loomed in her mind. Why was *she* staring at *him*? She valued her privacy!

At first glance, his eyes looked like those of many other men—dark, unveiled, almond shaped. At second glance, the lack of distinction between his pupils and irises lent him a trace of mystery. Though his lips pressed together in displeasure, those eyes beckoned.

Her soul lay exposed to his gaze. The slight tilt of his head, the jut of his chin, the shoulders straight and broad—all suggested a quality beyond surety. His face absorbed and reflected her *essence* and left her breathless. Her lips curled up, and a euphoric wave washed over her. Somehow she knew that just as she exceeded the ordinary, so did he. The connection she felt to this stranger delved beyond normal.

Lara forced air into her lungs and stood her ground. She reversed his power. Her gaze held him locked in place; his soul was drawn in her direction.

The night-shift meeting ended abruptly, and when she blinked, he'd disappeared.

What had just happened? Lara stood in the hall in front of the nurses' station. People headed in four directions. She twisted, but no one's back matched the face and body of that ethereal male nurse.

She asked the desk nurse.

"You mean Bobby? Don't waste your time. He's gay."

No way. She didn't believe it. Nonetheless, Lara refused to dwell on the mysterious male nurse.

She lay in bed later, gazing through her skylight. Clouds with eyes paraded across her vision, and an owl hooted. She'd spent hours in a semiconscious dream-world, where it was difficult to distinguish between reality and fiction. One thing was sure—the staring contest meant nothing.

She promised herself not to think about him at work the next day, and no way would she be at the second-floor front nurses' station at 9:50 P.M.

She arrived at 9:45. Not *there* exactly. Down the hall. Curiosity drove her, though nothing would come of it.

What if he experienced the same strange feeling I did?

Lara paced the hall. She pretended to be busy, but she'd finished her rounds early. She straightened wheelchairs parked near the elevators. She glanced at her watch. 9:47. She didn't usually wear a watch, but time had concerned her particularly as she went through today's shift. Why?

This is ridiculous. I'm acting like a schoolgirl.

Her watch ticked. 9:48.

Night-shift nurses milled about, chatting, laughing. Not him. She refused to admit that his image haunted her. She'd never experienced this feeling before. She'd read about it in books, seen it in movies, but neither of those experiences made it real. Until last night.

Call it professional curiosity?

Yes, that satisfied her denial.

When she saw him tonight, would he glance away? What about the gay facade? She laughed. It *had* to be a charade, but why would he pretend to be something he wasn't? Their common bond made him mysterious and appealing.

Tall, lean, silent. His nursing scrubs didn't fit his aura. That tight-lipped smile and self-assured stance reminded Lara of someone from her nightmares. Was it the faceless man who *might* exist? Robert? Jake insisted on his existence.

Impossible. Lara was now living two hundred miles plus a lifetime from her Washington, D.C. home, and she'd taken a circuitous route to get here. She'd been out of sight for two months. The twenty-plus pounds she'd lost, the haircut and makeover made her look like a different person. If Robert existed, he'd never recognize her. This mysterious male nurse who snagged her attention might be anyone, but he wasn't Robert.

The meeting started. Lara checked her watch again. 9:51. She picked up a chart and pretended to read it as she insinuated her way closer to the group. He'd turn his head, she'd catch his eye and hold his gaze. If he held hers as he had last night . . .

It didn't matter. None of it mattered. He wasn't there.

Fifteen

Every time they exchanged shifts, Lara caught his eye. Scuttlebutt yielded his name, Bobby Eyre. Scuttlebutt also insisted Bobby was gay. What were these nurses thinking?

Lara encountered Bobby numerous times in her first week. His male aura overwhelmed her senses, but attempts to engage him met with limited success. Bobby remained reluctant to reveal himself. Like Lara, he hid his real identity. He answered questions with questions, and he quoted Shakespeare instead of making real contact. Yet those strange eyes excited Lara's mind and made butterflies flit across her stomach. His mysterious nature made her more determined to unmask the man she sensed beneath the facade.

Marty Connor from human resources reappeared in the middle of her second week. Old enough to be her father, maybe her grandfather, he had a round freckled face that always maintained a smile. She couldn't help but smile, too, every time she saw him with his pants hiked up high in a style beyond even Marty's years.

"Ms. Jones, how'd your first week go?"

"I'm pleased to see you again, Mr. Connor. You're the welcoming committee *and* the follow-up committee?"

"Checking to make sure you're acclimated and comfortable. There's also a few areas of the hospital that weren't on the opening-day tour and may not've come up during your time here. Ms. Esher asked me to be sure you were familiar with all hospital departments."

They boarded an elevator, and Mr. Connor punched *B.* He pointed to a red emergency switch. "This is the floor-call override button."

The bell dinged as the doors opened on the basement. Two nurses boarded as Mr. Connor and Lara got off. "Hello, Kara. Hello, Christina." Mr. Connor maintained his same smile. "Did you just move to our area, Ms. Jones?" He directed her down the hall.

"A week ago."

"Where from?"

Lara recalled her plane ride, and decided to lie by telling the truth. "I came here from Cleveland."

"Family?"

"Excuse me?"

"Do you have family in the area? Is that why you came here?"

"No family. This just seemed like a nice place. Not as fast-paced as the city." She caught herself, then, realizing she'd given away too much. What had Jake said about answering questions? *Answer a question with a question.* Just like Bobby. A small laugh escaped Lara's lips.

"Sorry?" Mr. Connor said.

"Your accent. New England?"

"Oh. New Hampshire. Moved here forty years ago. Thought I would've lost the accent by now."

They stopped in front of an open door. Mr. Connor peered in. "Doesn't seem to be anybody home." He walked inside.

Lara followed, entering a large lab very much like a dozen other hospital labs she'd seen. Long, black Formica counters lined the walls, with cabinets above and below, and there was an island down the center with sinks, littered with test tubes and flasks and microscopes. In the middle of the back wall, another doorway led to a giant refrigerated walk-in unit.

"This, of course, is the blood bank. Don't know where everyone is. Someone could just walk in."

"Like us," Lara murmured in agreement. The sun tattoo flared on her back. In most hospitals, the blood bank was on the main floor, near the emergency room. She wondered why this one was placed here.

They headed down the hall in the opposite direction. Lara offered a wan smile. "I can guess where we're going next. Pretty much the same in all hospitals."

Mr. Connor offered an apologetic shrug. "Orders from Ms. Esher. Have to show you everything. Not all hospitals are the same. Doesn't seem right, but in this one . . . the kitchen's down here, too."

He greeted an orderly and two doctors by name as they passed.

"Do you know everyone in the hospital?" Lara asked. Her guide just smiled.

They walked through swinging doors into the outer office of the morgue. Mr. Connor cleared his throat.

"Good evening, Dr. Raymond. I see we're keeping you busy this weekend."

A young woman with long black hair framing an oval face glanced up. "Hello, Mr. Connor. I see you're on the tour circuit again. Just don't let me catch you down here for any *other* reason." She refocused on her work without a word to Lara.

Mr. Connor chuckled as they passed through another set of swinging doors into a room lit only by two nightlights. Metal tables posed like statues in the middle of the floor. Bizarre arms were attached to the sides of the tables at oblique angles, with cutting saws and drills dangling from them. A scale, petri dishes, clamps, forceps—Lara recognized an autopsy work area. Mr. Connor spoke under his breath. "Don't worry, Dr. Raymond, you won't get me for a long time."

Lara smiled. She'd realized Mr. Connor would be the person to ask, but she'd controlled the urge—until now. She wanted to know about Bobby. She could wait no longer.

She repeated her previous question with a different inflection. "You know everyone in the hospital?"

"Not quite, but everyone hired in the past five-and-a-half years has taken this tour with me."

"Remember all their names?"

"Whom would you like to know, Ms. Jones?"

She smiled, unmasked. Mr. Connor wouldn't mind her inquisitiveness. He might even understand. "The male nurse on the night shift. We've spoken several times, but I still don't know much about him."

The old man gave her a glance. "There's two male nurses on that shift, but I'm guessing you don't mean Philippe D'Paltrow."

"Why wouldn't I be asking about Philippe D'Paltrow?"

"For the past week, Philippe's been dressed like one of the nurses."

On the far wall were three rows of square metal doors. The unsubtle smell of formaldehyde overwhelmed Lara, even though she knew the drawers to be airtight. She cocked her head. "I thought you said he's a nurse. Why would—"

"Dressed like a *female* nurse."

"Oh."

Mr. Connor's smile returned. "So . . . you must mean Bobby Eyre. He's been off schedule the past few days."

Lara shook her head. "You just happen to know everyone's schedule too?"

"Only the unusual ones. Like Dr. Raymond and Bobby."

"What's so unusual about Dr. Raymond's schedule?"

"I guess you'd call her schedule . . . morbid. On the other hand, she's a pathology doctor, so maybe it isn't that unusual that she wants to be here during the busiest times."

"There's a busy season in the morgue?"

Mr. Connor's chuckle sounded nervous. "Like I said, it's a little morbid. Always more car accidents during holiday weekends, snowstorms and school proms. Dr. Raymond is scheduled during every holiday weekend and every local prom."

Lara laughed. "And how does she schedule snowstorms?"

"She comes in whenever it snows. We can always count on her four-wheel drive."

Lara paused. "I suppose Bobby Eyre comes in during rainstorms?"

Mr. Connor shook his head. "Full moons. Been here five years, hasn't missed working a full moon yet."

"You notice things like that?"

He glanced at her. "Not usually, but he has the strangest work schedule of anyone here: twelve nights on, one off, twelve on, three off. Then he repeats: twelve on, one off, twelve on, three off. Puts him here for every full moon."

"Why? Hoping to see a case of lycanthropy?"

"Excuse me?"

"A joke."

Mr. Connor offered a weak smile. "I don't know why he works every full moon." He wheeled suddenly, grabbed her shoulders and growled. Lara let out a little scream, and Mr. Connor's grin broadened. "You could ask him, but then he'd bite you."

Lara took a deep breath and exhaled, genuinely relieved. She pushed her shoulders back. "Mr. Connor!" she said, but she laughed.

They rode the elevator to the fourth floor. Lara exhaled again, purging the morgue air from her lungs. "Have you been a tour guide here long?" she asked.

"Since I retired, six years ago. This is my second career. Mrs. Connor and I have lived here in this town forty years. Been married forty-seven." He pulled out a wallet and flashed a picture. "Five children and three grandchildren so far."

"That's a beautiful family."

His smile broadened but he didn't say anything.

The bell dinged, and the elevator doors slid open. "What's on four?" Lara joked. "Weather reporting and the wild animal clinic?" Before Mr. Connor could answer, a chorus of babies crying and a young woman screaming in pain confirmed their location, and Lara answered her own question. "Maternity."

"Ever been?"

"Not in this hospital, but I've been in maternity wards in other hospitals."

Mr. Connor laughed. "No, I mean, have you ever been a mother?"

Lara laughed, too. "Nope. Never thought about it—not seriously, anyhow. I would want a father involved, and there isn't anyone under consideration."

Mr. Connor looked abashed. "Sorry, didn't mean to pry."

"It's okay."

"The right guy is out there, you just haven't met him yet. Bet you've heard that a thousand times. Maybe that's why you came to Bucks County." Marty hooked his thumbs through his suspenders and asked, "Do you believe in fate?"

Lara took the question as rhetorical and didn't answer.

They walked the hallways, peeked into the only one of five birthing rooms in use. "We have beds here for nineteen new moms, including three single rooms," Mr. Connor added. "The hospital also uses some of these rooms for psych patients."

"Psych patients on the maternity ward?"

"The psych ward is under construction," Mr. Connor said. "We have to use whatever space is available. *This* room seems to get a steady dose of psych patients." He pointed to the propped-open door of 431. "Females only, on the maternity floor."

"Where does the hospital put male psych patients?"

"Proctology."

Lara laughed. "What about overflow?"

"Hasn't happened yet. Although . . . now that you mention it, that's surprising."

"Why's that?"

"The full moon. More births and more loonies." He took her to a different room, flipped on a light switch to reveal broad windows, an easy chair with soft cushions, a bureau and a double bed. "In case a dad wants to stay overnight with the new mom. We're a progressive hospital. When my kids were born, dads stayed in the waiting room and tapped on the glass at the nursery. Now dads catch babies, cut umbilical cords and film it. Whom do you show that to—your drinking buddies? You pull out the DVD after Thanksgiving dinner?" He cupped his hand to his mouth, playing the role of Dad at a holiday. " 'Who wants to watch Mom give birth to your sister again?' I mean, I think that's taking it too far."

"It is the miracle of life, Mr. Connor."

"Birth is the miracle of life, filming it is a documentary—and please call me Marty."

"I will, Marty, if you'll call me . . ." She'd been about to say *Lara*, still unused to the name Jake had saddled her with. "If you'll call me Meridian."

Sixteen

Lara said good night to Marty a half hour after the end of her shift. She collected several things from her locker and paused at the second-floor nurses' station to sign off charts. As she did, a caress of air brushed the short hairs on the nape of her neck. A sense of familiarity crept up her spine, and she turned. She got a glimpse of a man six feet tall, lean, with dark hair. He was standing beyond the double doors at the end of the hall. They swung shut and obscured him from view.

Intuition made her spin 180 degrees. Bobby Eyre was there, about to enter a patient's room, the tilt of his head suggestive. Their eyes locked, and Lara drew a deep breath. From this distance she could not distinguish between his pupils and irises.

Bobby shook his head and disappeared with a scowl. Anger? What had she done to make him angry? And had it been him at the other end of the corridor? How had he moved so quickly?

When the doorbell first rang, Lara rolled over and drifted back to sleep. She'd never heard this doorbell before, so the sound didn't register. When it rang a second time, realization dawned, and Lara cursed and drew her consciousness into line. She peeked at the clock. 4:21. She peeked at the skylight. 4:21 A.M. On Tuesday morning—her day off.

She took a mental inventory, found no recollection of extending any predawn invitations. The doorbell continued to ding, and Lara cursed as she slid out of bed and gathered her robe.

Halfway down the steps she gasped and clutched the robe to her chest. The last time she'd been wakened in the middle of the night, terrible things had happened. What if Tony had found her? She stopped. A pulse throbbed in her temples.

No, wait. Tony hadn't rung the bell, he'd broken into her home. Whoever leaned on the doorbell now couldn't be Tony.

Not that it mattered. No one she knew would be ringing her bell at this hour.

Lara hurried back up the stairs, found her cell and pushed the contacts button. The only programmed number belonged to Jake. She hit dial.

He answered on the first ring. "City morgue. You stab 'em, we slab 'em."

"That's not funny," Lara snapped.

"What can I do for you at this ungodly hour, Nurse Jones?"

"There's someone at my door."

"Who?"

"If I knew, I wouldn't be calling you."

"Why don't you answer the door and find out?"

"Just like that?"

"You're worried it's Robert?" Jake answered his own question before Lara could. "Robert wouldn't knock."

"So . . . just answer the door?"

"Go for it." He sounded much too blasé for Lara's taste.

"Will you stay on the line?"

"Of course."

The porch light burned outside, its sensor activated, and Lara edged down the first few steps. A microshade blocked the view through the window next to the front door. Lara sensed a shadow behind it. She jumped as the doorbell rang again. Her heart pounded, and she pressed the cell tight against her ear. "Jake?"

"Yes, dear?"

Her face screwed up. "Aren't you worried about me?"

"Answer the door."

"What if . . . ?"

"Answer the door."

Lara caught her breath, licked her lips and finished descending the steps. She pushed the shade aside, peeked . . . then yanked the door open. Agent Jake Plummer was perched on the porch, arms raised in mock innocence, one hand still holding his cell phone.

"For an ER surgeon, you're such a wimp."

"You're such a child." Despite efforts to the contrary, Lara's lips curled. "Did your watch break?"

Jake glanced at his wrist. "Does this mean I'm not invited in for breakfast?"

Lara rolled her eyes and pushed open the screen door. Jake marched into the kitchen, tilted his head back and sniffed. "Fresh coffee?"

Lara stared, hands on her hips. "I suppose you want bagels and cream cheese."

Jake pretended not to notice her sarcasm. "Toasted, please."

Lara filled a measuring cup with water and placed it in her microwave, then pulled a small tin from a cabinet next to the stove. "I have French vanilla decaf. Instant. It'll have to do." She spooned some of the crystals into two mugs while the microwave counted down, tugged open the refrigerator door and shielded her eyes against the light. "I really do have bagels."

"And a toaster?"

"Didn't you furnish this house?"

"How'd your first week at work go?" He didn't wait for a reply. "Time for your real job to begin."

"You want me to pull shifts in another hospital, too?"

"I want you to investigate coworkers."

Lara snorted. "I'm a nurse, not a detective. Investigate them for what?"

"We'll begin with their habits." He drummed his fingers on the counter. "I want you to look for anything suspicious."

Lara leaned next to him, arms crossed. This conversation didn't make sense. "Suspicious in what way?"

Jake bared his teeth, raised his hands like vampire claws and growled.

"Oh, for heaven's sake, when are you going to grow up?"

The Fed straightened. "I'm not joking. Look for someone with an aversion to sunlight."

"Someone who shrinks in terror at the sign of a cross?"

Jake offered a patronizing smile. "Despite Dog's opinion, I think you'll find that cross stuff nonsense."

"Ohhhh." Lara gave a big nod as the microwave

beeped, and she poured hot water into their mugs. "Vampires are serious, but the cross is nonsense."

Jake nodded. "If you look closely, you'll see the same signs I saw that indicate a vampire feeding in the vicinity of your hospital."

"Dead people drained of blood?" She stared at him.

"Not usually, no. Vampires today are smarter than that. Bodies draw attention, and with modern investigative techniques and agencies like ours dedicated to finding them, they can't afford to be noticed. Most vampires only drink a pint or two, which leaves the victim dizzy and fatigued, but alive. They wipe the victim's memory, and no one's suspicious."

"Except you."

Jake ignored her and sipped his coffee. "Occasionally vampires do kill, so you should also look for unexplained sudden deaths involving great losses of blood. More likely you'll find colleagues and patients complaining of inexplicable dizziness. Look for people with nonhealing wounds, or wounds that heal too fast."

"I need to peer at people's necks?" She held her hand at eye level, wrist limp, index finger pointing at Jake. "Excuse me, sir . . . umm, how long have you had those bite marks?"

Jake waved a dismissive hand. "I told you, too many movies. Neck bites are easy to spot. Vampires hiding their existence will bite somewhere less obvious, though near major arteries." He tapped his chest. "Here, just above the heart." He pointed toward Lara's chest. "On a woman, it's often the underside of the breast. Sometimes they'll go for the wrists or the soles of feet."

"I need to look for people who're limping?" she asked. "Or should I be checking out the girls in the locker room?"

He shook his head. "You're a real wise guy, aren't

you? Don't worry. Victims won't be difficult for a doctor to spot. As a starter, their appearance is pale and their lips are gray and dry."

"Duh, it's a hospital. That's just about everybody!"

"Exactly," he said. "You think vampires don't know this? Over the past few decades they've been popping up as hospital employees, because the side effects of a vampire bite aren't as easily noticed in that environment. *You* need to notice." Jake sipped his coffee and shook his head. "Don't underestimate our foes, Ms. Jones. Vampires are cunning and ruthless. One almost killed you."

"Tony—"

"Tony is a servant. Let me show you something." He pulled some papers from an inside jacket pocket. "This is the police report filed the night your house burned. The notes are from the officer who interviewed you." He handed the papers to Lara and continued as she scanned them. "You didn't mention Tony to the police, did you? You described a slightly older, much thinner man, whom you treated for a gunshot wound. Later, in the hospital, you told me the man's name. Robert. That's when you first mentioned Tony. You don't remember Robert because before we could get you out of the hospital, somehow, Robert performed a memory wipe."

Lara flipped the papers onto the counter. "You're suggesting that I saved the life of a man whom I can't remember, by removing a bullet from"—she picked up the papers again and scanned the page—"from his shoulder, and just for good measure he bit me and drank my blood before torching my home."

Jake shook his head. "We checked you thoroughly in the hospital. As far as we could tell, you've never been bitten."

Lara waved a hand. "That's a relief." She turned her back to Jake and leaned over the counter, as much to ground herself in reality as for physical support. This didn't sound like a joke anymore. The police report looked real, even if none of this made sense.

"Why didn't you show me this report during training?"

"That was then. It wasn't important. It matters that you believe now."

"How will I know when I meet a vampire?" Lara asked. She expected a laughable answer. *When he sinks his fangs into you.* She suddenly remembered something Jake said when she first met him in the hospital. *Once Robert Helstrom sinks his fangs into you, he doesn't let go.* Jake had laughed. Lara didn't think it was so funny.

Jake squinted and peered at her. "It's something about their eyes." He shrugged. "I can't pinpoint it. It's not like vampires carry a sign around proclaiming what they are. Their eyes are just . . . different. Otherwise they can pass for anybody on the street."

"As long as it's nighttime," Lara said.

"Duh. Everybody knows that. Sunlight and vampires don't mix."

Lara forced a smile. "How come you didn't rename me Buffy?"

"You're not a slayer. Your job is to find the vampires. I'll take care of them afterward. You know what Dog always says—the only good vampire is a dead vampire. Dog commands, I obey. My job is to keep Dog happy."

"Whatever happened to due process?"

Jake chuckled. "The *process* is pretty much as Dog explains it. Every once in awhile it's determined that it's in the best interest of society to keep a vampire incarcerated. You wouldn't believe the bombshell we have locked up now."

Lara nodded. "So, how does one become a vampire these days?"

Jake shrugged. "Like in the old days. A vampire drinks most of your blood, then you drink the vampire's."

"Ah." Lara peered over her shoulder at him. "That a wooden stake in your pocket, or are you just happy to see me?"

Jake frowned. "You've been joking for two months now. It's time to get serious."

Seventeen

Lara began her third week as Nurse Meridian Jones at St. Mary's Medical Center without a smile. She showered and changed in the hospital health club after her daily two-hour workout.

The more she exercised, the more she wanted to exercise. She'd lost almost twenty-five pounds. She had a new home, a new identity . . . and a new life as a vampire huntress. She laughed out loud. Jake couldn't be serious. He was distracting her from memories of the fire and Tony's lethal intentions, creating this impossible scenario to make her feel better. He'd realized she was worried about Tony finding her and finishing the job, but there didn't seem much chance of that, not after being cloned in Atlanta, then flying to half a dozen cities before here. He could give it up.

She glanced in the locker-room mirror. The person staring back didn't look anything like Dr. Lara West, and she spoke to the stranger. "Next time you see Agent Plummer, tell him thank you, but I'm distracted enough as it is. I don't have time to hunt vampires."

A toilet flushed, and an elderly woman emerged from the end stall, cast a suspicious look at her and shuffled out.

Lara spoke to her reflection again. "Great. Let me introduce myself. I'm Meridian Jones, wacko nurse."

Lara usually spent the first few hours of her shift focused on the job, on the needs of her patients. Ms. Michael wasn't her patient, so Lara didn't know why she stopped in the woman's room. Perhaps it was the unusual metal halo she wore to support weak neck muscles, which made her look like a robot under construction.

Lara scanned the chart—healthy appetite, nothing to account for her pale complexion or dry, cracked lips. The patient also complained of dizziness, which could often be explained, except it was covered by nothing the physicians had thought of yet. Ms. Michael's neck muscles had been in a weakened state for six months. There was no reason given for how the weakness began, and no reason why muscle tone hadn't returned.

One other thing on the chart caught Lara's attention. Ms. Michael had a nonhealing wound on the sole of her left foot. Antibiotic creams, salves, compresses— nothing changed the disposition of the wound.

She had to see for herself. Lara angled toward the end of Ms. Michael's bed, glancing over her shoulder before lifting the blanket and peering at the sole of the sleeping patient's foot. She saw pale skin, scar tissue, some oozing . . . nothing she could identify as puncture marks.

Warmth rose in her face. Nonsense. Jake was making her imagine things. She eased the blanket back into place, smoothed down its edges and poured a fresh glass of water, then scurried into the hall before anyone noticed her presence.

She picked a random room next, second door on the left. It held Ms. Kelly DiRico, a pretty woman in her twenties, admitted seven days prior. Her husband had brought her in for a psych evaluation. After several days, no grounds had been found to keep her as a psych patient, so she should've been released. But . . .

Lara reread the chart. Sudden, inexplicable fatigue had kept Ms. DiRico a guest at St. Mary's. Blood tests had ruled out the usual suspects, like mono and iron deficiency, and the psych evaluation ruled out . . . well, the psych stuff.

Kelly's eyes drifted open and focused on Lara. She had a nice smile. "I keep having the strangest dreams," she said. Her voice was sleepy.

Lara smiled at her. "Mind if I ask what you do on the outside?"

"I'm a dental hygienist."

Lara nodded. "Do you enjoy your job?"

"I work for the nicest doctor. He's been here three times to visit me."

The woman's speech slurred, and Lara checked the chart again. No meds. "Do you live alone?"

"With my husband, of course."

"Do you two get along?"

"Sure."

"What do you enjoy doing when you're not at work?"

"Dancing."

"When's the last time you went?"

"Can't remember. It's been months."

Hm. No dancing in months. Lara pondered. If the woman had been having an affair, some torn allegiance might explain depression. Lara took a shot, trying to find some explanation other than Jake's. "Do you have a boyfriend?"

The patient shook her head and smiled weakly. "I

have *two* boyfriends." She held up two fingers in confirmation. "My husband and my son."

Lara flashed the woman a smile. Okay, there went her theory that maybe Ms. DiRico's husband or lover wasn't paying her enough attention. She had no medically valid reason for lethargy, and no emotional reason to explain it, either. Jake's comments were getting scarier.

"Are you my new doctor?"

"Meridian Jones. I'm a nurse. Why do you think you're tired all the time?"

"I don't know," the woman said. "It didn't start until after I spent a couple of nights on the maternity ward."

Lara gulped and tried to fight down her fears. So what if two patients in a hospital of hundreds supported Agent Plummer's ridiculous notions? She patted Kelly DiRico's hand. "Get some rest. I'll check on you again later." She turned to go.

"Wait. Please, can you get me something for the itch?"

"What itch is that?" Nothing on Ms. DiRico's chart mentioned an itch.

"My doctor is a man. I'm too embarrassed to ask him. That's why I thought you might be my new . . ." The woman kicked the sheet off with difficulty, and hiked up her hospital gown. Her legs spread slightly apart, she pointed to two small welts high on her inner thigh. "I must've been bitten by a couple of mosquitoes on the maternity ward. These itch like crazy. Can you please get me something for it?"

Lara stared, mouth agape. Since when did mosquitoes hunt in pairs? "Of course. I'll have a nurse—a female nurse on this shift—bring you something right away." She squeezed Kelly's hand.

She left then, but she couldn't focus on work. Every brain cell was fighting off Jake's theory. A couple of patients with inexplicable symptoms from his list were coincidence, nothing more. Lara scoffed. A surgeon couldn't entertain such outlandish ideas. Puncture marks high on the inner thigh of a beautiful young woman?

She headed to the cafeteria. Nothing was more sobering than hospital food. She rode the same elevator she'd taken with Marty, and it gave her an idea. After her shift ended tonight, she would visit Dr. Raymond in the morgue and ask about deaths. That would give her some more information, and it'd be easy to obtain:

"Hiya, Doc. Any unexplained bodies lying around?"

"Why do you ask?"

"Professional curiosity. I'm not a nurse. This is a clever disguise. I'm really a vampire hunter, and Agent Jake Plummer says a series of inexplicable deaths may be a sign there's a vampire in the community."

"I see." Dr. Raymond would don a mask and rub her chin. She'd pick up the phone and punch a few numbers.

"Who're you calling?"

"Psych consult."

Piece of cake.

"Mind if I join this conversation?"

"Excuse me?" Lara replied.

Philippe grinned. "You seemed to be enjoying the conversation between you and . . . yourself. . . . I'm really glad I ran into you down here. Both of you! Are you headed to the cafeteria, too? Silly me, no one just drops in to visit the morgue. Anyway, I couldn't help but notice, you're more versed in medicine than most nurses, and I need advice about a patient. . . ."

Lara's shift had ended about an hour before, and she was unsettled. She'd enjoyed the conversation with Philippe. He was intuitive, and a creative nurse from what she'd seen. Still, she'd been surprised when he asked her to go shoe shopping at the In-Step over the weekend. She'd been more surprised to hear herself agree. Lara West didn't make many friends. Who was she though, Lara West or Meridian Jones?

She'd finished her shift full of doubt about her plans, but hung around the hospital. She'd filled in charts, visited nameless patients while they slept, straightened bedcovers and fluffed pillows, and she'd inventoried the supply room. Well, she hadn't actually inventoried the supply room while killing time. She'd done that three hours earlier while on duty. After shift, she merely recounted the inventory, which was what she was doing now.

Eighteen bedpans? Check. If no one knew she planned to conduct an interview in the morgue, how could anyone know she was avoiding it?

Do it now and report to Jake.

"Sorry, no data to support your theories." That's what she wanted to say.

She remained in her scrubs. Perhaps her chat with Dr. Raymond would feel less like an interview that way.

She headed into the bowels of the hospital, refusing eye contact. The elevator dinged, and the doors slid open onto the empty basement corridor. Lara's footsteps echoed off the walls. She pushed the swinging doors open enough to peek into Dr. Raymond's outer office. No one was home.

"Dr. Raymond?"

No answer.

She entered the coroner's office. The doors swung back and forth behind her. A single lamp revealed reports smeared across a large desk, several words underlined in red or highlighted in neon yellow.

A large brown envelope partially hidden beneath the papers caught Meridian's attention. She reached across the desk and slid two papers aside, exposing writing on the envelope. CONFIDENTIAL. SENSITIVE MATERIAL.

Lara stopped to consider. What constituted sensitive material in a morgue, anyway?

No sounds emerged from the morgue workroom. She was alone in the basement, and this was what Jake wanted her to do—spy on her colleagues.

She extricated the envelope without disturbing the other reports and bent the prongs of the clasp straight up so they'd fit through the hole without tearing the unsealed flap. She slid out a police report with photos of a young woman who'd been found in Tyler State Park. Candi Malloy. The report indicated the woman had bled to death. There was no blood at the scene, though, so police concluded the murder had occurred elsewhere, the body dumped. Time of death, 1:30 A.M., night before last.

Lara shook her head. Unexplained murders happened all the time. She imagined that criminals often dragged bodies far from the crime scene to confound authorities. Nothing surprising in that. She slipped the papers and photos back into the envelope.

The morgue doors swished open. *Bobby.*

A surge of adrenaline overpowered Lara. She hadn't heard the elevator. How else could he get to the basement? More important, what did he want? Why didn't he speak? Did he think staring would provoke her feelings? Her heart raced because he'd startled her, no other reason.

Yeah, right.

He erased the space between them with extraordinary speed, and his mouth covered hers. His hand kneaded her back, mounting her spine until his fingers tangled in her hair. His tongue danced around her mouth and captured her breath. Her flesh quivered. Instead of objecting, instead of pushing away his advances, she moaned when his other hand slid into the band of her pants, drowning her in a sea of sexual tension pent up for much longer than she cared to think about.

How could this be happening?

She groaned and struggled, not attracted by his overpowering male aura. *Not?* Right. There was no way she could give herself to a suspicious and mysterious man. There was also no way to stop herself.

Lara slipped in the moment, lost in the lips that slid down her neck, lost in the hand that caressed her scalp, lost in the finger that delved into the warm place between her legs. Her juices were flowing freely now. He found her spot, and as her breath became ragged, as her purring turned to moans escaping from deep in her throat, he exploited her hunger. Every touch elicited a reaction, magnified sensations, repeated and magnified them again.

She felt herself dissolve into him. Bobby's mouth peppered kisses across her skin as he raised her scrub shirt off first one shoulder, then the other. His finger circled inside of her, applying a pressure that weakened her legs. How had he known to touch her like that? No longer in control of her will, no longer able to prevent the surge of emotion that left her in a state of euphoria unlike any she had ever experienced, surrender became Lara's only option. These feelings extended beyond simple fantasy sex with a stranger.

She panted, her hips gyrating with his motions, pleading with him to take her . . . where? She didn't know how to describe someplace she'd never been. Certainly she'd experienced orgasms before, but what she knew had felt so very different. There'd never been a buildup like *this*.

Her moaning grew louder, torn from her throat with every breath. She felt an urgency in his movements, though his pace hadn't changed. His kisses became deeper. His tongue licked the salty perspiration that dotted her skin. He licked it with relish—the relish of a man hungry for her explosion and not his own. The fingers that strummed inside her sang a song she had never heard before: slow, soft, an unexpected falsetto with the deep bass of manhood beneath, the voices of both Bobby and . . . what, his alter ego?

There was nothing she could do but wait for the culmination of her feelings. What had begun as separate sensations—his hand on her scalp, the moisture of his breath in her ear, his fingertips caressing her cheek, his tongue gliding across her shoulders and exploring every plane of her neck, and the constant pressure of his other fingers barely inside her, swirling—all blended together as if being sucked into the black hole that had become her consciousness. He hadn't even touched her breasts.

She sucked in air. She couldn't imagine what would happen if his mouth slipped lower and he pulled on one nipple, his fingers tugging lightly on the other. She couldn't get enough oxygen. Her feelings compressed into a dot, and that dot pressed on her entire being in a crescendo of unending urgency.

Bobby licked her ear again, and he licked her chin. His lips brushed against her shoulder and traced lower. His hand caressed the back of her head one more time and slipped onto her other shoulder. As if he'd read her mind, his tongue found one nipple at the same moment his free hand found the other. The pressure between her legs increased. Her knees buckled. The explosion that rocked Lara delivered her to an alternate reality. She collapsed against the desk, breath ragged.

She grasped his shoulders, trying to bring some semblance of order to her thoughts as Bobby disengaged. How could she have allowed this man to touch her? She'd never felt anything like that.

What did he do to me?

"I didn't plan this," he whispered, his eyes locked with hers. "I missed you when we exchanged shifts tonight. I missed that look you give me that says you understand I'm keeping a secret, the look that says you'll share your secret if I'll share mine." He held her shoulders. "When I spotted you two hours into my shift, I could tell you'd had better days. I wanted to gather you in my arms, caress your cheek and assure you that, whatever your issues, I'll be here to support you. I want to celebrate *us*, Meridian, whatever this connection is that we both feel."

Lara held her breath.

"I followed you down here without thinking of reasons. You're becoming part of my life, and I want you to know my real nature, if only for a moment."

With unfathomable speed, Bobby pulled her away from the desk, twirled her around and maneuvered behind her. He massaged her shoulders and kissed her neck. The edge of his teeth grazed her flesh, and a shiver arced across her.

What if . . . ?

When he whispered in her ear, his breath caressed her skin and his voice wrapped around her consciousness. Her eyelids drifted shut.

"I've thought about bringing you across," he said.

Lara opened her eyes. Why couldn't she speak? Across what?

"Into my world," Bobby responded, as if she'd spoken aloud. "A life of darkness, but a life of eternity. We'd belong to each other." His voice remained a whisper.

Lara's mind raced. Bobby's lips brushed her neck. She braced against the wall. He massaged her arms, his hands tracing a line to her fingertips, then back across her palms and pausing on her wrists. He increased pressure there, on her veins, as if he could feel the blood pulsing through her.

His breath tickled her ear. "The temptation to take you is overwhelming."

Sensations flooded her mind. Waves of pleasure rolled over her, pleading for the destruction of a barrier he'd not yet penetrated.

Take me.

Every touch, every caress, sent surges of electricity arcing across her flesh and between her legs. His breath on her skin, his lips on her shoulders, his fingers—

He stopped.

Don't stop!

She sensed more than hesitancy, and peered over her shoulder at him. She read the struggle on his face. The eternity he spoke of stared out of those unfathomable eyes. Eyes the like of which she'd seen once before, when she'd saved a man's life in her home.

He gathered her into his arms and spoke, their bodies pressed tight. "I have no right to choose that life for you, despite my feelings."

What feelings?

"I don't know if I can stop myself, stop my beast from taking what I want."

The words made sense, but they didn't, they couldn't. *I don't understand,* her mind said.

Her body pleaded, *Take me.*

"I can't," he answered again as if she'd spoken. Anguish contorted his features. "This can't be my choice. I have to protect you."

Protect me from what?

"I have to make sure that . . . someone like me can't take you against your will." He stared into her eyes as if begging her to understand.

I'm giving myself. Take me! But her words didn't match his meaning.

He caressed her cheek. "Your thoughts can focus this way." The oddest sensation filled her mind, as if her thoughts were retreating behind a wall, an impenetrable barrier that would keep her safe from . . . what?

Someone like you?

He kissed her. Lara's eyes closed, and her mouth yielded to his will, inflamed by desire, swollen with passion. Theirs was a kiss of longing. A kiss of passion. A kiss that lasted a lifetime.

He broke their embrace and steadied her shoulders. "Focus your thoughts," he commanded. She felt how the barrier in her mind strengthened. "This way, someone like me can't take you against your will."

Someone like you?

"I'm sorry, you will not remember."

Lara's thoughts swirled, and every atom of her essence exploded outward, refusing control or understanding. Her mind wanted to collapse, as had her body, sucked into the sleep that often followed an orgasmic encounter. She sensed a passage of time— seconds or hours, it defied comprehension.

A nudge shocked Lara awake. Dr. Raymond peered over wire-rimmed glasses. "Lost from your tour?"

Lara jumped. She didn't know what to say. "I didn't mean to startle you."

"I think that's my line," the coroner said. "What can I do for you, Nurse . . . Jones?"

Lara froze. Her right hand clenched a large brown envelope, and her shirt was rumpled. Why did she feel drained? Where had Bobby gone? Why were orgasmic contractions making her flesh tingle? Nothing had happened between them!

"Call me Meridian, p-please," she stammered. Bobby had been talking about . . . what?

Dr. Raymond put down a tray of instruments and pointed at the envelope in her hand. "There's a reason it's stamped confidential."

Lara thought about denying seeing the contents but decided a direct approach would be better. "I'm interested in pathology, and I hope . . ." Her eyes strained into the dark corners of the office. Where *had* Bobby gone? She decided not to ask Dr. Raymond.

"You hope what?" Dr. Raymond asked.

Lara raised the envelope. "I hope to be a surgeon one day. Did you examine this corpse? The girl bled to death? How much blood was missing?"

Dr. Raymond answered after only the slightest hesitation. "We don't get many murders in this part of Bucks County. The few that do occur don't often end up on my desk." She grabbed more instruments from a shelf, picked up the tray and headed for the inner sanctum. "What struck me as peculiar about this death . . . That is what's captured your interest, the strangeness?" She didn't wait for an answer but continued to walk. "Was the lack of blood on the body."

Lara followed her. "You mean *in* the body."

"Ms. Jones, the English language is precise. If I'd meant in the body, I would've said, 'in the body.' The lack of blood *on* the body surprised me. Death by sudden blood loss should be messy. A few drops on her clothes suggest she died in them, but lack of any other spillage leads me to conclude that the victim was deliberately drained."

"That's ridiculous. Who would do that?"

"That's the oddity, isn't it, Meridian?" The coroner raised an eyebrow and made it clear that Lara was dismissed.

Lara stalked up to the locker room and recomposed herself. She wasn't quite sure what had just happened, or what to make of it all, but she had lots to think about. Her memory didn't match the physical sensations still arcing through her body. At last, glowering into the mirror above the sink, she spun on her heel and strode across the tiled floor. She shoved open the nurses' locker room door, only to have it bounce back at her.

"Ouch!"

"I'm so—"

Bobby. Face-to-face with him, she found herself unable to speak. She finally growled, "There's a reason this is labeled the women's locker room."

His eyebrow arched. His lips curled as if he masked a secret, an expression torn between a smirk and a smile. His nostrils flared, as if he were an animal taking a scent. The tilt of his head, the jutting chin. His hair was tousled, and she wondered where he'd been. His eyes glimmered, and again the distinction between pupils and irises blurred.

Someone like you?

Her head tilted to match his, and she sniffed as he had. A subtle odor, like salt on a sea breeze, carried her away. For a moment she drifted in a fog, forgetting the hospital, forgetting Meridian Jones, Lara West or any other damn persona. As with salty peanuts, the more she took, the more she wanted. She was at that moment impaled by the singularity of his focus.

He spoke as if he'd just regained speech control. "I'm meeting Philippe here."

"Excuse me?"

"I'm meeting Philippe."

An odd sensation followed. She wanted to talk about seeing Bobby in the morgue, ask him what had happened, but her thoughts were suddenly directed elsewhere.

Nice kid, Philippe. The first time he'd approached her, he'd flashed a picture of his puppy. He acted like one of the girls and sometimes dressed like one of the girls. It made sense he'd introduced himself as "one of the girls." Pleasant, chatty—and Bobby Eyre wanted to meet him in the women's locker room?

Lara fought for control of her thoughts. She could understand the other nurses accepting Philippe, but rumors about Bobby's sexuality persisted.

I'm safe . . . from someone like you? Lara focused her mind.

Bobby gripped the edge of the door, holding it open. He pulled back farther, indicating his desire to pass. Meridian continued her imitation of a statue.

What attracted her to this man? Why did she sense an overwhelming maleness in him, contrary to everyone else's opinion? What could possibly be dangerous about him, a thirty-something male nurse named Bobby? Of course, the name didn't fit the man. In a guttural voice he'd once told her some women called him Roberre. That didn't fit, either. All she knew was, his presence ignited the sun tattoo on the small of her back and made her tingle.

"I said, are you the warden?"

"The what?" Had she zoned out? How many times had he asked? She had no way of knowing.

"The warden of the women's locker room."

His words finally registered. She stepped aside with a grandiose flourish and a nod of her head. Permission granted.

He brushed by, and for a split second she smelled his musky male heat—sweet, sensual, like a vanilla candle when you blow out the flame and a wisp of smoke rises to your nostrils before vanishing in a wash of air. Lara focused all her will not to let a moan escape her lips. Then she fled.

Marty Connor was delivering a stack of papers to the nurses' station. His face lit up and he waved as Lara approached. He pointed toward the locker room. "I see you met Bobby."

Lara smiled. "You're here kind of late, aren't you?"

"Sometimes I work a late shift, six to midnight. Not many people in my office want to work that shift. Most of the time our office isn't open then, but when we need to catch up, I volunteer. Don't sleep much anymore."

He sighed. "Sue—that's my wife—she sleeps a lot. Likes to have an early dinner, four o'clock, and by seven she's ready for bed. Says she doesn't mind if I work a couple late nights. Long as I don't make a ruckus when I come home." Marty displayed a broad grin. "I enjoy it, having the office to myself. Speaking of late, didn't your shift end two hours ago?"

"Checking on patients before I leave."

"They won't pay, you know."

"Who won't pay?"

"The hospital. Far as they're concerned, if they didn't call you in, you're off duty when your shift ends. They won't pay."

Lara smiled. "Doesn't matter, Marty. I'm not doing it for the money. If I wanted the money, I'd've become a surgeon."

Marty laughed, hitched up his pants and glanced at the wall clock behind the nurses' station. "I have to punch out and grab my keys. If you'll come to the office with me, I'll walk you to the parking lot."

"An offer I can't refuse." Lara winked. Marty crooked his arm and she encircled it with her own.

Lights in the administrative offices had already been dimmed for the night. Marty veered Lara to the right. "This is my desk," he said with the pride of a first grader. "I keep the personnel records, histories, profiles. I also copy the scheduling paperwork. Head nurses keep schedules four weeks in advance." He shuffled some papers around his desk and uncovered a Monopoly mouse pad.

Lara noticed all the office computers except for Marty's were on screensaver. His machine was running a program. "You leave the computers on all night?" she asked.

Marty shrugged. "That's how they've been doing it since I got here. I guess it's easier than shutting them down and rebooting every morning." He sat at his desk. "I just have to close this program and log off."

Personnel files. That's what he'd been working in. Marty moved the mouse and clicked a couple of times, logging himself off. "Oh!"

"What's wrong?" Lara read over his shoulder.

"Silly me. I always forget that before I log off, I have to register I made entries in the personnel file. Otherwise my boss gets angry. Sorry, I have to sign on again."

"Doesn't security bother you when you work here at night?"

"Nope. They peek in around ten o'clock, and then I

don't see them. I don't know if they bother after midnight. I guess there's not too much that can be stolen from this office. The hospital *is* having a problem, though. No one's talking about it, but they're going to have to do something if it doesn't stop soon."

"What kind of problem?" Lara asked.

Marty's gaze shifted from side to side, as if he'd said something that he shouldn't have. "It's kind of gruesome. You won't tell anyone if I tell you? It could be an issue for me."

"You don't have to tell me, Marty. I don't want you to get into trouble."

Marty waved his hand at her. "That's why I like you, Meridian. You remind me of my wife, Sue. She's more concerned about the people around her, too. We should have you over for dinner one night." He chuckled. "I mean one afternoon, if you can stand to eat dinner at four o'clock. That's Sue, though, likes to eat and go to bed early."

Lara peered at Marty. He didn't seem to realize that he'd repeated himself. How old was he? Seventy? Seventy-five?

The old man spun around in his chair. "I'd better sign back on before I forget. I seem to be forgetting a lot of things recently."

Lara couldn't help noticing his password: ILOVESUE. "I'd love to meet your wife, Marty," she said.

"Good, but don't tell her what I'm going to tell you now. It would make her worry about my safety."

Lara crossed her heart. "I promise."

Marty motioned her closer, glanced again at the office door and whispered, "Someone is stealing blood."

Eighteen

Lara strained against the Universal weight machine, perspiration soaking her sweats. She hadn't slept well after Marty's startling news, and she'd gotten nowhere sorting everything out. Ms. Michael presented a sallow complexion, cracked lips, unexplained dizziness. Ms. DiRico exhibited inexplicable tiredness and displayed two welt marks high on her inner thigh. Dr. Raymond was examining the body of a young woman deliberately drained of blood. All coincidences, nothing related to any of the impossible nonsense Jake suggested.

Blood stolen from the hospital was one coincidence too many.

A rational explanation had to exist. When Lara had first graduated from med school, reality had appeared black-and-white, easy to decipher, easy to understand. The real world of an urban ER taught her shades of gray.

Suppose . . . No, how could she do that? Not even hypothetically. It was ridiculous.

Lara stepped into the shower. The hot water soothed tired muscles. A really good shower would have washed ludicrous notions down the drain, but maybe she'd used the wrong soap. Too many coincidences. So many mysterious situations. Were any of her coworkers slaves to the night? Dr. Raymond acted ghoulish, a slave to the morgue after dark, but Marty said she came in during day shifts, too, whenever enough bodies enticed her. Did Lara owe it to herself to open her mind to the possibility of . . .

No. There is no such possibility.

Lara lathered under her arms and across her hips. She'd lost a couple more pounds, and the curves she'd kept were more pronounced. The after-workout muscle sting meant endorphins were still flowing. Awareness expanded. She liked the feeling—except when confounded by evidence contrary to rational thought.

Bobby Eyre had worked twelve days on, one off, twelve on, three off for five years' worth of night shifts. He was at the hospital for every full moon. But what did the full moon have to do with anything?

Nothing. Another absurd notion.

Did Bobby have an aversion to sunlight? Where had he come from? Were there unexplained deaths and missing blood at his previous job? Where did he live now? There were no castles with towers or dungeons in Bucks County. Lara laughed.

See? Ridiculous.

Also, something about Bobby appealed to her. He had a mysterious charm and, despite the belief of coworkers, was not gay. He exuded a male aura, seductive, elusive. There was something strange about his eyes—dark, intriguing, and the line between his pupils and irises remained indistinct.

One thought she refused to consider, although it kept pounding against the wall of her consciousness. Jake had said she'd know by the eyes when she met a vampire.

There were all these questions for which rational answers must exist. How could she get them? Simply

walk up to Bobby or bang another door in his face?
*Oops, excuse me, didn't mean to run into you, but since
you're standing right here, would you mind answering a few
questions? You're not really gay, are you? And by the way, do
you drink blood?* Ha, ha. The direct interview approach
left something to be desired.

As Lara bent one knee at a time and washed her
feet, she remembered something Jake said about soles
once. When she'd joked about checking for neck
bites, he'd said smart vampires bit less obvious parts—
wrists, breasts, the soles of feet. When she'd first met
Jake in the hospital, he'd peeked under her sheet and
inspected the soles of her feet before ever joking
about vampires. Didn't that lend more credence to
the possibility that he was telling the truth?

Okay, how could she investigate Bobby? Marty knew
everyone. She could ask him. Of course, that seemed
only one step less absurd than asking Bobby himself.
*By the way, Marty, have you noticed Bobby flying to work?
Does he keep an extra pint of blood in his thermos?* Some
questions she considered weren't totally out of line.
And if he caught on . . . *Do I suspect Bobby of* what? *Of being a vampire? How silly is that?*

She switched the shower to cold and realized she
had to go back to the hospital. Tonight.

As the summer night closed around her like a shroud,
Lara hugged the bare flesh of her arms and shrugged
to shake the yoke of guilt. Did vampires live and work
in Bucks County? It was clear enough that she
couldn't ask Marty ghoulish questions, but his computer wouldn't be so quick to judge. She kept telling
herself this was what Jake wanted her to do, and Jake
was with the government.

Her footsteps echoed in the hospital's empty corridors. *It's not breaking and entering if the door is unlocked,* she told herself. The computers were left on, and Marty had shared his password just last night, hadn't he?

She glossed over that thought. She wouldn't *steal* anything. Just read. Private files. No one would ever know.

The personnel program whirred into operation, and the opening screen asked if she wanted to search the files by name. Two fields, first name and last name. Lara typed in *Bobby Eyre.* The mouse passed over *Go,* but she didn't collect two hundred dollars. Not funny. Perspiration rolled down her ribs.

As she waited, she refused to acknowledge Jake's intended role for her. It wasn't vampires. She was just searching out blood thieves, and he didn't want her thinking about the more realistic side of the process. She was just an investigator researching for the WPAVU—

Uh-oh. It suddenly sank in what the *VU* embossed on Jake's badge stood for. She had a feeling Dog wouldn't let him carry a fake badge.

A new screen flashed.

No matches were found.
Try narrowing or expanding your parameters.
Search by first name or last name.
Women who marry or divorce after their files
have been created may change their names.
This program may not recognize diminutives
or nicknames.

Of course the computer wouldn't recognize *Bobby.* Meridian smacked the side of her head. Was she braindead? She needed to use *Robert.* Adrenaline surged.

Robert.

Her first instinct was to call Jake. Her second instinct

was to ignore her first. This couldn't be the same man who Jake claimed was Tony's boss. Could it?

Robert Eyre. The file dared her to read it. Lara bit her lip.

Robert Eyre's file listed a rare skin condition that required him to avoid direct sunlight, hence his requested and granted permanent nighttime assignment. It also listed a previous job as a nurse at St. Francis Hospital in Memphis, Tennessee. He'd left Memphis five years ago.

Memphis. Jake had reported a vampire there biting women's inner thighs, but they'd lost track of him—*five years ago.* They now believed him to be on the East Coast. As she had just seen, East Coast patient Kelly DiRico had two puncture marks high on her inner thigh. Lara gulped and continued reading.

No reason was given for Bobby's twelve on, one off, twelve on, three off work schedule—no family history of lycanthropy, at any rate. "Okay, not funny," Lara told herself. "I'm looking for vampires, not werewolves."

Really not funny.

She flipped open her cell and hit the only number on the call list. Jake answered on the first ring.

"Trouble?"

"I need to be transferred to the night shift."

"Can't sleep?" he asked.

"Research."

"I knew it! You've found something."

Lara paused, wondering if she could allow herself to believe. "Too many coincidences, that's all. I'm going to disprove them."

"Dog's anxious. Coinciding with the time you entered our program, hospitals have been reporting missing blood in an arc spreading north from D.C."

"It's reached Bucks County."

"How do you know?"

"St. Mary's is having a problem."

"They haven't reported it." Jake sounded upset. "How do you know?"

"Research."

"Full of surprises, aren't you?"

"When I get transferred, I'll be assigned a new mentor. Make sure it's Bobby Eyre."

Jake groaned. "You aren't chasing him just because his name is Robert, are you?"

Lara bit back a curse. It had taken her two weeks to stumble her way to this conclusion, and Jake had reached it in ten seconds. She raised the pitch of her voice. "No, I'm not chasing him because his name is Robert." Her voice returned to normal. "One other thing. The police found the body of a young woman, Candi Malloy, in a local park a few days ago. You might want to look into it."

"Gotcha covered," Jake said. "Transfer, mentor, Candi."

Lara wasn't sure whether to be pleased or terrified.

Nineteen

How many people did Bobby have to help before he repaid his debt to society? Lots, apparently. Lots of patients, lots of coworkers, lots of problems. That's why he'd made "friends" with Philippe D'Paltrow. Well, it was one reason. Bobby had made mental suggestions, and Philippe had responded each time as if Bobby had no influence over him. While refreshing to discover someone over whom he could not exert his will, it was also disconcerting. It made Philippe both interesting and a problem.

Philippe liked to talk. He fortunately saved chitchat about fashion and makeup and hairstyles for the female nurses. He talked to Bobby about his feelings—not just about being gay in a heterosexual world. They also discussed religion, art, and the psychology of dealing with power-hungry bosses. When Dr. D'Lorien, an outspoken staff physician, suggested euthanasia as a remedy for a terminal patient with unmanageable pain, Bobby and Philippe had begun a weeklong debate on the ethics and efficacy of such action. Bobby secretly found similarities between the terminal patient and periods in his own tortured existence.

Tonight they discussed anthropology and sociology, and whether or not such a thing as a societal secret could exist.

Though the conversation wasn't quite over, hunger licked at Bobby's throat. If he wanted to feed, he'd have to lose Philippe, not to mention avoid the increased security and Meridian. For all this time, feeding on the night of the full moon and the nights on either side had made for a barely livable existence. If he missed one of those . . .

Bobby chuckled, chiding himself. Vampires were dead. Nothing at all about their existence was "livable."

His hunger grew. Thirst for blood danced along his spine. It gripped his shoulders and shook with a force so overpowering, so terrifying, Bobby realized he had no choice. He *had* to feed. Tonight. He'd gone as long as he could without tasting blood.

He closed his eyes with the memory of sinking his fangs into the soft flesh of that psych patient's inner thigh. Her blood, rich with life, had squirted into his mouth, sating his hunger. The explosions of blood and sex had coincided in stage five of Vampirical Harmony. His existence was maintained for another month. He was grateful to Kelly DiRico . . . but he'd thought about Meridian Jones.

"I don't think a society could keep a secret—I don't even think an individual could keep a secret—indefinitely," Philippe said.

Bobby had suggested the opposite. He questioned himself, though. In a way, twenty-six nights ago he'd shared his secret with Ms. DiRico for a moment, before wiping her memory.

Hunger lashed out. Obstacles were everywhere. Guards roamed the halls, security cameras kept constant vigil, locked doors prevented access to stairs. The full moon attracted people to the hospital and, research accomplished, Bobby knew seven mothers had given birth in the last twenty-four hours, and two more were in labor now. He could hear their screams. He could smell the musk of the newborns and sense their desire for existence. St. Mary's also drew a cyclical influx of young female psych patients, and three had been admitted that morning. Bobby had walked the maternity/psych ward earlier and picked his victim, Diana Loztic. Her womanhood appealed more than the others'. Long, wavy, blonde hair, pale skin, blue eyes that penetrated beyond the sight of the doctors and nurses surrounding her—all had left a vital impression. Bobby wanted her blood. He needed her blood. Now.

He jumped to his feet.

Philippe jumped. "Where're we going?"

Bobby shook his head. "Work," he said.

The two of them finished their rounds and all of the extraneous duties Nurse Cron had assigned. Scut work. If nothing else, in Nurse Cron's mind, being gay was a venial sin punishable by Nurse Cron. How would she punish Bobby if she learned of his mortal sins with psych patients? Bobby laughed.

"Aren't you going to share the joke?" Philippe asked.

Bobby smiled, but desire for blood swelled up inside him and stopped him from speaking.

"How do you know that anthropologists haven't discovered the secret of the Inuit people?" Philippe asked after a moment. They'd been talking of it earlier.

"I've lived with the Inuit. I know their secret."

"Anthropologists have lived with them, too."

"As outsiders. They never became part of Inuit society."

"What kind of secret could be kept for decades, let alone generations?"

Vampirical Harmony remained a secret. If Bobby wanted to torment a woman, he could treat her to the first stage without wiping her memory. A woman who experienced stage one just once, memory intact, would be like a crack addict undergoing withdrawal. The deeper he took a woman into Vampirical Harmony, the more severe the withdrawal. The intensity of stage two often rendered women unconscious. Stage three, the suspension of disbelief, couldn't begin until she regained consciousness.

Remorse trickled through Bobby. He'd shared all five stages of Vampirical Harmony but the memory wipe with Marilyn. He'd never make that mistake again.

Before Marilyn, only the beast had killed. Bobby felt as responsible for her taking her life as if he'd sunk his fangs into her milky white flesh and drunk her last ounce of blood. He closed his eyes and fought back swelling emotion.

"What were you doing living with the Inuit, anyhow?"

"For three months, the Inuit live in eternal night. A long time ago I needed to escape from society, and the darkness suited me."

Philippe scuffed the floor. His fingers fiddled, and

Bobby could sense his apprehension. "I know what you mean," he said. "Sometimes I'd just like to get away from everyone I know. It seems like, when you're gay, everyone makes every issue about sex. It's not all about sex."

Bobby understood. He wouldn't want women chasing him for the sex they'd had if he ever allowed them to remember. Thankfully, Freud had never written down the five stages of Vampirical Harmony. As long as Bobby kept Roberre's sexual activities confined to a dreamworld and always performed a memory wipe, he was safe. He never brought women to his home. Even the hospital administrator didn't have a real address for him.

Bobby rolled his tongue over his growing teeth; thinking about sex had aroused the beast in him. He kept his lips pressed together so Philippe couldn't see. But he had to feed. Soon. It was a good thing that he'd never been aroused by a woman and lost control of himself.

Meridian Jones?

The thought popped into his head as he was reminded of his past actions. No. She was an interesting challenge, the first in a long time, but that was all. It had been easy to surprise her in the morgue, to get the emotional taste of her he needed. And maybe later he'd get more. He'd investigate this mysterious woman, discover her secret, and perhaps he'd again treat her to stage one of Vampirical Harmony before wiping her memory. That was all.

He pushed thoughts of Meridian into the recesses of his mind. His already-heightened senses extended farther, and every female in the vicinity became potential prey. Male blood didn't interest him. Female blood tasted sweeter.

Something else tasted sweeter still—the blood of a

woman with whom he was involved. For the last half century, Bobby had fed in an emotional vacuum, a night creature, alone. He saw a chance to have that delicacy once again. The woman named Meridian called to him as he'd never before been called, but . . . he couldn't get involved with her. He wouldn't risk her life.

Yes, it was better if he kept his partners unaware. He could leave a sleeping woman with a dreamworld satisfaction and two mosquito bitelike welt marks that itched for a few days, that was all. Instead of being a murderer, he traded a woman her blood for unconscious pleasure—which appealed to Bobby, if not to Roberre. While she slept, he would search for his victim's sexual trigger. Every woman had fantasies, even the Inuits Bobby had visited. Bobby would touch a woman's soul, feel her thoughts . . . then Roberre would take her to that place—luscious, often exotic. Sometimes, though, in the mind of a nonreader, the place would be her own bed. He could always tell nonreaders: they lacked imagination.

Every time the scent of lavender floated on the air, every time her voice wrapped around his spine, Bobby sensed Meridian's unleashed mind. Her essence was compelling, mysterious and challenging. He spent hours thinking about it. It made him feel alone. It heightened the extent of his solitude.

For the first time in almost fifty years, since that beautiful actress had committed suicide, the temptation to share his secret raged. He glanced at Philippe in pink scrubs and matching pink clogs. Philippe, this tormented young man who seemed so desperate for connection. Could he share his secret with Philippe—or with Meridian?

Not Meridian!

Bobby recoiled at the memory of the last time he'd

shared his secret. He'd become emotionally involved. Oh, how involved! He remembered Marilyn's surprise— and his own equal surprise at her acceptance of his beast.

It would be safer to share his secret only with Philippe.

Don't worry, Roberre said. *If he doesn't accept you, I'll take care of him.*

No, Bobby said. *If he doesn't accept me, I'll change my identity and we'll move on.*

Roberre laughed.

"Excuse me," Philippe said. "Is this a private conversation, or can anyone join in? You know, you remind me of my parents."

"How so?"

"When I was in elementary school, my parents dragged me to *Star Trek* conventions."

Bobby stared at him. "I didn't drag you anywhere."

"They dressed in uniform and spoke to Starfleet through fake communicators. The only difference is, you're not using a communicator." Philippe giggled. He glanced at the clock behind the nurses' station. "Oh, my! I forgot to tell you, Nurse Cron volunteered us to be doorstops tonight."

"What?"

"At one o'clock, security all over the hospital is shutting down while they upgrade the computer system or something. The stairwell doors lock automatically, and if there happens to be a fire while the system is down, the doors won't unlock. The security guards have to take care of other things, so Nurse Cron volunteered us to keep the fire doors open for an hour, just in case. I guess it's for liability reasons." Philippe smiled mischievously. "I call this floor. You have to go to the maternity ward. Those women howl for a full moon."

An hour on the maternity ward without Philippe? Perfect. He couldn't have asked for better.

"Who's taking care of the third floor?" he asked, his hunger screaming to be sated.

"Don't know, don't care. Not our responsibility," Philippe answered. "But I called this floor. You go on up to four."

Bobby held up his hands in mock defeat. "I'm going, I'm going."

"You better hurry. It's almost time. Nurse Cron said to wait until exactly one o'clock, then open the stairwell door and hold it open. Once they shut off the system, opening the door won't set off the alarm."

Bobby nodded and grabbed a box of adult-sized diapers from a supply cart.

"What's *that* for?" Philippe asked.

"I forgot." Bobby invented an excuse. "One of the fourth-floor nurses asked me to bring this up earlier."

He rode the elevator up. The corridor lights were dimmed on the fourth floor. Befitting the full moon, a soon-to-be-new mother howled in one of the birthing rooms before receiving an epidural. Bobby smiled and his tongue traced his fangs. He allowed the sharp points to tear into his flesh.

Bobby glided down the corridor toward the emergency stairs. He paused as he approached room 431. His palm caressed the door, and he could sense the presence behind it, female, vulnerable, asleep. A psych patient, *his* psych patient, Diana. His palm caressed the next door, and he could sense the presence there, too. A new mom, Cindy Birdby, vulnerable but awake.

The clock struck one. Bobby dashed across the hall to the stairs and yanked open the door.

"Are you there?" Philippe's high-pitched voice echoed up the stairwell.

"Just a minute," Bobby called. He glanced at the security camera that captured the fourth-floor landing, the red light unlit. He pulled a diaper from the box, covered the locking mechanism on the doorjamb, stretched the adhesive tape ends onto the walls and fastened it in place. The door shut not quite all the way, and Bobby could push it open from the inside.

"Excuse me," Philippe's voice sang in the night. "I'm waaaaiting."

"'How poor are they that have not patience!'" Bobby quoted Shakespeare.

A third voice interrupted, one of the janitors who'd been pressed into doorstop duty on the third floor. "I'm not going to listen to you two faggots all night. I'm goin' for a cup of coffee. Keep an eye on my door." They could hear wheels squeak across the floor as Davey Blissockiss pushed his bucket and mop cart into place to block the door.

"I'm using a crash cart," Philippe called. "What're you using to keep your door open?"

"Still working on that," Bobby said. It would be a problem if Philippe wanted to talk the whole time. "Back in a few." He didn't wait for a response.

Diana Loztic slept, but the mom in the room next to her lay awake. She might hear Bobby and Roberre and Diana. Probably overanxious about a late-night feeding that hadn't happened yet because baby Birdby slept.

Easy cure for that.

Bobby glided to the nursery. Like a mother hen, an old nurse hovered over the bassinets. If a baby so much as whimpered, she coddled it, doing her best to protect new moms from late-night feedings. Unfortunately, Bobby needed Baby Birdby awake and inconsolable.

"Sorry," he whispered as he read the tag. Jedediah Birdby.

What do babies like?

Bobby narrowed his eyes and projected the image of a puppy into Jedediah's mind. The baby woke with a start but didn't scream. Bobby pressed his face against the glass and stuck out his tongue. Still no reaction. Of course, newborns didn't see well.

He drifted off the ground, bringing his face higher, hovering in the infant's narrow vision field. He pounded on the glass, and Nurse Hen spun around, frowning. Bobby flung himself onto the ceiling, out of sight. When the nurse turned away, he crept down the wall and over the window, upside down. He rolled his eyes. He made every funny face he could think of. Jedediah remained stoic.

Frustrated from lack of blood, Bobby tried one more time to touch the baby's mind with his thoughts. "I'm really sorry," he whispered, "but I have to feed." He projected an image of Janitor Blissockiss. The baby screamed. Nurse Hen scuttled over. Jedediah wanted nothing to do with her.

"I guess you're hungry," the nurse clucked. She bundled the wailing baby in a blanket and trundled him off to visit his mommy.

Bobby had already taken up a station in the alcove across from room 431. Feeding didn't take long, as Jedediah wasn't hungry, just in need of the comfort of his mother's bosom. Soon the nurse carried him back to the nursery, again asleep. His mother, relaxed after her successful breast feeding, entered her own dream-world within minutes.

Thirst gnawed at Bobby. It twisted his spine and lifted him off the floor. He floated there, and in his mind, Diana became Meridian.

He imagined the warm gush of liquid exploding in his mouth. He pictured Meridian lying in her bed, legs spread, back arched in exquisite pain and delight as his fangs sank into the rounded flesh of her inner thigh. His desire for blood pressed down on his inner being, forcing him along an unalterable path.

Screams in the birthing room faded into a distant reminder of future meals, but other sensations rose to the fore. A neon exit sign buzzed in the dim light at the end of the hall. Nurse Hen clucked over her charges in the nursery, and a singularity of focus swept Bobby into the moment as he glided forward across the corridor and for the second time that night caressed the door of room 431.

His fangs ached. His fingers gripped the doorknob and twisted. The unlocked door offered no resistance, and Bobby floated into the room. His eyes, like those of a wolf, pierced the darkness and devoured his sleeping prey. He tugged on the sheets and they slipped away, revealing the milky white vessel before him.

A sudden scream ripped into his consciousness. Diana twitched and struggled in the dark, mouth closed—the terror wasn't hers. Bobby recognized the shriek: Philippe. His surprise overrode his bloodlust, and he hurried to discover the cause.

The diaper had kept the stairway door unlocked. Without thought, Bobby leaped over the railing and glided down two stories to the second-floor landing. Philippe stood on his tiptoes, his back pressed against the wall, his eyes wide and flicking back and forth between Bobby and . . . the twelve-inch-long creature weaving on the concrete floor near his feet.

The rat stood up on its hind legs and sniffed, its nose twitching in that peculiar rodent fashion. Bobby thrust his head forward and hissed through his fangs. The rat squealed and ran away. Philippe squealed and fainted.

Bobby swooped forward and caught Philippe's crumpling body. He lifted him effortlessly, carried him to the steps and sat him down, leaning him against the wall. He kept a hand on Philippe's shoulder to steady him. The nurse's eyes fluttered open.

"Can you teach me how to do that?" Philippe asked, his voice soft and hesitant.

Bobby shook his head. "No."

Philippe tried to smile. "I hate rats."

Bobby nodded. "Me, too."

"I didn't bump my head, did I?"

"You're not dreaming," Bobby said.

"You must have a hard time finding a dentist."

"Ready to stand?" Bobby lifted Philippe to his feet.

"Are you really . . . ?"

Bobby nodded again.

"You were supposed to shake your head," Philippe said as he steadied himself.

"Hey, fags, I thought I told you to get my back." The third-floor janitor, Davey Blissockiss, sauntered into the stairwell. "Nurse Cron just ripped me a new one."

"That makes three or four you have now?" Philippe asked. His hands shook.

The janitor stopped, his feet spread apart, hands on hips. "I don't need no lip from a couple of bony-ass fags."

"Who do you need it from?" Philippe trembled, but Bobby tightened his grip on Philippe's shoulder.

"Whom," he corrected.

"*Whom,*" Philippe repeated. "Whom do you need it from?"

With two-inch heels on his logger boots, Blissockiss barely stood at five and a half feet. He puffed himself up as much as he could, though. "Why don't you two suck each other's dicks?"

Philippe took another step forward, but Bobby stopped him again.

Nurse Cron marched through the doorway. Chin down, she peered over her glasses. "Well, we already know Mr. Blissockiss isn't where he belongs. What about you, Mr. D'Paltrow? Where're you supposed to be?"

Philippe answered quickly—glancing at Bobby. "On four, ma'am."

"So, only Mr. Eyre is where he belongs. Congratulations, Mr. Eyre. Mr. Blissockiss, get back to your job," Nurse Cron growled.

Blissockiss glared at Philippe and stomped up the stairs, mumbling.

"Mr. D'Paltrow, I'm sure I made it clear to you that for one hour you were not to leave your post. You've left the hospital open to a huge liability. There'll be consequences in your permanent record."

Bobby opened his mouth, but Philippe spoke over him. "I don't know what got into me. I'll just hustle my bony ass back up to maternity. Sorry, Nurse Cron. Sorry to have bothered you, too, Bobby." Philippe's clogs flapped as he marched up the stairs.

Nurse Cron continued to talk, but Bobby tuned out the drone and focused on the man who now carried his secret to the fourth floor. Hunger stole through his mind and settled in his throat, but he continued to listen. Philippe reached the third-floor landing, and Blissockiss gave him another shot. "Hey, gay boy, bend over. I'll give you something real to squeal about." Philippe didn't comment, but continued climbing to what had been Bobby's post.

"And so," Nurse Cron concluded, "I've decided that you'll be her new mentor."

"What?" Bobby said.

"Mr. Eyre, sometimes you exist in a world of your

own." Nurse Cron turned her head to glance over her shoulder. "Ah, here she comes now."

A pretty woman with short hair and penetrating eyes stepped into the stairwell. "Let me introduce your mentor. Meridian Jones, this is Bobby Eyre."

Twenty

Roberre understood Bobby's intentions: leash the beast, make love, feed without killing. Roberre sneered at the whole process, though he acquiesced. Practicality had taught him not to kill. As the world had evolved, so had human danger to vampires. Religious groups, fanatical groups, even a clandestine American government agency sought to destroy those of his kind. Killing elicited their scrutiny.

Roberre also understood domination. He could bide his time, be it decades or centuries. Eventually, Bobby's desire to continue his existence would diminish, then end. When Bobby had no will left, Roberre would submerge the other personality so deep that Bobby would never resurface, and Roberre the vampire would dominate. For now, he remained content to let Bobby think he was in control.

A long time had passed since Roberre had drunk from the inner thigh of a woman when she wasn't sleeping. Bobby insisted they be asleep. Roberre still relished Vampirical Harmony. He would slide down his lover's body and his tongue would tickle her ankle as his powerful hands massaged her feet. He would caress her skin, feel every tingle that she felt as he edged up her legs, and by the time he reached her inner thigh, she would arch her back, pushing her hips toward him, imploring him to go on.

Stroke, fondle—these were physical sensations to most, but stage two of Vampirical Harmony applied an emotional caress, the stroking of the mind, the fondling of the woman's soul. No woman could resist this inner caress. Few women had the courage to go on, but all developed the need.

Bobby thought *his* beast reined. He drank female blood, killed no one. Roberre smirked.

The terrible events of the last world war had proven a boon to bloodsuckers. Many vampires migrated to battlefields. Under Roberre's subtle influence Bobby had migrated to America. Land of the free, home of the brave . . . and fewer men.

The women of 1940s America showed moral fiber. Enlightened and educated, they'd proved themselves profoundly stable under dire conditions. They demanded romance. After being manless for months, sometimes years, some women's emotions grew stronger, their passion verging on explosion. These were women most worthy of Vampirical Harmony. This continued over the next two decades.

The last great woman to experience Vampirical Harmony with Roberre, memory intact, had been a blonde-bombshell actress. The official report: suicide. Bobby believed he'd killed her just as certainly as if he'd sucked all the blood from her body. Roberre approved. He understood Bobby well enough to know that without involvement, his alternate personality would grow lonely. Decades of loneliness would lead to despair, and despair would allow Roberre to claim dominance.

Did Bobby really think it had been his idea in the morgue to teach Meridian to steel her thoughts against vampire mind control? Emotional intimacy would strengthen Bobby, reinforce his will and the power to control consciousness. Roberre wouldn't allow that. He wouldn't let Bobby create the emotional connection with Meridian or anyone else. Bobby believed he'd reached an equilibrium with his beast, allowing him to make love to sleeping women and thus protect himself. Roberre snickered.

The physical connection remained a serious matter. Hunger gnawed at him differently than it did at Bobby, and desire welled up in Roberre.

He hungered for a woman who wasn't asleep.

There were many things in the world that Bobby no longer expected—to walk openly in the midday sun, to become intimately involved with a woman . . . and for Meridian Jones to follow him.

Tonight, the night before the full moon, doorstop duty almost over, Philippe had seen something irreversible. But maybe that was okay. Diana Loztic slept peacefully in room 431, and now Nurse Cron had assigned Bobby to be Meridian's mentor for a month, to show her the night-shift ropes. How could he feed? Meridian had managed to insinuate her way into his life. Bobby's fangs ached with the relentless gnawing of hunger.

Decades of danger had taught Bobby to focus on feeding, to ignore his emotional and sexual needs, simply to maintain his existence. The serious increase in bloodsuckers under the Nixon administration led to the subsequent increase in vampire hunters, many rumored to work for the government. Vampires were slaughtered, and many more left civilized areas. Not practicing full Vampirical Harmony for the past fifty years with a woman awake had been the smartest thing to do. He had to leave no trail.

Meridian stepped on his heel.

"Ouch!" What were his alternatives? Animal blood maintained a vampire's existence but never satisfied bloodlust, and it brought horrific nightmares to him as well.

"Sorry. Guess I admired your clogs too close. They look a lot like Philippe's. Did you get yours at the In-Step? I know that's where Philippe shops." Meridian caught up and touched his shoulder. A jolt of electricity rifled through him. "You have an unusual relationship with Philippe."

Bobby shrugged off the beast that sought to overwhelm him. "How so?"

"Most of the male staff keeps a distance."

"Philippe has a peculiar way of viewing the world," Bobby explained. "Others find it . . . off-putting." No options remained. Cold blood equaled stale food, only half a step above animal blood. Warm male blood was only half a step above that. There was nothing he could do except accept the fate to which he'd been relegated.

"His view appeals to you?"

"Philippe appeals to me as a person." What appealed to Bobby most was drinking hot blood from a woman. He could feel Roberre's agreement.

"That's what I mean."

"What?" Bobby asked, torn in two directions, unable to focus.

"Most men wouldn't admit that about another man. Certainly not about a gay man."

He imagined Diana Loztic calling in vain to him from two floors above. "Are you implying something about my sexuality, Nurse Jones?"

Crimson expanded from her face to her chest. "I'm sure I don't know anything about your sexuality."

Why don't we schedule a lesson? Roberre begged.

The moon, a day past full, smiled on the St. Mary's Medical Center. Bobby frowned. After all this time, he had yet to feed, and Meridian had been waiting tonight as he came on duty. Bobby sighed. How hard could it be to shake one nurse with duties of her own to perform?

Much harder than he realized. Through the first two nights of their shared shift Meridian had clung to him. He'd come to work an hour early yesterday to find her already there, eager to learn—though not the ropes. She wanted to know about *him*.

"Brothers?"

"No."

"Sisters?"

"No."

"What about your parents?"

"What about them?"

"Are you close?"

Bobby hesitated, dredging up centuries-old memories. His voice softened. "They've been dead a long time."

Emotion played across Meridian's face. Tears blurred her eyes. Perhaps she empathized?

"I lost my parents almost ten years ago," she said. "Sometimes a memory surfaces and it feels like my mom or my dad is in the room with me. It's like I hear voices." She touched his sleeve. "You ever hear voices?"

What's she asking us? Roberre laughed.

The moon waned. Ms. Lynne Reiss now occupied room 431. The floor nurse at the end of the hall, two hours away from checking on Lynne to see if she was sleeping okay, peered over a chart at Bobby. He'd worked fast tonight and was an hour ahead of schedule. He had the time, he had the urge, he had the victim . . . and he had Meridian tagging along. Unshakeable.

On the fourth night of captivity, she had Bobby playing twenty questions again.

"Where do you live?"

"None of your business."

"Where'd you used to live?"

"Can't remember."

"Where'd you grow up?"

"I haven't grown up."

"Kind of like Peter Pan?"

"There're similarities. Maybe I should call you Tinkerbell."

"Ha ha. What kind of car do you drive?"

"I don't drive."

"You don't drive?"

"Never learned."

"How can you get by in today's world without driving?"

"Walk—or fly."

"Oh, right, Peter Pan. I forgot."

"Yeah, that's kind of a bad memory you have."

Twenty-one

By the fifth day of captivity, a hunger unlike any he'd ever known pierced Bobby's unbeating heart. Between enhanced hospital security and Meridian's tailgating, he still hadn't been able to feed. Craving caused the monster to war with him, and hunger fed that craving.

He needed to do this on his own terms, and he just hadn't been able to see those terms met.

Roberre made his desires clear. "I want to take *her*."

Bobby would not surrender Meridian. Emotional intimacy with the actress had helped him control his beast. Emotional intimacy with Meridian would likely have the same effect. How could he know for sure? How could he get there without putting her at risk?

I can't allow myself to fall in love with her.

Bobby knew Roberre drove a wedge between them, encouraging her barrier against mind control. That didn't matter. All he needed to do was protect her from his hunger, protect him from his need.

Hunger. It rode him back into the moment. Somehow he had to feed. He had to try something, and try it quickly. He could move on, start a new life, if something went wrong. Meridian didn't keep him; he liked it here. Staying had nothing to do with Meridian. His presence was a danger to her. Bobby would protect Meridian at any cost, another new life a last resort.

Roberre snorted.

The craving, it drove Bobby with expanding urgency. It reminded him of his past, of how he used to be. Over the centuries and when necessity demanded, Bobby had gone a few days beyond a month without feeding. The pain of this hunger extended beyond human experience. Anger accompanied it. The longest time Bobby had ever gone without feeding, a month and two weeks, he had nearly lost permanent control to his beast. London, in the 1890s. Roberre had ripped the throats from three women in one night, seven in total. Bobby had then fled to Vienna. Freud had saved him.

Few feeding choices remained that wouldn't draw attention. St. Mary's authorities needed to lighten up, because from what he'd heard, their extra security had netted no results. Was the only way to ease hospital security for Bobby to uncover the blood thief? He had no idea who it was, nor any ideas on how to capture the criminal. Especially not with Meridian clinging to him like writing on a balloon. No viable plan existed to slow her.

She had only been following him in the hospital so far, but what if she decided to tail him home? He didn't want anyone to know where he lived, especially her. She was too dangerous.

He'd arrived at St. Mary's five years ago, armed with references from a previous hospital job and an official-looking medical document stating that he suffered from severe skin melanoma and had to avoid sunlight. His remodeled church home allowed him to come from and go to work without drawing attention, and his official address was a post office box. He lived with all the anonymity a vampire required. Now Meridian was attempting to unravel his anonymity. That couldn't be allowed . . . and Bobby had to feed. Soon.

Night six was his first night off since Meridian had become an extra appendage. She shared his schedule so that mentoring would work, which meant it was her night off, too. Thank you, Nurse Cron.

Bobby waited until 2:00 A.M. before he entered the hospital. Less conspicuous in nursing scrubs, he tilted his head back and sniffed. Bandages, medicine, blood. His fangs erupted. He strode toward the elevators. The urge to drink gripped him and narrowed his focus. No one would interfere. He imagined warm blood squirting into his mouth, thick liquid swirling down his throat and satisfying his lust, the urge so powerful Roberre would be superfluous tonight. Bobby didn't need to trade personalities to make it possible to feast.

The elevator door chimed. No one noticed him.

Bobby pushed the button for four, and the door slid shut. The elevator stopped on two, dinged, and the doors opened.

No escape.

"What're you doing here?" Philippe's high-pitched voice echoed too loud for Bobby. Philippe's arms were loaded with supplies, and he hopped into the elevator. He glanced at Bobby's working garb. "I thought you had the night off. Would you mind pushing four for me?"

Bobby forced his fangs to withdraw. Since Bobby's revelation they'd had little time to talk, and Philippe always had almost as many questions as Meridian. Bobby hadn't told him much. His mouth now remained frozen somewhere between a smile and a grimace.

"Seriously, you're not working tonight . . . Ohhh. You *are* working." Philippe's gaze crossed the elevator buttons to find the fourth floor already lit and ended on Bobby's eyes. Surely he saw the hunger there. Bobby growled.

Philippe jumped. "Don't scare me," he begged, then he sighed. "I know we didn't exactly talk about this, but you're not going to . . . you know, kill anyone, are you? I just can't believe that—"

"No." Bobby's voice was low and guttural. His fangs were bared. "I'm not going to kill anyone."

Philippe sighed in relief. "You're headed for four? There's nothing there except maternity and psych. Ohhh . . ." Philippe scrunched up his face. "You're not going to drink blood from a baby, are you?"

"No babies."

"Oh. Maybe a new mother? Weak, innocent, young?" Philippe's eyes were questioning. "Or . . . a psych patient? Yes." He nodded as he realized. "Because no one would believe them if they claimed they were attacked by a . . ."

Philippe suddenly cocked his head, his tone half accusatory, half solicitous. "You're not even gay, are you?"

"Never said I was."

Philippe's weight shifted back and forth across his skinny hips. "Right, that little walk you do in front of the other nurses . . . I suppose that's because you have hemorrhoids?" He nodded again in understanding. "You just want to be left alone."

After a moment he asked, "This is where you always disappear to?"

Bobby shook his head. "I don't 'always disappear.' One or two times a month."

"It's always around the full moon, isn't it? Right before your three days off." Philippe's face screwed up as he asked another question. "I thought the full moon brought werewolves?"

"Don't be ridiculous," Bobby snapped, disconcerted by Philippe's insights.

"Werewolves are ridiculous but vampires aren't?" The nurse raised his eyebrows and thrust his head forward.

"Over the centuries I've just gotten used to feeding around the full moon. It's a habit."

"The other night, when we were playing doorstop and you jumped over the railing and saved me, that's what you were doing on four? Feeding? Only you didn't have time, did you?"

Bobby shook his head.

"Then Nurse Cron made you Meridian's mentor, and Meridian hasn't let you out of her sight for a moment. No wonder you're here tonight. You're hungry!" Philippe smiled as they stepped off the elevator. "Come on, let's find you a loony."

Bobby shook his head. "I can feed myself, thank you very much."

"Maybe not." Philippe pointed. Security guards now patrolled the fourth floor hall, one at each end.

Philippe approached the closest. "Excuse me," he said. "We can't help noticing extra security tonight. Anything going on we should be concerned about?"

Bobby stalked up behind his friend.

The security guard shook his head with a smirk. "Nothing for you to worry about, honey."

The second security guard disappeared down a side hall. Bobby stepped around Philippe so fast that Philippe couldn't see him move. He stopped in front of the guard, his eyes wild, his lips parted, fangs bared. His voice emerged low and guttural, the same tone Philippe had heard a moment before on the elevator. *Why is there extra security tonight?*

The guard paled, his eyes gone glassy and almost as wide as Bobby's. He spoke as if he had no choice in the matter. "Blood thief."

"Where?"

"Blood bank."

"Has anyone seen him?"

"No."

"What happened?"

"Tech pulled a unit to test. Animal blood, not human."

"What kind of animal?"

"Canine. Someone switched the two."

The elevator dinged, and another guard stepped off and glanced in their direction. Bobby made sure it looked like their trio was just chatting.

"Why so many guards?"

"Entire force called in tonight. Chief Bradley thinks it's someone who works here. Wants him caught now."

Bobby loomed up beside the guard, like an animal on the hunt, his voice low, his eyes penetrating orbs.

"This end of the hall is clear. Move away." There was one final suggestion. As Philippe blinked, Bobby stood behind the guard and whispered in his ear, "You will not remember . . . ."

The guard wandered away, and Philippe whistled. "Can you teach me how to do that?"

Bobby laughed. "No."

"It must be useful in the girls' locker room." Philippe winked.

"I never went into the girls' locker room until you invited me."

"Did I tell you, you remind me of my parents?"

"Once."

"I'm gonna tell you again. When I was in junior high, my parents dressed in robes and took me to dinner."

"You're *not* going to feed with me."

"They were Jedi robes, and they brought lightsabers. A policeman stopped us. Dad pointed at me and mom, then waved his hand in front of the officer and said, 'Jedi business. These aren't the droids you're looking for.' The policeman gave us this queer look and walked away." Philippe hummed *Star Wars* music, danced around Bobby and waved his hand in the air like a Jedi. "You won't remember anything about my parents."

He laughed then stopped suddenly. "You've been feeding here for years and no one's ever noticed. It's because you feed without killing and then wipe their memories." He turned his head and smiled at Bobby. "You could've wiped my memory and I wouldn't know. . . ."

Bobby sighed and shook his head. "You're not susceptible like that."

Philippe paused. "You didn't have to jump over the railing though, did you?"

Bobby didn't respond.

"Thank you." Philippe's eyes teared up. "More important than saving me from that monster rat, thank you for trusting me. That must be . . . difficult."

"More than you can imagine."

The second guard reappeared at the end of the hall.

"What're we going to do?" Philippe asked. "If it's not the guards, it's Meridian."

Bobby considered alternatives for Meridian. Philippe thought of them much faster.

"Why don't you just compel her in the opposite direction? Or let her tag along, then wipe her memory."

Because it wasn't in Meridian's nature to tag along quietly—he was sure she'd mess something up. "I think I'll go back to the second floor and wait a couple of hours. The guards will have finished their sweep of the hospital by then, and I'll be able to come back up here."

Philippe nodded. "I have work to finish. Good thing you don't take off too many nights. Nurse Cron is tougher on me when you're not here. You'd better stay out of her sight." He walked off with a nod and a small smile.

With stair access denied, Bobby had no choice but to ride the elevator. It dinged on the second floor, the doors slid open, and Nurse Cron entered waving a clipboard.

"Mr. Eyre! Here on your night off, and I see you're dressed for work. How convenient. We've been calling in everyone we could get hold of tonight, and I'm reminded again that your phone number is conspicuously missing." She peered over her glasses at him. When he didn't respond, she continued, "Administration is in an uproar. We've had uninvited guests. There's an issue with the blood bank, work is getting backed up all over, and the staff on call has patients to take care of."

She ran her fingers down her clipboard. "Dr. Raymond is next on the help list. You're the next volunteer, so that puts you on duty in the morgue tonight. Off you go. I'll beep her and let her know you'll be there in a moment." She pulled out her hospital pager and pushed a couple of buttons.

"I can't do that tonight." Bobby's mind searched for control of Nurse Cron's.

Doctors strolled around the corner and lingered at the second-floor nurses' station. Bobby had on occasion helped Nurse Cron make decisions with a suggestion or two. He couldn't do it tonight. Not with witnesses.

Nurse Cron peered over her glasses again. "I suppose there's an alternative. Ms. Jones is in room 223 helping with Ms. Michael. She seems to be having a great deal of difficulty. You could work with Ms. Jones. Help calm down Ms. Michael, relieve her anxiety. She thinks she's Mary Magdalene. Perhaps the two of you could escort her to the chapel."

Bobby stared at the head nurse for a moment, weighed his options. "I'll see what I can do for Dr. Raymond."

Nurse Cron smirked. "I knew you'd see things my way."

Dr. Raymond didn't look up, and Bobby stood in front of her lab bench for several moments in silence. She glanced at him and arched an eyebrow.

"You must be Mr. Eyre, my assistant tonight."

"What can I do to help?"

"I've got five bodies lined up. Can you drain them of blood, please?"

Bobby's eyes widened.

Dr. Raymond cracked a smile. "Morgue humor.

Actually, we've had an unusual number of deaths in the past twenty-four hours. We have to perform three autopsies. The others have to be examined, but we don't have permission for autopsies." She slid off her stool, picked up a scalpel and headed toward the body of a young woman laid out on a metallic table. "You can give me a hand over here. I don't recall seeing you before. Been here long?"

"About half an hour."

Dr. Raymond glanced at Bobby and frowned. "No, I mean, how long ago did you start working at the hospital?"

"I know what you mean. It's nurse humor. I've been working at this hospital for five years."

A thin smile creased Dr. Raymond's lips. "And before that?"

"Before that I was somewhere else. Where were *you* five years ago, Doctor?"

"New Orleans. Lots of work in the aftermath of a hurricane. Lots of violence covered up by people in charge, too."

Bobby had to keep asking questions, stay one step ahead of Dr. Raymond's. He eyed the body. "Whom do we have here?"

"You tell me."

Bobby picked up the corpse's hands and looked under her fingernails. He studied both sides of her neck, her wrists, her breasts and the soles of her feet. "Already drained of blood. Cause of death?"

"Heart failure. Total organ failure to be precise, brought on by the sudden loss of blood . . . telling you what?"

"She was still alive when her blood was removed."

"Who would do something like that?"

Bobby continued his examination under the arms,

rolled the body onto its side and inspected her back. "I think a better question might be why?"

"Speculation?" Dr. Raymond made a cut, removed organs and handed them to Bobby.

"Thirst?" Bobby suggested. *That's a little vampire humor.*

Dr. Raymond gave him an amused look. "Seriously, any ideas come to mind?"

"It would have to be the work of a sick mind." He weighed, measured, and cataloged whatever the coroner handed him.

"I'm concerned it's tied in to what's going on here in the hospital," she said.

"Someone stealing blood from the blood bank?"

"I doubt that's all that's happening. The hospital cracked down on blood-bank security a month ago, when they received a warning from the government."

Bobby tensed. "What kind of warning?"

"I don't know if it was a terrorist threat or what. It came from Washington."

"Which agency?"

"Don't know. FBI? CDC?"

"I heard human blood had been replaced with animal blood. That way, no one would notice anything missing until the blood was called into use and retested."

"And since it's tested initially . . ."

"The blood is being swapped after the first test, but before it's put into the blood bank."

"That would be the natural conclusion," Dr. Raymond agreed.

"Does the hospital collect most of its own blood?"

"Very little. Most of the blood comes from the Red Cross." Dr. Raymond donned a face shield. She picked up the buzz saw and sliced into the cranium of her subject, and several minutes passed before she spoke again. "Most nurses and even the physicians are a little squeamish in the morgue. You aren't. Have you been around death much?"

Bobby put two fingers on his carotid artery. No pulse. "Some." *A little more vampire humor.* "Who was this woman? Where was she found?"

Dr. Raymond pushed back her face shield. She put down the saw, picked up a file and riffled through a few pages. "Candi Malloy. Discovered a week ago in Tyler State Park. No blood at the scene."

"Dumped." Bobby nodded. "What kind of work did she do?"

Dr. Raymond scanned the paper. "Worked for the state." She tossed the file onto the bench and angled toward the next table and a man Bobby estimated to be in his late forties, flabby and flaccid, all of his blood still in place. His toe tag named him Earle Cathcart.

"Also heart failure?"

"No, but just as tragic. Broken neck. Police report said he fell down the stairs at work."

"Where did Mr. Cathcart work?"

Dr. Raymond picked up a different set of papers and read. She stopped suddenly and tossed this file onto the bench on top of the other file. She cocked her head and her dark hair spilled across her shoulders. "Red Cross."

The hospital was missing blood, the Red Cross supplied the blood, and a Red Cross employee's neck was broken? Bobby suddenly had something to check out tomorrow evening. He just hoped Dr. Raymond would release him from duty in time to feed tonight.

The sun set before he arrived at the Newtown office of the American Red Cross, and Bobby licked his lips. He glanced at the sign above the door. The Red Cross personified him as a vampire. They too took blood from people and the people lived.

Bobby still hadn't been able to feed; the coroner had kept him busy all night. In a few days his strength would be completely sapped. Still, he couldn't risk feeding outside of the hospital. That was too likely to draw attention, especially if Roberre's will prevailed. He'd made his predicament worse by waiting so long, by making himself so vulnerable to his beast. He didn't want to add to the area's already skyrocketing body count.

He jerked open the door and glided into the lobby. The Red Cross office stayed open weeknights until nine. Earle Cathcart had been found at the bottom of the steps yesterday morning when the day shift had come on duty. Nothing had been reported missing, and Earle's wallet was in his back pocket loaded with twenties, so foul play was ruled out. Earle had slipped, fallen down the stairs, neck broken. After the autopsy, the police were satisfied. Bobby remained suspicious. He'd called the Bucks County detectives office in Doylestown, pretending to be a freelance reporter. He'd spoken with Detective Ed Farley, who'd provided details and assured him it was an accident. Ha.

Bobby studied the inside stairs. They made two ninety-degree turns. Bloodstains had been cleaned but not totally dissolved at the bottom.

He mounted the steps. A droplet of blood scarred the fourth step from the top. Not surprisingly, the rural police had missed it. This suggested that Earle had fallen at the top, turned a corner twice and tumbled to the bottom. Not likely. The detective believed Earle had tripped on the steps near the bottom. Bodies don't turn corners by themselves, though. The detective could be forgiven for not searching for blood near the top.

Bobby closed his eyes and imagined Earle's neck being snapped, his limp body being thrown down the steps, then kicked around the corners to be discovered at the bottom. It had been a brutal death. Why had the man been killed?

Bobby opened the inside office door and stepped into what looked like a doctor's waiting room. Magazines were on a coffee table. There were rickety wooden chairs and outdated posters on the walls. The carpet was threadbare, and a large glass jar with a slit in the lid sat on the counter. Nickels, dimes, quarters and a few dollar bills made it clear the jar begged for donations.

An elderly soul sporting a VFW pin on his lapel smiled from behind the counter. "Hello, young man." His wrinkled face glanced up at the wall clock. "You've made it just in time to be our last donor tonight." He pushed a clipboard with a pen on a string across the counter. "If we could just get you to fill out this form . . . that way we can bug you in a couple of months for more blood."

Maybe the women I feed from should fill out forms.

"I'm sorry, I'm not here to make a blood donation. Just a monetary one." Bobby pulled a bill from his pocket and flashed it so that Ben Franklin winked at the old man before he got stuffed into the jar. "Is this where you get most of your blood donations? In this office?"

The old man waved a hand. "Nah, people don't seem to know we're here. Most of our blood is collected by our bloodmobile. We hang posters, arrange to be at a school or sometimes a supermarket parking lot on a Saturday afternoon, and people just show up."

"What happens to the blood after you've collected it?"

"Earle—he was our driver—took it to a lab in Warminster to be tested and cataloged before we deliver it to a hospital. Our office mostly supplies St. Mary's, but if some other hospital is running low and their local office can't meet the demand, we respond."

"Blood goes directly from the lab to St. Mary's?"

"Nah." He waved again. "Usually comes back here for storage till the hospital calls for it. Big refrigerator in the back." He jerked his thumb over his shoulder.

"You said Earle *was* your driver?"

The old man winced. "Terrible accident. Right here." He pointed toward the door. "Broke his neck on the steps night before last. Shame."

"Were you working with him that night?"

"Nah." He shook his head. "Office wasn't open when it happened. Earle brought a load back from the lab kinda late. He's never here that late. No one is. Shouldn't've been here that late."

"Sorry for your loss. Hope you find a new driver." Bobby headed for the door.

"Already have. Tony. Nice fella, bigger than Earle. Temporary, though. Made that clear. Wouldn't be around long. Said he could fill in until we found a regular driver. Nice fella. Goes to the bathroom a lot."

Bobby managed a smile as he left. He had a clearer picture of what was happening to the hospital blood. It wasn't being switched in the hospital; it was being switched here in the Red Cross office. No security cameras, no night guards. Easy enough for a vampire to break into this office without leaving evidence, swap the blood packets and labels, and no one would know. The blood had already been tested. So . . . Earle had arrived later than usual the other night and surprised whoever was switching the blood. A vampire would likely kill out of instinct, then realize the need to cover up.

This vampire collected dog blood and used it to replace human blood that no self-respecting vampire would drink. The dog blood wasn't discovered until days or perhaps weeks later, when the blood packets were retested before use in the hospital. Why would a vampire do that? Why not just steal the blood?

Because stealing the blood would draw immediate attention. *Unwanted publicity* was what the security guard at the hospital had called it. This vampire wanted human blood and time. Why?

It didn't matter, did it? Whatever the reason, hospital security had been upped, and that interfered with Bobby's feedings.

A plan formulated. This vampire avoided the hospital because of security. The Red Cross had only a few locked doors . . . and the occasional unexpected late-night delivery. The latter had been taken care of. No reason for the vampire to stop. It would just be more wary.

The vampire was undoubtedly using dog blood because dogs were easily accessible and a few dead dogs wouldn't raise anyone's suspicions. The vampire would be least cautious when collecting dog blood. Bobby could trap it then.

He landed in a field near his residence and took ten steps before his senses registered a warning. He emitted a low growl. Someone had invaded his territory. He rushed along the ground with the speed of a wolf, chasing an unmistakable human scent tinged with hospital aromas.

The trespasser was hunched over, face pressed against a stained-glass window, peering inside his dwelling.

Bobby approached from behind. He grabbed the intruder's shoulder. The man jumped, shrieked and spun around.

"Oh, Bobby, jeezus, you scared me!" Philippe's hand splayed over his heart. "What're you doing here?"

"I think that's my line."

"Oh. Right. I wanted to talk. I'm in trouble. I need your help. I didn't want to talk in the hospital, but they don't have a phone number for you."

"How would you know that?"

"Marty Connor in Human Relations. Friend of mine. How do you get away with no phone number?"

"No phone. I suppose Marty gave you my address?"

"Strange thing. The hospital didn't have an address for you, either, just a post office box. How'd you get away with that? How do you live without a phone?"

"How'd you find me without an address?"

"I followed you home the other morning. I didn't have the guts to talk to you then." Philippe kicked the ground. His head was bowed, and he fidgeted with his hands. "I didn't want you to know I followed you. Do you really live in this church? This is perfect. I mean, magnificent." He averted his gaze. Guilt riddled his expression.

"You'd better come inside."

Bobby unlocked the door and pushed it open. He opened a second door to his left, then another door down a short hall. Renaissance paintings hung on stone walls. On a small stand, where one might expect a Bible, sat a bound handwritten manuscript of *Romeo and Juliet*, autographed on the first page. His footsteps and Philippe's echoed across the vestibule's slate floor.

French doors of heavy glass swung open into the main room. It was one hundred feet to the opposite wall, and four stories to the arched ceiling. Stained-glass windows, six feet wide and two stories tall, lined each side wall. Bobby flicked a switch and outside spotlights reflected through the windows.

Paintings, statues, a suit of armor. The floor sloped down from the vestibule toward what used to be the main altar, replaced by a half dozen broad steps that led to a wide landing. Two modern sofas, a glass table and several chairs contrasted with fifteenth- and sixteenth-century art. The entire back wall was a stone fireplace tall enough for a person to stand in. Halls led off either side of the dais. A staircase spiraled to a dark hallway near the ceiling.

Philippe's mouth remained agape before he finally found his voice. "Are there secret passages?"

Bobby didn't answer.

Philippe twirled around. "This is like Hogwarts."

"I'm not magical."

Philippe cocked his head. "Did I ever tell you, you remind me of my parents?"

"I'm afraid to ask."

"The last time I saw them, they took me to a Harry Potter movie."

"Lots of adults like Harry Potter."

"My parents brought wands. When they reached the front of the concession line, Dad tapped the counter, flicked his wrist, and tried a spell. 'Popcorn leviosa.' Of course, the popcorn didn't move. Mom stepped right up. 'No, dear, you're saying it wrong. It's levio-*sa*, not levi-*o*-sa.' "

Bobby studied his friend. "The last time you saw them? I thought your parents were alive?"

Philippe bowed his head. "They are. In a way, this makes it tougher for me to ask."

"Ask what?"

"A favor. My parents—"

"No, you can't bring anyone to my home, not with wands or lightsabers or Starfleet communicators."

"That's just it. Could it be *my* home?"

Bobby wasn't sure he understood, but it didn't matter. "No."

Philippe continued as if Bobby hadn't spoken. "My parents think I'm a physician."

"Tell them the truth. You're an excellent nurse. They'll be proud of you."

"I told them the truth about being gay, and they've hardly spoken to me for ten years, but they've been struck by some kind of epiphany and they want to visit this weekend. I haven't seen them for ages."

"This epiphany wouldn't have something to do with a slight misrepresentation of your job?"

Philippe shrugged.

"They missed all of med school? Graduation? What did they think you were doing?"

"I told you, we've kind of been out of touch."

"You said you didn't speak much for the past ten years."

"That might've been an understatement. I'm not sure we've actually spoken at all in the past ten years." Philippe talked faster, as if getting it out in one breath might make the idea more palatable. "They're coming to visit this weekend. They think I'm a physician. They think I have a great practice and a great home. Couldn't we pretend this is my house for the weekend? This would really impress them."

"I'm sure it would. What else?"

"What do you mean?"

"There's something else. What haven't you told me yet?"

Philippe looked away. He stared at the ceiling for a moment. He shrugged and his head bobbed. He finally refocused. "It's possible I might've implied I might actually not be, you know, gay anymore. In which case, they couldn't find you here. That would make them suspicious, if we were roommates."

Bobby's voice was laced with sarcasm. "Yeah, we wouldn't want your parents to be suspicious."

Philippe cocked his head. "Does that mean you're going to do it?"

Bobby sniffed, and his nostrils flared. He studied Philippe's clothes. "That depends. I . . . I believe you have a dog?"

Philippe shrugged his shoulders, arms bent, palms up, his brow furrowed at the unexpected question. "Fluffy. How'd you know?" He brushed dog hair off his T-shirt.

"I need a favor from you in exchange. Actually from you and Fluffy. It might be dangerous. I need bait for a trap."

Twenty-two

So what if two patients in a hospital of hundreds matched the description Jake had given? Lara had interviewed Ms. DiRico, and had conducted a brief exam—for which she was embarrassed—of Ms. Michael.

In the morgue, she'd read a police report about Candi Malloy, found dead in a park. The woman was bled out. So what? The killer had left her in such a position that her wound was the lowest point, and gravity did the rest, to the last drop. No blood stained the scene or the body. Big deal?

She'd met a male nurse who only worked nights, explained ostensibly by a medical condition. He worked every full moon—but moons had nothing to do with vampires. He had no address, no phone number, and he was evasive when asked personal questions. All this made him a recluse, not a bloodsucker. He had no traceable history before his job here, and in five years he'd developed no friends except for Philippe D'Paltrow, the only other male nurse on the night shift.

She felt a strange attraction to Bobby Eyre. Something about him quickened her pulse and made butterflies flit across her stomach. Maybe she did spend an unusual amount of time thinking about him, but that didn't make her obsessed. The sense of familiarity notwithstanding, he seemed to feel the same attraction to her. So far, he'd refused to act on it.

Bobby. Robert Eyre. Jake had told her about *a* Robert. She'd read the police report she'd filed herself after someone, maybe this Robert, burned her house down. Her description of Robert matched Bobby. Tall, lean, thirties, dark eyes. It matched a million other men, too.

Jake believes I'm tracking a real, live—umm, excuse me, dead—vampire.

It was total nonsense. It had to be. She knew Jake would give up only if she proved for good that Bobby wasn't a vampire.

It would be easy enough to do, she decided. Vampires—if they truly existed—didn't eat or go out in the sunlight. Bobby had to go food shopping. Since he worked twelve nights in a row, he had to shop during the day. She'd lived alone for years and needed to grocery shop at least once a week, and Bobby probably did the same. There was a simple solution. All she had to do was follow him. How hard could it be to follow someone who didn't drive?

It turned out to be more difficult than she'd thought. The first morning she lost him in the hospital parking lot. She stopped for a car to pass, and when she looked up, he was out of sight.

The next morning, hard rain limited visibility. She was only twenty feet behind him as they exited the hospital. He scuttled past a group of five nurses huddled under two umbrellas and again vanished out of sight. She'd read enough about vampires—something she'd never confess to Jake—to know they moved with uncommon speed. This wasn't uncommon speed. This was coincidence of traffic and weather.

Lara was determined the next morning would be different . . . and it was. Bobby left the hospital and headed in a different direction. He maneuvered around a tall hedge, and when Lara scurried around the hedge, he was gone. She kicked the ground and stomped off.

The following morning, she sat near the lobby door so Bobby would think she wasn't tailing him. He stepped off the elevator and refused to make eye contact, walking past her without acknowledgment. Her eyes followed him to the end of the sidewalk. He crossed the parking lot in the same direction he'd gone the first two mornings.

Lara grabbed the bag at her feet, rushed to the elevators and punched the up button. "Come on, come on." She bounced from one foot to the other. She peered out the front windows, but reflecting headlights and a rush of people obscured the view.

The elevator arrived. She hopped in and struck the controls. Space confined her pacing, and she studied the digital numbers as they changed in slow motion, as if her will actually affected elevator operations.

She got out on the top floor and headed for the stairs. A security guard stood at a stairway door already propped open. Yeah, Jake. She requested stairway access, he arranged it without question. Steps led to the roof door, which was also propped open. She discarded her bag after removing binoculars and hurried to the southeast corner. There she scanned the horizon. A dark figure, silhouetted in the pale light, strode beyond the parking lot. He angled toward the corner of a field and, without pausing, glided across Route 413. He stopped on the far side and turned.

A SEPTA bus approached. She imagined the squeal of its brakes in the predawn silence. Lara refocused on the bus windows to see if Bobby had boarded, but the tinted glass made that impossible. The bus pulled away with grinding gears and a puff of dirty exhaust. Lara kept her binoculars trained on the departing vehicle.

No success. "Shit."

Out of the corner of her eye she spotted a figure standing where he had, and she refocused her binoculars. Bobby? He raised his head and stared at the southeast corner of the hospital roof, at her, as if daring her to acknowledge she watched him.

A barreling 18-wheeler blocked her view for less than two seconds. When it passed, Bobby was gone.

Frustrated and starving—it was a bad combination. Between hospital security and Meridian's tenacity, Bobby remained unable to feed. Far past the full moon, his hunger resonated in every aspect of his existence. It was much too far from the next full moon to wait.

Meridian's attempts to follow him home had been clumsy. Philippe had managed it in one try. How had

Bobby allowed that? It didn't matter, he supposed. Meridian was the immediate problem. When he'd come to the hospital on his night off, she was there. She'd tried to follow him home in the mornings. It had been a mistake to disappear in front of her like that.

The more Bobby thought about Meridian, the more he wanted to sweep her into his arms and kiss her. He wanted to caress her skin, wanted to sink his fangs into the soft flesh of her inner thigh and drink the intoxicating blood of her passion. No, he couldn't do that, and the more he thought about it, the angrier he became. Why wouldn't she leave him alone? Couldn't she sense how much danger she was in?

If he wasn't able to feed soon, he'd have to resort to animal blood. Years of tortured dreams reminded him he didn't want that. He wanted the blood of a human female . . . and yet he wouldn't risk feeding outside the hospital.

He checked—St. Mary's would receive their next blood shipment from the Red Cross in a few days. The vampire would most likely switch the blood the night before. That meant he'd probably search for replacement canine blood the same night. It would be several days then before Bobby could spring his trap to capture the blood thief, several days before he could even hope that hospital security would be eased. He couldn't wait that long to feed. He had to do something now—about feeding, about Meridian. What could he do to slow her down?

Vampirical Harmony. What if he used stage one and didn't wipe her memory? It would drive her nuts. She wouldn't be able to concentrate on following him around the hospital. She wouldn't be able to do anything. It was the only solution.

He would track her the next morning. That posed

another problem. He'd have to spend the day at her house. Stage one could take several hours, and then it would be daylight. Afterward he could induce her to sleep. He'd leave as soon as the sun set, before she woke up. Tomorrow night at the hospital he could feed without Meridian tagging along, and then he'd worry about catching the blood thief.

Lara dismissed the idea of calling Jake for help. Despite her failures, and even though she knew his people would be happy to tail Bobby, she wanted to do this on her own. She had to. Part of her wanted to unravel the mystery of the man, and part of her . . . well, part of her wanted the mystery. She felt that somehow she knew Bobby, though she'd never known him. How was that possible? Why did the sense of familiarity linger?

She stayed close to him during that night's shift, but remained silent. Once, when her fingers brushed his, she felt his cold skin, sensed the strength in his hands and the surety of his motions. A muscle twitched in his neck. He kept his mouth tightly closed as if guarding a secret. Pupils blended with irises. It lent a strange aspect to his face and an unfathomable depth to his gaze.

When their shift ended, she left the hospital and hurried to hide in the southwest corner of the field she always saw him cross. Bobby had headed this way three of the four mornings she'd tried to follow him. Maybe it would be easier to follow him from this point.

She waited for nearly half an hour. Bobby didn't appear. Emptiness such as she'd never before experienced filled every pore. The pale blue eastern sky draped over her shoulders. She knew something of Bobby the nurse, but at this moment she wanted to know Bobby the man. That might never happen. She

trudged back to the parking lot, found her car and
drove the short distance to 432 Blackrow Court.

Screen door propped on her hip, she slid the key
into the lock. The door opened. She stepped into the
kitchen foyer, but a strange sound jerked her head
around. Lara's heart jumped into her throat. A figure
loomed in the dim light, feet apart, hands dangling at
his sides, silhouette outlined by the sunrise. Bobby
Eyre, or a wisp of smoke? How could he have moved so
fast that she hadn't seen him approach?

He reached out, found the edge of the door and
flung it shut behind him, shrouding the kitchen in
darkness. Light from something, she didn't know
what, reflected in his eyes, and those eyes focused on
her. She felt the pulse in the soles of her feet. Fear
should've wrapped itself around her and squeezed until she couldn't breathe. Instead, that emotion lingered in the distance and desire welled up. She
couldn't possibly want this, but she did.

His presence here confirmed the unspoken attraction was mutual. Her pulse quickened. An inexplicable familiarity made her tingle. Bobby wasn't just any
man—he made her palms itch and the sun tattoo burn
on the small of her back. His mysterious background
appealed to her sense of adventure, but she wanted to
know more about the man behind those unfathomable eyes.

He must want to know me, too, or he wouldn't be here.

Desire burned in her mind. She wanted to hold
him, to caress his shoulders and kiss his lips—

Before she could move, his posture changed; the
predator spoke with his eyes. A silent message passed
between them. She understood that Bobby wanted to
take her with pretend force, and he wanted her to
fight him with pretend resistance. She'd never been in

a position like this—not in real life. Of course, she'd faced it in her dreams. She'd never confessed this dream to anyone. How many times had she fantasized being taken by a lover, fighting her attacker with every ounce of strength she possessed, hoping it wasn't enough to overcome him? It was a fantasy she'd never expected to experience.

When she finally found her voice, it came out hoarse and cold. "Get out of my house."

Bobby twisted the dead bolt. Lara grabbed a stack of mail off the island counter and threw it at him. He neither ducked nor flinched. The mail struck his chest and bounced off. He edged several steps closer, so close she could almost feel him. She glared into the eyes of a nocturnal hunter. She was the prey.

In that moment she realized something else: he offered a reality she'd never shared with anyone, and it was a reality she feared to explore.

"What do you want?" she demanded. She already knew.

"Take your clothes off." His voice was calm and controlled. When she didn't respond, he repeated the command.

"No way."

Bobby reached up to caress the hair just behind her ear. Lara pushed his hand away. He reached up with his other hand, and she pushed that away, harder. He reached out a third time, and she slapped his face. He buried his fingers in the short bristles of her hair and massaged her scalp. He caught her wrist before she could slap him again.

They stared at each other, and he twisted her arm behind her back. She swung with the other hand but he caught that wrist, too, and twisted it behind her back. He pulled her close to him, her hips pressed against his thighs. She leaned back to keep her face away from his.

"Kiss me," he ordered.

"No."

"Kiss me." The command was harsher. He pressed her wrists together and held them with one hand, while his other hand found the back of her head. She could feel his fingers dig into her flesh as he forced her mouth closer. She tried to twist her neck, but his grip was like a vise. He brought her mouth within inches of his.

"Kiss me."

"Never."

In a blur, his mouth covered hers. She struggled for breath and, as she did so, his tongue raked across hers. She wriggled and squirmed to no avail.

His was a kiss of hunger and passion. Her response was unavoidable. Her hunger was as great as his, her passion as torrid. Some undefinable quality rendered him irresistible. When he released her mouth, they both gasped for breath.

"Take your clothes off."

"No." Her response lacked its earlier conviction.

He reached around and seized the bottom edge of her scrub shirt. She wriggled out of his grasp. He grabbed the fabric, and the sound of rending cloth tore through the early-morning air.

Lara hunched over, but Bobby had both hands on the garment as she backed away. He pulled. The last of the fabric ripped, and her back and shoulders were exposed. She crossed her arms and held on to the garment. He pulled so hard that her arms were flung in front of her, and he peeled the garment off.

She grabbed her shoulders to hide her breasts.

"Take off your pants."

She took a step back. He advanced, and she backed

up until her legs pressed against the kitchen cabinets.

"I said, take off your pants." The words floated around her, compelling her to action.

"Don't give me orders."

His hands shot out, and he caught both sides of her scrub pants. She squirmed away, their arms tangled, and he slipped her bra straps off her shoulders. He leaned against her and unfastened the garment so fast she thought she was dreaming.

As he stepped back, her bra went with him. She covered up, but he had her torn scrub shirt in his hand. He wrapped the sleeve of the shirt around her wrist twice, then pulled her other wrist close, wrapped the sleeve around that and tied what was left to the other sleeve. Not so tight that she couldn't wiggle out of it, but tight enough to hold her for a few moments.

His gaze captured hers. His voice was cold, the words more a statement than a question.

"This is what you want."

"You can't do this," she whispered.

He gestured, palm up. "All evidence to the contrary." He leaned against her so that her arms were pinned between them. He cradled her head with both hands, massaging her scalp with a slow, circular motion. When his mouth covered hers this time, it moved with a deliberate action that said, *You're mine, and there's nothing you can do about it.*

She resisted his kiss, keeping her lips pressed together, but he nibbled at her mouth and licked and played with her, encouraging her to open herself to him. His mouth glided across her cheek, down her neck. Her head was thrown back and she was unable to suppress the moan that escaped her lips.

Excitement surged through her. She stepped out of

her shoes. Her toes flexed in anticipation of greater pleasure. The sun tattoo shot solar flares.

He held her close and she melted into him. The sensation of security overwhelmed her. This man could protect her from anything. She felt safer with Bobby than with Jake. Jake might hide her, but Lara had never felt he could protect her.

The image of a wounded man flashed across her memory. She could not distinguish his face. Was it the enigmatic Robert? The police report she'd filed never mentioned Tony, who was the true face she feared, but had told of a man she'd described to Jake in the hospital. If Robert existed and Robert had tried to kill her, then Robert was more dangerous than Tony. Why didn't she remember him? Why was she remembering him now? Were these flashes from her nightmares?

Another scene flashed in her mind. She walked into the living room of her old home, dressed only in a robe, except this woman didn't look anything like Meridian Jones. For a moment Lara thought these were someone else's memories. Tony loomed out of the shadows and grabbed her wrist.

Why had she been unaware that Tony lurked in her living room? Her wrist ached now, and she twisted to escape Bobby's bonds. What if Bobby was—

He must've sensed her uncertainty, because at that moment he leaned back. She peered up at him, lost in his eyes. She'd seen eyes like that before. In her house? The blurred image of that man flashed across her memory again, that man in her house with Tony. Tall, lean, with dark eyes like the ones before her . . .

Bobby spun her 180 degrees, keeping her trapped between him and the kitchen counter. His legs pressed against the back of hers. He kissed her shoulder. His hands slid over her waist, then her stomach.

She could feel him tugging the skin on her back, his teeth nibbling her flesh. His hands cupped her breasts and stole her breath.

The memory of another man cupping her breasts flashed through her mind. Had it happened in her home or in the morgue? The vision was hazy. It seemed a lifetime away, too—a world away. No face, but the hands felt familiar. Slender fingers, cold, edged with strength despite the circumstances. What circumstances?

Bobby teased her nipples to life, and a jolt rocketed through her memory. Excitement and alarm. Bobby, the coworker. The nurse. A nurse with unusual eyes that sent inexplicable tingling racing through her at first contact. Eyes she had seen before. Eyes that had sent the same tingling feeling arcing through her.

Coincidence? Bobby couldn't be Robert.

No, Jake had brought her to St. Mary's to work, a place where Tony couldn't find her. Jake had no prior knowledge of Bobby. Bobby *couldn't* be Robert.

Bobby's fingers teased her flesh. His lips and his tongue traced across her back, and her excitement expanded. "You have no idea what you're about to experience."

She'd heard a voice like this not very long ago. She'd been in her house. Asleep. No, woken by a sound.

What sound?

Her cell. A voice called to her, a voice low and guttural like Bobby's. A different kind of anticipation had built then to an unbelievable crescendo, much like the excitement she felt now. And there was blood everywhere.

Bobby pulled her out of the kitchen and into the bathroom. He searched the cabinets below the sink and emerged with a transparent plastic bottle in hand. Lavender-scented baby oil. It jolted her into the reality of the moment.

Her eyes flashed and narrowed. She growled at him between clenched teeth. "No."

Bobby propelled her out of the bathroom, around the corner past the dining room table and into the living room. Lara stumbled, but Bobby tightened his grasp and kept her up. She wriggled furiously to free her hands.

Bobby laughed. "You can't escape." Saying the words aloud magnified their truth. It also magnified her desire.

He lifted her arms above her head. One hand held her dangling, the other found its way to the back of her scalp. He kissed her hard again, pressing her head toward his. She tried to gain control of her emotions, to back away, to kick his legs, but she'd taken off her shoes, and kicking barefoot hurt. Every fiber of her was conflicted about what she wanted.

He didn't break the kiss. She opened her mouth to . . . what? Scream? No sound emerged other than tiny moans she was unable to keep trapped. Her body was ravished with pleasure.

His tongue plundered her mouth—she couldn't have described it any other way. Her heart sounded like a Ping-Pong ball bouncing off walls too close together.

The hand that held hers must have released her, because it caressed her breast again, and she wasn't sure when that had started. Her arms were still high above her head, their bonds as tight as ever. Bobby was too close to squeeze her arms between their bodies, and when she brought them down, they could only drape over his shoulders.

His mouth nuzzled against her neck. He nibbled at her flesh, each time raising goose bumps up and down her arms and legs. She could feel his lips on her skin.

His hands slid lower and cradled her hips. When he whispered in her ear, it tickled.

"You have the most beautiful ass I've ever seen."

That wasn't what she'd expected to hear.

Before she could respond, his mouth found hers again, and she felt herself surrender to the moment. She dissolved into him. This couldn't be the man who'd tried to kill her. He *was* the man she wanted to make love with her.

Another flicker of memory creased her mind. She had crept out of her bedroom, terrified, gripping something in her hand. Her cell? She remembered approaching the steps, not wanting to go down but unable to stop herself. Someone sat in the shadows of her living room. A stranger. She couldn't tell who it was, then or now. She'd surrendered in that moment to a will not her own.

Her mind jerked back to reality. She found herself facedown, bent over the broad arm of her sofa. Her toes barely touched the floor. Her hands, still bound, were stretched above her head and her cheek was pressed against a seat cushion.

Bobby's hands caressed her waist. He untied her scrub pants, grabbed the top edges on both sides and tugged. She wriggled, trying to free herself, and instead made it easier for him to get her pants down.

God, she wanted this. She didn't and she did.

This can't be the man who tried to kill me.

He hooked her underwear along with the pants, and both clung to her legs now just above her knees. His body pressed down on top of hers. When had he taken his clothes off?

His cold flesh made her shiver. She could feel his excitement pressed against her, and she imagined the sensation of . . .

For a moment she'd forgotten his intention, why she was in this precarious position. His hands refound her breasts and his fingers discovered her nipples, filled with another onrush of blood. His tongue laved the skin on her neck and back, and the urgency to have him fill her expanded like wildfire. Her blood burned, and it was as if he sensed it. Her mind screamed, *Take me!*

He poured the lavender-scented oil onto her back to cool the flames, but it had the opposite effect. She felt the thick liquid absorbed into her pores as some spilled up her back toward her shoulders and spilled across "the most beautiful ass" he'd ever seen. Like a star going nova, Lara collapsed inside herself, focused into a discrete point, that point containing every nerve ending and every sensory perception she was capable of feeling.

Wave after wave of pleasure swept through her and carried her into an unknown sea of emotion. Uncharted depths and volcanic eruptions created havoc in her consciousness. Reality drifted in and out. What had he penetrated? Nothing she'd ever read, nothing she'd ever experienced, nothing anyone had ever described or intimated felt like this. She wanted to hold him, to wrap her arms around his back and pull him so close that their bodies merged into one. She wanted to drift into oblivion entwined in her lover.

She couldn't. She was facedown, and he embraced her back. His arms snaked around hers and he caught her shoulders. Kisses peppered her neck.

She couldn't tell if she was moaning or purring. He grew lighter each moment, as if he floated above her and she floated with him. Her body convulsed, burning in the fires of heaven and hell.

She struggled to maintain consciousness. A voice argued with her. *His* voice, but Bobby didn't speak aloud.

Sleep, the voice urged inside her head. It was the same voice, deeper and more guttural. *Build a wall with your thoughts. Protect your mind.*

It was a voice of passion and a voice of command. The passion coiled around her.

Protect my mind from what?

Someone like me, the voice answered. *Now, sleep.*

Lara refused to obey. *I must stay awake.* She fought his will. She was sure it was his will. Bobby wanted her to sleep. Why?

"Sleep," his voice intoned. Terrible things had happened the last time she was in this position.

Another flash of memory teased the edges of her mind. Caressing hands and a soothing voice, a similar sense of urgency that rode her body from here to eternity . . . and then sleep. Smoke burned her lungs and she remembered coughing, her wrists tied together—

Her wrists were no longer bound. When had he untied her?

Her head nestled against Bobby's shoulder, one arm draped around his neck. He carried her up to the bedroom, but she swore neither of them touched the steps. Her blinds were closed, but midmorning sun streamed through the skylights. He placed her on the bed in a shadow, cradling her head onto a pillow, then draped a blanket over the four posts of the bed, creating a canopy. Why did he do that? His voice urged her to sleep, though his lips didn't move.

Consciousness folded in on itself, and reality slipped away as the room spun around her. Footsteps trampled in her memory—two sets, Tony's and . . . Robert's! Smoke obscured his face, but it had to be him. Lara struggled to stay awake.

This couldn't be the same man. This man massaged her temples in a slow, circular motion as if he could rub the unwanted memories from her mind. She swooned and sank into the folds of her pillow and the coolness of his touch.

She woke minutes or hours later. She was unsure which, until her eyes focused on the dark skylight. Night seeped into her bedroom. She no longer felt the pressure of a body snuggled against hers. No sounds disturbed the silence. Bobby wasn't in her bathroom, and he wasn't in her kitchen.

She glanced at the clock. 9:00 P.M. An hour to get to work. Less. Shift meetings started at 9:50. The warm bed didn't want to yield her up, but she had to shower and dress. Darkness surrounded her and flittered off her tingling skin. Half a day later. How could she still feel the sensations caused by his touch?

Lara stood and took a step, but her knees nearly buckled. She imagined him pressed against her back, his hands caressing her, his breath in her ear. She remembered her body exploding with more pleasure than she'd ever known. She could think of nothing else.

Shivering, she ventured into the bathroom. She propped herself up against the tile wall and the water beat down on her, unable to wash away his hands or his scent. A voice squeezed into her memory of the night of the fire—but events didn't blend into a pattern. A collage of sounds rang in her head. A voice on the phone? Whose voice was that? Not Tony's. It was a voice of pain, and yet a voice of command. Lara recalled leaving her bedroom that night, but she hadn't wanted to.

As she dressed, she imagined Bobby's hands helping her, caressing her flesh, touching her in places no one had ever touched before. Her skin burned. She ached with the desire of a long-abandoned lover. What felt like weeks or months past had only occurred hours before.

How could his touch remain so vivid in her mind, as if he were still here? How could ripples of pleasure sweep across her flesh the same way they had moments after making love? Had they even made love? She remembered only the feelings of passion, of pleasure, of fulfillment . . . but none of penetration or the act.

She wanted his touch again. She needed to feel him pressed against her—his skin, his hands—to know that he desired her as much as she desired him. As amazing as it had been, the deed felt incomplete. She closed her eyes and forced those thoughts to the side.

New images appeared. Ever since that morning, along with her pleasure and those memories, visions had also popped into her consciousness, pictures of the man who'd tried to kill her. She was sure of his existence now. Robert. She wasn't sure that Robert was Bobby, however, and she had to find out. She had to get closer to him. She needed to look around his house. It should be easy after the morning's events. All she had to do was wangle an invitation. Hadn't he enjoyed himself as much as she? Why else would he have done it? Had she imagined him screaming with pleasure?

She headed to work. As she walked into the main entrance of the hospital, her thoughts again returned to sex. New memories, not those of the fire, filled her thoughts. She hadn't considered how this situation would affect her job. She'd never had a relationship with a coworker. How awkward would it be when he smiled at her, knowing the intimacy they'd shared just a few hours ago? He would smile at her, wouldn't he?

Nurse Cron cleared her throat as Lara approached the back of the group assembled for the nightly meeting. Philippe stood next to Bobby. He stretched up on his toes and whispered in Bobby's ear, then turned and gave her a quick up and down.

"Good day?" he asked.

Lara blushed. "Nice to see you, too, Philippe. Hello, Bobby."

Philippe's grin expanded into a wide smile. Bobby didn't make eye contact, acknowledging her only with a jog of his head. She found this unnerving. Why wouldn't he turn and look at her? He certainly hadn't been shy earlier.

As the meeting broke up, Philippe waved good-bye to Lara. "Don't forget, we're going shoe shopping again this weekend."

Lara followed Bobby. He grabbed a stack of charts off the counter at the nurses' station and strode down the hall. Lara hurried after him. She figured he probably wanted to wait until they were alone before saying anything.

"Wait a minute!" She caught his arm and tugged. Strength rippled in his muscles. He turned and held her gaze. "Aren't you going to say anything to me?"

"Get a new mentor."

Twenty-three

A pang of compassion swept through Bobby as he stared down into Meridian's eyes. This had been the plan. He'd completed the first stage of Vampirical Harmony with no memory wipe. To be a true distraction, he had to ignore her.

In that moment, standing in the second-floor hall just past Ms. Michael's room, Nurse Cron frowning at them from the nurses' station, he realized that he wanted to make love to Meridian again as much as she wanted it. Emotions had overwhelmed him this morning. Meridian had exposed layers of her inner being, tastes of the humanity Bobby craved. Tastes of the *human* Bobby craved. Would Meridian have the strength of character to accept him?

Bobby frowned. What did it matter? He couldn't share himself.

Remember what happened last time.

Meridian's veins stood out. A flush rose in her neck. Her eyes questioned him. Bobby simply licked his lips. Hunger gnawed at his stomach. His fangs erupted. He could hear the blood surging through Meridian's arteries. He wanted to take her. Now.

He couldn't bite her! He wanted to now, to make love to her, to share with her the other four stages of Vampirical Harmony that would end with him parting her legs and sinking his fangs into the warm flesh of her thigh. Drinking her blood would coincide with the most incredible orgasm either of them would ever experience. Meridian would scream with release, and he would again drink the blood of involvement. How sweet the taste.

No! He would not allow himself this. He would protect Meridian Jones. He forced his fangs to retract.

Another possibility toyed with his consciousness. What if he brought her across?

We'd be together for eternity.

He could share thoughts and feelings with a woman he—what? Loved? He growled. His fangs emerged and pierced his tongue. Blood splattered in his mouth, bittersweet.

The wound healed and he shook his head. *I can't bring her across.* He stared at his hands, then clenched them into fists. *If I'm still capable of love, then for her sake I have to let go.*

He turned and headed down the hall. Meridian

would likely run away to nurse her anger—that's what he'd planned would happen. Bobby would then have the chance to feed, assuming he could avoid hospital security. He *had* to avoid hospital security.

Footsteps followed. The timbre of Meridian's voice wound around his spine and squeezed. Her words didn't matter; her presence caressed his mind.

"Don't you want to talk about this morning?" No anger.

He closed his eyes for two seconds to enjoy the sensation of her interest. . . . No involvement. He had to cut her loose. He had to feed. "No."

"Okay."

It wasn't the response he'd expected. Nor did he expect her footsteps to continue close behind him. Understanding that she'd never make love with him again should have been gnawing at her worse than Bobby's own hunger gnawed at him. She shouldn't be able to focus on her work. She shouldn't be able to concentrate on her surroundings. She should be forlorn and angry. Bobby would have no trouble slipping away, even if she tried to stay close.

He hadn't turned to look at her again. Maybe she didn't understand. Maybe she thought they'd meet after the shift ended, and he just didn't want to discuss it now. He had to make her understand.

"Leave me alone," he said.

"I can't. We're assigned."

"I told you, find another mentor."

Meridian sounded calm and lucid. "Hospital procedures. You know what a stickler Nurse Cron is. It would take an act of Dog—I mean God—to make a change."

Bobby didn't understand. Meridian seemed unmoved. This wasn't the reaction of a woman who'd experienced the first stage of Vampirical Harmony and believed she'd never experience it again.

He ducked into Kelly DiRico's room. Meridian trailed after him.

He stared at Ms. DiRico for a moment, trying to find his bearings. The woman shouldn't still be here. Maybe he'd spent too much time on her in the maternity/psych ward. Perhaps he'd drunk a little too much of her blood. That had been almost six weeks ago. She should've recovered from any side effects by now, and have been either released or moved to a real psych ward. Kelly remained lethargic, but she turned her head and a smile creased her lips when she saw him. "You look familiar," she said, her words slow, slurred.

"I've been your night nurse since you were moved to this floor two weeks ago. I should be familiar by now."

The woman managed to shake her head, her smile dissolving. "No, something else. Not my nurse."

Meridian stepped around to the side of the bed. "You think you've seen him somewhere outside of the hospital? Before you were admitted? Do you remember where?"

Kelly's head slid from side to side against her pillow, but her eyes remained focused on Bobby. "Not outside of the hospital." As if an epiphany washed over her, the smile returned. "You're the man in my dreams." Her smiled widened. "I haven't had dreams like those since I was a teenager. Maybe I've *never* had dreams like this." She blushed.

Bobby knew what she referred to. Her subconscious had somehow held on to memories of Vampirical Harmony and regurgitated those memories while she slept. More than a century ago Freud had warned this might happen. Bobby never revisited any of the women with whom he'd shared Vampirical Harmony to find out. Perhaps he was paying the price.

"What kind of dreams?" Meridian asked.

Before Kelly could answer, Bobby grabbed her chart. He turned his back on the patient and took a couple of steps away, beckoning Meridian to follow. He spoke in a whisper. "Look, she came to the hospital as a psych patient. Inexplicable fatigue for almost six weeks. Whatever she's dreaming about doesn't make any difference."

Meridian took the chart from Bobby and read. "Wow. I didn't notice before, but Ms. DiRico was admitted the day before a full moon. Weird, huh?" She scanned the second page. "And she was hyped up enough on lithium to slow down a vampire."

"Excuse me?" Bobby said.

"You know." Meridian stuck out her chin, bared her teeth and growled. "A vampire."

"That's an odd analogy. Wouldn't it be 'enough lithium to stop a rhinoceros'? Or you said it was a full moon. Maybe she was given enough lithium to stop a werewolf?"

"Trouble is, there's never a werewolf around when you need to test one," Meridian replied. Was she staring at him in challenge? "She's not on lithium anymore. There has to be some other explanation for her continued lethargy."

"They probably took her off the lithium too fast."

Meridian glanced at the chart again and shook her head. "Nope. Weaned her. The hospital has tested her blood for everything known to man. Haven't found anything. Maybe the lethargy is related to her dreams."

"Why don't you stay here, interview her and discover if that's true."

"Where're you going?"

Bobby grabbed the stack of charts he'd put down when he entered the room. "There's lots to do besides this detective work. I have other patients to check."

Meridian nodded. "You're right. It's too late to conduct an interview. I'll help you run through the other patients. We should let Ms. DiRico get a good night's rest. We can come back together tomorrow to talk with her. . . . Maybe early in the afternoon."

Bobby hesitated only a moment. "Sure. Tomorrow afternoon." He'd have to think of an excuse later.

He pressed his lips together. He itched without any good place to scratch. Seeing Kelly evoked images of feeding. Those images heightened his need, and Meridian hadn't reacted to withdrawal from Vampirical Harmony the way he'd expected.

She dogged him as he completed his rounds. She followed him to the morgue on an errand for Nurse Cron. Dr. Raymond glanced up when they interrupted her. "Ah, two of my favorite people, together at last."

"What did she mean?" Meridian asked when they were back in the elevator.

"I'm sure I don't know," Bobby said.

She stayed with him in and out of the women's locker room to talk to Philippe, but stopped at the door when he entered the men's bathroom. Inside, Bobby took a deep breath. This was the first time he'd been out of her sight all night. Maybe he could float out a window, feed on the fourth floor and return before she barged in looking for him?

Great plan. If only the men's bathroom had windows.

Fists clenched, eyes closed, fangs erupting, Bobby forced his tongue over the jagged edges. The pain of the ripped skin and the taste of his own blood helped— but not much. He had to feed! Meridian wanted to spend so much time with him, he was reconsidering taking her.

She should've been so distracted by stage one of Vampirical Harmony that feeding would no longer be an issue. She wasn't distracted. What was going wrong?

What if he continued? What if he went back to her house after their shift ended this morning, what if he shared stage two with her, and still no memory wipe? After the stage-two orgasm rendered her unconscious, Bobby could make sure she slept for the rest of the day. She'd be crawling out of her skin by the time she arrived for work at the hospital. Bobby would have no trouble eluding her in order to feed.

Too many visitors, especially in maternity, to feed before his shift began. Few other options existed. The only issue was moral. Could he do this to her?

Hell, yes. He wasn't taking her life, just driving her a little wacky as she went through withdrawal. What if withdrawal never ended? He'd worry about that later. He *had to feed*. He had the right to maintain his existence . . . even at the expense of Meridian's sanity.

Twenty-four

As Lara reached the parking lot, Philippe caught up with her, out of breath.

"Meridian, honey, before you go, I have the biggest favor to ask you." He gulped air before he continued. "My parents are coming to visit, and I have to find—"

"No. Sorry, I can't put them up, Philippe. Find a hotel." She fished in her pockets for car keys.

"That's not it. I have a place for them to stay. That's not it at all." Philippe fidgeted with his hands. He kicked the ground, and he looked everywhere but at Meridian. "You see, well, I might've exaggerated a certain situation to my parents."

"What's that?"

Philippe spoke faster, as if that might make anything he asked less of an issue. "I kind of let them believe I was no longer gay, and to prove that I need to find—"

"A girlfriend." She finished his statement. "No, sorry, I can't be your girlfriend, Philippe. I'd be perpetrating a hoax on two people I don't know, who are probably very nice and don't deserve to be fooled by me. Probably not by you, either. It's not my position to tell you what to do, but as your friend, I think you might consider telling them the truth. They're your parents."

"Kind of late for me to be confessing anything. They're arriving this afternoon." His mouth twisted into something between a grimace and a frown. "I suppose I could tell them you're sick or something."

"I suppose you could tell them the truth. Or find someone else to play your girlfriend."

Philippe tilted his head and stretched his neck way out to the side. He spoke in a whisper. "I sort of told them your name. They're expecting to meet you this weekend."

"What!"

"I described you to them. Just a little bit. I don't think anyone else can play you. Can't you do it?"

"No." Lara shook her head. "No, no, no. Absolutely not. You have no right to involve people you know in a masquerade like this."

"I—I'm sorry," Philippe stammered. "I really am. I didn't realize this would be such a big deal. I'm glad you have the courage to stand up to my bullying. That's why I like you so much, Meridian, and it's why I suppose if I was a guy, I mean a 'straight' guy, I'd want you to be my girlfriend. Maybe Bobby didn't want to hurt my feelings? Do you think that's why he said okay?"

"Bobby said okay, he'd be your girlfriend?"

"No!" Philippe laughed. "Bobby said okay, I could borrow his house for the weekend. You know, to pretend it's mine, to impress my parents—since I'm a physician and all."

"You're a physician now, too?" Lara's mind raced. She hadn't found Bobby's house, but now Philippe was inviting her to spend the weekend there? "Okay."

"Okay, what?"

"Okay, I'll be your girlfriend." She squinted at him. "Did you tell Bobby you were asking me to do this?"

Philippe shook his head. "Oh, no."

"Do us both a favor. Don't. It would involve him in one more hoax he doesn't need to be involved in."

Philippe still had that sheepish, I-haven't-told-you-everything-yet look. "What?" Lara asked.

"You and I are living together."

Lara nodded and gave a rueful smile. "I'll pack enough for the weekend, so I'll have everything I could possibly need."

Philippe's face lit up. "I call the right side of the bed!"

Lara pulled into her short driveway, grabbed the mail and dragged the recycling can up to the porch just as the morning sun creased the horizon. A sense of déjà vu swept over her as she propped the screen door with her hip and slid the house key into the lock. Stepping into the kitchen foyer, she pivoted at an unusual sound.

No one was there, but the screen door was closing again as if someone else had entered.

"I must be really tired," she mumbled.

She turned to put her mail on the counter and

gasped. Bobby stood in her kitchen, feet apart, arms at his side, a cocky tilt to his head.

"You didn't think we were finished, did you?"

How could he have sneaked past her?

She could settle this now. The morning sun streamed through the back blinds. What if she ran outside? If he was a—She couldn't even say the word in her head. But if he was what some people suspected, he wouldn't be able to follow her. If he wasn't, and this was simple sexual play, he'd chase her to eternity.

She hesitated. What about the skin melanoma listed in his file? If what that claimed was true, direct sunlight would have an adverse affect either way.

She'd get him back inside quickly enough. The question was, would he come out to play?

She made a lunge for the door. Before she could reach it, he grabbed her wrist and pulled her back toward him. He held her off-balance, pressed against his torso. "You're not going anywhere until I make you feel better than yesterday."

"Better than yesterday?" That wasn't possible.

His mouth covered hers before she had time to consider the consequences. Their tongues met, and she could taste his desire. She could taste her own, expanding like a brushfire out of control. His arms encircled her shoulders, and she melted.

How had he gotten into the house without her seeing him? Why had he acted so distant last night at work? What did he expect this morning? Not a repeat performance of yesterday, certainly. That had been the most powerful experience of her life. It was an experience during which she'd given up power freely and been rewarded for it. In part it had been abetted by his surprise appearance, and in part it was that it had seemed he was reading her mind. They'd shared a sexual experience out of her fantasy world. She'd never shared a fantasy before. His desire had been as strong as hers, but she'd sensed he focused on *her* pleasure—not typical male behavior.

Her knees weakened, and a strange tingling flitted across her stomach. When had he stopped kissing her mouth and moved to her neck? He nibbled at her flesh, and his tongue traced a line that tickled from her chin to her ear. It wasn't a straight line.

No! Yesterday, passion had swept her away. She wasn't going to surrender this morning. She needed information. She needed to know the real Bobby.

His hand slipped beneath her scrub shirt and rubbed the small of her back. The sun tattoo burned at his touch. Lara's mind swirled as her thoughts conflicted with sensations.

His assault on her senses intensified. His hand found hers, but instead of grasping it, he massaged her fingers one at a time, then kneaded her palm and the back of her hand. A moan escaped from between her lips. She loved to be touched on her hands and feet. She liked the feeling of skin on skin, the warmth of flesh massaging flesh.

He lifted her scrub shirt over her head and dropped it on the floor. Finding the hook on the back of her bra and with practiced expertise, he unfastened it and slipped it off her shoulders. It dropped to the floor on top of her shirt. His shirt was added to the pile, and he pulled her close against his chest.

How had he known to do that so perfectly?

With a light touch, Bobby swept his hands up over her back and across the short hair on her scalp. He traced every crease and fold of her ear, first with his fingers, then with his tongue. The weaker her knees grew, the more he supported her. His strength seemed effortless, his intensity focused in the moment, solely on her pleasure. A quiver rippled through Lara when he lifted her in his arms and carried her upstairs.

He laid her on the bed and rolled her onto her stomach. She expected him to pull her pants off, but instead he straddled her and began a deeper back massage. The tension in her shoulders melted with his touch. He rubbed each arm up to her fingertips and back, not with professional disinterest, but with the surety of a longtime lover. How could he know more of her pleasure spots than she herself did? He discovered another. And another.

Instead of her breath growing calm with relaxation, it became ragged with excitement. Bobby's hands manipulated her flesh, and he continued to search for the pinnacle of her ecstasy. He found a spot on her neck that made her purr. Another spot on her head, and still another in the small of her back.

Lara had no idea when they'd taken the rest of their clothes off, but she watched his naked torso move with the grace of a wild animal. He rubbed her feet and her ankles. She neared the verge of explosion.

He backed off then. Each time he found a different spot to touch her, it heightened her excitement. Each caress, each kiss, each embrace drew her closer to him and the brink of fulfillment. Lara felt herself surrender—not to the moment, but to the man who held her immobile in the moment. She could no more have walked away from the bed than she could have flown. Each time he brought her to the edge of a climax, he backed off, and each edge was higher up the mountain. Her imagination lost itself in the intensity of feelings.

When the threshold of anticipation became unbearable, she leaped off the edge into an abyss of sensations and emotions. He didn't just catch her—he embraced her.

She didn't know if she screamed. The feeling was like nothing she'd ever encountered. It was as if one orgasm topped another five or six times, each stronger than the previous. When the sensation overwhelmed every part of her, she collapsed on the bed, drained, heart pounding, unable to catch her breath and unable to remain entirely conscious.

She was sure this time. He'd touched her only with his tongue and his fingers and his mind.

Her mind swirled. The room spun in one direction while the bed spun in the other. Lara floated above the sheets, unable to ground herself in any kind of meaningful reality.

Holy freakin' cow, what had she just experienced?

Twenty-five

The intensity of Bobby's feelings surprised him. He'd intended to remain controlled, but the more he touched Meridian, the more she responded, the more his emotions intensified. She composed her soul, shared thoughts and feelings as well as flesh. He'd carried her to the edge and back numerous times. Each time her thoughts had magnified, each time his mind had enveloped her, each time she'd pleaded for more.

His feelings stretched beyond anything in experience. Meridian's bare soul ignited passion that transcended naked flesh. The beast in him stirred, and Bobby quashed the urge to take her blood.

Roberre refused to be ignored. *Take her,* he commanded. *Bring her across. Yours for eternity . . . No one will stop you. No one will know. Take her now.* Roberre paused. *I can smell her blood.*

Bobby's nose twitched.

How sweet the scent. Bring her across. Roberre toyed with him. *Make her yours.*

Bobby's fangs pierced his tongue, and he sucked the blood down into his throat. The urge to take Meridian swelled. She lay naked beside him, asleep, lost in the orgasmic sea of stage two.

Now is the moment to bring her across, Roberre urged.

He caressed her inner thigh. A moan escaped her lips. The smell of sex laced with lavender lingered in the air. Meridian could be his for eternity.

This moment, these feelings, could last a hundred lifetimes.

"Take her," Roberre whispered, his voice a mixture of subtle tones and temptation.

Long-lost emotions surged through Bobby and centered in the forefront of his mind. A smile creased his lips, and warmth spread outward from his stomach. He didn't understand, but the feelings empowered him. His smile broadened, and Roberre submerged, defeated. Bobby collapsed on his back, arms spread to the sides, eyes closed. He hadn't succumbed to his beast. This remained his experience from start to finish.

Meridian moaned as if his thoughts had wakened her. She snuggled closer and tugged at his hips. She caressed his cheek, and her fingers glided down his neck. "I just had the strangest dream." Her voice was husky with sex. "You shared your body—and I don't mean with me. I mean, it's like there's two of you, only the other you isn't *you*." Her fingers traced a line down his chest and circled his heart. "It's hard enough being one person. At work all night, you have to pretend you're something you're not. Outside of work, you're free to show the real you." Her hand slipped lower. "I understand what it's like to pretend at work. Once, in the elevator, you said some people call you Roberre."

Bobby tensed. What did she know? It couldn't be as much as he feared. He couldn't allow her to connect with Roberre. Never.

"Part of the attraction is the threat that you may uncover the other me," he admitted. His voice emerged calm and controlled.

"I'll never be a threat to either of you—either side of your personality. The real you is neither a Bobby nor a Roberre. We all exceed the sum of our parts."

Bobby laughed. "If there are two people in here, how would you know whom you're talking to?"

Meridian shrugged. "You may run an internal dialogue between the two of you, but I'm talking to the sum of your parts. I'm telling you, Bobby is as important to Roberre as Roberre is to Bobby. I don't know why you separate yourself, but you need each other to—"

"Enough!" He pinned her shoulders flat on the bed. He fought to keep his fangs from emerging. "Sleep," he commanded.

Anger raged. Why? Because she understood too much?

No! The beast is not a part of me!

"Sleep." His voice softened to a faint tone that wove a delicate pattern of suggestion. "You will not remember . . ."

Had he just surrendered to *her* will?

Lara woke up snuggled against Bobby's back. She rolled off the bed and glanced at the clock. The bright midday sun streamed in through the skylight, though it didn't fall on her or Bobby. He had draped a blanket across the bedposts like a canopy. To protect his sensitive skin from melanoma, or because he's a . . .

Philippe would be here soon to guide her to Bobby's house, and she hadn't packed yet. That was no problem. She could do that without waking him.

She'd showered, dressed and packed by the time Philippe arrived in her driveway. He waved, and she held the screen door propped open for him.

"This is a lovely little neighborhood, and so close to work! You could roll out of bed and be there. Did you pick this tile?" He pointed at the kitchen floor. "I wanted to put tile like this in my kitchen, but it was so expensive. How can you afford it on a nurse's salary?"

He didn't give her time to answer. He walked around the corner and into the front breakfast nook. He pulled up the shade over the garden window. "You know, your plants look a little dried out. Well, not really dried out, so much as parched. They're dying. What's up with that, Meridian?"

"I've never been able to keep plants alive, no matter what I do. When I think I'm watering them enough, it's never enough. Any suggestions?"

"Yeah, try a plant psychologist."

"A what?" Lara stared at him.

"A plant psychologist."

"You're joking."

Philippe shook his head. "I keep her on speed dial." He patted his pockets. "Oops, I left my cell in the car again." He spied a phone book on top of the refrigerator, pulled it down and looked in the Yellow Pages under *Psychology*. "I came across this a few months ago. I know it sounds a little odd, but here it is." He stabbed his finger at a bold listing.

DR. KERRY RAND
PLANT PSYCHOLOGIST
NEWTOWN, PENNSYLVANIA

"I'll keep that in mind," Lara said. Hadn't Jake mentioned his niece, a Newtown psychologist with strange ideas? Bobby had certainly shared some strange ideas, too. And other things.

"What?" Philippe cocked his head as he studied her. "You have a Cheshire-cat grin. Care to explain?" He picked up one of her bags.

Lara's gaze jumped to the stairs, then refocused on Philippe. She grabbed her other travel bag and her keys. "I'll follow you."

"It's not far," Philippe said. "Bobby lives closer to the hospital than you do. Wait until you see his house. It's incredible."

They arrived in less than five minutes.

Lara stared. "He lives in a church?"

Philippe shook his head. "It's not a church anymore. Come on, I'll show you. My folks won't be here for an hour or so."

A small section of porch with a heavy wooden door jutted out on the side. Philippe palmed a key and opened the door into what looked like a tiny waiting room without chairs. He flipped a switch, and a small bulb lit the entrance as the door closed behind them. He opened a second door to his left, then another door down a short hall. The sequenced doors seemed designed to keep natural light from penetrating—at least to Lara's suspicious mind.

Shadows grew as they stepped inside. "Wait a minute," Philippe said. His hand slid to a control panel near the door. At the press of a button, metallic shutters slid open, exposing a half dozen two-story-tall stained-glass windows on each side. Light streamed into the room.

Lara dropped her bag in the vestibule. Her eyes widened as she admired the room's expanse.

Philippe pointed to a bookstand. "That isn't a Bible, either."

Lara forced her legs to move. She'd never seen a house like this. She glanced at the sheaf of parchment Philippe had indicated. It looked old, but not brittle.

Act I, Scene 1. A play of some kind.

Philippe gently turned the pages back to the title and the author's signature.

"This is an *original*?" Lara gasped.

Philippe shrugged. "Sure looks like it."

Lara cut an angle across the great room. Paintings, sculptures, statues, a grand piano—too much to take in. "This place is a museum. Talk about a nurse's salary. Is he independently wealthy? If he is, how come he's working?"

"So he can spend more time with us?"

"Nice sentiment, but somehow I don't think it's the answer."

A bark echoed off the high ceiling, so loud it made Meridian jump. "What was that?"

"Fluffy." Philippe raised his voice. "C'mere, boy!"

Lara recalled the picture Philippe had shown her when they'd first met. "That deafening boom came from a puppy?"

A dog the size of a small cow bounded forward, barking.

"What is that?" Lara shrieked.

"I told you, that's Fluffy. He's half St. Bernard, half Great Dane." Fluffy skidded to a halt, his tail thrashing, his mouth open and drooling and his tongue licking

Philippe and Lara simultaneously. It was hard to tell which end of Fluffy was happier.

Lara scratched the head behind its mass of tangled hair. "Fluffy, you have to calm down. You're getting me wet." She laughed.

"Don't worry," Philippe said. "He's very well trained." He pointed a finger at the dog. "Fluffy, sit."

Much to Lara's surprise, Fluffy obeyed. His head rose up, eyes eager to play, but he sat and didn't move.

"Very impressive," she said. "What else can he do?"

Philippe rocked back and forth on his heels. He put his hand out, palm down. "Fluffy, play dead." The dog stretched huge paws in front of him, lay down, and rolled onto his side.

"Fluffy, play *really* dead," Philippe commanded. With what sounded like a grunt, Fluffy rolled onto his back and let his paws dangle limp in the air above him. His head lolled to one side.

Lara laughed and clapped. "Good doggie!" Fluffy's saucer-shaped eyes stared at her, upside down, to see if she meant that, okay, he could get up and play again. At her nod, he scrambled to his feet, both ends of his body wagging.

"Come on," Philippe said, laughing, "I'll show you the bedroom." He pointed to a massive circular stair-case at the rear of the chamber. The steps climbed to a door near the ceiling.

Lara tilted her head back to stare at a landing four floors above. "That's a lot of steps. I might get dizzy," she warned.

"Don't worry," Philippe said. "We can take the elevator."

Nothing about Bobby had suggested wealth. He acted like any other normal nurse.

No, he didn't. No other nurse had made love to her

so exquisitely the past two mornings. The experience transcended lovemaking. Somehow she didn't recall the specific act, but she had vivid recollections of the sensations. She'd never felt anything like the way Bobby had made her feel, making love to her mind while he was doing such wonderful things to her body. He was inside her head, sharing thoughts while they shared physical sensations. That wasn't possible. Was she remembering correctly?

She glanced over her shoulder at the works of art. None of this was possible. This was the accumulated wealth of generations. That was the only plausible explanation. Bobby had inherited all this from his great-great-grandfather. The question popped into her head again.

What if he is a . . . ? Go ahead, say it. I dare you.

Okay, why would anyone work the night shift for five years and never change? Not perfectly compelling. It was circumstantial evidence. Lots of people worked only the night shift, and not all of them had a possible skin condition.

Why would anyone refuse to give his employer a home address or a phone number? Why would anyone become such an obvious loner? Why would they install remote-control metallic shutters on such beautiful windows? Move so fast that at times they couldn't be seen? Make love in such a way that few other men could compare? Did this all lead to the inescapable conclusion that Bobby was a vampire?

There, I said it. Is Bobby a vampire?

Jake had said she'd told him someone named Robert had almost killed her. He'd shown her the police report. She'd seen images, flashbacks—lost memories? Yes, she believed they were. Shortly after it happened, Jake had sent her to St. Mary's Medical Center because he believed a vampire worked there. Was that vampire Bobby?

Jake had been dismissive when she'd first mentioned Bobby, almost sneering when he'd found out her suspicions and that the two figures shared a name. Jake had said that Robert was a vampire, but Robert had tried to burn her to death, not drink her blood. Why would a vampire do that? Was this him again, having recognized her? Was he toying with her now, showing her the heights of pleasure before he came for her life? Did vampires do that? Why hadn't Jake given her more training than simple workouts? Why hadn't he warned her that the first step to doom would be seduction? Maybe she should've read more of the vampire books Jake had plied her with.

Philippe opened the door to the master bedroom. He pulled the cord to slide back curtains that concealed six shuttered windows. He pressed a button and the shutters unfolded. "You can see the hospital from here." He pointed out the corner window.

Lara shook her head, dismissing everything. The concept was nonsense. Vampires were nothing more than mythical creatures created to scare children and old women. The myth was perpetuated in culture—movies, books, television shows—because it made money. People loved to be scared, and vampires scared them. If vampires existed, Bobby's room would have a coffin, not a bed.

Vampires don't scare me because I know they don't exist.

The WPA was real, but the VU had to be a joke. But why? And for whom?

She barely heard Philippe say something about putting food in the refrigerator, his parents, shopping . . . for her to look around with Fluffy, but not get into trouble. She remembered that part. *Don't get into trouble.* It sounded like a conversation she'd once had with Bobby.

"Trouble is my middle name," she said to Fluffy.

Trouble; that starts with T, that rhymes with D, and that stands for . . . door. Which was where she stood now: in front of a door.

Philippe had promised to be back before his mom and dad arrived. Fluffy was parked on a sofa, and his body language promised he'd be attentive as soon as that pair—or anyone else—showed up. Lara had felt safe to explore the house. She'd discovered this locked door, the only one, behind what would have been the main altar in the building's previous incarnation. Why would an inside door be locked?

Something's behind that door that he doesn't want anyone to see.

That was motivation enough for Lara to want the door opened.

Judging by the architecture, there was no space for a full room behind the door. It had to be a staircase. Lara reached up on her toes and felt the top edge of the frame. No key rested there. That would've been too easy.

She rattled the handle. Seemed like a simple enough lock. How did they open locked doors in the movies? They picked the lock. She couldn't do that, though. Slide a credit card and release the latch? She could do that.

The dog's gigantic eyes fixed on her as she marched across the room armed with a credit card. "Don't worry, Fluffy, I can handle this myself," she waved.

Opening the door turned out to be much easier than expected. She pushed and wiggled it a bit, the card slid against the latch and the door pulled open. There were stairs. Straight down and dark. She flicked a switch. A meager light cast dim rays down the steps . . . which squeaked, of course. Wasn't this the stereotypical scenario—locked door, dark basement, squeaky steps? What was next? Monsters in the shadows?

She laughed. If vampires didn't exist, and she'd decided they didn't, what did she expect to find down here?

Bobby didn't remember falling asleep. When he woke, Meridian was gone. He snarled. How could this be?

Dizziness caught him as he sat up. The room swirled. His stomach grumbled, and his fangs erupted. Weakness such as he'd never before experienced settled in his legs and arms. He needed to feed—*still*. How had it progressed so far without relief?

Night approached the darkened bedroom, reminding him that he had other issues. The hospital was due to receive a new shipment of blood from the Red Cross tomorrow. The blood thief would have to switch packets tonight, and he'd need animal blood to do that. It was time to spring his trap.

A coffin. That's what Lara expected to find. Isn't that what everyone kept in their locked basement? Maybe a pile of bodies? Unfortunate victims? What if a coven of vampires lived down there?

No, a coven is witches.

What did you call a group of vampires? A horde? A family? A dentist's delight?

The bottom two steps turned sharply right. Darkness spread out before her. No light switch presented itself. Childhood fears of the family basement filled with monsters swept through her mind. Monsters had scared her then. An icy line arced across Lara's shoulders.

Another image flashed through her brain. She'd descended a familiar flight of steps. A man sat across the room, cloaked in shadows, his back to her, his left arm bent and pressed against his right shoulder. He'd called for help. It had been her duty as a physician to assist him.

A shadow scurried across the floor, and Lara jumped. Had she imagined that? The click of toenails? A cat? Is that why the door was locked? To keep the dog away from the cat?

Lara reminded herself that she hadn't seen a cat, just a shadow. She also reminded herself that neither cats nor dogs could open doors, even if they weren't locked.

Why was her heart thumping so hard?

A new image flashed through her thoughts: a man, sitting in her living room, blood spilling from a wound. She tried to focus on his face, but the image eluded her. What did he want? Why was this man in her house? She tried to imagine Bobby's face on the man, but the image wouldn't resolve itself.

She refocused on basement exploration, took a deep breath. Must've been a cat. Or a rat.

Ewww! She needed a flashlight. What else that big would be running around?

She hurried up the stairs, closed the door and exhaled. A flashlight. Right. She headed for the kitchen and searched drawers and cabinets. No flashlight— and not much else, either. Dishes, bowls, cups, courtesy of Kmart. A single pot hung on the wall above an unused stove. "I guess Bobby doesn't do a lot of entertaining," she told Fluffy. The silverware looked cheaper than the dishes.

Of course there was no flashlight in the refrigerator, but she needed to look. She found a couple half gallons of milk, one open, one sealed, and a dozen water bottles. Philippe had been right, when he'd called it barren. Was she disappointed there weren't rows of cork-stoppered wine bottles filled with cow's blood?

The pantry contained a box of Kellogg's Frosted Flakes and six bags of Oreo cookies. Like the milk, one bag was open. Not the diet of champions. Not the diet of vampires, either.

Her mind whipped around and . . . snagged images of the past two mornings. Sexual images. The images evoked feelings, and the feelings made her tingle. The first morning had been a buildup for the second, but they were no more finished after the second than they were after the first. As fantastic as Bobby made her feel, she lacked a sense of fulfillment, as if Bobby withheld it. She wanted to hold Bobby now, to stroke his cheek and caress the back of his neck.

She refocused. What was in the basement that made Bobby keep an inside door locked? *Please, let it be a cat.*

Candlesticks on the dining table would work as a flashlight replacement, if only she carried matches.

Turn a stove burner on high, roll up a piece of paper, touch the burner until the paper ignites and light the candle.

Bobby didn't keep paper lying around, though. Tons of books, but no loose paper.

Lara went outside and searched her car for something flammable. The late afternoon sun streamed through the windshield and cast an interesting reflection off the stained-glass windows beyond. At the sound of a car engine and tires scraping across the stone driveway, she turned and gasped.

I hope it's not Bobby.

He'd said he didn't drive. How had he gotten to her house, anyway? There'd been no car parked outside when she'd left.

She didn't have long to worry. A Lincoln or a Cadillac—she couldn't tell the difference—pulled up next to her SUV and parked. An elderly couple emerged. They were short and skinny, their hair was thinning, and they acted like two kids on fifteen extra minutes of recess. Both were smiling, and they talked to her the way parents might talk to their five-year-old's friend.

"*Hi-i-i!* You must be Meridian. We're so pleased to meet you. I'm Hildie D'Paltrow, Philippe's mom. This is my husband, George, Philippe's dad. We can't tell you how happy we are that Philippe has finally made a friend like you."

Like me? You mean, not gay?

Lara frowned. It wasn't her place to judge or preach. She recovered before they noticed, but knew her basement expedition was postponed.

"You just missed Philippe," she said. "He went food shopping, but he'll be back in a few minutes, I'm sure."

George stood with hands on hips and stared. "Philippe didn't say anything about living in a church."

"Oh, dear." Hildie waved at him. "I don't think it's a church anymore."

"Wait until you see the inside," Lara said. "Come on. Philippe won't mind if I begin the tour without him."

She ushered them through the winding entrance. Neither of the D'Paltrows said much during the tour. As they passed the basement, George rattled the locked door. It had relocked itself when she'd closed it after her earlier expedition.

Fifteen minutes later, they were seated on the sofa across from Fluffy. Lara commanded the dog to sit and stay with the small hand gestures Philippe showed her. Fluffy looked like he wanted to jump into the D'Paltrows' laps and snuggle, only he was bigger than the pair combined.

George eyed him. "That's a very well-trained animal. How do you do it? Mind control?"

"Oh, George." Hildie pushed his shoulder. "Hush up now. Aren't you happy to be here?" She faced Meridian. "Philippe has told us so much about you, dear. So, you're a nurse in his hospital? Do you help with a lot of his operations?"

She silently laughed. "I'm helping him with a really big one right now."

George frowned. "It's the night shift, right? Philippe only works the night shift?"

Lara didn't understand why George was agitated. She tried to remain pleasant. "Yes, the night shift. Would you like some bottled water? I'm afraid we don't have much else until Philippe gets back." She glanced toward the windows. "He should be here soon. It's almost dark out."

George pressed his lips together, nodded his head and scanned the immense room. "Yes, odd thing that. Hardly any food in the refrigerator. And remote-control shutters. Not too many houses come equipped with those. How did Philippe acquire all this?" He gestured with his hand, hopped up, marched across the room and pointed in the general direction of the basement. "What's with the locked door?"

I'd like to know that, too.

Lara couldn't believe she had to lie for Philippe to protect whatever secret Bobby kept hidden down there. She could hardly pick the lock again in front of the D'Paltrows.

"Rats," she said.

"Excuse me?"

"We have a rodent problem."

"And you keep the door locked because you think the rats might open it? What's really down there? Bodies?" George waved both hands in the air. When Lara didn't answer, he arched an eyebrow and pressed on. "Coffins?"

"George, you're being rude," his wife said. "This is Philippe's house, not Meridian's. She's not responsible for what he does. You can ask your son when he gets here, if it's bothering you so much."

George approached a window and peered through the colored glass. "When he gets here. I imagine it'll be just a few more minutes, because the sun is almost below the horizon."

"George D'Paltrow, you've been watching too many movies!"

"With you," the man retorted to his wife.

"If you're not careful, you're going to get your blood pressure cranked up. She's a nurse." Hildie pointed at Lara. "Ask her."

"If you have high blood pressure, Mr. D'Paltrow, you do want to be careful about getting excited," Lara agreed.

George glared at his wife, who shrugged.

"What? You want to find him while it's still light outside?"

"I'm sure he'll be home any minute," Lara said.

Hildie sighed at her husband. "You want to look for him at the grocery store?"

"If he's even at the grocery store—which I doubt," George insisted.

"Mr. D'Paltrow," Lara asked, "why would you think Philippe isn't at the grocery store?"

Hildie pushed up off the sofa. "Honey, George has some strange ideas about a lot of things, and if we don't indulge him, neither one of us is going to get any peace. Can you give us directions to the store?"

These vampire connections were getting to be too much. She had to put them to rest. "Better than that, I'll *take* you."

"Oh, no, that's not necessary, dear."

"Mr. and Mrs. D'Paltrow. Please. If you're worried about your son, the least I can do is take you to him. I assure you, though, he was quite healthy when he left here, and I'm sure he's not doing anything dangerous. He was just going to buy groceries." Lara jangled her car keys. "Come on. I'll bet we can catch him in the checkout line."

She only wished she could spy Bobby there, too.

Twenty-six

Philippe slid the packages into the car's backseat. It was way more than he'd expected to purchase, but Bobby's kitchen had been really empty. He mopped his brow. Behind the shopping center, the sun was setting in a huge fiery ball. Philippe got into the car, angled it out of the parking lot and headed toward his pretend home.

When he arrived, Meridian's SUV was gone and a shiny Lincoln Town Car was parked in its place.

Must be Dad's. But where's Meridian?

Philippe grabbed as many of the plastic bags of food as he could handle, pushed open the church's first front door and the second, and then the third. "Mom? Dad?"

No response.

"Dad?" he called again.

He headed for the kitchen. Fluffy galloped toward him.

"Where is everybody?" Philippe asked. He flung the packages onto the counter. Fluffy barked. "Can you translate?"

Fluffy cocked his head. Philippe shrugged. "I guess

not." He shuffled back and forth to his car to finish with the groceries.

"I don't know where they could've gone," he said to Fluffy as he collected the last load. "Maybe she's showing them the hospital?" He finished loading the refrigerator. Fluffy barked. He barked again and again. "You have to hush up," Philippe said.

"I didn't say anything."

Bobby knelt next to Fluffy, ruffling his ears.

Philippe flung his hand over his heart. "You scared me! Where'd you come from? How'd you get in here?"

"This is my house, you know."

"Right. I know, I know. I'm sorry. I'm just flustered. Mer—" He'd been about to say Meridian and his parents were gone, but thought better of it. Meridian had asked him not to tell Bobby she was here. "My parents must be taking a stroll. I'm not sure when they'll be back. I'd like you to meet them. Heck, at this point, *I'd* like to meet them."

"Not now," Bobby said. "That's why I'm here. Time for you and Fluffy to do your part. I need you to drive to the eastern entrance of Tyler State Park."

"Now? I haven't seen my parents for ten years."

"Another half hour shouldn't be a problem, then. Take Fluffy for a walk. Don't go too far. I doubt you'll be alone for long."

Philippe glanced at the stained-glass windows. "It's dark. Doesn't the park close at sunset?"

"Exactly why you'll become the perfect bait. No one will be around."

Philippe's heart pounded. "Where will you be?"

"Around."

"We'll be safe?"

"As safe as I can keep you," Bobby said. He stared into Fluffy's huge eyes. The dog licked his face.

"M-maybe I should've mentioned something when you first told me about this plan," Philippe stammered.

Bobby glanced at him. "What's that?"

"In case you didn't notice in the hospital stairwell, I'm a coward." Philippe stared at his feet and spoke as if the words were being dragged out of him. "In high school, I used to get beat up. A lot. You know, not just because I'm gay. I like to cross-dress. I always have. The boys in school didn't approve." A tear rolled down Philippe's cheek. "Dad didn't exactly understand, either. That's why I left home."

"Sorry." Bobby's tone softened. "There's no time to make alternate plans. This has to do with my survival."

"I can't go through with it." Philippe's voice squeaked. "I can't stand up to anyone."

"I'll protect you."

"I think I need to wait for my parents."

"I think you need to go now. You'll see your parents as soon as you get back. They'll understand, I'm sure."

"Understand what? That I'm bait for a vampire?"

"Leave them a note. Tell them you had to take Fluffy for his evening constitutional in the park, otherwise the dog won't sleep. You'd better put Fluffy on a leash, too."

Skepticism and a touch of fear filled Philippe, but he'd promised a fair trade for use of his friend's home, and he didn't want to renege. He scribbled a note and left it on the empty counter where Meridian would notice. "Come on, Fluffy, we have a job to do." He turned to ask Bobby another question, but Bobby had vanished.

Night had settled on Bucks County by the time Philippe pulled into the Tyler State Park entrance off the Newtown-Richboro Road. The park did indeed close at sunset, and the gate was down. Philippe drove around it. He found the parking area long, narrow, not far from the busy road, and butted up to a grove of trees.

A cool summer breeze caressed his cheek as he got out of the car. An owl hooted high above. A nocturnal symphony was played by a thousand crickets interspersed with frogs and Philippe wasn't sure what else. Nor did he really want to know. He shivered as it dawned on him what he was doing. A path meandered across a small bridge, then sloped upward, winding around the trees and out of sight.

"I think that's where we're supposed to go." Philippe pointed and spoke to his dog. "No one will see us from the road." He remembered Bobby saying something about putting Fluffy on a leash, but he never walked Fluffy with a leash. He leaned in through the open car door. Fluffy sat in the passenger seat. "Come on," he said. "We have to take our evening constitutional."

Fluffy looked at Philippe, glanced at the woods, looked back at Philippe. He didn't move.

Philippe glanced into the woods, too. Branches rustled, and a cool puff of air raised goose bumps on his flesh. He shivered. "I don't want to go in there, either, but we promised to help Bobby. He's helping us with Mom and Dad, so we owe him. Come on."

Fluffy hopped up and stepped out of the car. He leaned against his master's legs and nuzzled his hand. Philippe scratched behind the beast's ears, took a deep breath, and found it difficult to swallow. He peered into the dark between the trees.

"We gave our word," he reminded Fluffy.

The owls and the fireflies, the beetles and the worms and whatever other creepy things crawled in the earth, accompanied them down the path into the trees. Philippe slowed his pace, and Fluffy, though he would normally bound around the park, clung to his side, tail down. When Philippe turned around, the road wasn't visible, and sounds of speeding cars were muted by the cacophonous music of the night's creatures.

A bare sliver of moon peeked between branches, casting its feeble light on the ground. Something whooshed through the air. Fluffy growled and edged closer to him.

Philippe had never before heard Fluffy growl, and he didn't know which startled him more, the dog or the sudden aftermath of silence. No crickets or cicadas. No owls. No thousand-legged creepy things.

A light thump behind him exploded in his ears, and he spun around to find himself face-to-face with a snarling man. Scant moonlight reflected off pointed fangs, but the rest of his face was in shadow. Philippe clutched his heart and fell to the ground in a half faint.

A smile curled the corners of the vampire's lips. His voice was a sepulchral growl floating on the summer breeze, and Philippe wondered if it wasn't the tiniest bit familiar. "Come here, little dog. I need your blood."

Fluffy's legs were slow to obey. His tail dragged, and his ears were pinned back. The vampire grabbed the dog's collar and pushed at the same time.

"Lie down," he commanded.

Fluffy whimpered but lay in the dirt, stretched on his side, ready to accept whatever fate had in store. The vampire maintained his grip on the dog's collar. In his other hand, a huge syringe glinted. He loomed over the animal. Fluffy whimpered again, but lay still.

"Let the dog go!"

The vampire's head shot up, his eyes glowing. He released the dog's collar, but Fluffy didn't move.

Philippe turned, too. He raised his head in recognition. "Bobby!"

"Run," Bobby said.

The other vampire growled, and his fangs glistened with saliva. His face contorted in anger, now that Philippe could see it in the moonlight.

Philippe struggled to his feet. The man charged with incredible speed. Philippe screamed.

"Run," Bobby shouted again, and he dashed forward.

At the moment the other vampire's hands tightened around his throat with absolutely inhuman strength, Bobby realized how long it had been since he'd last fed. This creature was more than his match.

Lara pulled into the long drive and parked next to the D'Paltrows' car. She'd assumed that Philippe went to Summit Square, the location of the closest supermarket. She and the D'Paltrows walked past the checkout lines, peered down all the aisles. No Philippe. Afterward, there'd been no point checking anyplace else. By the time they reached the next-closest shopping center, Philippe would be home. So . . . why wasn't his car here now?

Night had settled over Bobby's house. Lara wanted to investigate the locked basement. She couldn't do that with the D'Paltrows tagging along, however, and candlelight wasn't what she wanted to use for her search, especially not after dark.

As they walked through the front doors, Philippe's dog did not bound forward. "Fluffy!" Lara called. He was probably asleep on the sofa.

No response.

"That's odd, isn't it?" George said.

They walked through the main room and spotted the empty grocery bags on the kitchen counter. Lara spied the note. "We must've crossed paths with Philippe. He probably got here right after we left," she said. "He's taken Fluffy to the park for his evening walk."

"Convenient, now that the sun's gone down," George mumbled.

"That's enough," his wife scolded.

"Let's go," George said. He dug for his car keys.

"Oh, George, we're not leaving yet. We haven't seen Philippe. We—"

"He's at the park. We're going to the park. Now." George pounded his fist into his palm and cocked his head toward Lara. "But she's not going with us. No more runarounds."

Hildie glanced at Lara and raised her eyebrows, gave an apologetic look. "Can you give us directions to the park, sweetie? My husband is a little anxious."

Directions to the park were simple, and Lara didn't volunteer to go along. Mr. D'Paltrow had an issue with his son that was probably best handled in private, and she wanted time alone to search the basement. It'd work out perfectly. She'd need a flashlight, though.

As soon as George and Hildie pulled their car out of the driveway, she bolted to her SUV and headed home. She didn't recall seeing one in her townhouse, but Jake was a Boy Scout. He would've supplied her with one somewhere.

"Honestly, George, I don't know what your problem is." Hildie D'Paltrow frowned in the dark car as they drove.

"My problem is that our son, the former *faygele*, seems to have a new career."

"You can't be serious."

"I am. Look at his house. Even on a doctor's salary, he couldn't afford that. Not on two doctors' salaries.

All those paintings. I don't know much about art, but some of those look old, and I recognize the artists from the Italian Renaissance. Not to mention a first-edition autographed Shakespeare manuscript. How could he acquire all this?"

"Are you suggesting he's a criminal? A thief?"

"More than that. Worse. Who has triple front doors on their house? Remote-control metallic shutters? No food in the refrigerator? He only works the night shift, and we can't see him until it's dark outside? Hildie, I think our son is one of the undead."

Hildie puffed her cheeks and blew air out in a rush. "That's nonsense. It wasn't long ago that we cradled him in our arms, you took the training wheels off his bicycle, he kissed his first . . . friend. When did he have time to become undead?"

"Doesn't matter, does it, Hildie? If he's turned, he's turned."

The pair rode in silence for a few minutes.

"It really doesn't make sense, George. Suppose, just suppose, Philippe was a . . . you know . . ." She hesitated. "One of them. It had to have happened since he left ten years ago. Where would he have gotten all that artwork? If those important pieces had been stolen in recent years, it would've been in the news. We haven't heard any such news report. What he has, that's the accumulated wealth of generations."

George stopped at a traffic light two blocks from the park. "What're *you* suggesting?"

"A more plausible theory. A mother knows her son, even if we haven't seen him forever. That bedroom, the kitchen . . . that's not his living space. The house belongs to someone else."

"Who? The girl?"

The light changed to green. "No," Hildie said, "It's

not her space, either. The only thing in that house that might've belonged to our son was the dog."

"The dog slobbered on everything."

"See what I mean?" They turned into the park entrance and had to drive on the grass to go around the gate. "You're right about one thing though, George. The remote-control shutters, triple front doors, no food and no owner during daylight hours. That house belongs to a"—she squeezed her lips into a thin line before she could say it—*"vampire."*

George stopped the car short in the parking lot. "We haven't seen Philippe since he graduated from high school. He calls out of the blue, invites us to visit, tells us he's now a doctor and he's had an epiphany—he's no longer gay. We think his house belongs to a vampire. It's dark out now, and our son is missing."

"Either he's really walking his dog or . . ."

"Or he's in trouble." George threw open his door. "Let's go, Hildie. Our son needs help!"

"There's no other cars here, dear."

"Doesn't matter. Don't assume anything. Grab that bag in the backseat and follow me."

"But—"

"No time to argue. Grab the bag." George reached across the seat and pulled a flashlight from the glove box. He hopped out of the car, popped the trunk and slung dual plastic tanks onto his back.

Hildie called from inside the car, "George, there's a cross and a half-dozen wooden stakes in this bag!" She held the container up as if accusing him of a crime. "You were expecting this?" She backed out of the car and stared at him beside the car's open trunk. "What's that thing?" Recognition dawned. "That belongs to the little boy across the street. That's his squirt gun!"

George cinched the straps. "This isn't a squirt gun,

Hildie. This is a Hasbro, long-range, dual-tank Super Soaker, and it's loaded with holy water. Let's go."

They charged down the path and up the other side into the trees. Hildie struggled to keep pace. A dog barked.

"This way, Hildie girl!"

Movement in George's peripheral vision grabbed his attention, and he angled left. Growling and sounds of a struggle echoed in the dark. George D'Paltrow burst through the underbrush and flashed his light on two men fighting on the ground. Fluffy had her teeth sunk into the leg of the man on top.

"Get off him!" George ordered. If Fluffy attacked the man on top, the man on the bottom was likely Philippe's friend.

The man on top twisted his head sharply and glared. He sprang from the ground and wheeled toward the interlopers, a movement that wrenched him free of the dog. He clutched a liquid-filled plastic bag. Red eyes glowed in his face, and blood smeared his mouth and dripped from his fangs. He leaped for George and Hildie D'Paltrow.

The man who'd been prone surged off the ground, too, blood erupting from his wounds. He knocked the attacking vampire off balance just as he was about to bite George. Then the D'Paltrows' savior dropped to his knees with the effort. "Run," he begged them. "I'll hold him here."

George's would-be attacker spun around. His fangs glistened in the moonlight.

The wounded stranger crawled again between them and the vampire. "Run. Please." He reached behind him to push them away. "Take Fluffy back to Philippe." He struggled and stood, but his legs shook.

The vampire growled and flew at the stranger, taking

him to the ground. The stranger's face contorted in pain, but he wrapped his arms around the vampire and held on with whatever strength remained. "Save yourselves," he gasped.

George glanced over his shoulder at his wife. She nodded. He spun around. "Die, you bastard!"

George fired the Super Soaker. Hildie charged forward, screaming, wooden stake in one hand, cross in the other. But as holy water splattered the vampire, he howled, leaped into the air and disappeared with a whoosh.

Fluffy barked and whined. George shone his light on the man on the ground, the one who'd tried to save them. He was motionless, blood spilling from his chest.

"Oh, my," Hildie said. "Oh, my. Where's Philippe? Where's our son?"

George shook his head. "Doesn't matter, does it, Hildie? He's not here. He's . . . he's probably home."

"Without his dog?"

George didn't have an answer for that.

Hildie refocused on the man on the ground. "We need an ambulance right away." She pulled a cell phone from her pocketbook.

George put his hand on top of hers. "No. Don't you see? This man can't go to a hospital. Look. Here." He edged closer and aimed his light at the man's mouth, at the fangs. "I don't think those are surgical implants. Give me a hand, Hildie. We've got to take him to Philippe. He's a doctor. He'll know what to do." He slid the tanks off his shoulders. "Put this on in case that monster comes back. It's the only thing we have that can stop him."

"You don't think he was frightened by my wooden stake?"

George helped his wife wiggle into the straps. "Point and squeeze this." He showed her the trigger. Bending over, he pulled the injured man to a sitting position and hoisted him onto his shoulders. He grunted with the effort and staggered toward his car.

Hildie patted her thigh. "Come with us, Fluffy!" She chased her husband. "George, I can't believe you told one of the undead to *die*."

When they arrived back at Philippe's house, Meridian's SUV was gone, but another car was in its place. "I hope that's our son," George said. Hildie helped him wrap the unconscious and bleeding man in a blanket and carry him into the house. Fluffy limped in beside them.

"Philippe. Are you here? Philippe!"

"Dad?" The voice came from upstairs. "I'm so glad you're finally here. I need your help. I left my friend and Fluffy at the park. I didn't know what to do. I was so—" Their son rushed down the spiral staircase and spied George and Hildie at the same time he spied the man cocooned in their blanket. "Bobby!" he shrieked.

George and Hildie deposited the wounded man on the sofa. "He needs a doctor, son. I don't know much about medicine, but he's lost a lot of blood."

"We couldn't take him to the hospital," Hildie added.

Philippe glanced from one parent to the other. "Mom? Dad?"

George's head bobbed. He pointed at Bobby's fangs. "You may not believe this, Philippe, but . . . he's a vampire. That's why we brought him back here to your house."

His son struggled to swallow. "This isn't my house, Dad. It's his." He stared into his father's eyes, and George stared back.

"It's okay. We figured that out." George sighed and gestured to the wounded man. "He needs help, son. Another vampire attacked him."

"The other vampire was trying to kill him," Hildie spoke up.

"No," George corrected. "Vampires are already dead. The other vampire was trying to *destroy* him. He—"

"Mom, Dad, I know. This is my friend, Bobby Eyre. He's the one who—Ahh!" Blood seeped through the blanket. Fluffy whimpered.

"Mom, in the kitchen," Philippe directed. "Find a pot. Bring warm water. Dad, upstairs, there's a linen closet in the hall. Bring towels. Go!" He shooed them off. He needed Meridian. Why wasn't she here?

Philippe talked to Fluffy while he unwrapped his friend. "Are you okay, boy? I'm sorry I left you. You forgive me, don't you? I was so scared. I didn't know what to do. Bobby ordered me to run. Are you okay? You look a mess—but Bobby looks worse."

He unraveled the blanket and unbuttoned Bobby's shirt, then put his hand on Bobby's cheek. "He's cold. But . . . I suppose he's probably always cold." He caressed Bobby's neck and forehead. Blood trickled from his friend's mouth. Philippe rubbed his forehead and stared at the chest wounds. "What happened back there, Fluffy? Those look like bite marks. Was the other vampire draining him?"

Hildie sloshed back with a pot of warm water. George returned with an armload of towels. Philippe had not yet removed Bobby's shirt, disconcerted as he was by the wounds that gashed his friend's upper torso. He pressed a towel against them.

"Keep pressure on this, Dad."

Philippe soaked the end of another towel in the pot

of water and cleaned the visible areas of Bobby's chest and shoulders. The bleeding didn't stop, though it was sluggish. He felt Bobby's neck. No pulse. What did that mean for a vampire?

Philippe tilted Bobby's head back and opened his friend's mouth. Fangs glistened there, red with blood. There was no sound of breathing.

He pinched Bobby's nose, covered Bobby's mouth with his own and forced air into his friend's lungs. He counted to three and did it again. He released the nose and pounded on Bobby's chest, above his heart. "He can't be dead," he said.

"Of course he's dead. He's a vampire!" his father growled.

Bobby's body twitched, clearly in distress. Hildie shrieked, "Do something!"

Philippe closed Bobby's mouth. Tears filled his eyes. "I don't know what else to do, Mom."

George D'Paltrow leaned forward. "You're a doctor. You have to know something."

Philippe bit his lip but held his father's gaze. "No, Dad, I'm not a doctor. I'm a nurse. A gay nurse. This is a sham. This whole weekend. The whole thing, me, everything. This is not my house, I don't have a girl-friend, and I'm not a physician. I'm nothing, nobody, just a . . ."

His father put his hand on Philippe's shoulder, voice soothing. "It doesn't matter. You're our son. This man is your friend. Help him."

Philippe stared at the floor, then banged the side of his head. He patted his pockets.

"What're you looking for?" his mother asked.

"I need my cell."

"Here." She pulled hers from her bag again. "Use mine."

Philippe punched in a number. "Come on, come on, pick up."

"Hello?"

"Meridian?" Philippe said. "Where are you? What do you know about the undead?"

"What?" Her voice sounded odd.

"No time to explain, get back here now."

"I'm turning into the driveway. I just went home to get something."

"Hurry up."

"What's wrong?"

"It's Bobby."

"What's wrong with him?" Her voice became even more strangled.

"He's been bitten."

"By . . . by Fluffy?"

"It's not an animal bite."

"What're you talking about?"

"Just get in here. You won't believe me if I say."

Twenty-seven

Lara's SUV skidded to a halt in the driveway. She kept her black bag under a blanket in the back. She'd been surprised that Jake had returned it to her, as it was a connection to her previous life—the life she was still determined to reclaim as soon as Tony and Robert were captured. Jake hadn't said anything about the bag, but she'd found it in the closet with her new wardrobe, and had shifted it here to this vehicle. Jake's people had removed the bullet, of course, her only safety net. They'd taken all her bullets, back at WPA headquarters.

She snatched up the bag and hurried into the converted church. She began her assessment immediately as she approached. Philippe and Mr. D'Paltrow gripped blood-soaked towels thrust against Bobby's chest and shoulders. Pale complexion, no rise and fall of his chest. His lips were slack.

She touched his hand. The skin was cold and he had no pulse. He had always felt warm to her. She could detect no respiration. She pulled up one of his eyelids. No need to use her opthalmoscope—pupil and iris blurred together, no way to distinguish if the pupil was fixed and dilated. She set her bag on the coffee table, pulled out latex gloves and slipped them on.

She backed Mr. D'Paltrow out of the way and peeked under the towel he'd shoved against Bobby's chest. She pushed Philippe's towels aside, too. Shocking, what she saw: multiple wounds, bite marks as if he'd been attacked by a sanguinary creature. But the bite marks were not like those of any dog she'd ever known. The wounds seemed too small for the amount of blood that soaked towels, clothes, and the blanket that lay beneath him.

Is this what I'm supposed to be looking for, Jake?

Philippe gasped. "That's really bizarre."

"What?" Lara demanded. At the same time as she asked, images of a similar scene flashed through her mind—her house, her living room, a man with a wound in his shoulder. No bite marks, but that man presented similarly, with pale complexion, cold skin, no pulse.

Philippe gaped.

"What?" Lara repeated.

"I swear those wounds were much worse five minutes ago."

"You've done a good job. The bleeding has nearly stopped."

"I didn't do anything," Philippe said. "That's why I called you. Meridian, he's not breathing."

"I know. How long has it been?"

Philippe glanced at his father. "Dad?"

George D'Paltrow shrugged. "Maybe fifteen minutes?"

"Is he on meds?" Lara asked.

"I don't know," Philippe said. "None that I'm aware of."

"You checked his airway?"

"I don't have anything to check with."

"We need to bag him. I need room to work. Push the table out of the way, move him onto the floor. I have a trach tube in my medical bag."

Hildie and George moved the coffee table. Lara cradled Bobby's head as Philippe and George grabbed the blanket beneath him and lifted him onto the floor. "Here, Philippe, hold his head tilted back like this." Lara rummaged in her black bag.

Philippe stammered. "Why do you have a physician's bag?"

She answered without pausing. "I'm a surgeon."

Philippe's eyes widened. "Why are you pretending to be a nurse?"

"Whatever her reason, it doesn't matter, does it?" his father asked. "She's doing her best to save your friend's life."

Lara glanced up and forced a tight-lipped smile. She opened Bobby's mouth . . . and gasped. *Fangs.* Everything she'd feared. Everything she'd decided she couldn't believe. It was all true, and she'd been an idiot not to see. But she hadn't wanted to see, because of the connection she'd felt with him. Because of the bond they'd shared.

She shook off her shock and focused again on the

task at hand. Should she proceed as if he were a human? Was that the correct protocol?

"I've got to get the trach tube in so we can start him breathing again," she said.

If he even breathes normally.

How had she not noticed before?

When people are walking and talking—and making love to you—you assume they're living.

She edged closer, the end of the tube inches from Bobby's mouth. His eyes popped open, he hissed, grabbed her wrist and sat up. Hildie screamed. George had to restrain himself. Philippe fainted.

Lara's hand covered Bobby's and gently relaxed his grip on her. Recognition seeped into his face, and he allowed her to ease his head back onto the floor. It lolled to the side.

Alive but not breathing. Someone else's thoughts—Bobby's?—were voiced through her mouth. "We won't need the trach tube."

She removed the towel from his chest. His wounds were sealed. It was unlike anything in her experience—in the same way that Bobby speaking inside her head was unfamiliar. None of this was logical. How could anything about a vampire be logical?

Philippe came to. "Are you okay?" Lara asked. "Bobby needs blood."

Philippe nodded. "What can I do?"

Lara glanced at Bobby, whose eyes were again closed. He wasn't communicating. She wasn't entirely sure what to do.

"We can't take him to the hospital, so we'll have to bring blood to him. I think we're going to need a lot—maybe ten units, maybe more. Do you think we can get that much, Philippe?"

The nurse shrugged his shoulders. "I don't know.

Two months ago we could've walked into the blood bank and no one would've noticed. Now, with all the cameras and locks, I don't know if I can get into that room without a written order. They certainly won't hand anything over to me."

Lara sat on the floor next to Bobby, her legs pulled up to her chest. "We have to think of something else, then. There must be some other source of blood."

Philippe's head bobbed, and his hands fluttered.

"What?" Lara asked.

"There is another source, but it's kinda gruesome."

Lara cocked her head and arched her eyebrows.

Philippe continued, "I happen to know the average birthrate in the hospital is three to five babies a day."

Lara shuddered. "We can't take blood from newborns! Even if we could get to them, and even if it were with their consent, they don't have enough."

"No, no. That's not what I mean. I've read that hospital death rates match their birthrates. That means there's probably three to five recently deceased bodies available at any time. We could drain blood from those in the morgue, and even if someone discovers it, no one would care."

Lara hesitated. Philippe's idea sounded almost plausible, and it wouldn't hurt anyone, but somehow she knew it wouldn't work. "I'm not sure exactly why, but I think . . . well, I think a vampire needs blood taken from a living source. Otherwise, wouldn't they be able to drink from the dead all the time? Yours is a good idea—a more *ethical* idea—but I don't think it'll help revive him."

"Why don't we give him *our* blood?" Hildie suggested.

Lara shivered, knowing she couldn't do it herself. She couldn't give blood for anyone. Hadn't she protected her *essence* her entire life? But how could she explain that to these people?

Thinking, she studied the gore-soaked clothes, blanket, towels, sofa and floor. She could only imagine how much blood Bobby had lost before the D'Paltrows brought him here.

"Judging by his blood loss, the small amount of blood each of you could donate won't help him enough." She recalled a line from one of the books Jake had wanted her to read. She'd only glanced at it. *Vampires maintain a significantly greater amount of blood than humans.*

Philippe deflated. "What're we going to do, then?"

Lara thought. "We'll get blood from the hospital, and a lot of it. And if that fails . . . well, Hildie, we'll use your plan as backup." As a very last option. "We'll get equipment for a transfusion while we're there."

She pushed up off the floor. "Come with me, Philippe. We're going to the hospital and see what we can scrounge. Mr. and Mrs. D'Paltrow—George, Hildie—you stay here with Bobby. He's vulnerable. If whoever did this tracks him here, he won't be able to defend himself. That's another reason you shouldn't donate blood. It'd leave you vulnerable, too." She hoped they didn't notice that she'd excluded herself from donating.

George put his hands on his hips. "It'll take an army of vampires to get through us." Hildie moved a step closer to her husband.

"Good," Lara said. "Close the shutters, including the upstairs. Lock the doors. Find blankets and keep him warm."

"You think that'll help, dear?" Hildie asked. She sounded doubtful.

Lara shook her head, realizing she was working by

rote. "I have no idea. You two are in charge of his safety. We'll be back as soon as we can."

"Where're you going?" Philippe asked as she headed for the stairs instead of the door.

"To put on scrubs. You do the same. We'll be less conspicuous that way."

Less than five minutes later they were in her SUV headed for St. Mary's. They rode in silence until Meridian turned into the hospital drive. "You knew?"

Philippe bit his lip. "He exposed his existence to me."

A pang of jealousy swept through Lara. She and Bobby shared something intrinsic, and they'd made love. Twice. She was sure. Even if she couldn't recall the moments of penetration, the sensations remained vivid . . . if somehow incomplete. How much more intimate could they get? But Bobby hadn't shared his secret with her.

Lara swept these thoughts aside. His life—or, as a vampire, his undeath—depended on her. He needed blood. At Jefferson Memorial, in the ER, security regarding blood was lax. Once delivered from the blood bank, no one stood guard over it. Perhaps the same was true at St. Mary's. She hoped it was.

They parked and entered as if they were on duty, except they headed for the emergency room. She'd explained her plan to Philippe.

"Maybe we'll be in luck," he said. "Friday night is the busiest time in the ER. What do you want me to do?"

"Let's look around first and see if we can spot any packets not in use. We'll see after that. Maybe we can just take them and no one'll notice. You might have to distract someone so I can swipe them."

Philippe touched her shoulder. "Can we save him, Meridian? He lost an awful lot of blood. I didn't know a human body could hold that much."

"He's not human," she reminded him. She was reminding herself, as well.

"He sure acts it."

Yes. He certainly felt human to her. Each morning they'd made love had transcended previous experience. Was it only because he was beyond human? Was it the accumulated knowledge of more than a lifetime, or was there something else, something . . . sweeter?

The sense of familiarity with Bobby never lessened. He might be a vampire, but he clung to humanity with as much ferocity as any human could generate. She realized then it was his human side that appealed to her, even more than the mystery of the inhuman. She wanted to know the man.

How old was Bobby, anyway? A hundred? A hundred and forty? More? Was there any way to tell with a vampire? Chop him in half and count the number of rings? Would blood in a packet even save his life? Would it be any more effective than blood from a corpse? She had no way of knowing. She had no way of finding out, other than testing it, and then it might be too late.

Wait. Yes, she did have a way. She could call Jake. This was his business. He'd know.

She pulled out her cell phone and flipped it open. His was still the only number in memory. She was about to push send, when she realized Jake wouldn't help her save a vampire. His business was to destroy vampires. She flipped the cell shut.

The ER was busy, but nothing like Jefferson Memorial. There was no constant influx of shootings and stabbings and beatings. There were three suspected DUIs having their blood-alcohol levels tested; a new mom who hadn't made it to maternity; an old man, whom age had finally caught; and two car accidents that between them yielded one person who needed a transfusion. Not a promising selection.

"We're going to have to think of something else," Lara said.

"What about the old man?"

"What about him?"

"Well, I don't think we could get in there right now and take much without getting caught, but . . . if he dies, we could take his blood. No one would care. It's not like he'd need it anymore. They'll embalm him. If we route him off as soon as he dies, take his blood right away . . . well, it'll be close to blood from a live donor."

Lara winced at the idea, but she didn't have a better one.

"We need an IV and empty packets to store the blood," Philippe said. "The typical death scenario in the St. Mary's ER is, once he's gone, the family gets a moment alone with him.

"The nurses won't let anyone stay too long. They'll pull the curtain. They'll call downstairs to the morgue. There's almost never a morgue orderly. The hospital can't afford it. If Dr. Raymond is on duty, and she almost always is, it'll take her a while to get here. She'd be here in a flash, if it was one of those people from the car crash who died. Old age won't pique her professional curiosity. We'll have time."

They headed off to gather the necessary supplies.

"Meridian," Philippe spoke up as they walked. "I just thought of something. What if he doesn't die in the next few minutes? What if he lingers? How long can we wait?"

The question led to another gruesome thought. She'd heard enough of the attending physicians' conversation as they passed. Total organ failure was imminent. He had no chance to regain his past function, but he could linger. Lara knew she couldn't take his blood while he was still alive, but could she help him over the edge? His plugs had already been pulled. The old man was going to die in a few minutes or a few hours anyhow. If he died in minutes, she might be able to save Bobby. It was an unpleasant dilemma, the worst she'd ever faced.

No one guarded the supply rooms, and they both had keys. Getting prepared was easy. Carrying out any plan would be more difficult.

"Won't someone notice we don't belong in the ER?" Lara realized.

"They didn't notice us in there before, why would they notice us now?"

"The guilty looks on our faces?"

Philippe grabbed her arm and squinted at her. "Suck it up, girl." He tapped his chest. "You don't see me fainting, do you?"

Lara fought a smile and prepared to act. Taking the blood of a man who'd just recently died—she could do that. But could she help a dying man die, even to save another life?

They returned to the ER in time to hear the old man's physician. "Your father is a real fighter, Mr. Goldberg. He's hanging in there." The doctor squeezed the other man's shoulder and nodded. This wasn't what Lara wanted to hear.

"Doctor, is there any chance at all he'll regain consciousness? I'd really like to talk with him."

The doctor was an older man, balding, with a patch of gray hair that wound around his ears and down the back of his neck. His glasses were thick, the frames black, and his nose was broad and flat, as if it had been broken in a fight. His eyes locked onto Mr. Goldberg's. "I'm sorry, son."

Lara watched the peculiar bob of Mr. Goldberg's Adam's apple, and she recognized a man struggling not to cry. "I think I'll get a cup of coffee," he said.

The doctor pulled the curtain, allowing the dying Mr. Goldberg whatever dignity was left to him, while his son sought peace. No one watched the closed curtain, and Lara and Philippe slipped behind it.

Lara handed the bag of supplies to Philippe and inched to the head of the bed. She studied the old man's face. His eyes were closed, his breath shallow and difficult. His complexion was pallid, his cheeks sunken, and dark bags drooped below his eyes. His hand twitched in sleep. Was he dreaming? Was she?

She needed to take the pillow from beneath his head, hold it over his face and press down. There'd be no sounds, no struggle. Mr. Goldberg would feel nothing. She was only hurrying his imminent departure— maybe making it easier for him.

Lara hesitated.

"We have to," Philippe whispered. "To save Bobby."

Lara closed her eyes and balled her hands into fists. She pictured Bobby as she'd left him, on the floor of his home, swathed in blood-soaked towels, his complexion not too different from Mr. Goldberg's.

I can't do this. I'm a physician, not a killer.

Then she heard something else. She didn't know if it was real or her imagination, but Bobby's face popped into her mind. His mouth didn't move but he spoke to her. He could only manage one word.

Please.

Lara's eyes popped open. She grabbed Philippe's arm and directed him from behind the curtain. "Let's go."

"But—"

"I'll explain later."

Twenty-eight

They arrived back at the church in minutes.

"Did you get the blood?" Hildie asked.

Lara shook her head. "Not exactly. You had the best idea, Hildie. We brought the necessary equipment." She pulled the catheter and IV line from a bag and handed it to Philippe, hoping that this was the right decision. She'd somehow sensed from that one word she'd heard in her head (Bobby's voice—had it been imagined or not?) that even gallons of blood transported back from the hospital would be less effective than a few liters fresh from a living body. With luck, the three willing donors around her would be enough.

She answered their questions before they could ask. "There're three of you. You're each going to donate a liter and a half. That much will be safe, but you'll need to remain lying down for a couple of hours. I'll take care of Bobby while you're resting." She hoped to excuse herself in their minds from giving any herself.

"What if it's still not enough blood?" Hildie asked.

Lara winced. "It'll be a good start—and it'll be fresh, not bagged or from the dead. Hopefully it'll be enough to revive him, and he can tell us whatever else we need to do. Mr. D'Paltrow, roll up your sleeve and lay down on the sofa." George obeyed at once.

Philippe leaned close to Lara and whispered, "You could give at least a liter safely and be up and about in twenty minutes."

Lara shook her head, annoyed. "No, I can't." She didn't want to explain that even to save Bobby's life, donating her *essence* was more than she could stand.

Philippe found a vein in his father's arm and inserted a needle. "Mom, would you get us a glass of orange juice from the kitchen, please? I'm so glad I bought some."

As soon as George finished donating, Lara drew blood from Hildie. Philippe started an IV into Bobby.

"Not like that," Lara said. "There're straws in the kitchen. Attach one on the end of the bag, put the straw in his mouth and let the blood run down his throat."

"It won't drip without a regulator," Philippe said.

"Squeeze the bag to get it started. If I'm right, he'll suck it in."

Philippe winced. "That's gruesome."

Lara shrugged. Part of her agreed, but . . . "Vampires drink blood. It's not the same as a transfusion."

Philippe started the bag as she'd directed. Even Lara was a bit surprised when Bobby's autonomic vampire response drew blood through the straw, but nothing changed after the first unit was transferred. Lara drew blood from Philippe and replaced the now empty IV bag with the bag she'd taken from Hildie.

Bobby groaned halfway through the third ingestion. His coloring became less pale, but his eyes didn't open. Lara looked under the towels. She took a deep breath and held it as she examined his torso. No trace remained of any wounds, not even a scar—another reminder of just how inhuman her lover really was.

After the last bag of blood was taken, the three donors slept. Lara struggled to keep her eyes open, even though as a surgeon, she'd been able to go all night without sleep. She was weak and tired, but needed to stay awake to monitor her patient. Tension had eased from his face, yet aside from a couple of groans, he retained the appearance of death.

In the end, sleep overwhelmed her, and Lara collapsed on the floor next to Bobby. Her dreams were restless, nightmares of women being attacked by a vampire—screaming, gruesome images too profane to relive. Lara had the impression that these women were not fiction created by her subconscious, but actual women and actual suffering. She didn't know how she was seeing them.

She woke with a start. Shielded by the steel shutters, the room was dark except for a single lamp that cast a dim light against the wall. Lara raised her head. Bobby lay peaceful. Philippe and his parents were still asleep.

She stretched and pushed herself up. Tiredness had left her body, and she felt a pang of hunger. Amazing, what a couple hours of sleep could do. Fresh night air would help, too.

She headed out the front doors and had to shield her eyes. No wonder she felt rested. She must've slept for eight hours. Sunlight glinted off the windshield of her SUV. There was a flashlight on the front seat, which reminded her. . . . Everyone else was sleeping. This was her opportunity to check the basement.

She realized suddenly that there was no need to go into the basement. She'd discovered Bobby's secret.

And yet . . .

A locked door, a mystery. She grabbed the flashlight from the car and headed back into the house, careful to bolt the doors behind her. The basement door was still locked, but she handled that again with her credit card. She flipped on the feeble light at the top of the stairs and switched on her flashlight before she reached the bottom.

The steps squeaked. She stopped on the last step and angled her light in a wide arc. There was the usual basement stuff: furnace, hot water tank, a few boxes piled up in a corner that she couldn't see around. The basement floor was a cement slab—no tile, no carpet.

A scratching sound like fingernails clicking on cement drew her attention, and she swung the light around to chase it. Nothing was visible. Even with the flashlight, did she want to venture onto the dark floor? What had she seen in the gloom the first time she was down here? What had she run into?

The flashlight cast eerie shadows and its beam revealed nothing significant, just gray cinderblock walls, a water stain, visible rafters, a few cobwebs. She estimated ten or twelve steps to be able to see around the corner. There had to be something down here besides old boxes to warrant the locked door.

Lara took a deep breath and ventured farther into the dark. Something squealed, and she jumped.

Damn it, that wasn't a cat!

Sounds echoed on both sides of her. She flashed her light in either direction, and something scurried through her vision.

Taking a deep breath, she charged around the corner. Ahead of her, standing open, was the thick metal door of a walk-in vault, but it faced the wrong way, as if she was already standing inside.

As she crossed the threshold, a jolt flared up her ankle and leg, a feeling like being zapped by an electrical outlet. She jumped back. She'd broken the red laser lines that had become visible, crisscrossing a foot and a half off the floor. Movement in the dark swept through her vision.

This must be some sort of electrical fence to keep out whatever's down here.

She held the side of the vault and lifted her leg high and over the lines, careful not to break them again. She didn't realize she held her breath until she was safely across. Plush carpet now was underfoot.

Indirect lights winked on, activated by her presence. She scanned a huge room with a curved ceiling and bookshelves that lined three walls. A Van Gogh hung between the shelves. Lara jumped when the stone fireplace whooshed to life. A glass desk in front of it held a computer and scattered notes. A high-backed, swiveling rocking chair eased up to the desk.

Another vault door to the left of the fireplace stood man height, though it was narrower than the first, as if this had begun as a true doorway. What was usually outside seemed to be on the inside of this vault, as if the vault was designed to seal the occupant in rather than to protect valuable property.

Lara stepped closer. "I wonder how I get this to open?"

Upon her words, one mechanism clicked, another tumbled. The huge handle spun, and the door opened into a short tunnel with a man-sized hole, into which Lara swung her flashlight beam. The stench of a sewer overwhelmed her.

"Yuck."

She backed out and forced the door shut. The mechanisms clicked and tumbled automatically, and the vault was again locked from this side.

Why would Bobby have a vault door to the sewer? No answer leaped to mind.

She maneuvered around the desk. The computer was asleep, and she jiggled the mouse. REALTOR.com.

Bobby had been investigating property in Santa Fe,
New Mexico. Why?

She read the papers on the desk. They were employee lists with shift schedules from St. Mary's and
architectural drawings of the hospital showing floor-by-
floor design. How had he obtained this information?
From someone like Marty.

He had highlighted the staircases, the positions of
recently installed security cameras and the blood bank.
There was an entrance to the sewer system through the
morgue.

Lara glanced at the sealed door and connected the
dots. She leafed through more papers on the desk.
Notes were scribbled across the pages.

Blood thief not stealing from hospital.
American Red Cross, Earle, broken neck not possible in
fall.
New driver: Tony.
Canine blood in blood bank.
ASPCA reports unusual number of missing large-breed
dogs in recent weeks.

These notes were followed by a list of questions,
some with answers, some without.

Why would V. want blood from blood bank?
Why steal from Red Cross? Less security.
Why replace with animal blood? Theft not noticed for
extended time.
No self-respecting V. drinks blood from a bank. Why
steal it?
Why else does a V. want human blood? Experiments.

This was what Jake wanted: information about a vampire stealing blood. Clearly, if Bobby was also trying to figure out what was going on, he wasn't the thief. If she helped lead Jake to the thieving vampire—likely the vampire who'd attacked Bobby in the park—she'd be protecting Bobby and the D'Paltrows.

Yes. Jake hadn't said anything about two vampires operating out here. If she delivered one, Jake should be satisfied. She could go back to her own life then. They had to have caught Robert by now—no one had said anything about him for ages. Bobby's notes mentioned a new Red Cross driver named Tony. That had to be coincidence.

She kept reading.

Set trap.
Philippe's dog.
Tyler State Park.

This seemed to be all the information Bobby had. She'd let Jake know that a vampire was stealing blood from the Red Cross and replacing it with dog blood. Let Jake set his own trap.

Lara stood up and marched around the desk. As she did, a question suddenly occurred to her. Why was Bobby trying to catch another vampire?

The answer didn't seem too difficult. Bobby had been at St. Mary's for five years. He'd been feeding all that time, and if no one had noticed, he likely felt safe. Hospital procedures had recently changed, what with all the locked doors and security cameras, and clearly it hadn't happened because they recognized Bobby was stealing blood, but because someone else was. Bobby's hunting ground had been compromised.

He can't feed easily. He must think that if he catches the blood thief, the hospital will lighten up, and he can go back to doing whatever it is he's been doing. I haven't seen him doing anything particularly incriminating . . . .

She wondered how long it had been since he'd fed. She would have been part of the problem. Since she'd arranged for him to become her mentor, she'd spent every moment at the hospital with him. Down a gallon or two of blood, it wasn't surprising he'd lost the battle in the park. That explained some of his actions.

When he made love to her, what was that about? Was he really interested in her? Or was he simply distracting her so that he could find his next meal?

The attraction was real! It had to be. Though it seemed a contradiction, her connection to Bobby had never felt stronger.

She reminded herself of how the D'Paltrows had described Bobby draining his last ounce of strength to save them. A vampire, he was also a man she was proud to have as a lover—even if the act had never been consummated in the traditional sense.

She chided herself. How could making love with a vampire ever be traditional?

Lara returned upstairs. Bobby showed no signs of waking. Neither did Philippe, nor his parents. Exhausted from fighting a vampire and down a quart or so of blood, no wonder they still slept. Lara had no idea if the four and a half units of blood she'd given to Bobby were enough. She had hoped he'd be awake by now to tell her if she needed to do anything else to help him. But perhaps it was a daylight thing. Maybe vampires didn't wake until sunset. She might go back to the hospital in the meantime and see if she could scrounge. Less effective than the freshly donated kind or not, more blood would still be useful.

She showered and put on fresh scrubs. In one sense, knowing about Bobby was a relief, but how could she have feelings for a vampire? Vampires weren't human. They weren't even alive.

He clung to some sense of humanity, though. He evoked genuine emotions in her. Genuine emotions she'd never before felt. Emotions like . . . would she share her *essence* with him? She'd been tempted, briefly—only briefly. Whenever their eyes met, there was no denying the sense of familiarity they shared. He made her heart pump faster and butterflies—or was that bats?—flit across her stomach. She wanted to be with him, to know him, to understand him. More than with any man she'd ever known, his touch excited her. He'd electrified her body and soul on those mornings they'd made love. They'd shared uncharted sensations.

She had to remind herself one more time: He's a vampire. He drinks human blood to survive. He's a monster! She stared at the mirror and reminded herself that Bobby would have no reflection.

She suddenly had an odd thought. It scared her. She raised her chin and twisted her head, studying her neck. No visible bite marks. But . . . what was it Jake had told her? No vampire would be so obvious. A vampire might bite a woman's breasts or wrists or the soles of her feet.

Lara pulled up her scrub shirt and her bra without unhooking it. She scrutinized her reflection, but no puncture marks were evident. She readjusted her clothes, held her hands at arm's length and turned her wrists over and back. Nothing there, either.

Balanced against the vanity, she picked up first one foot, then the other, to inspect the soles. Nothing.

What about her inner thigh? She yanked her scrub

pants down and pushed her flesh to the side. Right leg, left leg . . . Okay, she hadn't been bitten. Whew!

She hadn't been bitten. He had been starving, they had been in close proximity and she had been in his control, and he hadn't bitten her. He'd had his mouth all over her! What did she owe Bobby? What did she mean to him—and what did he mean to her? She would do almost anything to save a patient's life, but this was different—as the past few hours had taught her. Still, Bobby was something special. He'd helped the D'Paltrows in the park. He'd been a starving vampire and he hadn't bitten her. There was good inside him.

And her *essence* remained intact.

But he unquestionably was a vampire. And Jake espoused Dog's theorem, the only good vampire is a dead vampire. Should she turn him over to Jake?

She drove to the hospital. As she turned her SUV into the parking lot, another thought struck her. Bobby had been feeding at the hospital for five years. What if his sparing her had been an aberration? What if he'd been killing others?

No. She didn't believe that. No medical evidence existed to suggest that innocent patients had been dying, and Jake would most certainly have passed that information along, or she would have heard it from some of the staff. Bobby had likely discovered a way to take enough blood to survive without arousing suspicion.

That raised another point. Did Bobby have the right to take blood, even if others weren't aware? What if he had taken Lara's blood? She'd feel violated! Didn't she feel violated just knowing how much he had kept secret from her?

The sun had cast its shortest shadow when she entered the hospital. Now it dipped below the horizon, and she'd managed to steal only one packet of blood. She'd barely had time to stuff it in her scrub pants before she'd been cornered by Samantha Esher, the head nurse of the day shift, and asked to pick up some duties. She obliged, hoping it would produce opportunities. No such luck.

She'd left a note, and Philippe had called a couple of hours ago to report that he and his parents were awake. No side effects, though they were hungry and eating without her. He'd call again the moment Bobby woke.

The inside door to the blood bank was locked, and an orderly and a technician maintained their posts in the outside lab. The ER still remained the most likely place to snatch blood. She'd been there twice without success. She'd try one more time before she headed home.

She stepped off the elevator into the first floor lobby just as a large man in his late thirties and with sweat dripping down his forehead entered through the sliding front doors. He wore a white uniform and a tilted-back Red Cross cap. Did she imagine the repugnant odor wafting across the space between them?

Almost at the same moment she saw him, the man's eyes swept across her. Lara's heart stopped beating. She exhaled . . . and her heart kick-started itself when his eyes moved on without recognition. He lumbered across the lobby.

Lara rubbed her wrist. It had been months since she'd seen Tony. According to Bobby's notes—it really was him!—he was driving for the Red Cross now. He wasn't here looking for her. He was probably making a blood delivery. This had to be coincidence.

A heartbeat later she heard a familiar voice growl over the lobby's din. "You."

She willed herself not to turn, not to respond.

Other heads glanced up. Not hers. She maintained a steady pace. She felt Tony's beady eyes boring into the back of her head. She'd lost forty pounds. Her hair was scalped and blonde, her muscles toned. He couldn't possibly recognize her.

"Dr. West," the voice called. "Lara West."

Heat streamed into Lara's cheeks. All eyes in the lobby focused on her. How could that be? No one knew her true identity. She resisted the urge as long as she could, but she had to see if Tony followed. She peeked.

A sly smile creased Tony's lips. As soon as their eyes met, he pivoted his huge frame and hustled toward her. Pretending not to recognize him, Lara turned and fled.

She maintained a steady walking pace, not looking back. St. Mary's was her hospital now. She knew her way around better than she had at St. Bonaventure's in Arlington. Tony wouldn't catch her—or so she pleaded. Saturday evening visitors crowded the hospital. They would run interference, slow his pursuit.

She peeked again as she passed the admittance desk. Tony had already closed half the distance between them. How could he move so fast?

She reached a long corridor and turned left, out of his sight, and ran. She pushed open the swinging doors in front of her, then went left again instead. When Tony rounded the corner, the movement of the doors would make him think she'd gone through.

She had to be out of sight, if by chance he glanced down this side corridor. At the third door on the left, she ducked into a storage room and locked the handle. No way would he expect to find her in here. She didn't bother to turn on the lights. No reason to draw attention to the room.

She counted. He wasn't far behind her—perhaps ten seconds? The door handle jerked, and breath caught in Lara's throat. Whoever it was gave up quickly.

Another twenty seconds. She couldn't wait too long, because Tony would backtrack. If that had been Tony trying the handle, he'd come back to this room.

She took a deep breath, ready to move out, when suddenly a key slid into the lock and the storage room door popped open. She was trapped!

A hand snaked into the dark storage room and tapped on the light switch. Lara stood like a statue. She didn't realize she'd closed her eyes, pinching them tight, but when she did, she squinted out through one eyelid.

Janitor Blissockiss, a true curmudgeon, stood in the doorway. He nodded his head with a leer. "I catch a lot of couples locked in here, but this is the first time I've caught a woman in here alone. Having a good time, are you?" He cackled between missing teeth.

Lara waited for her heart to reengage. She forced her legs to move. Tony would be back this way soon. She brushed by Blissockiss. He was barely as tall as she, even with his logger boots. "Pig," she managed to say as she turned into the corridor.

She glanced through the swinging doors as she passed. Tony's massive back was visible far down the hall, so she angled right again, toward the main lobby, and walked as fast as she dared without drawing attention.

She glanced back as she exited the sliding main doors and stepped into the night air. Tony was not in sight, probably still deep in the bowels of the hospital, searching for her room by room. Lara breathed a sigh of relief. Half walking, half running, she headed for the front lot. She'd call Jake just as soon as she was safe in the car. Maybe his people could get here fast enough to trap that bastard in the hospital.

The orange glow of a parking-lot light cast her SUV in nearly daylight brightness. She fumbled for her car keys.

"Lose something, Dr. West?"

Lara spun around and jumped back, keys in hand. A handsome man, lean, perhaps six feet tall, in his midforties, stood close. Dark clothes hugged his body as if custom made. The orange light reflected in his eyes.

Those eyes bore the mark of a nocturnal hunter. They narrowed in focus, glowing, their pupils and irises blended together. She'd seen eyes like these before. They had caressed her soul.

"You," Lara said.

"Best you can do? Quote Tony?"

A rash of memories flooded back. She knew this man. She'd carved into him with a scalpel. He'd touched her in an intimate way.

Robert. Not Bobby, but Robert.

This was the man from whom she'd removed an unusual bullet. This was the man whose face had eluded her for the past few weeks. This was the man Jake wanted.

This was the man who'd hog-tied her and burned her house down. Tony worked for this man.

Uh-oh.

She ran. Robert grabbed her wrist. Lara winced. "I can scream."

"I can rip your arm off." Like a vise, his grip tightened in confirmation.

Lara's eyes darted around the parking lot. No one was close. She pressed her lips together in acquiescence, and Robert relaxed his grip. He didn't release her.

"Let's sit in your car, shall we?" Without confiscating her keys, he opened the driver side door and guided Lara onto the seat.

She grabbed the wheel to steady herself. She'd expected him to push her across to the other side and slide in after her, but instead he closed the door. Dumb move. All she had to do was hit the door lock button, start the car and drive away.

The passenger door opened before her hand came off the steering wheel. How could anyone move that fast?

Robert climbed in, slammed his door and pushed the lock button. "Is that what you were trying to do?"

"What do you want?" she growled.

"I confess I'm surprised to see you, Dr. West." He touched his lips, then gestured toward her, leaning back as he did. "I like what you've done with your hair."

Pleasure disappeared from his expression. A shadow passed over his face, and his voice grew deeper. "I was quite displeased that you gave Tony the wrong bullet. Horrified, when I thought you were dead and the bullet was missing. Imagine my elation to discover your empty grave."

"Imagine mine."

"I concede that you gave me an idea when you cut off my shirt that night."

"What idea?"

"My own blood purified when the wound healed. Blood on the shirt, however, was tainted. While that was not as good as having the bullet, it was good enough to begin experiments." Parking-lot light reflected through the windshield and glinted in his eyes. "My experiments require a large amount of blood. I've been working my way through hospital blood banks north from D.C." He smiled, and his fangs glistened. "What brings *you* here, Doctor? Searching for me?"

"It was you who attacked Bobby in the park last night?"

"An interfering fool. Friend of yours?"

"You nearly killed him."

Robert laughed. "He's already dead. We're vampires, remember? But I nearly destroyed him, yes. Odd that he happened to be there at that moment. More odd, the old fools who came as well. No one *happens* to carry squirt guns filled with holy water. That had to be planned. More friends?"

"I—"

Robert waved to dismiss her answer. "Since you're here, you can return my property. The bullet, if you please, Dr. West."

"I don't have it anymore. Jake—"

"Oh, I'm sure you still have the bullet, Lara, and I'm sure Agent Plummer has doctored it—excuse the poor pun. Knowing I'd find you, he probably added a homing device. When I take the bullet from you, he thinks he'll be able to track me. Come, Dr. West, the bullet, please." Robert cocked his head. His eyes narrowed. "In your pocket? The glove box?"

They'd taken the bullet out of her medical bag the first night in WPA headquarters. Surely Jake wouldn't risk her life by putting it back.

"Ah, your medical bag. That's how you switched it that night. The bullet you removed from my shoulder dropped in the bag, and you retrieved a different bullet. Neither Tony nor I suspected. Very clever."

"Are you a mind reader, too?"

"Let's say I can sense thoughts." He reacted before Lara could blink. He pinched her throat between thumb and forefinger, forcing her head back. He leaned forward, eyes locked onto hers, voice dark and menacing.

"Where is your medical bag?"

Twenty-nine

The SUV skidded to a halt in front of the church.

"Who's inside?" Robert demanded.

Lara's mind worked fast. "Bobby, unconscious. Philippe, a nurse attending to Bobby in case he wakes up before I get back, and the couple from the park last night, the vampire hunters."

They're vampire hunters, they're vampire hunters. They'll destroy *you.*

Lara focused her thoughts. A wall formed around her mind, protecting her from . . . what? *Someone like me.* Bobby. Robert was someone like Bobby. Bobby had armed her for this!

She bit back a sob and refocused. If Robert believed the D'Paltrows were true vampire hunters, he'd be less likely to go inside.

Robert sprang forward. His fingers strangled her throat again, and her head banged against the car seat. He hissed, "It'll be simpler for everyone if you do as you're told. You can alert them, we'll have another fight, and I promise your friends will get hurt. Or you can go get your medical bag and come right out. It's up to you."

He released her, opened the car door and pushed her out of the vehicle. He leaped out behind her, snagged her arm, dragged her toward the front door and all but shoved her inside. He paused in the third doorway. "You've got one minute."

Lara understood what she had to do. She'd get the bag and come right out. At least she was protecting Philippe and his parents. This monster wasn't willingly going into the house.

She glanced at the autographed copy of *Romeo and Juliet*. Was Robert as old as Bobby? Hildie hurried forward. "I was worried about you, dear!"

"Meridian, I'm glad you're back. He's restless," Philippe said.

Lara headed for the sofa. Her medical bag rested on the coffee table. Bobby still slept, his brow creased, his mind obviously engaged in nightmares. No pulse, still. No respiration.

"Wait another twenty-four hours. If he's not awake, you'll each need to give one more unit. No more than that, you understand, Philippe?" She grabbed the bag, took a closer peek at Bobby's face, and headed out.

"Meridian, wait! Where're you going? Did you get any blood?" Philippe called.

"Sorry." She stopped without turning. "The man who did this"—she jerked her head ever so slightly— "he's . . ." Realizing what she was doing, she shut her mouth and hurried toward the door.

Hildie's jaw dropped.

"Meridian. You can't go!" Philippe caught her.

Lara spun on her toes. She gripped Philippe's shoulder. "Trust me. Keep your parents inside." She suddenly remembered the single blood packet stuffed in her scrub pants, took it out and pressed it against Philippe's chest, forcing him to back up.

Then she broke away. "Don't follow me. Help Bobby!" She pointed to the blood packet, then slammed the first of the three doors behind her as she escaped.

Robert stood in the doorway of the second. "Smart choice," he said. He snatched her bag, grabbed her arm and rushed them to her SUV. "You're driving."

Lara composed her mind. The wall solidified. Bobby, Philippe and his parents would be safe if she had anything to say about it.

"You're fighting my will, Dr. West?" Robert laughed. "Don't worry, there're other ways to coerce you." He shoved her into the car and gained the passenger side before she could even straighten up in her seat. "We have a lot of work to accomplish." He bared his fangs and growled. "I have a fully equipped lab, and with your medical knowledge, I'm sure we can deconstruct this bullet in no time." He dug the bullet out of the bottom of the bag.

Lara gasped. "I can't believe Jake did that!"

Robert laughed. "Your buddy's a real charmer."

Thirty

Bobby opened his eyes. He could sense the moonlight caressing his home. It was time to feed.

Other thoughts flashed through his mind, contradicting the first. It couldn't be the full moon. That was still more than two weeks away. But centuries of training his circadian rhythms assured him a full moon floated in the heavens. He stared at the bedroom ceiling.

Park memories surfaced. He was confronting a vampire of enormous strength, losing consciousness . . . but not before someone attacked his attacker.

He studied the shadows. Meridian had entered his

dreams. She'd cradled his head and rubbed his brow. How long had he been asleep? *Examine well your blood. . . . Chanting . . . to the cold fruitless moon.* Shakespeare spoke to him across the centuries. His stomach knotted with bloodlust, screaming the answer. Had he really been asleep for two weeks?

He stood, not as steadily as he'd hoped. His fists clenched and unclenched. Weakness prevailed. He needed to feed, and he needed answers.

Voices drifted up the stairs. He recognized Philippe. At least he'd been able to protect his friend. The other two voices were unfamiliar, a man and a woman. He dressed and managed the circular staircase in silence.

Philippe spun around on the sofa. Two strangers stood nearby, their mouths agape.

"Bobby, he's taken Meridian," Philippe said. He hopped up, waving a piece of paper. "A note arrived this afternoon. It's just an address and a fingerprint. I think the fingerprint is in blood. What's it mean?"

Bobby's eyes narrowed. "It's a way vampires send warnings to each other. If I don't show up tonight, exactly two hours before sunrise, the next note will include a finger."

Bobby stumbled, and Philippe lurched forward to catch him. He eased Bobby into a chair. "We have to get you more blood."

Bobby frowned and flicked his chin toward the two strangers.

Philippe shook his head. "Don't worry about them, they're cool. Mom, Dad . . . this is my friend, Bobby Eyre. He's a vampire." The D'Paltrows continued to stare, mouths wide. "See?" Philippe said. "No reaction."

Philippe's father finally collected himself. "Excuse us. It's just that we've never sat in a room with a *conscious* vampire before." He pushed out of his seat and approached, hand extended. "I'm George D'Paltrow, Philippe's father. This is my wife, Hildie. That's some of our blood inside you. Philippe and Meridian couldn't get any from the hospital, so we all donated."

He hesitated as Bobby clasped his hand. Bobby wasn't sure whose skin was colder. He closed his eyes, then opened them and relaxed his grip. "In the park?"

George nodded and pointed at his wife. "Both of us."

"I'm in your debt." He dipped his head.

George regripped the handshake and stared into Bobby's eyes. "Young man, you stepped between us and that monster. I'd say we're in your debt."

"You have to save her!" Hildie shrieked.

"I'll do what I can," Bobby said. "First I need to feed."

George pushed up the sleeve of his shirt and held out a wrist. "As long as you promise to stop before it gets dangerous."

Thirty-one

Robert locked Lara in the basement before sunrise every day for two weeks. The basement stairs had been removed. She climbed down a ladder, which he then hauled up. The first morning, when he closed the basement door and jumped down, she'd cried out.

"You'd better just sleep, Doctor. You'll be operating on my schedule for a while." He'd pointed to a mattress on the floor. A lamp burned next to it, a wooden chair and two stacks of books were piled next to the lamp. "In case you need to do research, there's your material. I think you'll find it sufficient."

He'd entered a dark chamber on the far side of the basement and swung a heavy metal door shut behind him. Three bolts clicked into place. A ticking clock echoed off the walls.

Lara had paced her cell. How could she sleep? Robert had brought her to a house twenty minutes away from Bobby's, in a secluded wooded area near New Hope. He had a fully equipped lab, and he made her work. She'd refused at first, but it didn't take much coercion. He knew where her friends were. He'd made it clear that he would see that harm befell them if she didn't cooperate.

His own research had been laborious and detailed, but out of focus. It wouldn't take Lara long to get things on track, she could tell. Was that really what she wanted to do?

Did she have a choice?

Robert understood each step she took, and he remained glued to her side through that first night of work. When sunrise approached he'd called a halt and herded her into the basement. She'd been surprised that first morning when he joined her. How the hell would they get out? She never believed vampires could fly. She never believed vampires could exist.

She'd paced the basement perimeter. The cinderblock walls were around twelve feet high. She couldn't reach the landing at the basement door, even if she stood on the chair in the middle of the floor. Not even if she piled books on the chair and balanced herself on them. She knew—she'd tried. The legs of the chair had been sawed short, the books carefully counted. Had Robert measured her height? The landing remained just beyond her fingertips.

What if she dragged the mattress over and put the chair on that, then the books on the chair? That would make her tall enough. It would, if she balanced the chair against a wall, but the landing jutted out into the room's center, the mattress was too soft, and with books on it, the chair wobbled too much.

She'd dragged the mattress back into place, and restacked the books on the floor next to the lamp. Damn. She stared at the sealed door.

What the hell was he doing down here?

Daylight. She understood that Robert slept, and that he preferred—or did he *need*?—to sleep underground.

"Well, I'm not sleeping. There's no reason to let that monster sleep." She'd marched to the metal door and pounded with the side of her fist, but the door fit so tight and the metal was so thick that her fist made virtually no sound.

Lara glanced around then. Not much to work with. The chair would do, however—the chair with the sawed-off legs. That bastard. She jerked the chair off the floor and slammed it into the door. Again and again.

The door sprang open, and a blur swept forward. Icy fingers pinched her throat and she dropped the chair. She was forced backward, off balance. When her feet left the floor, she realized she'd really gotten to him. He held her by the neck at arm's length. She kicked and squirmed to no avail, struggling for breath.

She steeled her mind against the onslaught of his will. Would that be enough to protect her?

"You think this is a joke, Dr. West? You know what I am. Yes, I need to sleep during daylight, undisturbed by you or anyone else," he snarled. "I don't know how you learned to keep my thoughts out of your mind, but I have another lesson for you. There are consequences for your actions." He dropped her. She landed on her feet, her knees gave way, and she crumpled to the floor.

He contemplated for a moment. "Not nearly good

enough, Doctor. You need to experience firsthand what I do."

As short as it was, he managed to grab a tuft of her hair. She winced and pried at his fingers. He dragged her across the floor. "The bite of a vampire is just as painful as the bite of any wild animal." He pushed. She sprawled onto the mattress. His eyes narrowed. He bared his fangs and hissed.

When he attacked, his movements blurred, Lara shrieked. She couldn't stop him. She didn't realize at first what he was doing, yanking her scrub pants down, her underwear hooked with them. The monster wanted to rape her!

It took a moment to realize that sexual assault wasn't what he had in mind. He'd pulled her pants down to midthigh and flipped her onto her stomach. He straddled her across the shoulders, his back to her head, keeping her chest pressed tight against the mattress.

"You've developed such exquisite buttocks since the last time I saw you, Dr. West. They deserve exquisite torment." He bent forward. His arms stretched down her legs to prevent her from kicking him in the head. He licked a rounded cheek just once. "Ready?" He growled and sank his fangs deep into the soft flesh. She screamed as stinging pain shot in all directions. Blood squirted across her skin and dripped between her legs.

Apparently already sated, he ignored the blood and hopped off her. "Just a prick—to grab your attention."

She writhed on the mattress. Blood greased her hands as she felt the wound. She pulled her pants up and pressed the material against her skin to stanch the bleeding, but she said nothing.

"Did you get the message?"

Unimaginable pain radiated outward. It felt as if fangs still pierced her flesh.

Robert's voice stabbed through the haze clouding her mind. He grabbed her hair again and jerked her head back, forcing her eyes to look into his face, inches from hers. "Fortunately for both of us, I'm not hungry." He discarded her like an old doll. "You'll remain in this room in silence. You'll learn obedience, or you'll learn that the pain you feel now is nothing compared to what I can force you to endure."

When he'd attacked her at sunrise of the second day, it had seemed without provocation. He'd shoved her onto the mattress facedown and sunk his fangs into her buttocks again. He withdrew after a moment. "Don't worry. It won't affect you. Much."

Lara had shuddered and cried. Her flesh protested. She pulled her pants up to cover the wound. Her feet tingled, and the sun tattoo flared in the small of her back. A voice inside her head yelled at her attacker, *Liar.*

He didn't attack her the third morning, and she thought perhaps he'd leave her alone from then on. Then came sunrise of the fourth day. He took only a small amount of blood, but the prickle seared her flesh and lingered for hours before she drifted into a disturbed sleep. The attacks continued again after that. She had no idea why he skipped a day here and there, but was grateful for any reprieve.

By the end of the first week she was weary even after sleep. Wretchedness seeped into her thoughts and refused to subside. He refused to allow her medication, claiming it would taint her blood. The wound didn't heal.

She found sleeping during the days easier, and sleep itself deeper, but punctuated by dark dreams. Occasionally she thought she heard footsteps in the house above, but she knew Robert must have taken measures not to allow anyone into the house while he slept in the basement with her. Maybe it was Tony?

While they worked, Tony occasionally tromped in and out of the house, dressed in his Red Cross uniform, cap pushed way back. He delivered stolen packets of blood. Each night that he appeared, the repugnant odor that rose from Tony grew stronger.

Food made her nauseous, and she was reduced to maintaining the barest subsistence on clear broth and oatmeal. Her eyes grew sensitive to light, and she draped the lampshades with towels and blankets.

Whenever she sat, stinging speared her buttocks and shot upward across her back and down into her legs. She had antibiotic ointment in her medical bag but, when she applied it, Robert grabbed the tube from her hand and tossed it away. For the few minutes she was allowed alone in the bathroom, she'd take her bowl of oatmeal with her. "I'm hungry," she told him.

She applied oatmeal to the wounds. It allowed respites from the incessant itching, but she knew the wounds still weren't healing. Scabs formed, only to be repunctured by Robert.

Hollow success rewarded her research at 10:22 P.M., two weeks to the day after Robert had taken her. Her head bowed and her shoulders sagged, as if the weight of the world truly rested upon her.

Robert held the test tube up to the dim lightbulb and inspected the contents. "Thank you, Doctor. Stage one is complete." His lips curled in a sinister smile.

Lara glanced up, her neck aching, her eyes focused on him. "What do you mean, stage one?"

He shook the tube. "We need someone to test this on, don't we?" He strode across the room and stood behind her, legs pressed against the back of her thighs, and he whispered in her ear. "Not some*one* so much as some*thing*. A vampire?"

He yanked her hair and she screamed. He grabbed her wrist, then her index finger, and bit the fleshy skin, drawing blood. He forced the finger onto a paper and rolled it as a policeman would a felon's finger across an inkpad. He pressed the finger against another blank paper, and a deep red fingerprint stained the page.

"You don't happen to know any vampires who might volunteer for our little experiment, do you?" he asked.

"No!" The cry was torn from her throat.

"I didn't think so. That's why we're sending this little message. You see, I'm not wasting blood. He'll understand, one vampire to another."

He forced her into the basement, hoisted up the ladder, and this time didn't jump down. The basement door locked above her, and she was alone with her new wound.

She stared at her finger. Deep red blood seeped from her flesh, and she cupped her hand to cradle it. She gritted her teeth and winced at the urge that rushed over her. Closing her eyes, she kept them squeezed shut to wash the image from her mind. The thought dwelt, however, and the urge shook her being. Her cry, much like the previous one, burst from her throat, but the lament was for herself. She wanted to put the wounded finger in her mouth and suck out the blood.

Her stomach knotted, revolted, then exploded with dry heaves. This couldn't be happening to her.

Thirty-two

She knew Bobby would come. Every nerve ending sensed it. Every synaptic relay confirmed it. Perhaps they had been linked by their lovemaking, or perhaps it had happened when he'd touched her mind when he was wounded. Either way, he would come. It was little comfort that she sensed he survived.

Robert emerged from his cell the next evening without looking at her. He'd returned while she was asleep. He leaped up to the landing, unlocked the basement door and brought back the ladder. Despite everything else she'd witnessed, Lara still shuddered when he leaped ten feet into the air.

She understood what he wanted her to be today. Bait.

No more.

She refused to climb. He didn't speak, but jumped down, rushed at her like the wind and slapped her hard across the face. Lara's knees buckled and she crumpled to the floor. He pulled her up by the hair and dragged her to the ladder. "Climb."

Her strength was sapped, perhaps not so much from the blow as from lack of nourishment for the past two weeks. Her hands could barely grip the ladder rungs, and her fingers slipped against the cold metal. She made no progress.

"Climb."

Fire burned somewhere inside, because she despised that voice. She despised what he'd done to her and what she knew he planned to do to Bobby. She had to stop him. She had to wait for the right moment.

She struggled up the first few rungs. Her bare feet ached from the pressure. All of her muscles ached. She refused to surrender to the desire that made her throat burn.

She sensed him climbing at her heels. She could manage only one step at a time, and he overtook her. His arms encircled her legs, then her thighs. "Climb!" This time the voice was guttural, dirty.

She stopped moving, sneered.

She screamed when he yanked her pants down to her thighs. The movement was so fast, there was nothing she could do about it. She couldn't let go, or she'd fall from the ladder. His fangs tore into her, and the pain was worse than any she'd previously experienced. Her face pressed against the harsh steel frame, and she fought back tears.

Perhaps her imagination played tricks, but Robert didn't remove his fangs as fast this time. She grew dizzy. She climbed, but wasn't sure how she made it up the ladder and out of the basement with her pants around her thighs. Robert shoved her into the sparsely furnished living room with its two-story ceiling and exposed beams.

He tied her wrists together with rope, ignoring her moans, then tossed the end of it into the air. It toppled over a beam; he caught it and hauled. Her arms stretched high over her head, she struggled to maintain contact with the floor to relieve the pressure. He tugged, and she writhed in misery. He yanked her scrub pants all the way off. Her underwear was taken as well.

She screamed again with embarrassment and rage. He wanted her exposed and vulnerable when Bobby arrived.

The monster loomed in front of her, leaned close to her face. Stretched as she was, and almost eye to eye with him, the blending of his irises and pupils dissolved into a total blur. She couldn't read his expression, either.

She hated Robert for using her to trap Bobby. She hated him for what he'd done to her. For what he was *doing* to her. She bent her head and shook it. What *was* he doing to her? And why?

"I thought you had a more adept mind, Doctor."

Her eyes widened as understanding dawned, something she hadn't even considered before when overcome with those horrible urges. "You're going to turn me."

Robert laughed from his belly, and the sound rang through the room. It bounced off the ceiling and encircled the beams, and then he trapped her with his eyes. "Please, you flatter yourself. What makes you think I'd want you around for eternity? Oh, no." He paced away from her, and sprang back with the quickness that she couldn't fathom. "I've been drinking your blood, draining your precious life force. You'll reach the edge of turning, but you'll never come across.

"You thought that last time on the ladder hurt? You can't imagine the pain that's coming. Your veins will ache as the blood of desire courses through them. Every inch of your body will be inflamed. You'll feel the bloodlust of a vampire, but you'll never be able to satisfy the craving." He nibbled on her ear, then, and his fangs traced two thin lines down her neck, drawing parallel red trickles that he lapped.

She didn't hear Bobby enter the house, but she sensed his presence. Robert's head came up, his eyes narrowed and his nostrils flared. He draped an arm around her shoulders, his icy fingers caressing her chin and scorching her flesh.

A chill raced down her spine. She wanted to cry out, but Bobby appeared before she could marshal her voice. His skin was as pale as when she'd left him, his hair tousled by the wind, his fangs bared, and his eyes focused on her.

A wave of despair broke over her, and she screamed his name.

Robert fired a gun before she realized he'd pulled it from his pocket. Bobby dodged, but he couldn't out-race a bullet. It pierced his right shoulder, and he sprawled to the floor. Lara suddenly knew it was the same bullet she'd removed from Robert's shoulder.

The same bullet. Had that been a lifetime ago?

She felt Bobby's pain. He writhed on the floor, and she took a moment considering the connection she felt to him. How was it possible? A vampire! Was he not a man, too? They'd made love twice, but what she felt went beyond physical pleasure, as if he existed inside her mind, as if they shared thoughts. When had that connection begun, and what had caused it? Or had it always been?

Bobby glanced up from the floor, his fathomless eyes staring at her, anguish etched into his face.

Robert spun her so that she faced backward. "I wanted to show you what we've been doing," he said to Bobby. She closed her eyes, beyond humiliation.

He pinched her buttocks. "See the bite marks? She's

close to turning. Twice more will do it. I think I'll just bite her . . . once."

She heard him snarl, and his fangs drove into her again. Pain arced in every direction. His fingers gripped her hips, pulled her against his mouth, and he sucked harder. Wave after wave of sensation ripped through her body, and she squirmed and whimpered. Robert released her and spun her around to face Bobby again. His tongue traced across his lips, licking the remnants of her blood. On one level, Lara didn't understand what Robert was intending. In another recess of her mind, she knew.

He smirked. "After you're gone, I'm going to leave her like this." His voice was a hiss. "I'm told the torment of being brought to the edge but not taken across is unimaginable, and can last for hours. I hope she enjoys it."

Bobby struggled to push up off the floor. Lara knew Robert stood ready with the antidote she'd synthesized. The antidote would work, but he'd only give Bobby a drop or two, just to see the reaction. She shunted her thoughts from what Robert would then do to Bobby. It didn't take much imagination. He planned to destroy them both, her death a lingering torture.

Robert patted her face and tossed his gun to the floor. She twisted her head away, and he raked his fingernails across her jaw. The heat of four fine cuts burned there. Blood dripped onto the hardwood floor.

"Such a waste," the vampire said. He released her and rushed at his fallen victim.

His fingers pinched the skin at Bobby's throat. Bobby pushed with his left hand to force the attack away, but his strength was no match. Robert stretched Bobby's neck and forced his head back, turned him to face Lara. "Don't you agree?" he demanded.

He knelt over Bobby then, one knee digging into Bobby's chest, the other pinning his right arm. He pinched Bobby's shoulder near the bullet, and Bobby snarled, defenseless.

The front door burst open, and Philippe sprang into the room, a Super Soaker strapped to his back, the barrel pointed right at Robert. "Get off him," he squeaked. Shaky hands made aiming problematic.

Robert laughed. "If you shoot me, you'll get your friend. He'll burn, too."

"I'll take that chance," Philippe stuttered. "If I don't shoot, you'll destroy him anyway."

"Such a bright little boy you are." He charged at Philippe, and twisted to the side as Philippe fired. The stream of holy water splashed Bobby, whose back arched and face contorted. Robert grabbed the end of the Super Soaker barrel and ripped it from Philippe's hands. He stripped the water tanks off Philippe's back.

Philippe swung with his left fist, but Robert caught that wrist and twisted both arms behind his back, drawing Philippe near to him. He hissed and bared his fangs, his mouth wide. "Such a delicate neck."

"No!" Lara shouted.

Without warning, George D'Paltrow charged through the open door, firing as he bore down on the vampire about to bite his son. It must've been a plan to distract the monster. Hildie D'Paltrow, also armed with a Super Soaker, crowded behind her husband. She yelled when she saw her son's precarious position, and opened fire.

Robert swung Philippe around like a rag-doll shield, but holy water splashed everywhere and caught him. He howled and gripped Philippe tighter.

George circled right. Hildie circled left. Bobby struggled to stand but couldn't. Pain carved his features.

Hildie stopped firing long enough to cut the rope that held Lara captive. Lara's arms fell to her sides, and she wriggled out of her bonds while the blood rushed back into her limbs.

A door behind George burst open.

"Watch out, it's Tony," Lara gasped.

Tony leaped from the darkness. He tackled George, grabbed the Super Soaker, and twisted it out of his hands.

Robert turned to face Hildie, still holding Philippe. Lara scrambled toward the door. She had to get help. Robert released Philippe and sprang forward to cut her off, but with surprising speed, Hildie stepped between them. She fired her rifle.

"Run, child, run!" she said.

Holy water splashed Robert's chest and burned the exposed flesh on his hands and face. He hissed and turned back, forced to focus on his attacker. Half naked, Lara fled into the night.

Philippe glanced around. Bobby lay on the floor, blood pouring from his shoulder and puddling nearby. His mother was being attacked by Robert, and his father was being squished by a man three times his size. Memories of childhood bullies flooded his mind.

He ran to his friend first, knowing Bobby needed the most help. Sounds of struggle surrounded him. He tore off his shirt and used it as a compress against the wound, took Bobby's hand to hold it in place. That would have to do for now.

He straightened, fists clenched, and turned to Tony. "Get off my father, you pig!" He ran hard at the fat man on the floor, who'd pinned his father beneath his oppressive weight, and pounded on Tony's back. He fought to no avail. Tony's massive arm whipped out into Philippe's ankle, sending Philippe sprawling to the floor. Tony then slipped a leg over him, pinning both father and son. "They're not going anywhere. I'll get the girl, Boss."

Robert had disarmed Hildie and now held her in a viselike grip. Pain filled her face. "Don't bother. I took enough blood. She's in agony. In an hour she'll be back begging me to finish." He pushed Hildie to the floor and straddled her. "Hold them all here. I can feed later." With a sneer, he turned his attention to Bobby, a vial produced with a flourish and held prominently in his hand. He held the vial up to the light. "I have to help a sick friend."

The sting of the last bite didn't dissipate. Lara could sense every ounce of remaining blood that coursed through her body. The night throbbed around her as she escaped the house, crashing through the woods, but she could see an owl sitting on the bough of a tree a hundred yards away. How was that possible? She heard a cricket near her foot, but the cricket wasn't chirping.

She glanced around. What had Robert done with her SUV?

While she didn't know that, she sniffed and suddenly knew where Philippe had parked *his* car. She ran in that direction.

There was only one possible way to save them all and herself: Agent Jake Plummer. Philippe always traveled with a cell phone. Hopefully, he'd left it in his car.

She found the vehicle a quarter mile from the house, unlocked. He must have parked a short distance away so that Robert wouldn't hear them coming. But the glove box yielded nothing, and there was no phone under the seats. Damn. How to contact Jake?

OnStar! She remembered that first night, Robert saying he'd used OnStar to find her in D.C. Hoping his habits or his car hadn't changed, she ran toward the house.

When she got there, another issue occurred to her. Jake's phone number was programmed into her cell, and she'd barely glimpsed it the two times she'd called him. She closed her eyes now, and there was the number, embedded in her mind. She wondered if that was another benefit of being assaulted by vampires. She sniffed and found Tony's car a hundred yards from the house.

The OnStar operator didn't cooperate until she said she was a physician, this was a medical emergency, and that Agent Plummer worked for the United States government. Lara was then patched through.

No one answered until the sixth ring.

"Who is this?" Jake demanded when he picked up.

"Jake, no time to explain. OnStar can give you the location. I don't know exactly where we are. He's got them. He'll kill them."

"Lara? It's about time, girl. You've been entirely out of sight for two weeks. We're already tracing your signal. Now . . . who's got who?"

"Robert. It's Robert."

She could hear Jake thinking. "Who does he have?"

"Philippe. Philippe D'Paltrow and his parents, George and Hildie. And my friend, Bobby. Bobby Eyre. Robert—he's the one who's been stealing blood here."

"I'm on the move. The team is following. Ya done good."

Lara took a deep breath. Hunger such as she'd never before experienced gnawed at her, but it wasn't hunger for food. She closed her eyes again, and the image of red liquid spurting from an open wound painted itself in her mind.

Something occurred to her that she needed to relay. "He made me synthesize an antidote, Jake. Your bullet won't work anymore."

The Fed sounded unfazed. "Dog figured as much. Hang tight. We'll be there soon."

Overcome by pain and hunger, Lara doubled over. She grimaced but managed to speak. "Jake, bring me some clothes. Jake? Jake!" She'd missed the click of disconnection.

She pounded the seat, grabbed the car door and held on. Robert had brought her to the maddening edge. Would she go insane and kill herself? Would she beg Robert to bring her across? He wouldn't, but he'd enjoy watching her crawl.

Another wave of agony washed over her. Instinct told her no hope remained for herself, but that didn't stop her determination to do whatever she could to help her friends. Nothing would stop her from rescuing Philippe and his parents . . . and Bobby, the man she loved.

Love. This had to be love. This overwhelming desire to hold him, to protect him, to save him. He'd come for her, too, though he'd surely known he was out-matched. Every time the pain forced her eyes closed, she imagined lying on the living-room floor near Bobby and could feel his wound in her shoulder as if it were her own. It was a different sensation than the tor-ture burning through her veins—anguishing in its own way, but she relished the connection nonetheless.

She ran back to Philippe's car in search of clothing. She found a set of pink hospital scrubs and matching pink clogs in an overnight bag. They would do.

She wanted to act, to do something helpful before

Jake arrived, but she wasn't sure what, and the throbbing of her body came in relentless waves. She couldn't take Robert on alone.

Eyes closed, she felt herself transported into Bobby's mind. It was an odd sensation, familiar yet new, and she did everything in her power to share her strength with him—the strength that had brought her this far against such preternatural beings and such impossible odds. This man, to whom she was so close, with whom she was so emotionally intimate that they shared senses . . . she could help bear his burden. It was nothing compared to her own.

She sensed his agony lessen with each breath. His strength was slowly returning, and sensations crept into his semiparalyzed flesh. He'd been more affected by the bullet because of his already-weakened state. She could feel his toes wiggle and the pressure of the floor against his skull. The antidote she'd synthesized worked, but Robert had only administered a small dose, not enough for a complete cure.

Enough for Bobby to escape?

Another bullet suddenly tore into his flesh, piercing the same shoulder. She felt Bobby writhe on the floor as blood gushed from the new wound. The antidote worked, so Robert could soon discard the guinea pig. It was clear he'd made other bullets like the one from the WPAVU. He hadn't let Lara know.

Her eyes sprang open, breaking the bond between her and Bobby. She glanced at the digital clock in the car dash. Jake said he'd be here soon. That had been . . . ten minutes ago! Bobby didn't have any more time. She had to help him now.

She stumbled out of Philippe's car, her feet flapping against the soles of his too-big pink clogs. She discarded the shoes and continued barefoot, running faster than she'd imagined possible. Each step on twigs and stones cut into her feet, and her knees ached. Her hips hurt, too, and her head throbbed at the verge of explosion, but a single goal kept her focused.

She edged around the house and peeked into a window. Tony was herding the D'Paltrows—still alive!—toward the basement. He forced them to climb down the ladder. They'd be safe there if she could stop Robert. A plan formulated.

George's vampire-hunting kit lay on the porch where, apparently, he'd discarded it. Crosses, vials of holy water, wooden stakes . . . One wooden stake would do, and a vial of holy water.

Tony hauled the ladder up and sauntered back into the living room. Robert didn't even look at him. "I was sure Dr. West would be back by now. You'd better go find her. She'll have gone for a car." Lara scurried around the corner of the house just as Tony emerged, ambled down the steps and disappeared into the woods.

Lara slunk across the porch. Robert knelt, his back to her, examining Bobby's wounds. She crept inside. With her new speed, she hoped to plunge the stake into Robert's heart before he moved.

"I'm glad you're back." The vampire stood and twisted to face her. "Later than I expected."

Lara's shoulders drooped.

"Sorry. Did you want to surprise me?" He laughed.

Despair squeezed her spine. Lara knew she'd have no other opportunity; her strength would soon fade. She charged without further thought, knowing only that she had to save Bobby, that she couldn't endure her anguish much longer. She screamed as she lunged, her arm raised, the stake poised to end Robert's miserable existence.

He sidestepped, avoiding the attack. Spinning

around, he snatched the stake from her hand and tossed it aside. Robert growled, fangs bared. His fingernails slashed at her throat, drawing blood. He grabbed her and choked her, lifting her feet off the floor as she fought to maintain consciousness.

A gunshot sounded. With the sickening thunk of a bullet's impact, Robert's shoulder exploded in a shower of blood. He dropped Lara, who sagged to the floor at his feet.

Jake Plummer crouched in the doorway, both hands on his gun, poised to shoot again. "Let her go." He flashed Lara a smile. "Oops, guess I should've said that before I fired." He flicked the barrel of the gun in a gesture of nonchalance. His voice was grim. "Doesn't matter."

Robert turned, but this time without unnatural speed. He hissed, and spoke with a grimace. "The infamous Agent Plummer . . . The government must learn there are places they shouldn't meddle."

Lara's gaze darted around the room, and she was overcome by a fear of the villain succeeding after all. Hadn't Robert escaped worse traps than this? Hadn't Jake remembered that and brought backup? Did he know Tony lurked outside? Tony might've heard the shot. Besides, Jake's bullets wouldn't be effective— she'd formulated an andidote.

Robert scoffed at Jake and palmed an antidote vial. He flipped the cap, raised his hand to his mouth and drank.

Another bullet jarred the half-empty vial from Robert's grasp. "Too late. Our charming doctor synthesized a cure. As you can see"—his gaze traveled to Bobby, nothing about his prone figure suggesting he was a vampire—"we've already tested it."

"Yeah—nasty effect on humans, eh? If that's the result you're hoping for, that's fine with me," Jake said.

Stop talking and shoot him again!

Lara lay motionless, holding her breath for long spurts, hoping Robert would think her unconscious.

Don't wait for him to regain strength and speed. My antidote works. Shoot.

"Keep your hands where I can see them and don't move," Jake warned. "I *will* destroy you."

Robert sneered. "I have the antidote. You have no weapon that can stop me."

Lara knew Robert's power would return shortly. Jake would stand no chance, unless she could distract the vampire.

Inside her pocket, the vial of holy water she'd brought from George's pack pressed against her leg. She inched her hand toward it while attempting to maintain the illusion of unconsciousness. She managed to unscrew the cap and withdraw the vial.

Robert was focused on his attacker. His upper body swayed. His focus narrowed. Why didn't Jake shoot?

Robert hissed. "Your time on this world has expired. You're about to join your girlfriend. Or is that *his* girlfriend?" He toed Bobby's body.

Lara's hand flew out toward Robert's foot. She dumped the vial on his ankle. Holy water soaked through the sock and found flesh. Robert howled. His foot lashed out, kicking Lara.

"Shoot!" she shrieked.

Jake's gun fired three times, each report followed by a thunk of a bullet hitting flesh. The third impact dropped Robert to his knees, his eyes wide in disbelief.

"Oh, I'm sorry," Jake slapped the side of his head, "I don't know what's gotten into me. I forgot to mention we changed the formula in the bullet. Though I'm sure that antidote you have works great. Look at your friend there." He pointed to Bobby's limp figure. "Picture of health."

Jake pulled another gun and reholstered the first. "These new bullets, you'll see . . . the effect's faster." He smiled sideways and raised the new gun. "Just in case," he said. "Didn't want to take time to reload."

Robert gasped for breath.

Lara struggled to her feet. "You're not cheating me out of *some* revenge," she said to Jake. She stepped in front of Robert, twisted her hips, and with every ounce of strength she could muster, punched his nose. Robert buckled.

Lara turned then toward Bobby. He had no pulse, no detectable respiration. Still, Robert had survived. All she had to do was remove the bullet, and Bobby would regenerate. She hoped.

Examining his wound, Lara exhaled, her shoulders slumped and her chin drooped. The bullet had crushed the top of Bobby's shoulder and gone straight down into his body. Even if she'd had surgical instruments, she wouldn't know where to cut. The bullet could be lodged two millimeters inside, or it could be as far as his stomach. Without X-ray equipment, she had no way of knowing where to search. There was no more antidote, and she didn't know exactly how soon this bullet would destroy him.

Across the room, Jake was rattling into his cell phone. She stared at Robert, who was lying prone. Hippocratic oath be damned, she should never have saved his "life."

Tears flowed down her cheek as she caressed the side of Bobby's head. She tore off part of her shirt to use as a compress against his wound, but nothing she did seemed to stop the poisoned bullet from tearing him apart. She laid her head across his chest and wept. Even if she didn't survive, she'd expected to save him. He'd come here for one reason only: to save her. He'd paid for that decision.

Vision blurred, she spied the half-empty antidote vial dropped by Robert. She blinked to clear her sight. What would half a dose do? She had no idea, but it was Bobby's only chance.

She struggled to stand, but the energy sapped from her legs and she collapsed. Pain swirled around her. She was unable to hold it at bay now that her adrenaline was fading. She crawled to the vial.

As her fingers closed around the glass, Robert's eyes flicked open. Fangs bared, he growled and lunged for her. Lara barely had time to move, but two shots rang out in quick succession. Robert crumpled again to the floor.

Lara inched around to face Jake, who remained crouched, cell phone in one hand and gun, still smoking, in the other, poised as if expecting another attack. She felt a wave of anger. "I can't believe you put that bullet back in my medical bag as bait."

"Dog's idea. You know me. Wouldn't use you like that." Jake closed his cell phone, grabbed a wooden stake and focused on Robert. "No more chances. Let's finish this. Maybe these bullets aren't as effective as we thought."

Lara crawled to Bobby but hesitated. Could she save him? If Bobby revived now, he'd realize the only way to save her would be to turn her. Jake would know they were both vampires. What would Jake do? Destroy them both. She had no doubt.

Bobby couldn't revive until her life had slipped away. No, as long as Bobby remained unconscious, Jake wouldn't know. If she waited for the right moment, she'd be doomed, but he might escape before Jake discovered the truth. What if the bullet destroyed him before she got the opportunity to deliver the anti-dote?

Lara stared at the vial. What if she drank it herself? Could the potion reverse the effects of Robert's bite?

If it worked, she could have her life back. She could escape from the WPAVU and the world of vampires and return to a normal life at Jefferson Memorial. Her goal, her dream. Dr. Byra's job beckoned.

Jake raised his wooden stake, poised to strike Robert's flesh. Robert's eyes popped open, and with inhuman speed he throttled Jake. There was no more time to think. Lara tilted the contents of the vial into Bobby's mouth and massaged his trachea.

Robert tossed Jake across the room. The Fed bounced off the wall and he slumped to the floor.

Blood dripped from Robert's multiple wounds and from the corner of his mouth. Lara stared up at him. Jake's gun lay near the agent's body, but the stake was closer still. Lara could barely move. Crawling, how could she get to either before Robert caught her?

The vampire rounded on her, his eyes narrow and burning. "I promise you're going to suffer," he said. His voice resonated with hatred and, as if obeying his command, renewed pain flowed through her every pore. "You should've died in the fire." He crept to-ward her, his eyes never changing focus.

Jake was unconscious or dead. Bobby hadn't re-vived. Lara couldn't think through the torment of her body, and she couldn't figure out what to do.

"You should've forgotten about me when I wiped your memory in the hospital," Robert said. He stalked close enough to touch her. His pupils and irises blended together into a fathomless fire. Lara forgot for a moment who she was. Images sprang into her mind.

Mom, Dad . . .

"Your parents can't help you now," Robert sneered. He grabbed Lara's ankle, jerking her toward him. She screamed. His fangs sank into the sole of her left foot, and she screamed louder.

He released her abruptly, his grotesque mouth drenched in her blood. "I promised you suffering." He spun her around like a rag doll. Her arms flailed, but he grabbed one and sank his fangs into her palm. She howled and twisted, trying to free herself. Her legs jerked out, kicking Bobby.

Robert again released her. "You don't know what suffering is yet, but I promise to be your teacher, Doctor."

Was that who she was? Dr. Lara West, surgeon extraordinaire? Or was she Nurse Meridian Jones? Her mind was awhirl, adrift. What of her oath to do no harm? Could she harm this monster?

Hell, yes!

It didn't matter. She was helpless, trapped and overpowered.

She had friends, people here who could help her if she helped them. What of Jake? She'd seen his body convulse. He was still alive—though for how long? And Bobby? Her love? He hadn't revived. What more could she give him besides the antidote to magic bullets?

Think!

Blood oozed from her wounded foot and dripped onto Bobby's shirt.

Robert growled. "You should've begged to become my mate for eternity when I brought you to this house and first drank your blood. I gave you a taste of seduction in your living room. You should've known that's what I wanted from you now."

Her thoughts swirled, but Robert gave her the answer she needed. He sank his fangs into her forearm, and she remembered the obvious.

Blood! Bobby needs blood.

Robert was taking her blood by force. She'd never shared herself this way before, never willingly given the essence of her life to anyone. But she could. And her blood was Bobby's only chance. It was *her* only chance.

She swung her leg over Bobby's chest, resting her foot on his face, blood dripping, she hoped, into his mouth.

Shaking his head, Robert pushed her arm away. "You've proven to be more trouble than you're worth," he said. He spun her 180 degrees—her leg now pointing away from Bobby—and flipped her onto her stomach. "Beg for death!"

He pulled on her hips, and Lara grabbed Bobby's shirt. As she was dragged toward Robert, Bobby was dragged toward her. She could feel Robert ripping at her scrub pants. She put her forearm over Bobby's mouth, closed her eyes, and grimaced, perhaps for the last time.

Come on, damn it, drink!

Blood poured from her wounded arm. Robert knelt on the floor and yanked her closer. Lara lost contact with Bobby, and she cried out.

Robert swung her around like a toy, pants draped around her ankles. Her consciousness dwindled. Death summoned.

"I thought I'd take one last bite out of that beautiful ass just to remind you what pain feels like." And with those words, Robert sank his fangs into her buttocks.

"Feel this!" said a new voice, deep and guttural.

Thirty-three

Bobby—or was it Roberre?—drove the wooden stake between the shoulder blades of the vampire sucking the life from the woman he loved. Through bone and sinew, into the heart muscle and out the vampire's chest, the stake skewered him. Robert roared, flailed and collapsed into a prunelike blob.

Bobby rushed to Meridian, cradled her head. He sensed her faint life signs slipping away. Multiple vampire bites, extreme loss of blood . . . There was only one way to save her.

He sank his fangs into Meridian's neck. This was no time for sexual pleasure or Vampirical Harmony. There was no time or possibility for love without blood. He needed the most direct route to what little life was left in her body. He took her to the edge.

He didn't have much blood, either. He didn't know how that would affect the turning, but there was no choice. He bit his left wrist, then let the blood drip into her mouth. It gurgled there. Her eyes popped open. She bared fangs, ravenous hunger dancing in her eyes, irises and pupils now blended together. Bobby withdrew his arm and cradled her shoulders.

"You'll be woozy, but it'll pass," Bobby said. "You

need more blood. I can't give you any more. I need it desperately, too.

"We could take blood from him," Bobby suggested, indicating the stranger lying against the wall.

Lara glanced across the room. A half-sinister smile creased her lips, and she arched an eyebrow as if seriously considering a blood transfusion. "Jake? No, I don't think so. He'd leave us both with a sour taste." What was Bobby saying? He wasn't talking about a transfusion!

She looked into Bobby's fathomless eyes.

"Yes, your pupils and irises have blended together," Bobby said. " 'Let us be . . . gentlemen'—and ladies— 'of the shade, minions of the moon.' A friend of mine, Will Shakespeare, wrote that." He answered her astonished look. "As close as I felt to you before, having shared blood brings us closer. Two of our kind . . . well, we can sense each other's thoughts—not in precise words, but I understand what you're thinking. When you're able to relax and concentrate, you'll be able to sense my thoughts as well. It happens when . . . when two of us know a special bond."

She nodded. "A bond is great. I've never felt this close to anyone, but what did you do to me?" She already knew the answer.

"You'd be dead if I hadn't."

Lara touched the puncture marks on her neck. Dawning awareness brought terror. "I don't want to give up my life. I don't want to be a vampire!"

Bobby sighed. "It'll take time to adjust. You've gained an eternity—and consider the alternative."

She had considered it, to be honest. She knew what she was doing when she poured the antidote down Bobby's throat, and she'd known this would be the consequence. Somehow those thoughts hadn't made the translation into reality. The idea of drinking human blood to survive revolted her . . . but she already felt the hunger. The urge to satisfy that need burned in her brain, and the idea of eternal life held a unique appeal.

Lara examined her hands as if she'd never seen them before. She managed her fear and glanced at Bobby. "Okay. But I want to be with you. I want to know who you really are, and I want to know that other side of you that you keep bottled up, the side that saved us both."

"We'll have a long time to get to know each other," he agreed as he glided closer. "I love you—but I can't expose you to my beast."

"You mean Roberre?"

Bobby didn't answer. His mouth covered hers. His tongue slipped between her lips and traced a line across her fangs. He pushed upward, allowing the points to rip into his soft flesh. She did the same thing with her tongue, and their blood mingled, a joining of body and soul. Lara swallowed, and the blood embrace fired her desire, made it impossible to distinguish between bloodlust and craving for Bobby's flesh. The room swirled around her.

As their lips parted, Bobby met Lara's gaze again. He caught her and lowered her to the floor as she swooned.

"I love you, too," she whispered, her voice weak. "I'll stay with you forever."

Bobby kissed her forehead. "We have to feed."

"Help me into the other room," she managed. "There's untainted blood from the experiments. It's not ideal, but you can drink that."

Bobby nodded. "You need it as much as I do."

Behind them, Jake groaned. Bobby whirled and closed in fast on the man. "I have to take care of him," he said.

"No!" Lara cried.

"Don't worry. I'm going to adjust his memory."

A moment later it was done. Jake leaned against the wall, barely conscious, and Bobby carried Lara into the other room to search for blood. He whispered to her, "He won't remember anything about me, and he'll have no suspicions about you."

Bobby drained a fifth packet of blood. With his help, Lara managed to down two. Her bloodlust expanded and strength flowed into her limbs. She could adjust to the heightened senses if she could learn to drink blood. Bobby would teach her.

She was jerked back to reality as a familiar squeaky voice reached her ears. "Can anybody hear me? We're in the basement."

Philippe!

They hurried into the kitchen and found the ladder. "Is everyone all right? Can you climb up?" Lara asked.

"Where's that big ox?" Philippe shouted.

"Outside," Lara answered.

"There was someone else here?" Bobby asked.

"Tony. He worked for Robert."

"Ah . . . the new driver for the Red Cross?"

Lara nodded.

Bobby put the puzzle pieces together. "Robert stole blood from the Red Cross. Tony was his personal delivery boy."

"I know," Lara said. "He tried to deliver *me* several times."

Bobby tilted his head back and sniffed. "He stinks. I could track him now."

"Excuse me, can we get some help down here?" Philippe called.

Lara put her hand on Bobby's sleeve. "We have to

make sure Philippe and his parents are okay, and I'm still too weak. You'll have to find Tony another time."

Bobby lowered the ladder into place, and the captives climbed up to the kitchen.

Philippe was first, and he fell into Lara's arms. "Oh, sweetheart, I'm glad you're all right. I was so worried about you." As he pulled back, Lara watched his gaze travel to the puncture marks on her neck, dried blood caked around them. He gasped, and she imagined that the wounds had sealed themselves before his eyes, leaving no trace.

"Meridian, what happened?"

She held his shoulders and stared into his eyes. "It was the only way Bobby could save me. Robert took too much blood. I would've died. Honest. There was nothing else Bobby could do. I didn't want to give up my life, but . . . but I had to save him." Her eyes pleaded for an understanding that had only now become clear to her. She'd made the choice, not Bobby. She'd known the consequences of feeding him the antidote when she had.

Bobby was helping George and Hildie to stand. Philippe glanced at his parents, then back at Lara.

George grinned. "We won't say anything. You've done more than save our lives. You've helped us, helped me, to understand my son. The lifestyle you choose is just that—it's your choice. The lifestyle Philippe chooses is his choice. I'm his father, and I'll accept whatever choice he makes." He grinned at Philippe. "Be whatever you want, wear whatever you want—we'll still love you. We made you wear Federation uniforms and wizard robes. I guess I should've realized when you preferred witches' costumes."

Tears pooled in Philippe's eyes.

George squeezed his shoulder. "Don't get all mushy

on me, son. We're just happy to finally meet some of your friends. After all, it's only been . . . what, Hildie, ten years since the boy left us? Sure, your friends may not be run-of-the-mill nurses. . . ."

Hildie swatted her husband's ear. "George D'Paltrow, why don't you get over it? We're here now. We have our son back. Does it matter if his best friends are gay or undead? Be happy."

Philippe laughed. "Yeah, Dad, come on, be happy. I feel terrific." He draped one arm around Bobby's shoulders and the other around Lara's. "I can't stand it. My two best friends are vampires. I swear, I'm never leaving the night shift. And Nurse Cron better not mess with me anymore. When Meridian and Bobby—"

Lara smiled, then shook her head. "Sorry, Philippe, but I'm not staying."

"*We're* not staying," Bobby corrected.

"We're not staying," Lara repeated. "I was on assignment at St. Mary's, but I have . . . a life in Washington, D.C. I'm not giving that up . . . even if I can't work days anymore." Heck, if Bobby could be a nurse, she could still be the head of the night shift in the ER. She wondered how he'd feel about working for her.

Philippe glanced from Lara to Bobby, then at his parents. "Mom, Dad, I'm moving to Washington. I'll get a night-shift job down there."

Lara smiled at him. "Get yourself to D.C., then call me. Maybe I can help." Voices and scuffling echoed from the living room. "Sounds like Jake's people from the WPA."

Bobby nodded. "They're vampire hunters. I've got to leave before they see me again."

Lara angled him toward the back door. Bobby stopped her. "There'll be agents outside. I escaped them once before. In Memphis." He answered her questioning glance before she could speak. "Upstairs. They won't be watching the sky yet."

As she walked back down the steps, Lara wasn't surprised to see Katie among the agents combing Robert's house. At the moment, she and Jake were standing with Philippe and his parents.

"Someone up there with you?" Katie asked.

"Nope."

Jake flicked his chin. "Check it out," he ordered. Katie hurried up the steps.

Lara studied the other agents scurrying around. Her enhanced senses took in everything. She saw a loose thread on the seam of Jake's shirt and a cat hair on Owen's collar. She could close her eyes and track each person from their scent. As they ran from room to room, searching, she could sense tension in all the agents—all except Jake. He remained calm, as if he knew the results before the search finished.

Robert's body had been carted away. Sunrise lay just beyond the horizon. The team soon reassembled in the living room, and Jake issued final commands. He turned again to Katie, who had come back downstairs. "Bring them all in for debriefing."

Lara shook her head. "Sorry, Jake. Too tired. I'm going home to sleep. Philippe, would you mind giving me a ride?"

Much to her surprise, Jake didn't argue. He flicked his chin in the direction of Philippe's parents. "Bring *them* in," he said to Katie. "Young Mr. D'Paltrow can follow as soon as he drops Meridian at home. Give him directions."

Lara followed Philippe toward the door. Her heightened senses detected a jump in Agent Plummer's heart rate as she neared him. She could smell the pheromones. Fear? No way. Fascination? Possibly. Just what exactly had Bobby suggested to the man? Or was this merely a product of a vampire's increased sensuality?

Jake leaned close and whispered, "Good thing I got here when I did. Who knows what would've happened to you."

Lara said nothing, her thoughts focused entirely on Bobby. She made her good-byes to the D'Paltrows and stepped out of Robert's house into the predawn. She could sense Bobby in his home, awaiting her arrival. She recalled his parting words as he'd flown off without her.

Hurry, my love, before the sunrise.

She sensed his emotions, felt his caress. She gasped and moaned. "I'm coming!"

Philippe drove her quickly back to Bobby's house. Her lips brushed his cheek and she tasted salt from a tear. "Don't worry about me," she said. "I'd have been dead otherwise."

Philippe choked. "Sweetheart, I think you *are* dead."

Reality peeked over the horizon. The sky had long since transformed from midnight blue to cerulean, and orange tentacles of light chased night creatures into shadow. Lara squeezed Philippe's shoulder and dashed for Bobby's house.

All three doors locked behind her, sealing her in darkness. Her eyesight adjusted like a dimmer switch dialed up partway. Sensations assaulted her. Across the expanse of what had once been a sanctuary, she spied a speck of dried blood on the sofa where Bobby had lain wounded. The ticking of the grandfather clock was almost deafening. She teetered past the pedestal and sniffed the span of centuries from the autographed manuscript of *Romeo and Juliet*.

A blur of movement snagged her attention. "Bobby?"

She edged across the massive room, uncertain how to trust her new vampire senses. Her hand grazed some nearby polished armor. The plush carpet hugged the soles of her feet.

Another blur, and she was twisted around. "Bobby?" She backed up against the sofa. A caress drove chills down her spine. Before she could turn, the hand disappeared. Another touch tickled her ribs. An arm encircled her stomach from behind and pulled her close. Lips kissed the nape of her neck, warm breath scattered goose bumps down her arms, and she turned into the embrace.

Bobby.

He massaged her back. She reached up and pulled his head down until their lips met, soft and tender, and she felt the tension ease in his muscles. His tongue danced in her mouth. His hand slipped under the scrub shirt, and she sighed when he caressed her breast, her nipples hard with anticipation. She eased back far enough to reach his belt buckle.

"You need to rest," Bobby said.

"Really?" Lara slipped her hand down the front of his trousers. "Doesn't feel like *you* need to rest."

The closeness transcended experience. His blood both flowed in her veins and pulsed in the flesh in her hand, and everywhere it burned with passion. Hunger knotted her stomach unlike any hunger she'd ever felt. Her thoughts swirled, and the room spun in a dizzying array of senses.

I have to adjust, she reminded herself.

"It'll take time," Bobby said.

"Are you really reading my mind? I sensed you before, was able to tell what you were feeling, but—"

"The bond between us will grow stronger with time," he replied. "As for the extent of it . . ."

"You don't know?"

"I've never sired another vampire, Meridian."

His words reminded her. What exactly did she have to look forward to? What exactly had she become? Were all her ambitions now simply pipe dreams? It was time to find out—and to be completely honest with Bobby. After all, hadn't she already shared with him her *essence*?

"I have to tell you something." She glanced into his eyes. "My name isn't Meridian Jones. It's Lara West. *Doctor* Lara West. I'm a surgeon. A damn good one. My life, back in D.C.—I'm in line to become the youngest chief of emergency medicine at Jefferson Memorial. I want to help people. It's been my goal for years, and I don't want to give it up. That's what I was saying back when we were with Philippe."

Bobby grinned, clearly unfazed. "You're a vampire. You can still be the youngest ever night-shift ER chief . . . and, eventually, the oldest."

Lara laughed, relieved. But there was more yet to reveal. "Robert—the vampire Roberre killed—he broke into my home, wounded, and I saved his life. He tried to kill me. That's how I met Jake. He's an agent with the WPAVU. He inducted me and assigned me to St. Mary's to hunt for vampires, but I wasn't hunting for you."

"I understand," was all Bobby said. Again, he seemed unsurprised. She wondered how much he had already read in her mind.

"And one more thing . . ." Her voice quavered, as this was the most difficult to verbalize. "I want you to know, I wouldn't trade this, what I've become, for anything. Not if it meant giving up being with you." That was why she'd given him her *essence*.

At the same time as she reassured *him,* her words scared *her.* What exactly had she become? A creature of the night? For eternity? What if she couldn't adjust? The thoughts suddenly overwhelmed her. She no longer had control over her life.

Bobby returned the favor and reassured her. His touch steadied her fears. And it inflamed desire.

His mouth curled in a smile, then it covered hers again, catching her unawares. She pulled away, grabbed the edges of his shirt, yanked it over his head and tossed it on the floor. Her nails raked across his chest. His flesh had regained some color, his arms again held strength.

She unzipped his trousers and pushed them down. Bobby stood naked and unabashed. Lara admired the lines and sensed the power evoked by eternal life. What would be the price for her? She had yet to learn. Loss of control? It had always scared her, but hadn't it led somewhere better? And what if they lost control together?

His fathomless eyes studied her. Clothed, she felt naked. Would she please him? She entwined her fingers in his and guided him onto the sofa. She kissed his ear and buried her face in his neck, felt his desire swell, trapped between them.

Passion tingled in nerve endings she hadn't even known she had. Her flesh burned with a craving that extended beyond human experience. She held him tight, longing for his strength to surge through her, his weight delicious against her skin and clothes.

Back arched, hips thrust high, she slid her scrub pants off and wrapped her legs around his ribs. "Take me," she whispered.

He pushed her legs higher, found the entrance to her body. He moaned and began the journey. In.

Deeper. She tightened around him, and he groaned, clearly unable to control his pleasure.

Lara kissed him and pushed herself closer. She caressed the back of his head. "How long does it take a vampire to recover?"

"To make love again?" Bobby wriggled and thrust into her. "We're quick enough."

Lara arched her eyebrows and decided to tell him what she wanted, what she imagined might bring about the fulfillment she'd found lacking in the other two times they'd made love. "What happened back at Robert's house, when you killed him . . . Well, I've heard you talking to yourself. You have two sides of your personality. You keep one submerged."

"Yes," he admitted.

"Let it out."

"What?" Bobby looked shocked.

"*Roberre.* I want to see both sides of you." Lara's voice grew husky. "I want to play. If I'm going to lose control of my life, so are you."

"Too dangerous," he said.

Lara twisted, caught Bobby by surprise and disengaged their bodies. She reversed their positions. Kissing his shoulder and his chest, she traced her tongue in a line low across his stomach. She wedged his legs apart, the urge to drink blood swelling. Her fangs erupted.

The inner thigh. She heard the low, guttural voice in her mind but didn't understand. She knew Bobby combined sex and feeding, but . . .

"The more we share our blood in the heat of passion, the less often we'll need to take blood from others," Bobby was saying. "It's yet another good thing to come from this."

Lara growled deep in her throat, and the sound startled her as much as it did Bobby, but as she moved to obey, the idea of puncturing flesh and drinking blood from his thigh revolted her.

"You need a lesson," a low, guttural voice said aloud. "And I'm going to enjoy giving it to you . . . Meridian." She was flipped onto her stomach.

Roberre! I'm going to enjoy learning.

I, Lara or *I,* Meridian? Had she not become two people, just as Bobby was both Bobby and Roberre? Would Lara accept life as a vampire?

Meridian would.

Which of us is going to play with Roberre first?

The supplementary team members of the WPAVU finished their investigation, cleaned up and left. Jake had gone into the basement, found Robert's sleeping cell, and saturated it with holy water. No vampire would ever use this house again.

He climbed up the ladder to the first floor. His team was gathered in the living room.

"You got a couple nasty bruises in that fight. Better have that looked at," Katie said to him. "What's up, Boss? You look especially pleased about something. I know we're supposed to destroy any vampires we come across, but I thought you wanted Robert alive. At least for a while."

"I got something better than Robert," Jake said. He was indeed fighting a feeling of intense happiness. "I learned something I never knew before."

"Yeah? What's that?" Owen asked.

"I'm totally resistant to vampire mind control."

MELANIE JACKSON

*GHOUL, n. A demon addicted to
the reprehensible habit of devouring the dead.*

Who would have guessed something he'd penned in jest would turn out
to be real and swarm his island retreat? Yet for Ambrose Bierce, renowned
nineteenth-century wit and author of *The Devil's Dictionary*, the joke was
on him. If he didn't want to be digested—and he didn't, much—he had to
stay alive.

His reputed disappearance and death in Mexico in 1914 had been. . .
enlightening, and his animalistic new nature gave Ambrose hope of escaping
the undead army. However, there was another to save. On this island was she
whom he believed to be his soul mate. And while Joyous Jones promised
to give her all for love, he doubted she meant her life. Stranded literally
between the devil and the deep blue sea, a past fraught with secrets and a
future full of questions, the world's eminent cynic would have to trust fate.
To every night sky finally came the dawn, and from this B horror movie
would rise a. . .

DIVINE FANTASY

ISBN 13: 978-0-505-52803-2

JANA DELEON

Maryse Robicheaux can't help heaving a sigh of relief at the news that her not-so-beloved mother-in-law has kicked the bucket. The woman was rude, manipulative and loved lording over everyone as the richest citizen of Mudbug, Louisiana. Unfortunately, death doesn't slow Helena Henry down one bit.

Being haunted—or more like harried—by Helena's ghost isn't even the worst of Maryse's problems. Close to making a huge medical breakthrough, she's suddenly been given an officemate, and the only thing bigger than Luc LeJeune's ego is his sex appeal. Maryse would bet her life the hot half-Creole is hiding something. Especially because it seems someone's out to kill her. But getting Luc to spill his secrets while avoiding Helena's histrionics and staying alive herself will be the ultimate bayou balancing act.

Trouble in Mudbug

ISBN 13: 978-0-505-52784-4

#1 *New York Times* Bestselling Author

CHRISTINE FEEHAN

"The reigning queen of paranormal romance."
—*Publishers Weekly*

They were masters of the darkness, searching through
eternity for a mistress of the light...

Julian Savage was golden. Powerful. But tormented. For the
brooding hunter walked alone, always alone, far from his Car-
pathian kind, alien to even his twin. Like his name, his existence was savage. Until he met the woman he was sworn to
protect . . .

When Julian heard Desari sing, rainbows swamped his starving senses. Emotions bombarded his hardened heart. And a
dark hunger to possess her flooded his loins, blinding him
to the danger stalking her, stalking him. And even as Desari
enflamed him, she dared to defy him—with mysterious, un-
paralleled feminine powers. Was Desari more than his perfect
mate? Julian had met his match in this woman, but would
she drive him to madness . . . or save his soul?

DARK CHALLENGE

ISBN 13: 978-0-8439-6196-6

To order a book or to request a catalog call:
1-800-481-9191
Our books are also available at your local bookstore, or you
can check out our Web site **www.dorchesterpub.com**
where you can look up your favorite authors, read excerpts,
or glance at our discussion forum to see what people have to
say about your favorite books.

◻ **YES!**

Sign me up for the Love Spell Book Club and send my FREE BOOKS! If I choose to stay in the club, I will pay only $8.50* each month, a savings of $6.48!

NAME: _____

ADDRESS: _____

TELEPHONE: _____

EMAIL: _____

◻ I want to pay by credit card.

◻ **VISA**   ◻ **MasterCard**   ◻ **DISCOVER**

ACCOUNT #: _____

EXPIRATION DATE: _____

SIGNATURE: _____

Mail this page along with $2.00 shipping and handling to:
Love Spell Book Club
PO Box 6640
Wayne, PA 19087
Or fax (must include credit card information) to:
610-995-9274
You can also sign up online at **www.dorchesterpub.com**.
*Plus $2.00 for shipping. Offer open to residents of the U.S. and Canada only.
Canadian residents please call 1-800-481-9191 for pricing information.
If under 18, a parent or guardian must sign. Terms, prices and conditions subject to change. Subscription subject to acceptance. Dorchester Publishing reserves the right to reject any order or cancel any subscription.